P9-CPW-621

The Shadow Sister

Also by Lucinda Riley

The Midnight Rose

The Lavender Garden

The Girl on the Cliff

The Orchid House

The Seven Sisters Series

The Seven Sisters

The Storm Sister

THE SHADOW SISTER

Star's Story

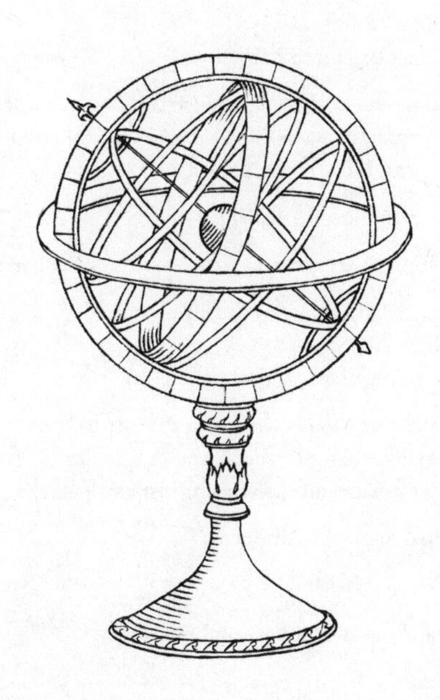

LUCINDA RILEY

ATRIA BOOKS

New York London Toronto Sydney New Delhi

An Imprint of Simon & Schuster, Inc.
1230 Avenue of the Americas
New York, NY 10020

This book is a work of fiction. Any references to historical events, real people, or real places are used fictitiously. Other names, characters, places, and events are products of the author's imagination, and any resemblance to actual events or places or persons, living or dead, is entirely coincidental.

Originally published in Great Britain in 2016

First Atria Books hardcover edition April 2017

ATRIA BOOKS and colophon are trademarks of Simon & Schuster, Inc.

For information about special discounts for bulk purchases, please contact Simon & Schuster Special Sales at 1-866-506-1949 or business@simonandschuster.com.

The Simon & Schuster Speakers Bureau can bring authors to your live event. For more information or to book an event contact the Simon & Schuster Speakers Bureau at 1-866-248-3049 or visit our website at www.simonspeakers.com.

Manufactured in the United States of America

10 9 8 7 6 5 4 3 2 1

Library of Congress Cataloging-in-Publication Data

Names: Riley, Lucinda, author.
Title: The shadow sister : Star's story / Lucinda Riley.
Description: First Atria Books hardcover edition. | New York : Atria Books, 2017.
Identifiers: LCCN 2016023125 (print) | LCCN 2016028840 (ebook) |
ISBN 9781476759944 (hardcover) | ISBN 9781476789156 (softcover) |
ISBN 9781476759951 (eBook)
Classification: LCC PR6055.D63 S53 2017 (print) | LCC PR6055.D63 (ebook) |
DDC 823/.914—dc23
LC record available at https://lccn.loc.gov/2016023125

ISBN 978-1-4767-5994-4
ISBN 978-1-4767-5995-1 (ebook)

For Flo

But let there be spaces in your togetherness.
And let the winds of the heavens dance between you.

—Khalil Gibran

List of Characters

ATLANTIS

Pa Salt—the sisters' adoptive father (deceased)

Marina (Ma)—the sisters' guardian

Claudia—housekeeper at Atlantis

Georg Hoffman—Pa Salt's lawyer

Christian—the skipper

THE D'APLIÈSE SISTERS

Maia

Ally (Alcyone)

Star (Asterope)

CeCe (Celaeno)

Tiggy (Taygete)

Electra

Merope (missing)

Star

July 2007

Astrantia major
(great masterwort—Apiaceae family)

Name derived from the Latin for "star"

I

I will always remember exactly where I was and what I was doing when I heard that my father had died . . ."

With my pen still suspended above the sheet of paper, I looked up at the July sun—or, at least, the small ray of it that had managed to trickle between the window and the red-brick wall a few yards in front of me. All of the windows in our tiny apartment looked onto its blandness, and despite today's beautiful weather, it was dark inside. So very different from my childhood home, Atlantis, on the shores of Lake Geneva.

I realized I had been seated exactly where I was now when CeCe had come into our miserable little sitting room to tell me that Pa Salt was dead.

I put down the pen and went to pour myself a glass of water from the tap. It was clammy and airless in the sticky heat and I drank thirstily as I contemplated the fact that I didn't *need* to do this—to put myself through the pain of remembering. It was Tiggy, my younger sister, who, when I'd seen her at Atlantis just after Pa died, had suggested the idea.

"Darling Star," she'd said, when some of us sisters had gone out onto the lake to sail, simply trying to distract ourselves from our grief, "I know you find it hard to *speak* about how you feel. I also know you're full of pain. Why don't you write your thoughts down?"

On the plane home from Atlantis two weeks ago, I'd thought about what Tiggy had said. And this morning, that's what I had endeavored to do.

I stared at the brick wall, thinking wryly that it was a perfect metaphor for my life just now, which at least made me smile. And the smile carried me back to the scarred wooden table that our shady landlord must have picked up for nothing in a junk shop. I sat back down and again picked up the elegant ink pen Pa Salt had given me for my twenty-first birthday.

"I will not start with Pa's death," I said out loud. "I will start when we arrived here in London—"

The crash of the front door closing startled me and I knew it was my sister CeCe. Everything she did was loud. It seemed beyond her to put a cup of coffee down without banging it onto the surface and slopping its contents everywhere. She had also never grasped the concept of an "indoor voice" and shouted her words to the point where, when we were small, Ma was once worried enough to get her hearing tested. Of course, there was nothing wrong with it. In fact, it was the opposite—CeCe's hearing was overdeveloped. There was nothing wrong with me either when a year later Ma took me to a speech therapist, concerned at my lack of chatter.

"She has words there, she just prefers not to use them," the therapist had explained. "She will when she's ready."

At home, in an attempt to communicate with me, Ma had taught me the basics of French sign language.

"So whenever you want or need something," she'd said to me, "you can use it to tell me how you feel. And this is how I feel about you right now." She'd pointed at herself, crossed her palms over her heart, then pointed at me. "I—love—you."

CeCe had learned it quickly too, and the two of us had adopted and expanded what had begun as a means of communication with Ma to form our own private language—a mixture of signs and made-up words—using it when people were around and we needed to talk. We'd both enjoyed the baffled looks on our sisters' faces as I'd sign a sly comment across the breakfast table and we'd both dissolve into helpless giggles.

Looking back, I could see that CeCe and I became the antithesis of each other as we were growing up: the less I spoke, the louder and more often she talked for me. And the more she did, the less I needed to. Our personalities had simply become exaggerated. It hadn't seemed to matter when we were children, squashed into the middle of our six-sister family—we'd had each other to turn to.

The problem was, it mattered now . . .

"Guess what? I've found it!" CeCe burst into the sitting room. "And in a few weeks' time we can move in. The developer's still got some finishing off to do, but it'll be incredible when it's done. God, it's hot in here. I can't wait to leave this place."

CeCe went to the kitchen and I heard the whoosh of the tap being turned on full blast, knowing that the water had most likely spattered all over the worktops I had painstakingly wiped down earlier.

"Want some water, Sia?"

"No thanks." Although CeCe only used it when we were alone, I mentally chided myself for being irritated by the pet name she had coined for me when we were little. It came from a book Pa Salt had given me for Christmas, *The Story of Anastasia*, about a young girl who lived in the woods in Russia and discovered she was a princess.

"She looks like you, Star," five-year-old CeCe had said as we'd stared at the pictures in the storybook. "Perhaps *you're* a princess too—you're pretty enough to be one, with your golden hair and blue eyes. So, I will call you 'Sia.' And it goes perfectly with 'Cee'! Cee and Sia—the twins!" She'd clapped her hands in delight.

It was only later, when I'd learned the *real* history of the Russian royal family, that I understood what had happened to Anastasia Romanova and her siblings. It hadn't been a fairy tale at all.

And nor was I a child any longer, but a grown woman of twenty-seven.

"I just know you're going to love the apartment." CeCe reappeared in the sitting room and flopped onto the scuffed leather sofa. "I've booked an appointment for us to see it tomorrow morning. It's a shedload of money, but I can afford it now, especially as the agent told me the City is in turmoil. The usual suspects aren't queuing up to buy right now, so we agreed on a knockdown price. It's time we got ourselves a proper home."

It's time I got myself a proper life, I thought.

"You're *buying* it?" I said.

"Yes. Or at least, I will if you like it."

I was so astonished, I didn't know what to say.

"You all right, Sia? You look tired. Didn't you sleep well last night?"

"No." Despite my best efforts, tears came to my eyes as I thought of the long, sleepless hours bleeding toward dawn, when I'd mourned my beloved father, still unable to believe he was gone.

"You're still in shock, that's the problem. It only happened a couple of weeks ago, after all. You will feel better, I swear, especially when you've seen our new apartment tomorrow. It's this crap place that's depressing you. It sure as hell depresses me," she added. "Have you e-mailed the guy about the cookery course yet?"

"Yes."

"And when does it start?"

"Next week."

"Good. That gives us time to start choosing some furniture for our new home." CeCe came over to me and gave me a spontaneous hug. "I can't wait to show it to you."

"Isn't it incredible?"

CeCe opened her arms wide to embrace the cavernous space, her voice echoing off the walls as she walked to the expanse of glass frontage and slid open one of the panels.

"And look, this balcony is for you," she said, as she beckoned me to follow her. We stepped outside. "Balcony" was too humble a word to describe what we were standing on. It was more like a long and beautiful terrace suspended in the air above the river Thames. "You can fill it with all your herbs and those flowers you liked fiddling around with at Atlantis," CeCe added as she walked to the railing and surveyed the gray water far below us. "Isn't it spectacular?"

I nodded, but she was already on her way back inside so I drifted after her.

"The kitchen is still to be fitted, but as soon as I've signed, you can have free rein to choose which cooker you'd like, which fridge, and so on. Now that you're going to be a professional," she said with a wink.

"Hardly, CeCe. I'm only doing a short course."

"But you're so talented, I'm sure you'll get a job somewhere when they see what you can do. Anyway, I think it's perfect for both of us, don't you? I can use that end for my studio." She pointed to an area sandwiched between the far wall and a spiral staircase. "The light is just fantastic. And you get your big kitchen and the outdoor space too. It's the nearest thing to Atlantis I could find in the center of London."

"Yes. It's lovely, thank you."

I could see how excited she was about her find, and admittedly, the apartment *was* impressive. I didn't want to burst her bubble by telling her the truth: that living in what amounted to a vast, characterless glass box overlooking a murky river could not have been farther from Atlantis if it tried.

As CeCe and the agent talked about the blond-wood floors that were going to be laid, I shook my head at my negative thoughts. I knew that I was being desperately spoiled. After all, compared to the streets of Delhi, or the shantytowns I'd seen on the outskirts of Phnom Penh, a brand-new apartment in the city of London was not exactly a hardship.

But the point was that I would have actually *preferred* a tiny, basic hut—which would at least have had its foundations planted firmly in the ground—with a front door that led directly to a patch of earth outside.

I tuned in vaguely to CeCe's chatter about a remote control that opened and closed the window blinds and another for the invisible surround-sound speakers. Behind the agent's back, she signed "wide boy" to me and rolled her eyes. I managed a small smile in return, feeling desperately claustrophobic because I couldn't open the door and just *run* . . . Cities stifled me; I found the noise, the smells, and the hordes of people overwhelming. But at least the apartment was open and airy . . .

"Sia?"

"Sorry, Cee, what did you say?"

"Shall we go upstairs and see our bedroom?"

We walked up the spiral staircase into the room CeCe said we would share, despite there being a spare room. And I felt a shudder run through me even as I looked at the views, which *were* spectacular from up here. We then inspected the incredible en suite bathroom, and I knew that CeCe had done her absolute best to find something lovely that suited us both.

But the truth was, we weren't married. We were *sisters*.

Afterward, CeCe insisted on dragging me to a furniture shop on King's Road, then we took the bus back across the river, over Albert Bridge.

"This bridge is named after Queen Victoria's husband," I told her out of habit. "And there's a memorial to him in Kensington—"

CeCe curtailed me by making the sign for "show-off" in my face. "Honestly, Star, don't tell me you're still lugging a guidebook around?"

"Yes," I admitted, making our sign for "nerd." I loved history.

We got off the bus near our apartment and CeCe turned to me. "Let's get supper down the road. We should celebrate."

"We haven't got the money." *Or at least,* I thought, *I certainly haven't.*

"My treat," CeCe reassured me.

We went to a local pub and CeCe ordered a bottle of beer for her and a small glass of wine for me. Neither of us drank much—CeCe in particular couldn't handle her alcohol, something she'd learned the hard way after a particularly raucous teenage party. As she stood at the bar, I mused on the mysterious appearance of the funds that CeCe had suddenly come into the day after all of us sisters had been handed envelopes from Pa Salt by Georg Hoffman, Pa's lawyer. CeCe had gone to see him in Geneva. She had begged Georg to let me come into the meeting with her, but he'd refused point-blank.

"Sadly, I have to follow my client's instructions. Your father insisted that any meetings I might have with his daughters be conducted individually."

So I'd waited in reception while she went in to see him. When she'd emerged, I could see that she was tense and excited.

"Sorry, Sia, but I had to sign some stupid privacy clause. Probably another of Pa's little games. All I can tell you is that it's good news."

As far as I was aware, it was the only secret that CeCe had ever kept from me in our entire relationship, and I still had no idea where all this money had come from. Georg Hoffman had explained to us that Pa's will made it clear that we would continue to receive only our very basic allowances. But also that we were free to go to him for extra money if necessary. So perhaps we simply needed to ask, just as CeCe presumably had.

"Cheers!" CeCe clinked her beer bottle against my glass. "Here's to our new life in London."

"And here's to Pa Salt," I said, raising my glass.

"Yes," she agreed. "You really loved him, didn't you?"

"Didn't *you*?"

"Of course I did, lots. He was . . . special."

I watched CeCe as our food arrived and she ate hungrily, thinking that, even though we were both his daughters, his death felt like my sorrow alone, rather than ours.

"Do you think we should buy the apartment?"

"CeCe, it's your decision. I'm not paying, so it's not for me to comment."

"Don't be silly, you know what's mine is yours, and vice versa. Besides, if you ever decide to open that envelope he left for you, there's no telling what you might find out," she encouraged.

She'd been on me ever since we'd been given the envelopes. She had torn hers open almost immediately afterward, expecting me to do the same.

"Come on, Sia, aren't you going to open it?" she'd pressed me.

But I just couldn't . . . because whatever lay inside it would mean accepting that Pa had gone. And I wasn't prepared to let him go yet.

After we'd eaten, CeCe paid the bill and we went back to the apartment, where she telephoned her bank to have the deposit on the flat transferred. Then she settled herself in front of her laptop, complaining about the inconsistent broadband.

"Come and help me choose some sofas," she called from the sitting room as I filled our yellowing tub with lukewarm water.

"I'm just having a bath," I replied, locking the door.

I lay in the water and lowered my head so that my ears and hair were submerged. I listened to the gloopy sounds—*Womb sounds*, I thought—and decided that I had to get away before I went completely mad. None of this was CeCe's fault and I certainly didn't want to take it out on her. I loved her. She had been there for me every day of my life, but . . .

Twenty minutes later, having made a resolution, I wandered into the sitting room.

"Nice bath?"

"Yes. CeCe . . ."

"Come and look at the sofas I've found." She beckoned me toward her. I did as she asked and stared unseeingly at the different hues of cream.

"Which one do you think?"

"Whichever you like. Interior design is your thing, not mine."

"How about that one?" CeCe pointed to the screen. "Obviously we'll have to go and sit on it, because it can't just be a thing of beauty. It's got to be comfy as well." She scribbled down the name and address of the stockist. "Perhaps we can do that tomorrow?"

I took a deep breath. "CeCe, would you mind if I went back to Atlantis for a couple of days?"

"If that's what you want, Sia, of course. I'll check out flights for us."

"Actually, I was thinking I'd go alone. I mean . . ." I swallowed, steeling myself not to lose my impetus. "You're very busy here now with the apartment and everything, and I know you have all sorts of art projects you're eager to get going on."

"Yes, but a couple of days out won't hurt. And if it's what you need to do, I understand."

"Really," I said firmly, "I think I'd prefer to go by myself."

"Why?" CeCe turned to me, her almond-shaped eyes wide with surprise.

"Just because . . . I . . . would. That is, I want to sit in the garden I helped Pa Salt make and open my letter."

"I see. Sure, fine," she said with a shrug.

I sensed a layer of frost descending, but I would not give in to her this time. "I'm going to bed. I have a really bad headache," I said.

"I'll get you some painkillers. Do you want me to look up flights?"

"I've already taken some, and yes, that would be great, thanks. Night." I leaned forward and kissed my sister on the top of her shiny dark head, her curly hair shorn into a boyish crop as always. Then I walked into the tiny broom cupboard of a twin room that we shared.

The bed was hard and narrow and the mattress thin. Though both of us had had the luxury of a privileged upbringing, we had spent the past six years traveling around the world and sleeping in dumps, neither of us prepared to ask Pa Salt for money even when we'd been really broke. CeCe in particular had always been too proud, which was why I was so surprised that she now seemed to be spending money like it was water, when it could only have come from *him.*

Perhaps I'd ask Ma if she knew anything more, but I was aware that discretion was her middle name when it came to spreading gossip among us sisters.

"Atlantis," I murmured. *Freedom* . . .

And that night, I fell asleep almost immediately.

2

Christian was waiting for me with the boat when the taxi brought me to the pontoon moored on Lake Geneva. He greeted me with his usual warm smile and I wondered for the first time how old he really was. Even though I was certain he'd been the skipper of our speedboat since I was a little girl, with his dark hair and bronzed olive skin covering a finely toned physique, he still didn't look a day over thirty-five.

We set off across the lake, and I leaned back on the comfortable leather bench at the stern of the boat, thinking about how the staff who worked at Atlantis never seemed to age. As the sun shone down and I breathed in the familiar fresh air, I mused that perhaps Atlantis *was* enchanted and those who lived within its walls had been granted the gift of eternal life and would be there forever.

All except Pa Salt . . .

I could hardly bear to think about the last time I was there. All six of us sisters—each one adopted and brought home from the far corners of the earth by Pa Salt and named in turn after the Seven Sisters of the Pleiades—had gathered at our childhood home because he had died. There hadn't even been a funeral, an occasion for us to mourn his loss; Ma told us he had insisted on being buried privately at sea.

All we'd had was his Swiss lawyer, Georg Hoffman, showing us what at first glance seemed to be an elaborate sundial, which had appeared overnight in Pa's special garden. But Georg had explained that it was something called an armillary sphere and that it plotted the position of the stars. And engraved on the bands that circled its central golden globe were our names and sets of coordinates that would tell us exactly where Pa had found each of us, along with quotations written in Greek.

Maia and Ally, my two elder sisters, had provided the rest of us with the locations the coordinates pinpointed and the meanings of our Greek inscriptions. Both of mine were as yet unread. I had stowed them in a plastic wallet along with the letter Pa Salt had written to me.

The boat began to slow down and I caught glimpses of the beautiful house we had all grown up in, through the veil of trees that shrouded it from view. It looked like a fairy-tale castle with its light pink exterior and four turrets, the windows glinting in the sunlight.

After we had been shown the armillary sphere and handed the letters, CeCe had been eager to leave. I hadn't; I'd wanted to at least spend a little time mourning Pa Salt in the house where he had raised me with such love. Now, two weeks on, I was back, desperately in search of the strength and solitude I needed to come to terms with his death and carry on.

Christian steered the boat into the jetty and secured the ropes. He helped me out and I saw Ma walking across the grass toward me, as she'd done every time I'd returned home. Just the sight of her brought tears to my eyes, and I leaned into her welcoming arms for a warm hug.

"Star, what a treat to have you back here with me," Ma crooned as she kissed me on both cheeks and stood back to look at me. "I will not say you are too thin, because you are always too thin," she said with a smile as she led me toward the house. "Claudia has made your favorite—apple strudel—and the kettle is already boiling." She indicated the table on the terrace. "Sit there and enjoy the last of the sun. I'll take your luggage inside and have Claudia bring out the tea and pastry."

I watched her disappear inside the house, and then turned to take in the abundantly stocked gardens and pristine lawn. I saw Christian walking up the discreet path to the apartment built over the boathouse, which was tucked into a cove beyond the main gardens of the house. The well-oiled machine that was Atlantis still continued, even if its original inventor was no longer there.

Ma reappeared, Claudia following with a tea tray. I smiled up at her, knowing that Claudia spoke even more rarely than I and would never start a conversation.

"Hello, Claudia. How are you?"

"I am well, thank you," she replied in her heavy German accent. All of us girls were bilingual, speaking French and English from the cradle at Pa's insistence, and we only spoke English to Claudia. Ma was French through and through. Her heritage was visible in her simple but immaculate silk blouse and skirt, her hair drawn back into a chignon. Communicating with them both meant we girls grew up being able to swap languages instantaneously.

"I see you still haven't had a haircut." Ma smiled, gesturing to my long blond fringe. "So, how are you, *chérie*?" She poured the tea as Claudia retreated.

"Okay."

"Well, I know that you are not. None of us are. How can we be, when this terrible thing happened so recently?"

"No," I agreed as she passed me my tea and I added milk and three teaspoons of sugar. Contrary to my sisters' teasing about my thinness, I had a very sweet tooth and indulged it often.

"How is CeCe?"

"She says she's fine, though I don't really know whether she is."

"Grief affects us all in very different ways," Ma mused. "And often, it prompts changes. Did you know that Maia has flown to Brazil?"

"Yes, she sent me and CeCe an e-mail a few days ago. Do you know why?"

"I must presume it has something to do with the letter your father left her. But whatever the reason, I am happy for her. It would have been a dreadful thing for her to stay here alone and mourn him. She is too young to hide herself away. After all, you know so well how travel can broaden one's horizon."

"I do. But I've had enough of traveling now."

"Have you, Star?"

I nodded, suddenly feeling the weight of the conversation on my shoulders. Normally, CeCe would be beside me to speak for us both. But Ma remained silent so I had to continue on my own.

"I've seen enough."

"I'm sure you have," Ma replied with a soft chuckle. "Is there anywhere you two haven't visited in the past five years?"

"Australia and the Amazon."

"Why those places in particular?"

"CeCe is terrified of spiders."

"Of course!" Ma clapped her hands together as she remembered. "Yet it seemed there was nothing she was afraid of as a child. You must recollect how she was always jumping off the highest rocks into the sea."

"Or climbing up them," I added.

"And do you recall how she could hold her breath underwater for so long, I'd worry she had drowned?"

"I do," I said grimly, thinking back to how she had tried to persuade me to join her in her extreme sports. That was one thing I had put my foot down about. During our travels in the Far East, she would spend hours scuba diving, or attempting to scale the vertiginous volcanic plugs of Thailand and Vietnam. But whether she was below the surface of the water or high above me, I would lie immobile on the sand reading a book.

"And she always hated wearing shoes . . . I had to force her into them as a small child," said Ma with a smile.

"She threw them into the lake once." I pointed to the calm water. "I had to persuade her to go and get them."

"She was always a free spirit," Ma sighed. "But so brave . . . And then, one day, when she was maybe seven, I heard a big scream from your room and I thought that perhaps CeCe was being murdered. But no, just a spider the size of a twenty-centime piece on the ceiling above her. Who would have thought it?" She shook her head at the memory.

"She's also afraid of the dark."

"Well, that is something I did not know." Ma's eyes clouded over and I felt I had somehow insulted her mothering skills—this woman who had been employed by Pa Salt to care for us adopted babies, who became children and then young women under her watch, to act in loco parentis when Pa was abroad on his travels. She had no genetic link to any of us. And yet, she meant so very much to us all.

"She's embarrassed to tell anyone she has bad nightmares."

"So that's why you moved into her room?" she said, understanding after all these years. "And why you asked me if you could have a night-light shortly afterward?"

"Yes."

"I thought that it was for you, Star. I suppose it only shows we can never know those we have brought up as well as we think we do. So, how is London?"

"I like it, but we've only been there a short time. And . . ." I sighed, not able to put my devastation into words.

"You are grieving," Ma finished for me. "And perhaps you feel that wherever you are just now wouldn't matter."

"Yes, but I did want to come here."

"And, *chérie*, it is a pleasure to have you, especially all to myself. That has not happened often, has it?"

"No."

"Do you wish it to happen more, Star?"

"I . . . yes."

"It is a natural progression. Neither you nor CeCe are children any longer. That does not mean you cannot stay close, but it is important for you both to have your own lives. I am sure CeCe must feel that too."

"No, Ma, she doesn't. She needs me. I can't leave her," I blurted out suddenly as all the frustration and fear and . . . *anger* at myself and the situation bubbled up inside me. Despite my powers of self-restraint, I could not hold back the sudden enormous sob that rose up from the depths of my soul.

"Oh *chérie*." Ma stood up and a shadow crossed the sun as she knelt down in front of me, taking my hands. "Don't be ashamed. It is healthy to let it out."

And I did. I couldn't call it crying, because it sounded far more like howling, as all the unspoken words and feelings locked inside me seemed to pour out in a torrent.

"Sorry, sorry . . . ," I muttered, when Ma pulled a pack of tissues from her pocket to mop up the tidal wave of tears. "Just . . . upset 'bout Pa . . ."

"Of course you are, and really, there is no need to apologize," she said gently, as I sat there feeling like a car whose gas tank had just completely emptied. "I have often worried that you keep so much hidden inside. So, now I am happier"—she smiled—"even if you are not. Now, may I suggest that you take yourself upstairs to your bedroom and freshen up before supper?"

I followed her inside. The house had such a very particular smell, which I'd often tried to deconstruct so that I could re-create it in my own temporary homes—a hint of lemon, cedarwood, freshly baked cakes . . . but of course, it was more than the sum of its original parts and simply unique to Atlantis.

"Do you wish me to come up with you?" Ma asked as I mounted the stairs.

"No. I'll be fine."

"We will talk again later, *chérie*, but if you need me, you know where I am."

I arrived on the upper floor of the house where all we girls had our bedrooms. Ma also had a suite just along the hall, with its own small sitting room and bathroom. The room I shared with CeCe was between Ally's bedroom and Tiggy's. I opened the door and smiled at the color of three of the walls. CeCe had been going through a "goth" stage when she was fifteen and had wanted to paint them black. I had drawn the line at that and suggested we compromise on purple. CeCe had insisted she would decorate the fourth wall by her bed herself.

After a day locked inside our bedroom, a glassy-eyed CeCe had emerged just before midnight.

"You can see it now," she'd said, ushering me inside.

I'd stared up at the wall and was struck by the vibrancy of the colors: a vivid midnight-blue background interspersed with splashes of a lighter cerulean, and in the center, a gorgeously bright and flaming cluster of gold stars. The shape was immediately familiar—CeCe had painted the Seven Sisters of the Pleiades . . . *us*.

As my sight adjusted, I'd realized that each star was formed out of small, precise dots, like little atoms combining to bring the whole to life.

I'd felt the pressure of her presence behind me, her apprehensive breath at my shoulder.

"CeCe, this is amazing! Incredible, really. How did you think it up?"

"I didn't. I just"—she'd shrugged—"knew what to do."

Since then, I'd had plenty of time to stare at the wall from my bed, and continued to find tiny details that I'd never noticed before.

Yet, even though our sisters and Pa had complimented her effusively on it, she had not repeated the style again.

"Oh, that was just something that came to me. I've moved on since then," she'd said.

Looking at it now, even twelve years on, I still thought the mural was the most imaginative and beautiful work of art CeCe had ever produced.

Seeing that my luggage had already been unpacked for me, the few clothes neatly folded on the chair, I sat down on the bed, feeling suddenly uncomfortable. There was almost nothing of me in the bedroom at all. And I had no one to blame but myself.

I walked over to my chest of drawers, pulled the bottom drawer open, and took out the old cookie tin in which I had stored my most precious keepsakes. Sitting back down on the bed, I put it on my knees and opened the lid, drawing out an envelope. After its seventeen years sitting in the tin, it felt dry yet smooth beneath my fingers. Sliding out the contents, I looked at the heavy vellum note card that still had the pressed flower attached to it.

Well, my darling Star, we managed to grow it after all.
Pa x

My fingers traced over the delicate petals—gossamer thin, but still containing a faded memory of the vibrant claret hue that had graced the very first flowering of our plant, in the garden I'd helped Pa create during the school holidays.

It had meant getting up early, before CeCe awoke. She was a heavy sleeper, especially after the nightmares—which tended to arrive between the hours of two and four—so she never noticed my dawn absences. Pa would meet me in the garden, looking as though he had been up for hours, and perhaps he had been. I would be sleepy eyed but excited by whatever it was he had to show me.

Sometimes it was merely a few seeds in his hand, other times a delicate fledgling plant he'd brought home from wherever he'd traveled to. We would sit on the bench in the rose arbor with his huge and very old botanical encyclopedia and his strong brown hands would turn the pages until we found the provenance of our treasure. Having read about its natural habitat, and its likes and dislikes, we would then hunt around the garden and decide between us the best place to put it.

In reality, I thought now, he would suggest and I would agree. But it had never felt like that. It had felt as though my opinion mattered.

I often recalled the parable from the Bible he'd recounted to me once as we worked: that every living thing needed to be nurtured carefully from the start of its life. And if it was, it would eventually grow strong and last for years to come.

"Of course, we humans are just like seeds," Pa had said with a smile as I used my child-sized watering can and he brushed the sweet-smelling peat from his hands. "With the sun and the rain . . . and love, we have everything we need."

And indeed, our garden flourished, and through those special mornings gardening with Pa, I learned the art of patience. When sometimes, a few days later, I'd return to the spot to see if our plant had begun to grow, and find there was either no change or that the plant looked brown and dead, I would ask Pa why it wasn't sprouting.

"Star," he would say, as he took my face in his weathered palms, "anything of lasting value takes time to come to fruition. And once it does, you will be glad you persevered."

So, I thought, closing the tin, *tomorrow I will wake up early and go back to our garden.*

Ma and I ate together that evening at a candlelit table on the terrace. Claudia had provided a perfectly cooked rack of lamb with glazed baby carrots and fresh broccoli from the kitchen garden. The more I started to understand about cooking, the more I realized how gifted she actually was.

As we finished our meal, Ma turned to me. "Have you decided where you will settle yet?"

"CeCe has her art foundation course in London."

"I know, but I am asking about you, Star."

"She's buying an apartment overlooking the River Thames. We'll be moving in there next month."

"I see. Do you like it?"

"It's very . . . big."

"That's not what I asked."

"I can live there, Ma. It really is a fantastic place," I added, feeling guilty about my reticence.

"And you will take your cookery course while CeCe makes her art?"

"I will."

"I thought you might be a writer when you were younger," she said. "After all, you took a degree in English literature."

"I love reading, yes."

"Star, you underestimate yourself. I still remember the stories you used to write as a child. Pa read them to me sometimes."

"Did he?" The thought filled me with pride.

"Yes. And don't forget, you were offered a place at Cambridge University, but you didn't accept it."

"No." Even I heard the abruptness of my tone. It was a moment I still found painful to dwell on, even nine years later . . .

"You don't mind if I try for Cambridge, do you, Cee?" I'd asked my sister. "My teachers think I should."

"Course not, Sia. You're so clever, I'm sure you'll get in! I'll have a look at unis in England too, though I doubt I'll get an offer anywhere. You know what a dunce I am. If I don't, I'll just come with you and take a job behind a bar or something," she'd said with a shrug. "I don't care. The most important thing is that we're together, isn't it?"

At the time, I had absolutely felt that it was. At home, and at boarding school, where the other girls sensed our closeness and left us to our own devices, we were everything to each other. So we agreed on other universities that had degree courses we both liked the sound of, which meant we could stay together. I did try for Cambridge, and to my amazement, was offered a place at Selwyn College, subject to getting the grades in my final exams.

I'd sat in Pa's study at Christmas, watching him read the offer letter. He'd looked up at me and I'd relished the pride and emotion in his eyes. He'd pointed to the little fir tree bedecked in ancient decorations. Perched atop it, there shone a bright silver star.

"There you are," he'd said with a smile. "Will you accept the offer?"

"I . . . don't know. I'll see what happens with CeCe."

"Well, it must be your decision. All I can say is that at some point, you must do what is right for you," he'd added pointedly.

Subsequently, CeCe and I each got two offers to universities we'd jointly applied for, then we both took our exams and waited nervously to get our results.

Two months later, the pair of us were sitting with our sisters on the middle deck of the *Titan*, Pa's magnificent yacht. We were on our annual cruise—that year sailing around the coast of the south of France—nervously clutching the envelopes with our *maturité* grades inside. Pa had just handed them to us from the pile of mail that was delivered by speedboat every other day, wherever we were on the water.

"So, girls," Pa had said, smiling at our tense expressions, "do you wish to open them here, or in private?"

"Might as well get it over with," CeCe had said. "You open yours first, Star. I know I'll have probably failed anyway."

With all of my sisters and Pa looking on, I'd opened the envelope with trembling fingers and pulled out the sheets of paper inside.

"Well?" Maia had asked as I took a long time to read the results.

"I got a five point four overall . . . and a six in English."

Everyone burst into cheers and applause, and I was squeezed into a tight embrace by my sisters.

"Your turn now, CeCe," Electra, our youngest sister, had said with a glint in her eye. We all knew CeCe had struggled at school due to her dyslexia, whereas Electra was capable of passing any exam she chose to but was simply lazy.

"Whatever it says, I don't care," CeCe had said defensively, and I'd signed "good luck" and "love you" to her. She had ripped the envelope open and I'd held my breath as her eyes skimmed over her results.

"I . . . oh my God! I . . ."

We had all collectively held our breath.

"I passed! Star, I passed! It means I'm into Sussex to study art history."

"That's wonderful!" I had replied, knowing how hard she had worked, but I'd also seen Pa's quizzical expression as he'd looked at me. Because he knew the decision I would now have to make.

"Congratulations, darling," Pa Salt had said, smiling at CeCe. "Sussex is a beautiful part of the world, and, of course, that's where the Seven Sisters cliffs are."

Later, CeCe and I had sat on the top deck of the boat, watching a glorious sunset over the Mediterranean.

"I totally understand if you want to take the Cambridge offer, Sia, rather than coming to Sussex and studying there with me. Like, I wouldn't want to stand in your way or anything. But . . ." Her bottom lip had wobbled. "I don't know what I'll do without you. God knows how I'll cope writing those essays without you to help me."

That night on the boat, I'd heard CeCe stirring and moaning under her breath. And I'd known one of her terrible nightmares was beginning. By now adept at recognizing the signs, I'd risen from my bed and slipped into hers, muttering soothing noises, but equally certain I would not be able to wake her. Her moaning had grown louder and she began to shout indecipherable words I had given up trying to understand.

How can I leave her? She needs me . . . and I need her . . .

And I did, back then.

So I had turned down Cambridge and taken up my offer at Sussex with my sister. And midway through the third term of her three-year course, CeCe had announced she was dropping out.

"You understand, don't you, Sia?" she'd said. "I know how to paint and draw, but I can't for the life of me put together an essay on Renaissance painters and all their endless bloody paintings of the Madonna. I can't do it. Sorry, but I can't."

CeCe and I had subsequently left the room we'd shared in halls and rented a dingy flat together. And while I went to lectures, she had taken the bus to Brighton to work as a waitress.

That following year, I had come as close as I had ever been to despair, thinking of the dream I had given up.

3

After supper, I excused myself to Ma and went upstairs to our bedroom. I took out my mobile from my rucksack to check my messages, and saw there were four texts and a number of missed calls—all from CeCe. As promised, I had texted her when the plane had landed in Geneva, and now I sent a short reply telling her that I was fine and having an early night and that we would speak tomorrow. Switching off the phone, I slid under my duvet and lay there, listening to the silence. And I realized how rare it was for me to sleep in a room alone, in an empty house that had once been full of noisy, dynamic life. Tonight, I would not be woken by CeCe's murmurings. I could sleep right through until morning if I wanted to.

Yet, as I closed my eyes, I did my best not to miss her.

Rising early the following morning, I threw on jeans and a hoodie, picked up the plastic wallet, and tiptoed downstairs. Quietly easing open the front door of the house and taking the path to my left, I walked toward Pa Salt's special garden, the plastic wallet containing his letter, my coordinates, and the translated Greek inscription clutched in my hand.

Slowly, I wandered around the borders we'd planted together, checking on the progress of our progeny. In July, they came to full fruition: multicolored zinnias, purple asters, sweet peas gathered together like tiny butterflies, and roses that climbed all over the arbor, shading the bench.

I realized there was only me to look after them now. Although Hans, our ancient gardener, was the "nanny" for the plants when Pa and I were not here to care for them ourselves, I could never be sure that he loved them as we did. Stupid really, to think of plants as children. But as Pa had often said to me, the nurturing process was similar.

I stopped to admire a dearly loved plant that sported delicate purple-red flowers, suspended on fine stems above a mass of rich green leaves.

"It's called *Astrantia major*," Pa had said as we'd planted the tiny seeds in pots nearly two decades ago. "Its name is thought to be derived from '*aster*,' the Latin word for 'star.' And when it blooms, it has glorious star-burst-shaped flowers. I must warn you that it is sometimes difficult to grow, especially since these seeds have traveled with me from another country and are old and dry. But if we succeed, it doesn't take much looking after, just some good soil and a little water."

A few months later, Pa took me to a shaded corner of the garden to plant out the seedlings, which had miraculously sprouted after careful nurturing, including a spell in the refrigerator, which Pa had said was necessary to "shock" the seeds into life.

"Now we must be patient and hope that it likes its new home," he'd said, as we wiped the soil from our hands.

The *Astrantia* took another two years before it produced flowers, but since then it had happily multiplied, self-seeding in any spot in the garden that took its fancy. Looking at it now, I plucked off one of the blooms, my fingertips trailing across the fragile petals. And I missed Pa more than I could bear.

I turned and walked toward the bench nestled in the rose arbor. The wood was still covered in heavy dew and I used my sleeve to wipe it dry. I sat down, and felt as if the damp was seeping into my very soul.

I looked at the plastic wallet that held the envelopes. And I wondered now if I had made a mistake by ignoring CeCe's original plea to open our letters together.

My hands shook as I took out Pa's envelope and, with a deep breath, tore it open. Inside was a letter, and also what looked like a small, slim jewelry box. I unfolded the letter and began to read.

Atlantis
Lake Geneva
Switzerland

My darling Star,

It is somehow the most fitting that I am writing to you, as we both know it is your preferred medium of communication. To this day, I treasure the long letters you wrote to me when you were away at boarding school and university. And subsequently, on your many travels to the four corners of the globe.

As you may know by now, I have tried to provide each of you with sufficient information about your genetic heritage. Even though I like to believe that you girls are truly mine, and as much a part of me as any naturally born child could be, there may come a day when the information I have might be of use to you. Having said that, I also accept it is not a journey all my daughters will wish to take. Especially you, my darling Star—perhaps the most sensitive and complex of all my girls.

This letter has taken the longest to compose—partly because I have written it in English, not French, and know that your use of grammar and punctuation is far superior to mine, so please forgive any mistakes I make. But also because I confess I am struggling to find a direct route to provide you with just enough information to set you on your path to discovery, yet equally, not disrupt your life if you choose not to investigate your origins further.

Interestingly, the clues I've been able to give your sisters have mostly been inanimate, yet yours will involve communication of the verbal variety, simply because the trail that leads back to your original story has been very well concealed over the years, and you will need the help of others to unravel it. I only found out the true details recently myself, but if anyone can do that, it's you, my bright Star. That quick brain of yours coupled with your understanding of human nature—studied over years of observing and, most importantly, listening—will serve you well if you decide to follow the trail.

So, I have given you an address—it's attached on a card to the back of this letter. And if you decide to visit, ask about a woman named Flora MacNichol.

Lastly, before I close and say good-bye, I feel I must tell you that sometimes in life one has to make difficult and often heartbreaking decisions that, at the time, you may feel will hurt people you love. And they might, at least for a while. Often, however, the changes that occur from your decision will eventually be the best thing for others too. And help them move on.

My darling Star, I will not patronize you by saying any more; we both know what it is I am referring to. I have learned over my years on this earth that nothing can stay the same forever—and expecting it to is, of course, the biggest single mistake we human beings make. Change comes whether we wish for it or not, in a host of different ways. And acceptance of this is fundamental to achieving the joy of living on this magnificent planet of ours.

Nurture not only the wonderful garden we created together, but perhaps your own elsewhere. And above all, nurture yourself. And follow your own star. It is time.

Your loving father,
Pa Salt x

I looked up at the horizon and watched the sun appear from behind a cloud across the lake, chasing the shadows away. I felt numb and even lower than before I'd opened the letter. Perhaps it was the sense of expectation that I'd felt, yet there was very little in the letter that Pa and I had not discussed when he was alive. When I had been able to look into his kind eyes and feel the gentle touch of his hand on my shoulder as we gardened together.

I unfastened the business card that was paper-clipped to the letter and read the words printed on it.

Arthur Morston Books
190 Kensington Church Street
London W8 4DS

I remembered I'd once passed through Kensington on a bus. At least if I did decide to go and see Arthur Morston, I wouldn't have far to travel, unlike Maia. I then took out the quotation that she had translated from the armillary sphere.

The oak tree and the cypress grow not in each other's shadow.

I smiled, as it perfectly described CeCe and me. She: so strong and intractable, her feet firmly rooted in the ground. Me: tall but wisplike, swayed by the slightest wind. I already knew the quote. It was from *The Prophet*, by a philosopher named Khalil Gibran. And I also knew who stood—outwardly at least—in the "shadow" . . .

I just didn't know how to go about stepping into the sun.

After refolding it carefully, I then retrieved the envelope that held the coordinates Ally had deciphered. She had written down the location they pinpointed. Out of all the clues, this was the one that frightened me most.

Did I want to know where Pa had found me?

I decided that, for now, I did not. I still wanted to belong to Pa and Atlantis.

Having replaced the envelope in the plastic wallet, I drew out the jewelry box and opened it.

Inside lay a small black figurine of an animal, perhaps made of onyx, which sat on a slim silver base. I took it out of the box and studied it, its sleek lines clearly denoting it was feline. I looked at the base and saw there was a hallmark, and a name engraved on it.

Panther

Set into each eye socket were tiny bright amber jewels that winked at me in the weak morning sun.

"Who owned you? And who were they to me?" I whispered into the ether.

Replacing the panther in its box, I stood up and walked toward the armillary sphere. The last time I'd seen it, all my sisters had been crowding around it, wondering what it meant and why Pa had chosen to leave us such a legacy. I peered into the center, and studied the golden globe and the silver bands that encased it in an elegant cage. It was exquisitely fashioned, the contours of the world's continents standing proud in the seven seas surrounding them. I wandered around it, noting the original Greek names of all my sisters—Maia, Alcyone, Celaeno, Taygete, Electra . . . and, of course, mine: Asterope.

What's in a name? I quoted Shakespeare's Juliet, pondering—as I had many times in the past—whether *we* had all adopted the personas of our mythological namesakes, or whether our names had adopted *us*. In contrast to the rest of my sisters, far less seemed to be known about my counterpart's personality. I'd sometimes wondered whether that was why I felt so invisible among my siblings.

Maia, the beauty; Ally, the leader; CeCe, the pragmatist; Tiggy, the nurturer; Electra, the fireball . . . and then me. Apparently, I was the peacemaker.

Well, if staying silent meant peace reigned, then maybe that *was* me. And perhaps, if a parent defined you from birth, then, despite who you really were, you would try to live up to that ideal. Yet there was no doubt that all my sisters fitted their mythological characteristics perfectly.

Merope . . .

My eyes suddenly fell on the seventh band and I leaned in to look closer. But unlike the rest of the bands, there were no coordinates. Or a quotation. The missing sister; the seventh baby we'd all been expecting Pa Salt to bring home, but who had never arrived. Did she exist? Or had Pa felt—being the perfectionist he was—the armillary sphere and his legacy to us would not be complete without her name? Perhaps, if any of us sisters had a child, and that child was a female, we could call her Merope and the seven bands would be complete.

I sat down heavily on the bench, casting my thoughts back through the years to whether Pa had ever mentioned a seventh sister to me. And as far as I could remember, he hadn't. In fact, he'd rarely talked about himself; he'd always been far more interested in what was happening in *my* life. And even though I loved him as much as any daughter could possibly love her father, and he was—apart from CeCe—the dearest person on the planet to me, I sat there with the sudden realization that I knew almost nothing about him.

All I knew was that he had liked gardens and had obviously been hugely wealthy. But how he'd come by that wealth was as much a mystery as the seventh band on the armillary sphere. And yet, I'd never felt for a moment as though our relationship was anything less than close. Or that he'd held back information from me when I had asked him something.

Perhaps I'd just never asked the right questions. Perhaps none of us sisters had.

I stood up and wandered around the garden checking on the plants and making a mental list for Hans, the gardener. I would meet him here later, before I left Atlantis.

As I walked back toward the house, I realized that, after wanting to be here so desperately, I now wanted to fly back to London. And get on with my life.

4

London in late July was hot and humid. Especially given that I was spending all day in a stuffy, windowless kitchen in Bayswater. In my scant three weeks there, I felt as though I was learning a lifetime's worth of culinary skills. I brunoised, batonneted, and julienned vegetables until I felt like my chef's knife had become an extension of my arm. I kneaded bread dough until my muscles ached, and delighted in that moment of "spring back," when I knew it was ready to proof.

Each night we were sent home to plan menus and timings, and in the mornings we would complete our *mise en place*—preparing ingredients and placing utensils on our workstations before we began. At the end of class, we would clean every surface until it was sparkling, and I felt a secret satisfaction that CeCe would never wander into *this* kitchen and cause a mess.

My course-mates were a motley bunch: men and women, ranging from privileged eighteen-year-olds to bored housewives who wanted to spice up their Surrey dinner parties.

"I've been a lorry driver for twenty years." Paul, a burly forty-year-old divorcé, chatted to me as he deftly piped *choux* onto a baking tray to form delicate cheese *gougères*. "Always wanted to be a cook, and I'm finally doing it." He winked at me. "Life's too short, isn't it?"

"Yes," I agreed with feeling.

Thankfully, thoughts of my own stagnant situation had been pushed aside with the pace of the course. And it helped that CeCe was as busy as I was. When she wasn't preoccupied with choosing furniture for our new apartment, she was off riding the length and breadth of London on the red buses that snaked around the city, gathering inspiration for her current creative fetish—physical installations. This involved her collecting a whole heap of clutter from around the city and dumping it in our tiny sitting room: twisted pieces of metal which she'd gathered from scrap yards, a pile of red roof tiles, empty and smelly gas cans, and—most disturbingly of all—a half-burned man-sized doll made of bits of cloth and straw.

"The English burn effigies of a man called Guy Fawkes on bonfires in November. How this one here lasted until July, I'll never know," she told me as she loaded a staple gun. "Apparently it's got something to do with the fellow trying to blow up the Houses of Parliament hundreds of years ago. Bonkers, as the English say," she added with a laugh.

In the last week of the course, we were put into teams of two and asked to prepare a three-course lunch.

"All of you know that teamwork is a vital part of running a successful kitchen," Marcus, our flamboyantly gay course leader, informed us. "You have to be able to work under pressure and not only give orders, but receive them too. Now, these are the pairings."

My heart sank when I was teamed with Piers—more a floppy-haired boy than a man. So far, he'd contributed very little to group discussions, other than jokey juvenile comments.

The only good news was that Piers was a naturally talented cook. And often, to the irritation of the others, the one who would receive the most praise from Marcus.

"It's just 'cause he fancies him," I'd heard Tiffany, one of the cluster of posh English girls, bitching in the loo a few days ago.

I'd smiled as I washed my hands. And wondered if human beings ever really grew up, or whether life was simply a playground forever.

"So, this is your last day, Sia." CeCe smiled at me as I drank a hasty cup of coffee in the kitchen the following morning. "Good luck with your competition thing."

"Thanks. See you later," I called to her as I left the apartment and walked along Tooting High Street to get on the bus—the Underground was faster but I enjoyed seeing London on the journey. I was greeted by signs telling me that my bus was being rerouted due to gas works on Park Lane. So, as the bus crossed the river to the north, we didn't go the usual way. Instead, we went through Knightsbridge and sat with the rest of diverted London, before the bus freed itself of traffic, eventually taking me past the magnificent domed Royal Albert Hall.

Relieved we finally seemed to be on our way, I listened to my habitual music: Grieg's "Morning Mood"—so reminiscent of Atlantis—as well as Prokofiev's *Romeo and Juliet* . . . both originally played to me by Pa Salt. I thanked God for the invention of iPods—with CeCe's taste for hard rock, the old CD player in our bedroom had regularly vibrated to the breaking point with clanging guitars and screaming voices. As the bus drew to a halt, I searched the street for a familiar landmark but recognized nothing. Except for the name above a shop front to my left as the bus pulled away from the stop. *Arthur Morston* . . .

I craned my neck to look back, wondering if I was seeing things, but it was too late. As the bus turned right, I saw KENSINGTON CHURCH STREET emblazoned on the road sign. A shiver ran through me as I realized I'd just seen the physical embodiment of Pa Salt's clue.

I was still thinking about it as I filed into the kitchen with the other students.

"Morning, sweetheart. Ready to cook up a storm?" Piers came to stand next to me and rubbed his hands together in anticipation. I swallowed hard. I was a feminist in the truest sense of the word—I believed in equality with *neither* sex dominant. And it was fair to say that I loathed being addressed as "sweetheart." By either a man *or* a woman.

"So." Marcus appeared in the kitchen and handed each pair what looked a blank card. "On the other side of your card is the menu you are to prepare between you. I will expect each course to be on your workbench and ready to be tasted by me at noon sharp. You have two hours. Okay, loves, good luck. Turn over the card now."

Immediately, Piers swiped the card from my hand. I had to peer over his shoulder to get a glimpse of what we were to cook.

"Foie gras mousse with Melba toast, poached salmon with dauphinoise potatoes, and sautéed green beans. Followed by Eton mess for dessert," Piers read aloud. "Obviously I'll do the foie gras mousse and poach the salmon, as meat and fish is my thing, and leave you to do the veggies and the pudding. You'll need to get started on the meringue first."

I wanted to say that meat and fish was *my* thing too. And by far the most impressive bit of the summer lunch menu. Instead, I told myself that one-upmanship didn't matter—as Marcus had said, this test was all about teamwork—and busied myself with combining the egg whites and caster sugar.

As the two-hour deadline approached, I was calm and prepared, while Piers was frantically repiping his foie gras mousse, which he'd decided to remake at the last minute. I glanced at his salmon still poaching in its kettle, knowing he'd left it in for too long. When I had tried to say something, he had brushed me off impatiently.

"All right, time's up. Please stop what you're doing," Marcus called, his voice ringing through the kitchen, and there was a clatter as the other cooks put down their utensils and stepped away from their plates. Piers ignored him as he hastily moved the salmon onto the plate next to my potatoes and beans.

Eventually, having praised and annihilated the other five offerings in equal measure, Marcus stood in front of us. As I knew he would, he lauded the presentation and the texture of the foie gras mousse, winking at his favorite chef.

"Wonderful, well done," he said. "Now on to the salmon."

I watched him take a bite of it, then frown and look directly at me.

"This isn't good, not good at all. It's way overcooked. These beans . . . and potatoes, however," he said, taking a bite of both, "are perfect." Again, he smiled at Piers and I cast my eyes toward my fellow chef, waiting for him to correct Marcus's mistake. Piers averted his eyes from my gaze and said nothing as Marcus moved on to my Eton mess.

In fact, it looked rather like a tulip about to open, the meringue itself forming the vessel in which the "mess" of strawberries—macerated in cassis liqueur—and Chantilly cream were hidden. There was nothing "messy" about it and I knew Marcus would either love it or hate it.

"Star," he said, having tasted a spoonful, "the presentation is creative and it tastes bloody delicious. Well done."

Marcus then awarded first prize to us for the starter and again for the dessert.

In the changing room, I opened my locker with slightly more force than necessary and retrieved my street clothes so I could change out of my chef's whites.

"I'm amazed you kept your cool in there."

I looked up, the words having just mirrored my own thoughts. It was Shanthi—a gorgeous Indian woman who I'd guessed was around my age. She was the only member of the group apart from me who hadn't joined the rest for drinks at the pub at the end of each day. Yet she was very popular within the group, always exuding a calm, positive energy.

"I saw Piers overcooking the salmon. He was at the bench next to me. Why didn't you say something when Marcus blamed you?"

I shrugged and shook my head. "It doesn't matter. It was only a piece of salmon."

"It would have mattered to me. It was an injustice done to you. And injustices should always be set straight."

I pulled my bag out of my locker, not knowing what to say. The other girls were already leaving, heading off for a final end-of-course drink together. They called their good-byes as they departed, until it was only Shanthi and me left in the changing room. As I tied my trainer laces, I watched her brush her thick ebony hair, then apply a dark red lipstick with her long, elegant fingers.

"Good-bye," I said as I headed toward the changing room door.

"How do you fancy a drink? I know a great little wine bar around the corner. It's quiet in there. I think you'd like it."

I hesitated for a moment—one-on-one conversations hardly being my thing—and felt her eyes on me as I did so. "Yes," I agreed eventually. "Why not?"

We walked along the road and settled ourselves with our drinks in a quiet corner of the wine bar. "So, Star the Enigmatic." Shanthi smiled at me. "Tell me who you are."

Given this was the sentence I always dreaded, I had a stock response to it. "I was born in Switzerland; I have five sisters, all adopted; and I went to the University of Sussex."

"And what did you study?"

"English literature. You?" I asked, deftly tossing the conversational ball back to her.

"I'm first-generation British from an Indian family. I work as a psychotherapist and mostly deal with depressed and suicidal adolescents. Sadly, there's a lot of them about these days," Shanthi sighed. "Especially in London. The pressure parents bring to bear on their kids to achieve these days is something I'm all too familiar with."

"So why the cookery course?"

"Because I love it! It's my greatest pleasure." She grinned broadly. "You?"

I understood now that this woman was used to drawing people out, which made me feel even more guarded.

"I love to cook too."

"Do you intend to make it your career?"

"No. I think I like it because I'm good at it, even if that sounds a bit selfish."

"Selfish?" Shanthi laughed, the musical timbre of her voice warm in my ears. "I believe feeding the body is also a way of feeding the soul. And it isn't selfish in the slightest. It's okay to enjoy what you're good at, you know. In fact, it will help the finished product hugely. Passion always does. So, what else are you passionate about, Star?"

"Gardens and . . ."

"Yes?"

"Writing. I like writing."

"And I love reading. That, more than anything, has opened up my mind and enlightened me. I haven't traveled much, but books take me there. Where do you live?"

"Tooting. But we're moving to Battersea soon."

"I live in Battersea too! Just off the Queenstown Road. Do you know it?"

"No. I'm still quite new to London."

"Oh, so where have you lived since university?"

"Nowhere really. I've traveled a lot."

"Lucky you," Shanthi said. "I hope to see more of the world before I die, but to date I've never had the money. How did you afford it?"

"My sister and I took jobs wherever we were in the world. She did bar work and I usually did cleaning."

"Wow, Star, you're far too bright and beautiful to have your hands down a toilet, but good on you. Sounds like you're the eternal seeker . . . unable to settle down."

"It was more to do with my sister than me. I just followed her."

"Where is she now?"

"At home. We live together. She's an artist and she's starting a foundation course at the Royal College of Art next month."

"Right. So . . . do you have a significant other?"

"No."

"Neither do I. Any previous meaningful relationships?"

"No." I looked at my watch, feeling heat spread through my cheeks at her barrage of questions. "I should be going."

"Of course." Shanthi drained her glass, then followed me out of the wine bar.

"It's been great to get to know you better, Star. Here's my card. Drop me a text sometime and let me know how you're getting on. And if you ever need to talk, I'm always here."

"I will. Good-bye."

I walked away from her swiftly. I was not comfortable discussing "relationships." With anyone.

"Finally!"

CeCe stood, hands on hips, in the cramped entrance to our apartment. "Where on earth have you been, Sia?"

"I went out for a quick drink with a friend," I said as I passed her to go to the bathroom, hastily shutting the door.

"Well, you might have told me. I've cooked you something to celebrate the end of your course. But it's probably ruined by now."

CeCe rarely, if ever, cooked. On the few occasions I hadn't been around to feed her, she'd eaten takeaway. "Sorry. I didn't know. I'll be out in a second."

I listened through the door and heard her marching away. After washing my hands, I pulled my fringe out of my eyes, bending my knees slightly to regard myself in the mirror.

"Something has to change," I said to my reflection.

5

By August, London felt like a ghost town. Those who could afford to had fled the temperamental UK climate, which seemed to oscillate inconsistently between humid and cloudy, sunny and wet. The "real" London was asleep, waiting for its occupants to return from foreign shores so its daily business could resume once more.

I too felt a strange sense of torpor. If I had not slept in the days after Pa Salt's death, now I could hardly rouse myself from bed in the mornings. In contrast, CeCe was all action, insisting I accompany her to choose a particular fridge or the perfect tile for the backsplashes in the new apartment.

One muggy Saturday, when I would have happily stayed in bed with a book, she demanded that I get up and dragged me on a bus to an antique shop, convinced I would love the furniture it stocked.

"Here we are," she said as she peered out of the window and dinged the bus bell for the next stop. "The shop is number one fifty-nine, so we're here."

We alighted and I gasped as, for the second time in the space of a couple of weeks, I had ended up a few feet from the door of Arthur Morston Books. CeCe turned left, heading to the shop next door, but I lagged behind, peering briefly into the window. It was full of old books, the kind that I one day dreamed of having enough money to collect and which would adorn my own shelves on either side of my imagined fireplace.

"Hurry up, Sia, it's quarter to four already. I don't know what time they close here on a Saturday."

I followed her, entering a shop that was full of oriental furniture—crimson stained and lacquered tables, black cupboards with delicate butterflies painted on the doors, and golden Buddhas smiling serenely.

"Doesn't it make you wish we'd bought a container-load when we were traveling?" CeCe raised her eyebrows as she looked at one of the price tags, then formed her hands into the sign for "lots of money." "We must be able to source them cheaper elsewhere," she added.

She led us out of the shop, and having perused the windows of the other quaint old-fashioned shops along the street, we headed back to the bus stop. While we waited for the bus to arrive, there was nothing to do but stare back across the road into Arthur Morston Books. My sister Tiggy would have told me that it was fate. At best, I thought it was indeed coincidental.

A week later, while CeCe went to the apartment to check on the progress of the tilers as we were due to move in a few days' time, I walked to the local corner shop to buy a pint of milk. As I stood at the counter waiting for my change, I glanced down at a headline on the bottom right-hand side of the *Times*.

CAPTAIN OF THE TIGRESS DROWNS IN FASTNET STORM

My heart missed a beat—I knew my sister, Ally, was currently sailing in the Fastnet Race and the name of the boat was horribly familiar. The photograph below the headline was of a man, but it didn't lessen my anxiety. I bought the newspaper and scanned the article nervously as I walked back to the apartment. And, having done so, breathed a sigh of relief that so far, at least, there was no news of any further fatalities. The weather, however, was apparently appalling and three-quarters of the boats had been forced to retire.

Immediately I sent a text message to CeCe and reread the article when I returned to the apartment. Even though my elder sister had been a professional sailor for years, the thought of her dying in a race was one I'd never even contemplated. Everything about Ally was so . . . *vital.* She lived her life with a fearlessness that I could only admire and envy.

I wrote her a short text saying I'd read about the disaster and asked her to contact me urgently. My mobile rang as I pressed "send," and I saw it was CeCe.

"I've just spoken to Ma, Sia. She called me. Ally was in the Fastnet Race and—"

"I know, I've just been reading about it in the newspaper. Oh God, Cee, I hope she's okay."

"Ma said she'd had a call from someone to say she was. Obviously the boat's pulled out of the race."

"Thank goodness! Poor, poor Ally, losing a crewmate like that."

"Terrible. Anyway. I'll be on my way home in a bit. The new kitchen's looking fantastic. You're going to love it."

"I'm sure I will."

"Oh, and our beds and the double for the spare room have arrived too. We're finally getting there. I can't wait until we move in. See you later."

CeCe ended the call, and I marveled at her ability to switch to the practical so quickly after bad news, even though I knew it was just her way of coping. I mulled over whether I should be brave and tell CeCe that, at the grand old age of twenty-seven, perhaps it would be more appropriate to have our *own* bedrooms rather than share one. If we ever had guests to stay, it would be easy for me to move back into her room for a few days. It seemed ridiculous to be sharing when there was a spare room.

One day, Star, you'll have to deal with it . . .

But, as always, it was not *this* day.

As I was packing up my few possessions for the move a couple of days later, I got a call from Ma.

"Star?"

"Yes? Is everything all right? Is Ally okay? She hasn't answered my texts," I said anxiously. "Have you spoken to her?"

"I haven't, no, but I know she's unhurt. I have spoken to the victim's mother. You probably read he was the skipper of Ally's boat. What a lovely woman . . ." I heard a sigh escape Ma's lips. "Apparently her son left her my number for her to call in case anything happened to him. She thinks he may have had some form of premonition."

"You mean, of his own death?"

"Yes . . . You see, Ally was secretly engaged to him. His name was Theo."

I was silent as I took in the news.

"I think Theo knew that Ally might be in shock and unable to contact us herself," Ma continued. "Especially as she had not yet told any of you that she was in a serious relationship with him."

"Did you know, Ma?"

"Yes, I did, and she was so in love. It's only been a few days since she left here. She told me that he was 'the one.' I . . ."

"Ma, I'm so very sorry."

"Forgive me, *chérie*, even though I know how life gives and takes away, coming so soon after your father's death, for Ally, this situation is particularly tragic."

"Where is she?" I asked.

"In London, staying with Theo's mother."

"Should I go and see her?"

"I think it would be wonderful if you could attend the funeral. Celia, Theo's mother, told me it is next Wednesday at two o'clock, at Holy Trinity Church in Chelsea."

"We'll be there, Ma. I promise. Have you contacted the other sisters?"

"Yes, but none of them can make it."

"What about you? Could you come?"

"I . . . Star, I cannot. But I'm sure that you and CeCe can represent us all. Tell Ally that we send our love."

"Of course we will."

"I will leave you to tell CeCe. And how are you, Star?"

"I'm okay. I just . . . can't bear it for Ally."

"*Chérie*, neither can I. Don't expect a reply to any message you send her—she isn't responding to anybody just now."

"I won't. Thank you for telling me. Bye, Ma."

When CeCe arrived home, I told her as calmly as I could what had happened. And the date of the funeral.

"Presumably you told Ma that we couldn't make it? We'll still be knee-deep in boxes so soon after the move."

"CeCe, we *have* to make it. We have to be there for Ally."

"What about our other sisters? Where are they? Why do *we* have to disrupt our plans? For God's sake, we didn't even know the guy."

"How can you say that?" I stood up, feeling all the latent anger I'd been harboring about to explode. "This isn't about her fiancé, it's about Ally, our sister! She's been there for us both all of our lives and now she needs *us* to be there for her next Wednesday! And we will be!" Then I left and headed toward the bathroom, which at least had a lock on the door.

Not wishing to see her as I was shaking with rage, I decided I might as well stay there and have a bath. In the claustrophobic concrete jungle that surrounded me, the yellowing tub had often provided a sanctuary I could escape to.

Submerging myself, I then thought of Theo and the fact that he hadn't ever escaped from the water. I sat up immediately, sending small waves splashing all over the cheap linoleum floor, my breathing ragged with panic.

There was a knock on the door.

"Sia? Are you okay?"

I swallowed hard, trying to take some deep breaths of air—air that Theo had not found and would never be able to breathe again.

"Yes."

"You're right." There was a long pause. "I'm really sorry. Of course we must be there for Ally."

"Yes." I pulled out the plug and reached over the edge of the bath for my towel. "We must."

The next morning, the moving van and driver CeCe had organized pulled up in front of our apartment. After loading up our few possessions—which mainly encompassed all CeCe's junk for her new art project—we set off to collect the pieces of furniture she had bought from various shops around South London.

Three hours later, we arrived in Battersea. And, after CeCe had signed whatever she'd needed to sign at the sales office downstairs, the keys to our new home were in her possession. She unlocked the door and let us in, then walked around the echoing room.

"I just can't believe that this is all mine. And yours, of course," she added generously. "We're safe now, Sia, forever. We have a home of our own. Isn't it amazing?"

"Yes."

Then she reached out her arms to me, and knowing this was *her* moment, I went into them. And we stood in the center of the cavernous empty space and hugged each other, giggling like the children we had once been at the ridiculousness of being *so* grown up.

Once we'd moved in, CeCe was up and out early every morning to gather more materials for her installations before the first term of college at the beginning of September.

Which left *me* alone in the apartment all day. I was kept occupied with unpacking the boxes of bedding, towels, and kitchen utensils CeCe had ordered. As I slid a set of lethally sharp chef's knives into the block, I felt like a newly married woman setting up my first home. Except I wasn't. Nowhere near it.

Once I had unpacked, I set to work on turning the long terrace into a garden in the air. I used what little I had left in my savings and almost my full month's allowance from Pa Salt to buy anything I could to create as much immediate greenery and color as possible. As I watched the man from the garden center heave a big terra-cotta pot—filled with a gorgeous camellia covered in tiny white buds—onto the terrace, I knew Pa Salt would be turning in his grave at the extravagance, but I pushed the thought away, telling myself that on this occasion he'd understand.

The following Wednesday, I dug out suitably somber clothes for both of us—CeCe had to make do with a pair of black jeans as she didn't own a single skirt or dress.

All the sisters had been in touch by text or e-mail, asking CeCe and me to send their love to Ally. Tiggy—the sister I was probably closest to after CeCe—called me in person to ask me to give her a huge hug.

"I so wish I could be there," she sighed. "But the guns are out up here and we have a lot of injured deer in just now."

I promised I'd give Ally the hug and smiled as I thought of my gentle younger sister and her passion for animals. She worked at a deer sanctuary up in Scotland, and I'd thought when she'd taken the job how apt it was for her. Tiggy was as light on her feet as the deer themselves—I remembered vividly going to watch her dance in a school production when she was younger and how transfixed I had been by her grace.

CeCe and I headed across the bridge to Chelsea, where Theo's funeral was to be held.

"Wow, there are even television cameras and press photographers here," whispered CeCe as we stood queuing to get into the church. "Should we wait for Ally to arrive and say hello, do you think?"

"No. Let's just sit at the back somewhere. I'm sure we can see her afterward."

The large church was already packed to the gills. Kind people shoved up on a pew at the back and we were able to squeeze in at the end. Leaning to one side, I saw the altar, a good twenty paces in front of where we sat. I felt humbled and awed at how well loved Theo must have been to draw these hundreds of people here to say good-bye to him.

A sudden hush silenced the chatter and the congregation turned as eight young men proceeded past us down the aisle bearing his coffin. Followed by a petite blond woman, who was leaning on the arm of my sister.

I looked at Ally's drawn features and saw the tension and sorrow etched onto her face. As she passed me, I wanted to stand up and hug her then and there, to tell her how proud I was of her. And how much I loved her.

The service was one of the most uplifting yet painful hours of my life. I listened to the eulogies on this man I had never met, yet whom my sister had loved. When we were told to pray, I put my head in my hands and cried for a life cut short so young, and for my sister, whose life had also been brought to a standstill by his loss. I cried too for the loss of Pa Salt, who had not given his girls the opportunity to grieve in the traditional way. It was then I understood for the first time why these ancient rituals were so vital: they provided structure at a time of emotional chaos.

I watched Ally from afar as she arrived at the altar steps, surrounded by a small orchestra, and her strained smile as she put the flute she had trained for years to play to her lips. The famous melody of "The Sailor's Hornpipe" rang through the church. I followed suit as everyone around me began to rise to their feet and fold their arms, before beginning the traditional knee-bending movements, until the whole congregation was bobbing up and down in time with the music. When it ended, the entire church erupted into applause and cheers. I knew it was a moment I would never forget.

I turned to CeCe as we sat down and saw that tears were pouring down her cheeks. It moved me further to see that my sister, who rarely showed emotion, was crying like a baby.

I grasped her hand. "You okay?"

"Beautiful," she muttered, wiping her eyes roughly on her forearm. "Just beautiful."

As Theo's coffin was borne out of the church, his mother and Ally followed behind it. I briefly caught Ally's eye and saw a shadow of a smile cross her face. CeCe and I took our turn to follow the coffin outside with the rest of the mourners, and stood on the pavement, both unsure what to do.

"Do you think we should just leave? There are so many people here. Presumably Ally will have to speak to all of them," said CeCe.

"We have to say hello. Give her a quick hug at least."

"Look, there she is."

We saw Ally, her red-gold hair falling in waves around her unnaturally pale face, emerge from the crowd and walk toward a man who was standing alone. Something about their body language told me that we shouldn't interrupt, but we moved closer so she would see us when she had finished.

Eventually, she turned away from him, and her face lit up as she came toward us.

Wordlessly, CeCe and I threw our arms around her. And hugged her as tightly as we could.

CeCe spoke to her, telling her how sorry we were. I found it hard to say anything; I knew I was close to tears again. And I felt they weren't mine to shed.

"Aren't we, Star?" CeCe prompted me.

"Yes," I managed. "It was such a beautiful service, Ally."

"Thank you."

"And wonderful to hear you playing the flute. You haven't lost your touch," CeCe added.

"Listen, I have to go with Theo's mum, but will you come back to the house?" Ally asked.

"I'm afraid we can't. But listen, our apartment's only over the bridge in Battersea, so when you're feeling a bit better, just give us a bell and pop round, yes?" CeCe suggested.

"We'd really love to see you, Ally," I said, giving her another hug. "All the girls send their love to you. Take care of yourself, won't you?"

"I'll try. And thanks again for coming. I can't tell you how much I appreciate it."

With a grateful smile, Ally gave us a last wave and then walked toward the black limousine that was waiting at the pavement for her and Theo's mother.

"We'd better get a move on ourselves." CeCe began to walk down the road, but I hung back to watch as the car pulled away from the curb. Ally, my wonderful, brave, beautiful, and—as I had thought of her up until now—invincible older sister. And yet she looked so fragile, as if a puff of wind could blow her away. As I hurried to catch up with CeCe, I realized it was love that had felled her strength.

And at that moment, I promised myself that one day I too would experience both the joy and pain of its intensity.

I was relieved when, a couple of days later, Ally was true to her word and called me. We arranged for her to come round for lunch and to see the apartment, even though CeCe would be off taking photographs of Battersea Power Station for one of her art projects. And that afternoon, I set to work on a menu.

When the doorbell rang the next day, the apartment was filled with what I hoped was the calming smell of home-cooked food. Shanthi had been right, I thought: I wanted to feed Ally's soul.

"Hello, darling, how are you?" I asked as I opened the door and embraced her.

"Oh, coping," she said, following me inside.

But I could see that she wasn't.

"Wow! This place is fantastic," she said, walking over to the floor-to-ceiling windows to look at the view.

I'd set the table on the terrace, judging it just about warm enough to do so. She admired my makeshift garden as I served up the food and my heart broke as she asked about me and CeCe, when I could see her *own* heart was breaking over and over again. But I understood that her coping mechanism was to continue as she'd always done, and never ask for sympathy.

"My goodness, this is delicious, Star. I'm discovering all sorts of hidden talents you have today. My cooking is basic at best and I can't even grow cress in a pot, let alone all this." Her hands gestured to my plants.

"Recently, I've been thinking about what talent actually is," I ventured. "I mean, are things that come easily to you a gift? For example, did you really have to try to play the flute so beautifully?"

"No, I suppose I didn't. Not initially, anyway. But then, to get better, I had to practice endlessly. I don't think that simply having a talent for something can compensate for sheer hard work. I mean, look at the great composers: It's not enough to hear the tunes in your head; you have to learn how to put them down in writing and how to orchestrate a piece. That takes years of practice and learning your craft. I'm sure there are millions of us who have a natural ability at something, but unless we harness that ability and dedicate ourselves to it, we can never reach our full potential."

I nodded, taking it in, and feeling at a loss about my own possible talents.

"Have you finished, Ally?" I asked. I could see she had barely touched her plate.

"I have. Sorry, Star. It was gorgeous, really, but I'm afraid I haven't had much of an appetite recently."

After that, we chatted about our sisters and what they'd been up to. I told her about CeCe, her college, and how her "installations" were keeping her busy. Ally commented on Maia's surprise move to Rio, and how wonderful it was for her that at last she'd found happiness.

"This has really cheered me up. And it's so great to see you, Star."

"And you. Where will you go now, do you think?"

"As a matter of fact, I might go to Norway and investigate what Pa Salt's coordinates indicate is my original place of birth."

"Good," I said. "I think you should."

"Do you?"

"Why not? Pa's clues might change your life. They changed Maia's."

After Ally had left, with a promise to return soon, I walked slowly upstairs to the bedroom and pulled my plastic wallet out of a chest of drawers that was shaped in a series of steps—CeCe's choice, not mine.

I unclipped the card attached to the back of Pa's letter and stared at it yet again. And remembered the hope I had seen in Ally's eyes when she had told me about Norway. Taking a deep breath, I finally reached for the envelope with the coordinates that Ally had looked up for me. And opened it.

The next morning, I woke up to see a slight mist hanging over the river. And as I tended to my plants, I found the terrace wet with dew. Apart from my small shrubs and fast-drooping roses, it was impossible to spot greenery unless it was through binoculars, but I took in the changing scents of the season and I smiled.

Autumn was most definitely on its way. And I *loved* autumn.

Going upstairs, I grabbed my handbag and dug out the plastic wallet from my bottom drawer. And then, not allowing my overanalytical brain to process the path my feet were taking me along, I headed for the nearest bus stop.

Half an hour later, I was once again alighting in front of Arthur Morston Books. I peered into the window, which held a display of antique map books, lying on a faded length of purple velvet. I noticed that the map of Southeast Asia that lay open still referred to Thailand as "Siam."

In the center of the display stood a small, yellowing globe on a stand, reminding me of the one that sat in Pa Salt's study. I couldn't see a single thing beyond the display—the day was bright outside, but the interior was as dark as any Dickensian bookshop I'd read about. I hovered outside, knowing that to enter would take me on a journey I wasn't sure I was ready to embark on.

But what else did I have at present? An empty, aimless life, providing nothing of value to anyone. And I *so* wanted to do something of value.

I drew out the plastic wallet from my leather rucksack and thought of Pa Salt's last words, hoping they would infuse me with the strength I needed. Finally, I opened the shop door and a small bell tinkled from somewhere within. It took my eyes a while to adjust to the shadowy light. It reminded me of an old library, with its dark wooden floor and a marble-topped fireplace halfway along one wall, forming the centerpiece around which two leather wing chairs were arranged. Between them stood a low coffee table piled high with books.

I bent down to open one, and as I did so, dust motes flew up and dispersed like minuscule snowflakes into a shaft of sunlight. Straightening, I saw that the rest of the room was taken up with endless bookshelves, their contents stacked tightly.

I glanced around, delighted. Some women might feel the same about finding a boutique full of stylish clothes. To me, this room was a similar nirvana.

I walked over to a bookshelf, searching for an author or a title I knew. Many of them were in foreign languages. I paused to peruse what looked to be an original Flaubert, then moved along to find the English books. I pulled down a copy of *Sense and Sensibility*—perhaps my favorite of Austen's novels—and leafed through its yellowing pages, keeping my touch light on the aging paper.

I was so immersed that I failed to notice a tall man surveying me from a doorway at the back of the shop.

I jumped at the sight of him and snapped the book shut, wondering if it was an "impropriety"—as I had just read in Austen—to open it.

"An Austen fan, are we? More of a Brontë devotee myself."

"I love both."

"Of course, you must know that Charlotte was not a great admirer of Jane's work. She deplored the fact that the literary supplements swooned over Ms. Austen's more . . . shall we say, 'pragmatic' prose. Charlotte wrote with her romantic heart on her sleeve. Or, should I say, in her pen."

"Really?" As I spoke, I tried to make out the man's features, but the shadows were too heavy to see more than the fact that he was very tall and thin, with reddish-blond hair, wearing a pair of horn-rimmed glasses and what looked like an Edwardian frock coat. As for his age, in this light, he could have been anywhere between thirty and fifty.

"Yes. Now then, are you looking for something in particular?"

"I . . . not really."

"Well, browse away. And if there's anything else you wish to take off the shelves and read, please feel free to sit in one of the armchairs and do so. We are as much a library as a bookshop, you see. I'm of the belief that good literature should be shared. Aren't you?"

"I absolutely am," I agreed fervently.

"Do call up for me if you need help in finding something. And if we haven't got it, I am bound to be able to order it in for you."

"Thank you."

With that, the man disappeared through the door at the back, leaving me standing in the shop alone. *This would never happen in Switzerland*, I thought to myself, *given that at any second I could snatch a book off the shelf and make a run for it.*

A sudden noise pierced the dusty silence and I realized it was my mobile ringing. Mortified, I made to grab it and switch it to silent, but not before the man reappeared, putting his finger to his lips.

"I do apologize, but it's the only rule we have here. No mobiles allowed. Would you mind awfully taking the call outside?"

"Of course not. Thanks. Bye."

My face flaming red in embarrassment, I left the shop feeling like a naughty schoolgirl who'd been caught texting her boyfriend under the desk. It was also ironic as my mobile hardly ever rang, unless it was Ma or CeCe. Outside on the pavement, I looked down and saw it was a number I didn't recognize, so I listened to the voice mail.

"Hi, Star, it's Shanthi. I got your number from Marcus. Just keeping in touch. Call me when you get a chance. Bye-bye, lovely."

I felt irrationally irritated by the fact her call had led to an undignified exit from the bookshop. Having spent so long plucking up the courage to actually go in, I knew I wouldn't find any more of it today. When I saw the bus that would take me back to Battersea, I crossed the road and jumped onto it.

You're pathetic, Star, you really are, I berated myself. *You should have just walked back inside.* But I hadn't. I'd even enjoyed the brief conversation I'd had with the man, which was a miracle in itself. And now I was on a bus back to my empty apartment and my empty life.

Arriving home, I stared at a bare wall, and decided that I needed to buy a bookshelf for it.

"*A room without books is like a body without a soul*," I quoted to myself.

But as I was stony-broke until next month after all the plant buying, I also knew that I must do something about finding a job. Relying on Pa Salt's posthumous funds wasn't helping anything, especially not my self-esteem. Perhaps tomorrow I would walk down the high street and ask in bars and restaurants if there was any work going as a cleaner. Given my lack of communication skills, I definitely wasn't cut out to be front-of-house.

I went upstairs to shower, and noticed the bottom drawer of my chest of drawers was still open from when I had retrieved the plastic wallet containing Pa Salt's letter, the coordinates, and the quotation. With a horrified jolt, I couldn't remember when I'd last seen it. I ran downstairs to search for it, my heart beating like a proverbial drum against my chest as I tipped out the entire contents of my leather rucksack, but it wasn't there. I tried to think whether I'd had it in my hands when I'd stepped into the shop and remembered that I had. But after that . . .

I could only hope that I had put it down on the table in the bookshop when I'd idled among the shelves.

Going to my laptop, I searched the bookshop's website to look up a telephone number. When I rang, it clicked through to an answering machine, the distinctive tone of the man I'd met telling me that someone would call me back as soon as possible if I left them a number. I did so, then prayed to God that he *would* call. Because if that plastic wallet was lost, so was the link to my past. And, perhaps, my future.

6

The next day, I woke up and immediately checked my mobile to see if there was a message from the bookshop. As there wasn't, I realized I had no choice but to retrace my movements to Kensington Church Street.

An hour later, I entered Arthur Morston Books for a second time. Nothing had altered since yesterday—and thankfully, on the table in front of the fireplace lay my plastic wallet. I couldn't help but give a small cry of relief as I picked it up and checked its contents, all of which were present and correct.

The shop was deserted and the door at the back of the room was closed, making it perfectly possible for me to leave without disturbing any occupant behind it. But however much I wished to do this, I had to remember the reason I had sought out this place originally. Besides, the tinkling bell must have alerted someone to my presence. And it was only polite to let them know that I had found what I needed before I left.

Again, my mobile shattered the silence and I ran to exit the shop before answering it.

"Hello?"

"Is that a Miss D'Aplièse?"

"Yes?"

"Hello, it's Arthur Morston Books here. I've just received your message. I'm going to go downstairs now and see if I can find your missing item."

"Oh," I said, confused. "Actually, I'm standing outside. I was in the shop a few seconds ago, and yes, I found it on the table where I'd left it yesterday."

"I do apologize. I must have missed the bell. I opened up, you see, then dashed back upstairs. There's a book coming up in an auction today—" A ringing noise interrupted him. "That's my representative on the landline now. Do excuse me for a moment . . ."

All went quiet at the other end before I heard his voice again. "Forgive me, Miss D'Aplièse, I just had to decide on my maximum price for a first edition of *Anna Karenina.* Fabulous copy, best I've ever seen, and signed by the author too, although I'm rather afraid the Russians and their rubles will most likely win against my paltry pounds. Still, worth a punt, don't you think?"

"Er . . . yes," I replied, nonplussed.

"As you're here, so to speak, do you want to come back in and take a cup of coffee?"

"No . . . it's fine, thank you."

"Well, come back in anyway."

The line went dead and I hovered yet again on the pavement, wondering at the bizarre way this bookshop was run. But as he'd said, I *was* here and now had an open invitation to go back inside and talk to the man who might or might not be Arthur Morston.

"Good morning." The man was entering through the back doorway of the shop as I arrived at the front. "Sorry about all that, and my sincere apologies for not getting back to you sooner about your lost property. Are you sure I can't persuade you into a coffee?"

"Positive. Thanks."

"Ah! You're not one of those young ladies who equate caffeine with heroin, are you? I must say that I don't trust people who drink decaffeinated."

"No, I'm not. If I don't have my morning cup, my day begins badly."

"Quite."

I watched him as he sat down. Now he was closer, and the light was brighter, I reckoned he was in his midthirties, very tall and thin as a rake, like me. He was dressed today in an immaculate three-piece velvet suit, the shirt cuffs peeking out from the jacket sleeves, starched and exact, with a bow tie at the throat and a matching paisley pocket square folded just so in the breast pocket. He was pale of face, as though he had never seen the sun, and his long fingers intertwined around the coffee cup he held between his hands.

"I'm cold. Are you?" he said.

"Not particularly."

"Well, it is almost September, and from what the weather forecaster said on the radio, below thirteen degrees. Shall we light a fire to cheer our senses on this misty gray morning?"

Before I could answer, he'd stood up and busied himself with the fire. Within a few minutes, the contents of the grate were alight and a blissful warmth began to emanate from it.

"Will you sit down?" He indicated the chair.

I did so.

"You don't say much, do you?" he commented, but before I could answer he continued, "Do you know that the worst thing in the world for the health of books is damp? They've dried out all summer, you see, and one has to nurse them and their fragile interiors so they don't catch paper jaundice."

He lapsed into silence then, and I stared blindly into the fire.

"Please feel free to leave at any time. My apologies if I'm keeping you."

"You're not, really."

"By the way, why did you come to visit the shop yesterday?"

"To look at the books."

"Were you just passing?"

"Why do you ask?" I said, feeling suddenly guilty.

"Simply because most of my business these days is conducted online. And the people who come into the shop are mainly locals whom I've known for years. Plus the fact that you're not over fifty, or Chinese, or Russian . . . Putting it bluntly, you don't resemble my average client." He peered at me thoughtfully from behind his horn-rimmed glasses. "I know!" He slapped his thigh delightedly. "You're an interior designer, aren't you? Furnishing some lavish flat in Eaton Square for an oligarch, and requiring twenty yards of books so that the owner can show his illiterate friends how cultured he is?"

I giggled. "No. I'm not."

"Well, that's all right then, isn't it?" he said with genuine relief. "Forgive me for seeing my stock as the equivalent of offspring. The thought of them simply being an adornment to a room—ignored and never read—is one I just cannot bear."

This was shaping up to be one of the strangest conversations I had ever had. And at least this time, it wasn't just down to me.

"So, let us rewind. Why are you here? Or should I say, why did you come here yesterday, then forget something and have to return?"

"I . . . was sent here."

"Hah! So you *are* working for a client?" the man said triumphantly.

"No, really, I'm not. I was given your card by my father."

"I see. Perhaps he's a client of ours?"

"I have no idea."

"Then why would he give you my card?"

"The thing is, I really don't know."

Again, I had the urge to laugh at the rabbit hole this conversation seemed to be heading down. I decided to explain.

"My father died about three months ago."

"My condolences, Miss D'Aplièse. Wonderfully unusual surname, by the way," he added as an afterthought. "Never heard it before. Not that that makes up for the fact your poor father is recently deceased, of course. In fact, that was a highly inappropriate comment to make. I do apologize."

"It's okay. May I ask, are you Arthur Morston?" I opened the plastic wallet and found the card to show him.

"Goodness, no," he said, studying the card. "Arthur Morston died over a hundred years ago. He was the original proprietor, you see; he opened the shop in 1850, long before the Forbes family—my family—took it over."

"My father was pretty old too. In his eighties when he died. We think, anyway."

"Good grief!" he said, studying me. "Then it just goes to show how men keep their fertility well into their dotage."

"Actually, I was adopted by him, as were my five sisters."

"Well now, that indeed makes for an interesting story. But taking that aside, why did your father send you here to speak to Arthur Morston?"

"He didn't actually say that I needed to speak to Arthur Morston specifically, I just presumed it, because that was the name on the card."

"What did he ask you to do when you arrived here?"

"To ask about"—I quickly consulted Pa's letter to check I said the right name—"a woman called Flora MacNichol."

The man surveyed me intently. Eventually he said, "Did he indeed?"

"Yes. Do you know her?"

"No, Miss D'Aplièse. She too died before I was born. But yes, of course I know *of* her . . ."

I waited for him to continue, but he didn't. Just sat, staring into space, evidently lost in his own thoughts. In the end, the silence—even for me—

became uncomfortable. Making sure I picked up the plastic wallet from the table, I stood up.

"I really am sorry to have bothered you. You have my number, so if—"

"No, no . . . I must apologize again, Miss D'Aplièse, I was actually thinking of whether I should increase my maximum offer on the *Anna Karenina.* They're so rare, you see. Mouse will throttle me, but I do want it so very much. What was it you asked me again?"

"About Flora MacNichol," I said slowly, perplexed by the way his mind seemed to dart from one subject to the next at lightning speed.

"Yes, of course, but for now, I am afraid you will have to excuse me, Miss D'Aplièse, as I've decided that I really should not let those Russians win. I'm just going to pop upstairs and telephone my agent to raise my bid before the auction starts." He rose from the chair and pulled a golden fob watch out of his pocket, clicking it open like the rabbit in *Alice in Wonderland.* "Just in time. Could you possibly mind the shop while I'm away?"

"Of course."

"Thank you."

I watched his long legs make short work of the walk to the door at the back. Then I sat there, wondering whether I was mad, or he was. But at least it had been a conversation, and I had said the words I needed to. *And set the hares running* . . .

I spent a very pleasant time acquainting myself with the stock, making a definitive mental list of what I would want to have on my own dream bookshelf. Shakespeare, of course, and Dickens, not to mention F. Scott Fitzgerald and Evelyn Waugh . . . And then some of the modern books I loved too, which hadn't yet had time to become classics but I knew would be just as valuable to any collector in a couple of hundred years' time, if not as beautifully bound in leather as they used to be.

Not a single person entered the shop as I wandered the shelves. Hunting through the children's section, I found a collection of Beatrix Potter books—*The Tale of Mrs. Tiggy-Winkle* being my all-time favorite.

I sat down by the fire and began to turn its pages. And had a vivid flashback to a Christmas when I must have been very young. I'd found a copy of this book under the tree from Père Noël, and that night, Pa Salt had taken me on his knee in front of the fire that blazed merrily in our sitting room all winter and read the story to me. In my mind's eye, I remembered looking out of the windows at the snow-capped mountains feeling warm, contented, and very, very loved.

"At peace with myself," I whispered out loud. *That is what I want to find again.*

"All done," came the man's voice, jolting me out of my memories. "Call me reckless, but I just had to have that book. I've been searching for it for years. Mouse will no doubt give me a tongue lashing, which I fully deserve, for bankrupting us even further. Goodness, I'm hungry! It's all that stress. You?"

I looked down at my watch and saw that over an hour had passed since he'd disappeared upstairs and it was now five to one.

"I don't know."

"Well, could I tempt you? There's an excellent restaurant just across the road which very kindly provides me with whatever the day's menu is. It's a set menu, you see," he clarified, as if this was important. "Always exciting to never be quite sure what you will get, rather than choosing it for yourself, don't you think?"

"I suppose so."

"Why don't I run across the road to collect the food and see if I can entice you? I owe you lunch at least, for being kind enough to stay down here while I sweated it out over the auction."

"Okay."

"Beatrix Potter, eh?" he said as he glanced down at the book in my hands. "How ironic. In all sorts of ways. She knew Flora MacNichol, but then nothing in life is a coincidence, is it?"

With that, he left the shop, and if I'd had any intention of disappearing while he was out, his parting words had prohibited it. I tended the fire in the way that Pa Salt had taught me, banking the coal close together so that it did not burn too fast and waste fuel but gave out a steady, constant heat.

Again, the shop remained deserted, so I read *The Tale of Jemima Puddle-Duck* and *Tom Kitten* while I waited for his return. I was just about to begin on *Jeremy Fisher* when my nameless lunch companion reappeared through the door holding two brown-paper bags.

"Looks excellent today," he said as he locked the door behind him and turned the sign to CLOSED. "I don't like to be disturbed when I'm eating. Bad for the digestion, don't you know. I'll just pop upstairs and get some plates. Oh, and a good glass of white Sancerre to go with the fish," he added as he strode across the shop and I heard him bound up the stairs.

I was amused at his mannered, old-fashioned use of language. Even though I'd become used to the clipped English spoken here by the upper classes, my new friend took this to another level. *A true English eccentric*, I thought, and I liked him for it. He wasn't afraid to be exactly who he was, and I knew only too well how much strength of character that took.

"Now, I hope you like sole, and the fresh green beans are no doubt sautéed to perfection," he said as he reappeared with a bottle of wine, condensation dripping off it; plates; cutlery; and two perfectly starched white linen napkins.

"I do, very much. And yes," I said, "green beans are surprisingly tricky to cook well."

"You're a chef?" he asked me as he removed the covering from two foil trays. They reminded me of plane food. I could only hope their contents tasted better.

"No, I just enjoy it. I took a course a few weeks ago and I had to serve green beans."

"You must understand I am not a food snob in the modern sense; I don't mind what I throw down my gullet, but I do insist it's well cooked. The problem is, I'm spoiled. Clarke's is one of the best restaurants in London and their kitchen has prepared this for us today. Now then, will you have a glass of wine?" he asked as he transferred the food onto a china plate and placed it carefully in front of me.

"I don't usually drink at lunchtime."

"Well, I always think it's good to break bad habits, don't you? Here."

He poured me a glass and handed it to me across the table.

"*Tchin-tchin!*" he toasted me, gulping back a large swig, before proceeding to take enormous forkfuls of his fish. I prodded mine gently.

"It really is excellent, Miss D'Aplièse," he encouraged me. "Don't tell me you are on a diet?"

"No. I'm just not used to eating at lunchtime either."

"Well now, as the saying goes, 'Eat breakfast like a king, lunch like a prince, and dinner like a pauper.' Such a simple maxim to follow, and yet the human race ignores it and then complains when it's unable to shift its fat. Not that weight seems to be a problem for either of us."

"No." I blushed as I continued to eat, noticing that he'd already vacuumed his plate clean. He was right—the food was excellent. He observed me closely as I ate, which I found extremely off-putting. I picked up my wineglass and took a sip, trying to garner my courage to ask the questions I needed to. I had come here to find answers, I reminded myself.

"You said Flora MacNichol knew Beatrix Potter?" I prompted him.

"Indeed, indeed. And so she did. In fact, Miss Potter once owned this very shop. Have you finished?" He eyed the one mouthful I had left on my fork. "I'll take the dirty plates upstairs out of the way. I do so hate looking at them, don't you?"

As soon as my fork was back on my plate, he swept it up, along with the bottle of wine. He took his own finished glass too, and seeing mine was no more than half drunk, he left it on the table and disappeared through the back door.

I took another sip of my wine, which I didn't really want, and remembered that I must ask him his name when he returned. Prizing information out of this man was a delicate operation.

When he reappeared this time, he was carrying a tea tray with two china cups and a *cafetière* on it.

"Do you take sugar?" he asked as he placed it perilously on top of an old dictionary. I briefly wondered how much the book was worth. "Love the stuff myself."

"I love it too. Three please."

"Ah, I always have four."

"Thank you," I said as he passed me my cup, and I felt as if I had been swept up in the Mad Hatter's tea party. "So how did Flora MacNichol know Beatrix Potter?" I asked again.

"She was once a neighbor of Miss Potter's."

"Up in the Lake District?"

"Indeed," he said approvingly. "Do you know about books and their authors, Miss D'Aplièse?"

"Please, call me Star. And you are . . . ?"

"Your name is 'Star'?"

"Yes." I couldn't tell from the expression on his face whether he approved or not. "It's short for 'Asterope.'"

"Ah! Aha!" A smile tickled his lips and he began to chuckle. "Again, how deliciously ironic! Asterope, the wife—or mother, depending on the myth—of King Oenomaus of Pisa. You are one of the Seven Sisters of the Pleiades, the third of Atlas and Pleione's daughters, after Maia and Alcyone, and before Celaeno, Taygete, Electra, and Merope . . . 'Many a night I saw the Pleiads, rising thro' the mellow shade, / Glitter like a swarm of fireflies tangled in a silver braid . . .'"

"Tennyson," I said automatically, recognizing the quote from one of Pa's books.

"Correct. My dear departed father, who owned this shop before me, studied classics at Oxford, so my childhood was full of myths and legends . . . although I was *not* the son to be named after a mythical Greek king, but that's another story . . ." His voice trailed off and I worried that his attention had wandered again. "No, I was named by my sainted mother, God rest her soul, who studied literature at Oxford. Which was where my parents met and fell in love. Books are in my blood, you might say. Perhaps that is the case for you too. So, do you know anything of the family from which you were originally adopted?"

My hand reached for the plastic wallet. "Actually, that's why I'm here. My father left me these . . . clues to find out where I came from."

"Ha! The game is afoot!" The man clapped his hands together. "I do so love a good mystery. Are the clues in there?"

"Yes, but all the information I have, apart from the bookshop card telling me to ask here about Flora MacNichol, is the place I was born. And this." I laid the jewelry box on the table in front of him, opened it, and took out the panther. My heart was beating in fear at the trust I was placing in this stranger, sharing information with him that I had not yet even confided in CeCe.

His long fingers pushed his glasses higher up his nose as he scrutinized the apparent address of my birth, and then the panther with great care. He returned them to me and leaned back in his chair. He opened his mouth to speak, and I shifted forward to hear his thoughts.

"It's time for cake," he said eventually. "Although, isn't it always?"

He vanished upstairs, then reappeared with two slices of gooey chocolate gateau. "Want some? It's awfully good. I buy it from the patisserie along the road in the morning. I find my sugar levels drop between three and five, so it's this, or a nap."

"Yes, please," I said. "I love cake too. By the way, what is your name?"

"Good grief! Have I not told you? I'm sure I must have done at some point."

"No, you haven't."

"Well now, well now . . . that is a thing, and I do apologize. My mother named me for her favorite books. Therefore, I am either a grossly fat marmalade cat, or a fictional embodiment of a famous female author who ran off to France with her female lover and presented herself as a man. So," he challenged me, "what is my name?"

"Orlando." *And it's perfect*, I thought.

"Miss D'Aplièse"—he gave me a bow—"I am deeply impressed by your literary knowledge. So, am I more fat marmalade cat or, in fact, a woman masquerading as a man?"

I suppressed a laugh. "I think you are neither. You are simply *you*."

"And I think, Miss D'Aplièse"—he leaned forward and cupped a hand against his left cheek—"that you know far more about literature than you are letting on."

"I took a degree in it, but really, I'm no expert."

"You underestimate yourself. There are few human beings on the planet who would know of the marmalade cat and the famous biographical novel by . . ."

I watched him search for the author's name. And knew full well he was still testing me. "Virginia Woolf," I answered. "The story was inspired by the life of Vita Sackville-West and her affair with Violet Trefusis. And the *Orlando the Marmalade Cat* books were written by Kathleen Hale. One of her closest friends was Vanessa Bell, Virginia Woolf's sister, who also had an affair with Vita Sackville-West. But you probably know all this . . ."

As my voice trailed off, I was suddenly embarrassed that I'd imparted all this information. I'd simply been carried away with the excitement of finding another obsessive book lover like me.

Orlando was silent for a while as he digested my words.

"I knew some of it, yes, but not all. And I had never made the connection between the authors of those two entirely different books. How did you?"

"I did my dissertation on the Bloomsbury Set."

"Aha! But then, as you may well have noticed, Miss D'Aplièse, my mind flits around like a flitty thing. It's a bee searching for nectar and once it has found it, it moves on. Yours, to the contrary, does not. I believe that you are hiding your light under a bushel. A word I still mourn the death of in the English language, don't you?"

"I—"

"Tell me," he continued, "how do you know so much, yet present so little? You're like the sliver of a new moon, and just as mysterious. Miss D'Aplièse . . . Star, Asterope, whichever nom de plume you wish to use, would you like a job?"

"I would. I need one, because I'm broke." I tried not to look too desperate.

"Ha! So am I, and the business too, after today's little purchase. Of course, the wages would be dreadful, but I would feed you well."

"Exactly how bad are the wages?" I asked him, in an effort to pin Orlando down before he zoomed off in another direction.

"Oh, I don't know. The last student I employed took home enough to keep a roof over his head. Tell me what you need."

In truth, I knew that I would pay *him* to just be here every day. "Two hundred and fifty pounds a week?"

"Done." Then Orlando smiled. And it was a big smile that showed his uneven teeth. "I must warn you, I'm not terribly good with people. I'm aware they think I'm a little strange. I seem to put them off somewhat when they walk in here. Better on the Internet, don't you know? Can't sell a nut to a monkey, but my books are good."

"When do you want me to start?"

"Tomorrow. If that's possible?"

"Ten o'clock?"

"Perfect. I'll run upstairs and bring you a set of keys." He stood up again and was about to dash upstairs when I stopped him.

"Orlando?"

"Yes?"

"Do you want to see my CV?"

"Why on earth would I want to see that?" he asked as he spun around. "I just gave you the most thorough interview possible. And you passed with flying colors."

A few minutes later, I had collected my clues back into my plastic wallet and a heavy set of brass keys had been pressed into my palm. Orlando ushered me to the door.

"Thank you, Miss . . . what do you wish me to call you?"

"Star will do fine."

"Miss Star." He opened the door for me and I walked through it. "See you tomorrow."

"Yes."

I'd started walking down the street before he called to me.

"And, Miss Star?"

"Yes?"

"Remind me to tell you more about Flora MacNichol. And her connection to that animal figurine of yours. Good-bye for now."

I felt as though I had just been turfed out of Narnia back through the wardrobe. Outside, Arthur Morston Books felt like a parallel universe. But as I took the bus home and inserted my key card to gain entry to the apartment, I felt a little bubble of happiness and expectation. I hummed as I cooked supper, and mulled over whether to tell CeCe about my extraordinary day. In the end, I only mentioned that I'd found a job in a bookshop and would be starting tomorrow.

"That's good for now, I suppose," she said. "But you're certainly not going to make a fortune selling old books for someone else."

"I know, but I like it there."

I excused myself from the table as soon as possible and went outside to tend to my plants. My new job may not have been much to anyone else, but it was an awful lot to me.

7

My first two weeks at Arthur Morston Books consisted of much the same pattern as the day I'd arrived. Orlando would mostly be upstairs during the morning—the space behind the back door and what lay on the upper floor remained unknown to me—and I was told to call up to him if a customer wanted to see one of the most rare and valuable books, which were kept in a huge rusting safe in the cellar, or if there was a query I couldn't answer. But there rarely was—a query *or* a customer.

I began to recognize what Orlando called his "regulars": mostly pensioners, who would pick a book off the shelf and politely ask me the price, which was always written on a card at the back of it. Then, formalities over, they would take the book to one of the leather chairs and sit by the fire to read it. Often, they were there for hours before looking up from the book, then leaving with a polite "thank you." One particularly ancient gentleman in a threadbare tweed jacket came in every day for a week to pick up *The House of Mirth* and sit down with it. I noticed he'd even added a slip of paper to mark where he'd got to before he slid it back onto the shelf each day.

Orlando had provided me with the *cafetière* to make coffee in the alcove at the back of the shop, which I was to offer to any "customer" who came in. One of my duties was to buy a pint of milk on my way to work, which I would often pour away unused, as there were so few takers.

And it was above the shelf in the alcove that a picture caught my eye, the style of the illustrations being as familiar as the palm of my own hand. I stood on tiptoe to take a closer look and saw from the writing—now faded to within a ghostly whisper of its original—that it was a letter. The tiny watercolors that peppered the page had fared better and I marveled at the perfection of them. My nose almost pressed to the glass to decipher the words, I saw a date and the faint outline of a name.

"My dear Fl—" The rest of the name was too faded to be conclusive. But the signature at the bottom of the page of small, neat writing was not. It was without a doubt proclaiming the author of this letter as "Beatrix."

"Fl . . ." I murmured to myself. Could this letter be to *my* Flora MacNichol? Orlando had said that Beatrix Potter and Flora had known each other. I was determined to ask him.

At one o'clock precisely, Orlando would hare down the stairs and disappear through the front door. This seemed to be an invisible signal to whoever was reading in the chairs by the fire to leave. When he was back, Orlando would lock the door behind him and swing the sign to CLOSED.

The china plates, cutlery, and starched white linen napkins would appear from upstairs and we would proceed to eat.

This was my favorite part of the day. I loved listening to him as his mind skittered between one topic and another, normally punctuated by a literary quotation. It became a game for me to try to work out what particular subject would lead on to the next. Yet I usually failed to guess, as he veered off on wild and obscure tangents. I managed in between to learn that his "sainted" mother, Vivienne, had perished in a tragic car accident when Orlando was merely twenty and in his second year at Oxford. His father had been so heartbroken, he had promptly taken himself off to Greece to "drown himself in the misery of his mythological gods, and ouzo." He had died of cancer only a few years back.

"So you see," Orlando had added dramatically, "I am an orphan too."

His conversation was also sporadically peppered with questions about my own upbringing at Atlantis. Pa Salt especially seemed to fascinate him.

"So who was he? To know what he knew . . . ," Orlando muttered once after I'd confessed that I didn't even know Pa's country of birth.

Nevertheless, despite his obsession with Pa, he never volunteered any further information on the subject of Flora MacNichol. When I'd brought up the framed letter from Beatrix Potter, there was not the reaction I'd hoped there would be.

"Oh, that old thing"—he waved a hand toward it—"Beatrix wrote rather a lot of letters to children." And off he went on another subject before I could pin him down.

One day soon, I promised myself I would find the courage to ask more. But even if I never learned more about Flora MacNichol, my days were filled with glorious books; just the scent and feel of them as I cataloged new stock in a vast leather-bound ledger with a heavy ink pen filled me with pleasure. I'd had to take a handwriting test before he'd actually let me put ink to paper. I'd always been complimented on my clear, elegant script, but I'd never thought that one day a skill that was fast becoming archaic and defunct would turn into an asset.

As I sat on the bus on the way to the bookshop at the beginning of my third week, I pondered whether I should have been born in a different era. One where the pace of life was slower and missives to loved ones would take days—if not months—to reach them, rather than arrive in seconds by e-mail.

"Good God! I loathe modern technology with a passion!" Orlando mirrored my thoughts as he strode through the front door at his habitual half past ten, patisserie box in hand. "Last night, due to a freak rainstorm, all the telephone lines went down in Kensington, taking the Internet with them. And I was unable to put in my bid for a particularly spectacular copy of *War and Peace*. I love that book," he sighed, turning to me with a crest-fallen face. "Ah well, Mouse will be relieved that I'm not spending more money we don't have. Talking of whom, I mentioned you the other day."

I'd heard about "Mouse" several times before, but had never managed to ascertain exactly who this person actually *was* to Orlando. Or even whether they were male or female.

"Did you?"

"Yes. Are you busy this weekend, Miss Star? I have to travel to High Weald for Rory's birthday. Mouse will be there too. Thought you could see the house, meet Marguerite, and chat about Flora MacNichol."

"Yes . . . I'm free," I said, realizing I had to grasp the opportunity while it was on offer.

"That's settled, then. I shall meet you at Charing Cross in the first-class carriage of the ten o'clock train to Ashford on Saturday. I shall have your ticket with me. Now, I must disappear back upstairs to discover whether Wi-Fi—our great modern god—has deigned to appear to us mortals."

"Where are we going, exactly?"

"Haven't I told you?"

"No."

"To Kent, of course," he said airily, as though it should have been obvious.

For the rest of the week, I was torn between excitement and fear of the unknown. I'd been to Kent once on a university trip to see Sissinghurst, the glorious house and gardens that had once been the home of the novelist and poet Vita Sackville-West. I remembered it as a gentle and mellow county—the "garden of England," as one of my fellow students had told me it was nicknamed.

As promised, Orlando was already in the carriage when I arrived at Charing Cross station on Saturday morning. His midnight-blue velvet jacket and paisley scarf—not to mention the enormous picnic hamper that took up the whole of the table we were supposedly to share with other passengers—made for an incongruous sight on the modern train.

"My dear Miss Star," he said as I sat down next to him. "Perfectly on time as always. Punctuality is a virtue that should be lauded more often than it is. Cup of coffee?"

He opened the hamper and produced a flask and two china coffee cups, followed by plates of fresh, still-warm croissants wrapped in linen napkins. As the train pulled out of the station and Orlando served me breakfast, chatting to me as usual about everything and nothing, I noticed nearby passengers looking at us in bewilderment. I was only thankful that no one was sitting in the seats opposite.

"How long is the train journey?" I asked him as he took out two further plates of perfectly arranged chopped fruit and removed the cling film.

"An hour or thereabouts. Marguerite will collect us from Ashford station."

"Who is Marguerite?"

"My cousin."

"And Rory?"

"A charming little boy, who will be seven tomorrow. Mouse will be there too, although, unlike your good self, the poor dear has no concept of timekeeping. Now, if you'll excuse me," he said as he returned the dishes to the picnic basket, then fastidiously wiped every last crumb off himself and the table into a napkin, "I must take forty winks."

With that, Orlando folded his arms across his chest as if to protect himself from being shot, and nodded off.

Thirty minutes later, just as I was beginning to get nervous about getting off at Ashford, but not liking to disturb Orlando, his eyes suddenly snapped open.

"Two minutes, Miss Star, and we will alight."

The platform was bathed in mellow autumn sunlight as we walked along it, dodging other travelers.

"Progress takes its steady toll," Orlando lamented. "With the Eurotunnel station they are building, we'll never have peace and quiet here again."

As we emerged onto the station forecourt, I noticed there had been a frost the night before, and I could see the faint smoky tinge of my breath.

"There she is," Orlando said, marching at full speed toward a battered Fiat 500. "Dearest Marguerite, it's so kind of you to come and sweep us up," he said as a statuesque woman, as tall as he, extricated her long limbs from behind the wheel of the tiny car.

"Orlando," she said haltingly as he kissed her on both cheeks. She pointed to the large wicker hamper. "How on earth are we meant to get that in the car? Especially as you have brought a guest."

I felt her large, dark eyes sweep over me. They were an arresting color—almost violet.

"Allow me to introduce Miss Asterope D'Aplièse, more commonly known as Star. Miss Star: my cousin, Marguerite Vaughan."

"What an unusual name," the woman said as she approached me, and I saw from the faint lines on her pale skin that she was older than I'd initially thought, probably in her early forties.

"It's a pleasure to meet you," she continued. "I can only apologize for my cousin's thoughtlessness by bringing this ridiculous hamper, which you'll now have to squeeze in next to. God knows what's wrong with the coffee at Pret," she said, rolling her eyes at Orlando, who was attempting to load the hamper onto the backseat. "But I'm sure you know what he's like." She smiled at me warmly.

"I do," I said, finding myself smiling too.

"Personally, I think we should make him walk the five miles home as penance so that you can sit in comfort." She patted my arm conspiratorially. "Come on, Orlando, I've got a lot to do when we get home. The beef isn't in yet."

"I do apologize, Miss Star." Orlando looked like a chastened child. "I am completely thoughtless." He held the door open for me as I clambered into the back and wedged myself into the tiny space beside the basket, my arms pinned to my sides.

We set off down the leafy country roads, Marguerite and Orlando in the front, both so tall that the tops of their heads almost brushed the roof. I felt rather like a child again, but busied myself by looking out of the window, admiring the beauty of the English countryside.

Orlando talked nineteen to the dozen about books he'd bought and sold, and Marguerite admonished him gently for overspending on *Anna Karenina*—Mouse had told her, apparently—but I could hear the affection in her voice. Sitting behind her, I was close enough to smell her perfume—a comforting musky scent that filled the car.

Her thick, dark hair fell in natural waves to her shoulders and when she turned to Orlando to speak to him, I saw she had what Pa Salt would have termed a Roman nose, which sat prominently in her striking face. She was certainly not classically beautiful and, from the look of her jeans and old sweater, did not care to make herself more so. Yet, there was something very attractive about her and I realized I wanted her to like me—an unusual feeling.

"Are you coping back there?" she asked me. "Not far now."

"Yes, thank you." I leaned my head against the windowpane as the thick hedges, their height exaggerated by the low car, flew by me, the country lanes becoming narrower. It felt so good to be out of London, with only the odd red-brick chimney stack peeping out from behind the wall of green. We turned right, through a pair of old gates that led to a drive so potholed that Marguerite's and Orlando's heads bumped against the roof.

"I really must ask Mouse to bring the tractor and fill in these holes with gravel before the winter comes," she commented to Orlando. "Here we are, Star," she added as she pulled the car to a halt in front of a large, graceful house, its walls formed from mellow red brick, with ivy and wisteria fringing the uneven windows in greenery. Tall, thin chimney stacks, which emphasized the Tudor architecture, reached up into the crisp September sky. As I squeezed myself out of the back of the Fiat, I imagined the house's interior to be rambling as opposed to impressive—it was certainly no stately home; rather, it looked as if it had gently aged and sunk slowly into the countryside surrounding it. It spoke of a bygone era, one that I loved reading about in books, and I experienced a twinge of longing.

I followed Marguerite and Orlando toward the magnificent oak front door, and saw a young boy wobbling toward us on a shiny red bike. He let out a strange muffled shout, tried to wave, and promptly fell off the bike.

"Rory!" Marguerite ran to him, but he had already picked himself up. He spoke again, and I wondered if he was foreign, as I couldn't make out what he was saying. She dusted him down, then the boy picked up the bike and the two of them walked back to us.

"Look who's here," Marguerite said, turning directly to the boy to speak to him. "It's Orlando and his friend Star. Try saying 'Star.'" She particularly enunciated the "st" in my name.

"Ss-t-aahh," the boy said as he approached me, a smile on his face, before holding up his hand and opening his fingers out like a shining star. I saw that Rory was the owner of a pair of inquisitive green eyes, framed by dark lashes. His wavy copper-colored hair glowed in the sun, and his rosy cheeks dimpled with happiness. I recognized that he was the kind of child that one would never want to say no to.

"He prefers to go by the name 'Superman,' don't you, Rory?" Orlando chuckled, holding up his hand in a fist like Superman taking off into the air.

Rory nodded, then shook my hand with all the dignity of a superhero, and turned to Orlando for a hug. After giving him a tight squeeze and a tickle, Orlando set him down, then squatted in front of him and used his hands to sign, also speaking the words clearly.

"Happy birthday! I have your present in Marguerite's car. Would you like to come and get it with me?"

"Yes please," Rory spoke and signed, and I knew then that he was deaf. I rifled through my rusty mental catalog of what I had learned from Ma over two decades ago. I watched as the two of them stood up and walked hand in hand toward the car.

"Come inside with me, Star," said Marguerite. "They could be some time."

I followed her into an entrance hall that contained a wide Tudor staircase, which I could see from the wonderfully turned and carved oak banister was not a reproduction. As we made our way along a passage, the old stone flags cracked and uneven beneath my feet, I inhaled the atmosphere, scented with dust and wood smoke, imagining the thousands of fires that had been lit over the centuries to keep its occupants warm. And felt a definite envy for the woman who lived in this incredible house.

"I'm afraid I'm dragging you straight to the kitchen, as I have to get on. Please excuse the mess in here—we have God knows how many for Rory's birthday lunch and I haven't even peeled the potatoes yet."

"I'll help you," I offered as we entered a low-ceilinged room awash with beams, an inglenook fireplace forming the centerpiece with a cast-iron range inside it.

"Well, you could certainly help by pouring us both a drink," she suggested, her open gaze mirroring the warmth and beauty of her home. "The pantry is over there; there's a bottle of gin, I know, and I'm just praying there's some tonic in the fridge. Otherwise we'll have to be inventive. Now, where on earth did I put the potato peeler?"

"It's here." I picked it up from the long oak table, strewn with newspapers, cereal packets, dirty plates, and one muddy sock. "Why don't you get the drinks, and I'll do the vegetables?"

"No, Star, you're our guest . . ."

I had already grabbed the bag of potatoes and taken down a saucepan from a rack. I pulled out what I saw was a week-old newspaper to put the peelings on and sat down at the kitchen table.

"Well"—Marguerite smiled in gratitude—"I'll go and get the gin then."

In the following hour or so, I peeled all the vegetables, prepared the joint of beef, and put it in the range, then set about straightening the kitchen. Having found the gin and added some rather flat tonic to it, Marguerite left me in charge as she floated in and out to tend to her son, greet arriving guests, and set the table for lunch. I hummed as I pottered around what—without the current disorganized detritus—was my dream kitchen. The heat from the range warmed the room, and as I looked up at the cracks on the ceiling, I imagined the old yellowed walls with a fresh coat of white paint. Clearing the oak table, which was pockmarked with wax from dripping candles, I then washed up what was probably a week's worth of pans and plates.

Once everything was under control, I gazed out of the window, with its uneven glass panes, onto a kitchen garden that must have once been the source of vegetables for the house. I stepped out of the kitchen door to look closer and saw that it was now overgrown and in disarray, but I found a hardy rosemary bush and clipped some of the herb off it to flavor the roast potatoes.

I could live here, I thought as Marguerite returned, having changed into a rather creased honey-colored silk blouse and a purple scarf that complemented her eyes.

"Oh my God, Star, you miracle worker! I haven't seen the kitchen look like this for years! Thank you. Do you want a job?"

"I already have one with Orlando."

"I know, and I'm so happy you're there for him. Maybe you could occasionally dissuade him from spending large amounts of money to fund what is becoming his own personal library."

"He does actually sell quite a lot of books online," I replied, defending him as Marguerite poured herself another measure of gin.

"I know," she said fondly. "Right, Rory's having a fine old time opening all his presents in the sitting room and Orlando's gone down to the cellar to get more wine for the guests, so I can sit down for five minutes." She checked her watch before letting out a sigh. "Mouse is late again, but we shan't postpone lunch. I presume you gathered this morning that Rory's deaf?"

"Yes, I did," I replied, thinking that, just like her cousin, Marguerite's brain flitted from one subject to the next like a butterfly.

"And has been since birth. He has a little hearing in his left ear, but his hearing aids only go so far. I just . . ." She paused, meeting my gaze. "I never want him to feel as if he can't do something, as if he's lesser than anyone else. The things that people say sometimes . . ." She shook her head and sighed. "He's the most wonderful, smart little boy there is."

"He and Orlando seem very close," I ventured.

"Orlando was the one who taught him to read when he was five, having mastered British Sign Language so he could speak to Rory and teach him. We've mainstreamed him—that is, placed him in the local primary school—and he's even teaching the other children to sign. He's got a fantastic speech therapist working with him every week to encourage him to talk and lip-read and he's doing brilliantly. Children at his age learn so quickly. Now, I should be taking you through to meet the guests, rather than keeping you locked away in the kitchen like Cinderella."

"Really, it's fine. I'll check the beef." I walked over to the range and bent down to retrieve the joint and the roast potatoes. "I hope you don't mind, but I've added some honey and sesame seeds I found in the pantry to give the carrots some flavor."

"Goodness! I don't mind at all. I've never been much of a cook and it's been heaven having you do the lunch. What with Rory, and this troublesome house, not to mention my job, which I desperately need to pay the bills on it, I'm constantly chasing my tail. I've been offered a fantastic commission to paint a mural in France, but I just don't know if I can leave Rory . . ." Marguerite's voice trailed off. "My apologies, Star, these aren't your problems."

"You're an artist?"

"I'd like to think I was, yes, although someone said to me recently that I merely design wallpaper." Marguerite raised an eyebrow. "Anyway, thanks for today."

"I don't mind helping, really. What time do you want to eat? The beef is done, it just needs to rest."

"Whenever you're ready. Everyone who comes to High Weald is used to waiting for as long as it takes."

"How about half an hour? If you have some eggs, I can make Yorkshire puddings."

"Oh, we have eggs; the chickens run free range around the kitchen garden. We live on omelets here. I'll get them for you," she said as she walked into the pantry.

"Mag! I'm hungry!"

I turned and saw Rory entering the kitchen.

"Hello," I signed, then tried to mimic Orlando's hand movements from earlier, clapping my hands together twice, then sweeping my palms flat upward and forward. "Happy birthday," I managed.

He looked startled, then smiled. "Thank you," he signed back. Then pointed at the range and tapped his wrist as if there was a watch, before shrugging his shoulders in a question.

"Lunch is ready in thirty minutes."

"Okay." Rory made his way over to look at the beef.

"Cow," I signed, putting my fingers against my head in little horns. Rory burst into giggles and made the sign back to me with the correct finger placements. I took a knife and sliced a little off the joint for him as Marguerite emerged from the pantry. Rory put it into his mouth and chewed it.

"Good." He gave me a thumbs-up.

"Thank you," I signed by placing my fingers against my chin and then moving my hand away, hoping the French and British signs were similar.

"Don't tell me you know sign language as well, Star?" Marguerite said.

"I learned some when I was young, but I'm not very good, am I, Rory?"

Rory turned to his mother and signed quickly to her, making her laugh.

"He says your signing is dreadful, but your 'cow' makes up for it. Apparently you're a far better cook than me. You cheeky monkey." She ruffled his hair.

"Mouse here," Rory said, as he gazed out of the window. He made a little darting motion with one hand, like an animal scurrying.

"And about time. Star, do you mind if I leave you here for a while and go and entertain my guests?" She put the eggs for the Yorkshire puddings down on the table.

"Of course not," I said as Rory grasped his mother's hands and dragged her out of the kitchen.

"I promise to be back to help you serve," she said over her shoulder.

"No problem," I said as I went to the pantry in search of flour.

During the next half hour, I put some of the tricks I had learned in my course into practice, and by the time Marguerite returned, lunch was ready. I'd sourced serving dishes from the pine dresser and Marguerite's eyebrows raised in surprise as I began handing her dishes to carry through.

"Goodness, I'd forgotten where all this china had got to. Star, you really are an angel to do this."

"I don't mind. I've enjoyed it."

And I had. It was rare I got to cook for anyone other than CeCe. I was just thinking that perhaps I should place a card in our local newsagent's advertising my services when a man appeared in the kitchen.

"Hello, I've been sent to carve the beef. Where is it?" he said shortly.

I took in his unruly hair, graying slightly at the temples, his strong facial features dominated by a pair of watchful green eyes that I felt sweep over me. He was wearing a moth-eaten V-neck sweater over a shirt with a collar that was fraying, and a pair of jeans. As he came toward me, I saw that he towered over me. There was a definite resemblance to Orlando, but this man was a far more rugged—and certainly unkempt—version, and I wondered if this could be the brother Orlando had mentioned to me.

Gathering my wits, I replied to his question. "It's there, on the range."

"Thanks."

I studied him surreptitiously as he walked past me, and noticed the tense way he held himself as he pulled a knife from the drawer. His silence as he began to carve told me that he possessed none of the easy warmth of his possible relations. I hovered in the kitchen, suddenly uncomfortable, as if he felt I was an intruder, and wondered if I should find my way to the dining room. Just as I was about to do so, Marguerite reappeared.

"Is that nearly done, Mouse? They're about to eat their plates if you don't hurry up."

"Such things take the time they take," came the reply, equally cold as his initial sentence to me.

"Well, you come through with me, Star, and we'll leave Mouse to perform his magic."

Of all the characters I'd imagined in my head that could possibly be the famous "Mouse," it wasn't *this* man, who, although handsome, could have frozen an atmosphere in a few seconds. As I followed Marguerite from the kitchen to a low-ceilinged dining room with a fire playing merrily in the grate, I only hoped I wouldn't end up sitting next to him for lunch.

"There you are, dear girl," said Orlando, whose flushed cheeks indicated he'd been enjoying the wine he'd brought up from the cellar. "This looks absolutely splendid."

"Thank you."

"Come and sit down by me. Mouse is on the other side of you and I thought you could chat to him about Flora MacNichol. He's done some research on her recently."

"Star, can I introduce you to everyone at the table?" said Marguerite.

She did so, and I automatically said hello to the half a dozen new faces, trying but failing to absorb all their names and how they were connected to Rory.

"Is Mouse a relative of yours?" I asked Orlando in an undertone.

"Of course he is, dear girl," he chuckled. "He's my older brother. Have I not told you that? I'm sure I must have done."

"No."

"And before you say it, I am aware that he stole all our parents' beauty and brains, leaving me to embody the runt of the litter. A role I fulfill comfortably."

Yes, but you embody warmth and empathy, while your brother has none of either . . .

Mouse strode around the table to sit down next to me. As he did so, Orlando stood up.

"My lords, ladies, and gentlemen, may I have the honor of proposing a toast to Master Rory on the occasion of his seventh birthday. To your health and wealth, young man," Orlando signed to Rory as he spoke. He raised his glass with the assembled company and I saw Rory positively glow with happiness. Everyone lifted their hands in the air to applaud, and swept up by the good cheer of the table, I lifted mine too.

"Happy birthday," muttered Mouse from beside me, making no effort to sign the words.

"Right, please, everyone, let's eat," Marguerite urged.

I was sandwiched between the two brothers—one who, as usual, ate his food like a human waste disposal, and the other who hardly appeared interested in the process. Glancing around at the wine-mellowed company, I experienced a sudden frisson of pleasure, and allowed myself to think how far I had come in the months since Pa's death. The fact I was sitting at a lunch table surrounded by strangers was akin to a miracle.

Baby steps, Star, baby steps . . .

I also felt transported back to the many Sunday lunches at Atlantis with Pa Salt, when all of us had been younger and living at home. I could never remember any strangers being present, but then, Ma, Pa, and we six girls made eight—easily enough people to produce the kind of warmth and chatter I was experiencing here. I'd missed being part of a family.

I realized the Ice Man on my right was speaking to me.

"Orlando told me you work for him."

"Yes, I do."

"I doubt you'll survive for long. They usually don't."

"Steady on, old boy," cut in Orlando good-naturedly. "Star and I muddle along together rather well, don't we?"

"We do," I said, in a far louder and more definite tone than I would normally have used, defensive of my odd but sweet employer.

"Well, he needs someone to sort him out. The shop's been running at a loss for years now, but he refuses to listen. You know the shop will have to go soon, Orlando. It's on one of the most expensive streets in London. It would fetch a very good price on the market."

"Could we possibly discuss this another time? I always find that mixing business with the pleasure of eating gives me indigestion," countered Orlando.

"You see? He always makes an excuse not to face up to it."

The words were murmured and I turned to see that Mouse's green eyes were staring directly at me.

"Perhaps you could make him see sense. The business could even go completely online. The property taxes on the bookshop are astronomical and the footfall, as we both know, is negligible. The sums simply don't add up."

I dragged my eyes away from what was a strangely hypnotic gaze. "I'm afraid I know nothing about the business," I managed.

"Forgive me, it's inappropriate of me to talk to an employee about it."

Certainly when the employer is sitting within hearing range, I thought angrily. He'd somehow managed to patronize and belittle me, negating his lukewarm apology.

"So, what exactly is the connection between you and Flora MacNichol, Miss . . . ?"

"D'Aplièse," Orlando answered for me. "And it may interest you to know that her real Christian name is 'Asterope,'" he said slowly, waggling his eyebrows at his brother like an excited owl.

"Asterope? As in one of the Seven Sisters of the Pleiades?"

"Yes," I said curtly.

"She goes by the name 'Star.' Which I think suits her very well indeed, don't you?" Orlando put in helpfully.

I doubted Mouse did agree. He was frowning, as though something about me was a huge puzzle.

"My brother told me your father died recently?" he said eventually.

"Yes." I put my knife and fork together, hoping to end this line of inquiry.

"But he wasn't your real father?" affirmed Mouse.

"No."

"Although he treated you as if he was?"

"Yes, he was wonderful to all of us."

"So you wouldn't agree that a blood tie provides an inextricable bond between a parent and a child?"

"How could I? I have never known one."

"No, I suppose you haven't."

Mouse lapsed into silence and I closed my eyes, feeling suddenly and ridiculously tearful. This man knew nothing of my father, and his probing had been entirely devoid of empathy. I felt a squeeze on my hand, gone as fast as it had arrived as Orlando withdrew his own hand swiftly, throwing me a sympathetic glance.

"I'm sure Orlando has told you that I've been trying to research the family history," Mouse said to me. "There's always been a lot of confusion about the various . . . factions, and I thought I should look into it once and for all. And, of course, I've come across Flora MacNichol." I noticed the derogatory timbre of his voice as he spoke her name.

"Who was she?"

"The sister of our great-grandmother Aurelia," said Orlando, but again there was a bleak silence from my right. Then, eventually, a deep sigh.

"That isn't quite the whole story, as you know, Orlando, but it's not for now," said Mouse.

"Do excuse me, Miss Star, I have been commandeered to help Marguerite clear the plates," said Orlando, getting to his feet.

"I can help too," I said, standing up with him.

"No." He gently pushed me back into my chair. "You cooked our exquisite lunch, and under no circumstances are you allowed to be kitchen skivvy as well."

As he left my side, I decided that scrubbing every toilet in this huge house would be more enjoyable than sitting next to the man called Mouse. My imagination had already downgraded him to a large sewer rat.

"Have you any idea what the connection is between your father and Flora MacNichol?"

The Sewer Rat was speaking again. I would reply. Politely. "None. I don't think there was one. My father left all us sisters with clues to our *own* heritage, not his. Therefore whatever connection exists is likely to be between me and her."

"You mean that you might be another cuckoo in the High Weald nest? Well, let me tell you, there have been a few in the Vaughan/Forbes history."

He grabbed his wineglass and drained it, and I wondered what had happened in his life to make him so angry. I ignored his insinuation and refused to give him the pleasure of seeing it had upset me. Using my well-honed technique of countering silence with silence, I sat with my hands folded in my lap. I knew I could win any battle he cared to wage on that front. And eventually, he spoke.

"I suppose I must apologize for the second time in our short-lived relationship. I'm sure you're not a gold digger, just following your dead father's trail. Orlando also mentioned he left you something else by way of a clue?"

Before I had a chance to reply, a large cake awash with candles appeared through the dining room door in Orlando's hands and the table struck up the refrain of "Happy Birthday." Photos were taken of Marguerite and Orlando smiling over Rory's shoulders. I chanced a glance at the Sewer Rat and read what I initially thought was a morose expression, and then, looking into his eyes as he watched Rory, realized they were full of sadness.

After we had eaten the fudgy chocolate cake Orlando had brought in the hamper all the way from London, and drunk coffee in a sitting room that, just to add to my house envy, sported two enormous oak bookshelves on either side of the wide chimney breast, Orlando stood up.

"Time to depart, Miss Star. We are due to catch the five o'clock train. Marguerite"—he walked over to her and kissed her on both cheeks—"a delight as always. Shall I call a taxi?"

"I'll take you," came a voice from the armchair opposite.

"Thank you, old chap," Orlando said to his brother.

Marguerite pulled herself to standing and I saw the exhaustion in her eyes as she turned to me. "Star, please promise you'll come again to visit soon and allow me to make *you* lunch?"

"I'd love to," I replied honestly. "Thank you for having me."

Rory appeared beside us, his hands opening and closing excitedly, and I realized that he was signing my name over and over again. "Come back soon," he added in his odd little voice, and then wrapped his small arms around my waist.

"Bye, Rory," I replied as he released his arms, and I looked over his head to see the Sewer Rat staring at us.

"Thank you for that incredible cake," I heard Marguerite say to Orlando. "It was worth lugging that ridiculous picnic hamper here after all."

We duly followed the Sewer Rat outside to a Land Rover as battered and ancient as his cousin's Fiat.

"Climb in the front, Miss Star. You have far more to talk to Mouse about than I do. It becomes so dull when one knows everything one needs to about a person," Orlando said as he stepped into the back with his hamper.

"He doesn't know me," the Sewer Rat growled under his breath, as he got in beside me and started the engine. "Even if he thinks he does."

I didn't comment, not wanting to get into a war between the two brothers, and we drove away from High Weald in a thick silence that continued for the rest of the journey. I distracted myself by looking out of the window at the gentle autumn sunset bathing the trees with an amber glow, which was slowly turning to twilight. And thought how much I didn't want to return to London.

"Thank you kindly, Mouse," Orlando said as we arrived back on the station forecourt and we stepped out.

"Do you have a mobile number?" came the Sewer Rat's voice out of the gloom.

"Yes."

"Put it in here." He handed me his mobile.

He saw my momentary hesitation.

"I'll apologize for the third time today, and I promise that if you give me your number, I will contact you about Flora MacNichol."

"Thank you." I promptly typed my number in, thinking it was almost certainly a show of good manners and that I'd never hear from him again. I handed his mobile back to him. "Good-bye."

On the train on the way back to London, Orlando fell asleep immediately. I closed my eyes too, reliving the events of the day and thinking about Orlando's unusual and interesting relatives.

And High Weald . . .

If nothing else, today I'd found the house in which I could happily live forever.

8

"You were rather a hit with my errant family," Orlando said as he arrived at the bookshop the next morning with his three o'clock cake.

"Not with your brother, though."

"Oh, take no notice of Mouse. He's always suspicious of anyone he can't find fault with. One never knows what lies behind another's reaction until, well, one does," Orlando equivocated. "And as for your majestic luncheon, I am considering sacking the foil tins and having your good self provide the catering for our little establishment. Although I doubt you'd feel that the cooking facilities upstairs would cut your professional mustard." He gazed at me thoughtfully. "Are there any other hidden talents you are keeping from me?"

"No." I could feel myself blushing, as I always did when someone complimented me.

"You really are awfully accomplished, you know. Where did you learn sign language?"

"My nanny taught me the basics of it in French when I was younger. But mostly my sister and I made up our own signs. It was because I didn't like to speak much."

"And there's *another* of your gifts. If one has nothing useful to say, one shouldn't say anything at all. That's why I do so enjoy speaking to Rory, he's so very observant about the world. And his speech is improving so quickly now."

"Marguerite said you've been wonderful with him."

It was Orlando's turn to blush. "That's sweet of her. I'm very fond of my nephew. Bright as a button and doing well at school, although sadly, lacking a father figure to guide him. Not that I would ever consider myself worthy enough to take on that role, but I do my best."

I was desperate to ask who Rory's father was, and also *where* he was, but I didn't want to pry.

"Now, I must get on, although I'm sure there was something I wanted to tell you. Never mind, it will come to me."

I could see Orlando's attention—held for far longer on one train of thought than usual—had moved on. So I lit the fire and brewed the coffee that no one would drink, then took the feather duster to the bookshelves, remembering the Sewer Rat's comments about the price of the property taxes for the shop. And how much money they would get if they sold the building. I couldn't even contemplate it. Whenever Orlando was out, his bookshop was like a nest without its roosting bird; it was his natural habitat and the two were inextricably linked.

The day was cold and wet and I knew none of the regulars would be in, so I took *Orlando* off a bookshelf and sat down by the fire to reread it. Unusually, my mind couldn't focus on the words. It kept drifting back to yesterday, trying to unravel the family dynamics, and even more vividly, the image of High Weald and its calm beauty kept appearing in my mind's eye.

There was no word from the Sewer Rat, just as I had expected. And slowly, I resigned myself to not seeing High Weald again, concentrating my energy instead on how I might one day manage to acquire my own similar home.

As the days grew shorter and a thick frost greeted me every morning on the way to work, our regulars appeared even more rarely. So, with my newfound spur, one day when there was nothing else to do, I sat down in front of the fire and made notes on the novel I wanted to write. I allowed Pa Salt's encouraging words to combat my doubts about my ability and was so engrossed in ideas for it that I didn't hear Orlando coming down the stairs. It was only when he cleared his throat loudly that I looked up and saw him standing above me.

"Sorry, sorry . . ." I closed the notebook with a snap.

"No matter. Miss Star, I've come to ask if you are otherwise engaged on this forthcoming weekend?"

I suppressed a grin at the formal Orlando-speak. "No. I'm not doing anything."

"Well . . . may I put something to you?"

"Yes."

"Marguerite has been offered a big commission in France. She must fly there for a couple of days to discuss terms, and to 'case the joint,' as some would say."

"Yes, she mentioned it to me."

"She has asked me if we would both go to High Weald for the weekend to take care of Rory while she is gone. She said she was happy to pay you . . ."

"I don't need paying," I countered, mildly insulted that she would see me as "staff."

"No, of course not, and forgive me, for I should have said her first thought was that Rory liked you and perhaps you could provide the maternal touch that eludes me while Marguerite is gone."

"I'd be happy to," I replied, my spirits leaping at the thought of returning to High Weald.

"Would you really? Goodness, now, that does make me happy. I've never had to care for a child alone. I wouldn't know where to begin with bath times, et cetera. May I tell Marguerite yes?"

"You may."

"Then that's settled. We will leave tomorrow evening on the six o'clock train. I shall book us into first class and reserve our seats. Commuting, especially on a Friday, is such a nightmare these days. Now, I am late to collect our foil-tin treats. But once I am back we shall eat, and then spend the rest of the afternoon brushing up on your signing skills."

Once the door had shut behind him, I stood in the middle of the shop and hugged myself with pleasure. This was better than I could ever have envisaged. An entire weekend—two nights—in my dream surroundings.

"Thank you," I said to the ceiling of the bookshop. "Thank you."

The train to Ashford was packed and there were even people standing in our first-class carriage. Thankfully, Orlando had refrained from bringing his picnic hamper, swapping it for a battered leather suitcase and a canvas bag full of supplies, from which he produced a half bottle of champagne and two flutes.

"I always celebrate the end of the week like this. To your health, Miss Star," he toasted as the train pulled out of Charing Cross.

Once Orlando had drunk his glass of champagne, he crossed his hands over his chest and fell asleep. My mobile pinged suddenly and I saw it was a text. I presumed it was CeCe, who had been disgruntled when I said I was going down to Kent again for the weekend with my employer.

But the text was from an unknown number.

Hear you are coming down to High Weald with my brother. Hope we can arrange a time to meet and discuss Flora MacNichol. O.

I pondered the initial at the end, fascinated that both brothers' names began with the same letter.

Just over an hour later, we emerged onto the station forecourt. Orlando headed toward a taxi and we drove along the pitch-black country lanes toward High Weald.

"Lando! Staah!" Rory was waiting to greet us.

With his nephew hanging like a chimpanzee from his neck, Orlando paid the driver. I turned to see a figure on the doorstep, already jangling his car keys.

"I'll be off then," Mouse said as Orlando and I trundled toward him with our overnight cases. "I fed him what Marguerite had left, but I'm afraid he didn't eat much. I'm sure he's glad you're both here. Anything you need, you know where I am," he said to Orlando. To me he said, "You have my number, contact me when it's convenient. If it ever is." With a curt nod, he walked to his car, climbed in, and drove off.

"Goodness, I feel that we are parents," whispered Orlando to me as he lugged both his suitcase and Rory inside and I brought up the rear with the supplies and my luggage.

"Do you like pancakes?" I tried to sign. Orlando chuckled as Rory looked at me uncomprehendingly. So I finger-spelled the letters carefully.

Rory nodded eagerly. "Chocolate and ice cream with them?" he added, spelling the words out patiently for me before wriggling out of Orlando's arms and taking my hand.

"We'll look for some. You go and unpack," I suggested to Orlando over Rory's head, knowing how he liked to be organized.

"Thank you," he replied gratefully.

There was no chocolate sauce, but I sourced a Mars bar from the pantry and melted it to put with the ice cream on the pancakes. Rory wolfed them down as I explained to him slowly that he would have to help me with signing because I was far behind him. Once I'd wiped him clean of chocolate smears, he yawned.

"Sleep?" I signed.

He frowned reluctantly in reply.

"Shall we go and find Orlando? I bet he tells the best bedtime stories."

"Yes."

"You will have to show me where your bedroom is."

Rory led me up the grand staircase and down a long, creaking corridor until he reached the door at the end.

"My room."

As he led me inside, the first thing I noticed amid the football posters, bright-colored Superman duvet, and general clutter were the paintings stuck haphazardly with Blu-Tack to the walls.

"Who did these?" I asked him as he climbed into bed.

"Me," he indicated with his thumb.

"Wow, Rory, they are fantastic," I said as I wandered around the room studying them.

There was a brief knock before Orlando entered.

"Perfect timing. Rory wants your best story," I told him with a smile.

"Then I will gladly oblige. Which book?"

Rory pointed at *The Lion, the Witch and the Wardrobe* and Orlando rolled his eyes.

"Again? When can we move on to the rest of the series? I've told you many times that *The Last Battle* is perhaps my favorite book of all time."

Not wanting to intrude on their bedtime ritual, I headed for the door, but as I passed Rory's bed, he opened his arms wide to me for a hug. And I responded.

"Nigh, Stah."

"Night night, Rory." With a smile and a wave, I left the room.

With Orlando and Rory happily occupied, I went downstairs and wandered into the dimly lit sitting room, where I paused to look at the pictures dotted on side tables around the room. Most were grainy black-and-white photographs of people in evening dress, and I smiled at a color photo of Rory sitting proudly on a pony, with Marguerite standing next to him.

Exploring the house further, I walked along a corridor to a room that appeared to be a study. An ancient partner's desk was strewn with paper, books were piled up on the floor, and an ashtray and an empty wine-glass sat precariously on the wide arm of a worn leather sofa. Various prints hung on the walls, whose faded striped paper told me it had been a long time since this room had seen refurbishment. Above the fireplace hung a portrait of a beautiful blond woman in Edwardian dress. I stepped over an overflowing wastepaper basket to take a closer look, then jumped as I heard the tread of feet on the stairs above me and scurried out of the room to the kitchen. I didn't want Orlando to know that I had been snooping around the house.

"One nephew tucked up safe and snug in his bed. Now . . ." He proffered me a bottle of red wine and six eggs. "I can see to one, if you can turn the other into an omelet for us."

"Of course," I said, and, since I already knew my way around the kitchen, it was only fifteen minutes before we were sitting at the table eating companionably. *Just like an old married couple*, I thought. Or perhaps brother and sister might be a more appropriate analogy.

"Now, tomorrow, Rory and I will give you a tour of the estate. Given your professed penchant for botany, you will almost certainly gasp in horror at the state of the gardens. But I find their muddle rather beautiful. The remnants of bygone days, et cetera," he sighed. "And at the root of it all—to use an appropriate metaphor—lies the lack of funds."

"I think this house is perfect as it is."

"That, my dear girl, is because you don't have to reside in it or pay for its upkeep. For instance, the great hall of High Weald, once the setting for elegant society gatherings, has been closed off for years due to lack of funds to restore it. And I am sure that after a weekend of a lumpy horsehair mattress and the lack of hot water to cleanse yourself, plus the fact that the bedrooms are toe-curlingly cold due to the absence of a modern heating system, you will perhaps alter your opinion. Aesthetically, I agree, but practically, the house is a nightmare to live in. Especially in the winter."

"I don't mind. I'm used to roughing it." I shrugged.

"That was in hot countries, which, I can assure you, is an entirely different matter. The truth is, after the war, like so many families, the Vaughans fell on hard times. I find it rather ironic that little Rory will one day become a 'lord,' when he has only a decrepit and ailing manor to preside over."

"A lord? I had no idea. Who will he inherit the title from? His father?"

"Yes. Now"—Orlando swiftly changed the subject—"what can we dig out of that pantry for dessert?"

I woke the next morning in a room I felt I had seen before in a period drama on television. The bed I'd slept in was made of brass and every time I turned over, the knobs on the four posts rang like Christmas bells due to the rickety construction, and the mattress was as lumpy as Orlando had warned me it would be. The patterned wallpaper was peeling back in places, and the curtains shielding the windows had tears in the fabric. As I climbed out of the bed, even my long legs dangled a few inches above the wooden floor, and as I tiptoed across it to go to the bathroom, I looked longingly at the cast-iron grate and wished I could light a fire to ward off the chill.

Last night I'd been plagued with odd dreams, which was unusual for me. I normally slept peacefully, remembering nothing of my brain's nocturnal machinations when I woke. Thinking of CeCe and her own nightmares, I dug out my mobile to tell her I'd arrived safely, then realized there was no signal whatsoever.

I looked out of the window, seeing the delicate fronds of frost that crept across the small square panes, through which glimmers of early morning sunlight heralded the dawn of a bright autumnal day—just the sort that I loved. I dressed in as many layers as I'd brought with me and went downstairs.

By the time I reached the kitchen, a yawning Orlando was already there, wearing a paisley silk dressing gown with a woolen scarf wound around his neck, and an outrageous pair of peacock-blue silk lounge slippers on his feet.

"And here is the cook! Rory and I have sourced some sausages and bacon from the fridge, and of course we have eggs aplenty. How about a full English breakfast to set us up for the day?"

"Good idea," I agreed. We all pitched in, with Rory stirring the mixture for eggy bread—something he said he'd never tasted, and pronounced "delicious" when he did.

"So, young Rory, this morning we shall take Miss Star on a tour of the estate, or at least what's left of it, and hope that Sunday lunch does not drop from the skies upon our heads," Orlando added.

"What do you mean?" I queried.

"It's pheasant-shooting season, I'm afraid. Mouse is bringing a brace for you to perform your magic on for our lunch tomorrow." Orlando stood up. "Perhaps while we men perform our ablutions, you would write a list of everything you need to complement the birds, and I will have the local farm shop deliver it. By the way," he said, halting as he arrived at the kitchen door. "The trees in the orchard still bear fruit that goes to waste on the ground. If it's not too much trouble, perhaps you'd like to make use of some in a pie?"

I found a piece of scrap paper and a felt-tip pen in the drawer and sat down to write a list. I'd never cooked pheasant before, so I had a search around the kitchen for some recipe books, but found none and decided I would just have to invent my own.

Half an hour later we were forging across the frost-hardened drive. Orlando had planned a route that would apparently take us to the farthest reaches of the land, and then into what he called the jewel in the crown of High Weald.

"At least it was seventy years ago, anyway," he added. Rory was cycling ahead of us, and as he reached the gate, Orlando shouted at him to stop because of the road, but he didn't.

"Good God! He can't hear me!" he cried as he went haring off in pursuit, and I had a glimpse into the dangers Rory would face as he grew up and the constant supervision he needed now. I ran too, my heart pounding, to find Rory grinning cheekily at us as he emerged from behind a bush on the grass verge along the lane.

"Hiding! Got you!"

"Yes, you most certainly did, old chap," Orlando signed vehemently, as we tried to recover our breath and equilibrium. "You must never cycle on the lane. There are cars."

"I know. Mag told me."

Orlando stowed Rory's bike inside the gate. "Now, we shall cross the road together."

We did so, Rory between us, holding each of our hands, and I was struck by the fact that Rory called his mother by a shortened version of her name; a truly bohemian family, I thought, as Orlando steered us through an opening in the hedge on the other side. Endless fields bordered by hedges spread on either side of us and I watched Rory turn his head to take in the sights around him. He spied the late blackberries first, and we picked them together, most of them ending up in Rory's mouth.

"This is the bridle path that borders the old estate," Orlando said as we walked on. "Do you ride, Miss Star?"

"No. I'm frightened of horses," I confessed, remembering my one and only riding lesson with CeCe, when I'd been too terrified to even climb on.

"Not one for the nags myself either. Mouse rides excellently, of course, just as he does everything else. I do feel for him sometimes, mind you. I'm of the opinion that having too many gifts can be as bad as having none at all, don't you think? Everything in moderation, that's my motto. Or life has a way of coming back to bite you."

As we walked on, I saw the hedges were fluttering with small birds; the air smelled fresh and clear, and I enjoyed breathing in its pureness after weeks in the smoggy city. The sun shone bronze in Rory's hair, mirroring the trees that were holding on to their last glorious color before winter.

"Look!" he shouted, spotting a red tractor in the distance. "Mouse!"

"And so it is," said Orlando, shielding his eyes from the sun and squinting over the fields. "Rory, you have the eyes of a hawk."

"Say hello?" Rory turned to us.

"He doesn't like to be disturbed when he's tractoring," Orlando cautioned as a sudden blast of shotguns rang out in the distance. "And the shoot has begun. We should head back. The pheasants will be falling around us hard and fast, and they have a horrible habit of denting anything below them, be it animate or not."

Orlando set off at a fast pace, retracing our footsteps toward the house.

"So your brother is a farmer?"

"I wouldn't define him as such, given the other strings he has to his bow, but due to the constant staff shortage caused by the family financial crisis, he often has no choice *but* to be."

"Does he own this land?"

"We both do, as it happens. The estate was divided in the forties between brother and sister. Our branch—that of our grandmother Louise

Forbes—got the land on this side of the lane, plus Home Farm. While our great-uncle, Teddy Vaughan, Marguerite's grandfather, inherited the main house and gardens. And, of course, the peerage. All very feudal, but that is England for you, Miss Star."

We crossed over the lane and walked back down the drive of High Weald. I wondered which branch of the family had drawn the short straw when the estate was divided, but I knew nothing of the price of farmland as opposed to property around here.

"Rory!" Again, Orlando ran to catch up with his nephew, who had raced off toward the house on his bike. "We should show Star the gardens now."

Rory gave a thumbs-up and careered away again at pace, disappearing down a path to the side of the house.

"Good grief, I shall be glad when this is over," Orlando said. "I'm living in fear of something happening to that precious boy on our watch. Awfully glad you're with me, Star. I wouldn't have been allowed here without you."

I was surprised at his comment as I followed him along the path to the back of the house. We emerged onto a wide flagstone terrace, and I drew in my breath as I looked down into the vast walled garden.

It was as though I had landed in Sleeping Beauty's castle grounds, and now had to fight my way through the forest of thorns and gigantic weeds that enveloped it. As we walked down the steps and along the overgrown paths that wound through the maze of what must have been spectacular shrubbery, I saw the wooden skeletons of pergolas that had once carried magnificent climbing roses. The endless borders and flower beds still held their original pattern, but could no longer contain the plants and bushes that had escaped their confines and whose dry, brown entrails covered the paths.

I stopped and looked up at an ancient and majestic yew tree that dominated the garden, its determined roots having broken through the stone paths that surrounded it. There was a wild yet desolate air of romance about it all. And, I thought, just a whisper of possibility that those specimens which—against the odds—had survived unchecked could be salvaged.

I closed my eyes and conjured up an image of the garden awash with roses, magnolias, and camellias, the straight lines of clipped box hedges giving way to powdery blue ceanothus . . . every nook and cranny filled with gorgeous, lavish *life* . . .

"You can see how glorious it must have been once," Orlando said, as if reading my thoughts.

"Oh yes, I can," I murmured. I saw Rory winding his way along the overgrown paths, expertly maneuvering his bicycle around the overhanging plants as if he were taking some form of proficiency test.

"I must show you the greenhouses where my great-grandfather grew and nurtured specimens from all over the world. But now," Orlando said, "do you think there is something that you could perhaps rustle up for lunch? Then for tonight I've ordered a tenderloin fillet. The farm shop's beef is quite the best I know." Orlando gave a large yawn. "Goodness, that walk has quite exhausted me. Thank God I live in town. There's little else to do but walk in the country, is there? And one feels so guilty if one doesn't."

After lunch, Orlando rose from the table. "I hope you'll excuse me if I take a short nap. I am sure the two of you will muddle along together while I'm gone."

"I like your cooking, Star," Rory signed as his uncle left the kitchen.

"Thank you. Help me with the washing up?" I indicated the full sink.

Rory pouted at me.

"If you do, I'll show you how to make chocolate brownies. They are delicious."

We set to work and just as I'd allowed Rory to lick the bowl, the back door opened and I heard the footfall of heavy boots outside. Thinking it must be the delivery from the farm shop, I turned and saw the Sewer Rat step through the kitchen door. Rory and I stared at him in surprise.

"Hello."

"Hello," I said.

"Rory." He nodded at the boy, who waved back, his attention taken by the last remnants of the chocolate mix. "Something smells good."

"We're making brownies."

"Then I'm sure Rory is in heaven."

"Can I get you anything? A cup of tea?" I muttered, his presence making me nervous.

"Only if you're having one."

"I am." I flicked the kettle on. "Rory," I said, turning to him, "let's get you cleaned up." As I took a cloth to his chocolatey mouth, the Sewer Rat didn't move, just stood and surveyed both of us with his unwavering stare.

"Star, can I watch *Superman*?"

"Is he allowed to watch a film?" I asked the Sewer Rat.

"Why not? I'll come and switch it on for you, Rory."

By the time the Sewer Rat returned, the tea was brewing in a large earthenware pot on the table.

"Bloody freezing in that drawing room. I've lit a fire. Thanks for the tea," he said, sitting down, still in his Barbour. "I presume Orlando is taking his nap. My brother is a creature of habit."

I saw a glimmer of an affectionate smile cross his features, but it was gone before it reached its full potential.

"Yes."

"As a matter of fact, it isn't Orlando I've come here to see, it's you," he continued. "Firstly, to offer my thanks for being here this weekend. It's saved me from playing babysitter when I've had the shoot on the land."

"I'm sure Orlando could have managed equally well without me."

"Marguerite would never have allowed it."

"Why not?"

"Hasn't he told you? Besides being asthmatic, Orlando has severe epilepsy. Has done ever since he was a teenager. It's more or less under control these days, but Marguerite was nervous that he might fit, as Rory can't make himself understood by phone. He's learning to text, of course, but as there's zero signal here at High Weald, that's not an awful lot of use."

"I didn't know." I stood up and walked to the range to check on the brownies and mask my shock.

"Then that's very good news, as it means Orlando's being a good boy and taking his medicine as he should. While you're working alongside him, I feel it's important that you know, just in case. Orlando is embarrassed about it. The bottom line is, though, if he does fit, without immediate medical attention, he could die. We nearly lost him a couple of times when he was younger. And the other thing is . . ."

He paused and I held my breath as I waited for him to continue.

"I wanted to apologize for being less than polite to you when you were last here. I've got a lot on my mind at the moment, one way or another."

"That's okay."

"No, it isn't. But as I'm sure you've already gleaned, I'm not a very nice person."

Of all the self-absorbed, self-pitying, and generally selfish excuses I'd heard over the course of my life, this one took the biscuit. I felt anger fill me, as if I were absorbing heat from the range.

"Anyway, I brought you this. It's my shortened transcription of Flora MacNichol's journals, written by her between the ages of ten and twenty."

"Right. Thanks," I eventually managed to say to the brownies on the range in front of me.

"Well, I'll leave you in peace." I heard his footsteps cross the kitchen toward the door. Then a pause. "Just one more question for you . . ."

"What?"

"Did you bring the animal figurine with you? I'd like to see it."

I knew it was childish, but my irritation at his infuriating manner got the better of me. "I'm . . . not sure. I'll have a look," I replied.

"Okay. I'll be back tomorrow. By the way, our Sunday lunch is in the lobby. Bye now."

Once I had recovered and drunk two glasses of water straight down to quell the burning heat from the anger I felt at my unwanted guest, I ignored the pile of pages set neatly on the table and looked into the lobby. There I found a brace of pheasants alongside a box of assorted fresh fruit and vegetables.

I'm ashamed to admit that the largest pheasant took the brunt of my wrath as I plucked its feathers viciously, gutted it, and chopped off its head, feet, and wings. Once that was done, I sat down at the table exhausted, wondering why a person who meant absolutely nothing to me could rouse the depth of anger and frustration I felt.

I fingered the manuscript in front of me, the very fact that his hands had touched the pages making me shudder. But here it was, a possible clue to the past I had been searching for. And whatever I felt for its transcriber, a far higher cause had led me to High Weald.

I found a plate and placed three brownies upon it, clamping the manuscript under my other arm. Then I went in search of Rory, whom I found glued to the television screen, watching Christopher Reeve zooming through the sky.

I tapped him on the shoulder to get his attention and indicated the plate of brownies.

"Thank you!"

I watched him help himself before turning his attention back to his film. And seeing that he was happily occupied, I stoked the fire, then I sat down in the deep armchair next to the hearth. Putting the manuscript on my knee, I began to read.

FLORA

Esthwaite Hall, The Lake District

April 1909

9

Flora Rose MacNichol ran full pelt across the grass, the hem of her skirt soaking up the early morning dampness like a sheet of fresh blotting paper. The mellow dawn light glinted on the lake and set the icy fronds—remnants of a late frost—aglitter.

I can get there in time, she told herself as she neared the lake and veered right, her long-suffering black-button boots dancing lightly across the familiar hillocks of hard Lakeland earth, which refused stubbornly to pretend it was a smooth lawn and paid no heed to the constant ministrations of the gardener.

Just in time, Flora arrived at the boulder that sat at the water's edge. No one knew how it had come to be there, or for that matter why; it was simply a lonely orphan separated from its plentiful brothers and sisters that populated the surrounding screes and valleys. Looking rather like an enormous apple that someone had once taken a bite out of, it had provided a convenient resting place for generations of MacNichol behinds as they witnessed the spectacle of the sun rising behind the mountains on the other side of the lake.

Just as she sat down, the first rays of sunlight lit up the watery blue sky. A lark flew in perfect synchronicity with its reflection on the lake beneath—a silver silhouette of itself. Flora sighed in pleasure and sniffed the air. Finally, spring had arrived.

Irritated with herself for being in such a hurry that she had forgotten to bring her sketch pad and tin of watercolors with her to capture the moment, she watched the sun break free from its tethers on the horizon and shine a light on the snow-capped peaks, bathing the valley beneath in soft gold light. Then she stood up, realizing she had forgotten her shawl too, and that her teeth were chattering in the bitter morning air. Tiny burning sensations began to prickle the delicate skin of her face, like barbs shot by a heavenly bow. She looked upward and realized it had begun to snow.

"Spring indeed." Flora chuckled as she turned to walk back up the hill toward the Hall, knowing she still had to change her wet skirts and sodden boots before making an appearance at the breakfast table. This past winter had seemed longer than any other, and she could only hope that the raw winds that blew the snow at a cruel angle would soon be just a memory. And as humans, animals, and nature came out of hibernation, so too would her universe come alive and fill with the vibrancy and color she'd longed for.

During the endless months of short, dark days, she'd sat to catch what light there was at one of the windows in her bedroom and used charcoal to sketch the view, feeling that if she were to paint it, it would only be in black and white anyway. And, just like the result of the recent photographic session Mama had insisted on for her and her younger sister, Aurelia, it would only result in a dull facsimile of the real thing.

Aurelia . . . beautiful, golden Aurelia . . . Her sister reminded her of a porcelain doll she'd once been given for Christmas, her wide blue eyes rimmed by coal-dark lashes, set in her perfect face.

"Peaches and cream beside gruel," Flora muttered, pleased with her apt description of their opposing looks. She thought back to the morning of the photographic session, when the two of them had dressed together in her bedroom, putting on their best gowns. Regarding their reflections in the gilt mirror, Flora noticed how everything about Aurelia had soft, rounded contours, whereas Flora's own face and body seemed sharp and chiseled in comparison. Her sister was inherently feminine, from her tiny feet to her delicate fingers, and she radiated gentleness. Despite eating porridge laced with cream, Flora could never seem to achieve the heavenly curves of Aurelia and their mother. When she had expressed that thought, Aurelia had given her a gentle poke in the side with her finger.

"Dear Flora, how often must I tell you that you are beautiful?"

"I can see myself quite clearly in the mirror. My only redeeming feature is my eyes, and they certainly aren't enough to turn any heads."

"They're like sapphire beacons, shining in the night sky," Aurelia had said, and given her sister a warm embrace.

Despite Aurelia's kindness, it was hard not to feel she didn't belong. Her father had the red-gold hair and pale skin of his Scottish forebears and her sister had inherited her mother's cool blond beauty. And then there was Flora, with what her father rather cruelly called a "Germanic" nose, sallow skin, and thick dark hair, which completely refused to stay in a neat chignon.

She paused as she heard the faint call of a cuckoo from far away in the oak trees to the west of the lake, and allowed herself a wry smile. *A cuckoo in the nest. That's me.*

Treading back lightly over the tufts of coarse grass, Flora approached the worn stone steps that led up to the terrace. Its heavy gravelike slabs were covered with a winter's worth of moss and leaves. The house rose above her, its many windows glinting in the pale morning light. Andrew MacNichol, her great-great-grandfather, had built Esthwaite Hall one hundred and fifty years ago, not to be a thing of beauty but to shield its occupants from the cruel Lakeland winters, its sturdy walls fashioned from rough shale rock quarried from the nearby mountains. It was an austere dark gray building, the roofs pitched low and defensively, their edges sharp and forbidding. The house loomed above Esthwaite Water, staunch and immovable amid the wild landscape.

Skirting around the house, Flora entered through the back door to the kitchen, where the delivery boy had already deposited the week's groceries. Inside, Mrs. Hillbeck, the cook, and Tilly, the kitchen maid, were already preparing breakfast.

"Morning, Miss Flora. I s'pose them boots of yours are soaked through again?" Mrs. Hillbeck said, eyeing her as she unlaced them.

"Yes. Could you put them to dry on the range?"

"If you don't mind them smelling of your father's breakfast kipper," the cook replied, as she chopped thick pieces of black pudding into a frying pan.

"Thank you," Flora said, handing the boots to her. "I'll come and collect them later."

"I'd be asking your mother for a new pair if I were you, Miss Flora. These have seen better days. The soles've worn right through," Mrs. Hillbeck clucked as she took the boots by the laces and hung them to dry.

Flora left the kitchen, thinking that it would indeed be a wonderful thing to have some new boots, but knowing she couldn't ask. As she made her way along the dark corridor, a strong smell of mildew assailed her nostrils. Just as there was no money for new boots, neither was there any to repair the damp that had started to seep through the thick stone walls, ruining the one-hundred-year-old chinoiserie wallpaper—a riot of flowers and butterflies—that adorned the walls of Mama's bedroom.

The MacNichols were "impoverished gentry," a phrase Flora had heard whispered by one customer to another as she waited to be served at the village shop in Near Sawrey. Which was why last year she hadn't been surprised when her mother, Rose, had told her there were simply no funds available for Flora to make a London debut and be presented at court.

"You do understand, don't you, Flora, dear?"

"Of course I do, Mama."

Flora had been secretly thrilled that she would be spared the rigmarole of being primped, perfumed, and dressed up like a doll for the duration of the Season. She shuddered at the thought of being surrounded by silly giggling girls who didn't understand that the whole event was no better than a cattle auction, where the prettiest heifer went to the highest male bidder. Which, in human terms, meant netting the son of a duke who would inherit a large estate on his father's death.

And she abhorred London. On the rare occasions she had accompanied her mother to visit Aunt Charlotte in her grand white house in Mayfair, Flora had felt overwhelmed by the crowded streets and the continual clip-clopping of the horses' hooves, mingling with the roaring sound of the motorcars that were becoming so popular, even up here in her beloved Lake District.

However, Flora was equally aware that since she hadn't been presented with the other young ladies, the chances of her finding a suitable husband of rank and status were heavily diminished.

"I may well die an old maid," she whispered to herself, as she mounted the wide mahogany staircase and hurried along the landing to her bedroom before Mama could spot her soaking skirts. "And neither do I care," she said defiantly as she entered the room and saw numerous pairs of tiny eyes studying her from inside their cages.

"I'll always have you, won't I?" she said, her voice softening as she walked over to the first cage and released the catch to allow Posy, a large gray rabbit, to jump into her arms. She had rescued Posy from the mouth of one of her father's gun dogs and she was the longest-surviving member of her menagerie. Flora cradled Posy on her knee and stroked the long, silky ears—the left one missing its tip from when she'd dragged it out of the dog's jaws. Leaving Posy to hop around the floor, she greeted her other roommates, who included two dormice, a toad named Horace who lived in a makeshift vivarium, and Albert, a sleek white rat, inherited from the groom's son and named after the late Queen Victoria's husband. Her mother had been horrified.

"Really, Flora, I have no wish to deny you your passion for animals, but it comes to something when you are knowingly sharing a bedroom with vermin!"

Rose had not told Alistair, her husband, about Albert, although she had drawn a line at a grass snake Flora had found in the woods. Her shrieks when she had seen it had reverberated around the drawing room and Sarah, the one remaining upstairs maid, had to run to fetch the smelling salts.

"Givin' us all a fright with that creature!" Sarah had scolded Flora, her thick Lakeland dialect more pronounced under duress. The grass snake had duly been returned to its natural habitat.

Undressing down to her bloomers, Flora fed her animals their various breakfasts, pouring small piles of hazelnuts and sunflower seeds into bowls, along with hay and cabbage leaves. For Horace, the toad, she had a handful of the mealworms her father used for fishing bait. Re-dressing hurriedly in a fresh poplin blouse buttoned up to her neck and a blue floral skirt, she surveyed herself in the mirror. Like the rest of her and her sister's everyday wardrobe, the fabric was somewhat faded and the style was hardly the latest in haute couture, but the garments, at their mother's insistence, were at least well cut.

Adjusting the tight collar, Flora regarded her features. "I remind myself of Sybil," she muttered, remembering the stick insect she'd kept for almost a year in her vivarium before Horace had moved in, and how overjoyed she'd been at the realization that darling Sybil had given birth. She hadn't noticed the offspring until they were almost fully grown, so well had they blended in with their environment.

Ghost creatures . . . Just like her: good at being invisible.

She tucked a stray strand of her hair back into the coil at the nape of her neck, replaced Posy inside her hutch, and went to join her family for breakfast.

When she entered the gloomy dining room, her parents and her sister were already seated at the worn mahogany table. As she joined them, a distinct tut of displeasure emanated from behind the *Times* newspaper.

"Good morning, Flora. I'm glad you finally thought to join us." Her mother's gaze immediately fell to Flora's feet, surveying their stockinged state. An arched eyebrow was raised, but nothing was said. "Did you sleep well, my dear?"

"Yes, thank you, Mama," Flora answered as Sarah put a bowl of porridge in front of her with a cheerful smile. Sarah had taken care of the sisters since they were babies, and knew that the smell of cooked meat was enough to turn Flora's stomach. Rather than the customary breakfast of kippers, black pudding, and sausage that the rest of the family ate, it had finally been agreed after years of Flora's refusing point-blank to eat any of it that she should have porridge instead. She vowed that when she ran her own household, no dead animals would ever be served on a plate.

"Aurelia, dear, you look pale." Rose's eyes flicked over her daughter in concern. "Are you feeling quite well?"

"I am well, thank you," Aurelia answered, before raising a small forkful of sausage to her mouth and biting into it daintily.

"You must rest as much as possible in the next few weeks. The Season can be very tiring and you are only just recovered from that nasty winter chill."

"Yes, Mama," Aurelia replied, ever patient of her mother's fussing.

"I think Aurelia looks positively glowing," announced Flora, and her sister smiled gratefully at her.

Always sickly as a baby, Aurelia was treated by her parents and the entire household staff like the doll she so resembled. And now, especially, no one could afford for her to be sick. Their mother had announced a month ago that Aurelia *would* make her London debut and be presented at court to the King and Queen. It was hoped that she would catch the eye of a suitably wealthy man from a good family like their own. That was, if her sweet temper and beauty could outweigh the dearth of family money.

Even though Flora had no wish to "come out" herself, she did feel slighted at the fact that Aunt Charlotte, her mother's sister, who was covering the cost of Aurelia's debut, had not thought to do the same for her eldest niece.

Breakfast continued in its usual virtual silence. Alistair did not like idle chatter at the table, saying it disturbed his concentration while he was reading of world events. Flora glanced at her father from under her eyelashes. All she could see was his bald patch rising like a half-moon above his paper, wisps of graying red hair sprouting from just over his ears. *How he has aged since the Boer War*, she thought sadly. Alistair had sustained a gunshot wound, and although the surgeons had been able to save his right leg, he walked with a bad limp, supported by a stick. The most dreadful consequence of his injury was that the ex–cavalry officer, who had spent his life on horseback, now found himself in too much pain to ride out with the local hunt.

Even though they had lived under the same roof for nineteen years, Flora could recall no more than one or two conversations with her father that had continued past basic politeness. Alistair used his wife as his emissary to impart any wishes he might have for his daughter, or to express his displeasure. For the hundredth time, she wondered just why her mother had married him. Surely, with Rose's beauty, intelligence, and good family name—she'd been an "honorable" before her marriage—she would have had a wealth of prospective suitors to choose from? Flora could only presume that her father possessed hidden depths that she'd never had the good fortune to find.

Alistair folded his newspaper meticulously, signaling the end of breakfast. A slight nod from Rose indicated that both girls could leave the table. They slid their chairs back and made to stand up.

"Remember the Vaughans are coming tomorrow afternoon to take tea, so it's baths for both of you tonight. Sarah, can you draw them before dinner?"

"Yes, ma'am." Sarah bobbed a curtsy.

"And, Aurelia, you shall wear your pink muslin dress."

"Very good, Mama," Aurelia agreed as the two girls left the dining room.

"The Vaughans' daughter, Elizabeth, is making her debut with me," said Aurelia as they crossed the hall, her footfall echoing in the silence while Flora's stockinged feet padded on the freezing granite slabs. "Mama says we visited them in Kent when we were younger, but for the life of me, I can't remember it. Can you?"

"Unfortunately, I can," said Flora as they mounted the stairs. "Their son, Archie, who must have been six to my four years, pelted me with crab apples in their orchard. I was bruised all over. He was quite the nastiest boy I've ever met."

"I wonder if he's improved," chuckled Aurelia. "He must be twenty-one now, if you're nineteen."

"Well, we shall see, but if he decides to pelt me with crab apples again, I shall simply return the favor with stones."

Aurelia giggled. "Please don't. Lady Vaughan is Mama's oldest friend and you know Mama adores her. Well, at least I will know one person before I go to London. I hope Elizabeth likes me, because I'm sure the young ladies are far more sophisticated down south. I shall feel like a country peasant in comparison."

"And I am absolutely certain that's not how you'll be seen when you're dressed up in all your finery." Flora opened the door to her bedroom and Aurelia followed her in. "You'll be the most ravishing debutante of the Season, Aurelia, I'm sure of it. Although I don't envy you," she added, crossing the bedroom to open Posy's cage and allow the rabbit to run free.

"Are you absolutely sure you don't, Flora?" Aurelia perched on the end of the bed. "Despite your protestations to the contrary, I've been worried that you might. After all, it's not fair that I'm to have a debut when you didn't."

"What would all my animals do without me?"

"True, although I'd like to see your future husband's face when you insist on sharing your marital bedroom with your menagerie!" Aurelia scooped up Posy in her arms.

"If he misbehaves, I'll set Albert the rat upon him."

"Can I borrow your pet if necessary, then?"

"With pleasure." Flora grimaced. "Aurelia, we both know the Season is simply about finding you a husband. Do you want to get married?"

"To be truthful, I'm not sure about the marriage part, but I'd rather like to fall in love, yes. Wouldn't every girl?"

"Do you know, I'm beginning to think a spinster's life would suit me well. I shall live in a cottage surrounded by my animals, who will all love me unconditionally. It seems far safer than ever loving a man."

"But rather dull, don't you think?"

"Perhaps, but then I think I *am* rather dull." Flora picked up the dormice, Maisie and Ethel, in one of her palms and they curled up contently with their bushy tails wrapped around their heads as she swept out their cage with her other hand.

"Goodness, Flora, when will you ever stop putting yourself down? You excelled in the schoolroom, you can speak French fluently, and you draw and paint like a dream. I'm a complete dunce in comparison."

"Now who's putting themselves down?" Flora teased. "Besides, we both know that being beautiful is a far more prized quality in a woman. It's pretty, entertaining girls that marry well, not plain old bones like me."

"Well, I shall miss you terribly when I do get married. Perhaps you could come with me to my new home, for I really don't know what I'll do without you. Now, I must go downstairs." Aurelia let Posy hop to the floor. "Mama wishes to speak to me about the London diary."

As Aurelia left the room, Flora imagined herself rattling about in Aurelia's future home—the maiden aunt that appeared so regularly in novels she had read. Sliding off her bed and going to her desk, Flora unlocked the bottom drawer and took out her silk-covered journal. Pushing up her sleeves so as not to get ink on the lace cuffs, she began to write.

10

The following morning, Flora hitched her pony, Myla, to the trap and drove into Hawkshead to collect the box of discarded cabbage leaves and old carrots kindly saved for her by Mr. Bolton, the greengrocer. She knew her parents didn't approve of her driving herself, feeling it inappropriate that the eldest daughter of Esthwaite Hall should be seen in anything other than a carriage, but Flora was not to be dissuaded.

"After all, Mama, since you and Papa let our driver go, there's only Stanley to drive me and I feel it's terribly unfair to ask him, when he has so much else to do in the stables."

Her mother couldn't disagree and had eventually acquiesced. Recently, she had even taken to asking Flora to run errands for her while she was in the village.

Poor Mama, Flora thought with a sigh, imagining how difficult the continuing slide into penury must be for her. She still remembered visiting her mother's childhood home when she was younger, which had felt like a veritable palace to her wide-eyed four-year-old self. Scores of footmen, maids, and a butler whose face had seemed carved from marble had stood to attention as the daughter of the house had entered with her family. Both Flora and Aurelia had been whisked off by her mother's old nanny to the playroom and Flora had never set eyes on her grandparents. Although, if she remembered correctly, three-year-old Aurelia had been taken briefly from the nursery to be introduced to them.

Having completed her business, Flora handed a penny to the boy whom she'd asked to mind the pony, and climbed back up onto the wooden bench with a crate full of vegetables and a paper bag of pear drops—Aurelia's favorite—next to her.

The day was bright, and as she steered the trap out of Hawkshead, she decided to take the longer way around Esthwaite Water via the village of Near Sawrey so she could see the wild crocuses and daffodils beginning to burst into bloom. Even the air smelled lighter and the brief snow flurry of that morning had barely kissed the ground before melting. As she took the lane out of Near Sawrey toward home, she glanced up at the farmhouse just visible at the top of the rise to her left.

For the hundredth time, Flora thought about stopping and introducing herself to its lone resident, and reminding her of how they had met so many years ago. And what an inspiration she had been since.

As usual, having slowed Myla down, her courage failed her. *One day I will stop*, she promised herself. For behind those sturdy farmhouse walls lived the embodiment of all her hopes and dreams for the future.

Myla trotted on past Hill Top Farm and Flora was so deep in thought that, as she steered the trap over the humpbacked bridge across the stream, bubbling noisily over its pebble bed, she failed to hear the pounding of hooves coming full pelt across the open ground to her left. As she rounded the bend just beyond the bridge, a horse and rider appeared a few yards in front of her. Myla took fright, rearing up so high that the front wheels of the trap left the ground for a few seconds, shunting Flora across the bench as it tipped perilously to one side. Hanging on to its edge, Flora tried to right herself as the rider brought his own horse to a standstill, only inches from Myla's flaring nostrils.

"What on earth do you think you're doing?!" Flora shouted as she attempted to calm her terrified pony. "Have you no road sense?" At that moment, Myla decided to gallop home as fast as she could, away from the plunging bay stallion blocking her path. Flora lurched forward, losing control of the trap as the reins were wrenched through her hands, and Myla flew past the horse and rider toward sanctuary. Flora caught a brief glimpse of the shocked expression in the rider's dark brown eyes.

It took all the strength she possessed to hang on to the bench with one hand while using the other to pull fruitlessly on the reins. Only when they entered the gates of the Hall did Myla slow down a little, sweat showing on her flanks. Flora arrived at the stables shaken and badly bruised.

"Miss Flora! What on earth happened?" Stanley, the groom, asked as he noted the whites of the pony's eyes and tried to calm her.

"A rider crossed our path out of nowhere and Myla took off," Flora said, close to tears as she handed the reins to Stanley and accepted his hand to help her climb from the trap.

"Miss Flora, you're as pale as a ghost," he said as, now on terra firma, Flora felt suddenly faint, and leaned on Stanley's broad shoulder for support. "Should I call for Sarah to help you up to the house?"

"No, let me sit down in the barn for a while. Perhaps you could be kind enough to bring me some water?"

"Yes, miss." After leading her into the barn and settling her on a hay bale, Stanley left to find her a mug of water. Flora found herself shivering.

"Here you are, miss," said Stanley as he returned. "Are you sure you don't want me to fetch Sarah? You're a rare color and that's for sure."

"No." Flora spoke with as much firmness as she could muster. Any whisper of her being seen out of control of the trap in public would mean her journeys—and, therefore, her freedom—would be instantly curtailed. "Please," she said, rallying her jelly-like limbs and standing up, "say nothing."

"As you wish, miss."

Flora left the barn, her head held high but her bones feeling as though they had been rattled around inside their bag of skin. As she crossed the lawns to the house, she knew that not a single flicker of her eye must betray to her parents what had happened.

Entering the kitchen, she saw Mrs. Hillbeck's harassed expression as she took a joint of lamb from the oven.

"Where on earth have you been, Miss Flora? Your mother came down not ten minutes ago to ask us if we'd seen you. They're already sitting down to luncheon in the dining room."

"I . . . was out."

"Miss Flora?" Sarah approached her.

"Yes?"

"There's a dirty smudge on your nose and your hair's all over the place."

"Do you have a cloth?"

"Of course." Sarah took one and cleaned her face, just as she had when Flora was a child.

"Gone?"

"Gone, but your hair . . ."

"No time, thank you." Flora ran out of the kitchen, blindly putting her fingers through her stray locks to fasten them back into the chignon. Pausing at the dining room door and listening to the dull hum of conversation beyond it, Flora took a deep breath and entered. Six heads turned to watch her.

"Please forgive me, Mama, Papa, Lady Vaughan, Miss Vaughan, and Ar—"

Flora's gaze had followed her words around the table until it came to rest on a pair of dark eyes, wide with alarm and surprise at the mutual recognition.

". . . Archie," she spat. So this was the wretch who had almost thrown her from the trap—the nasty little boy who had bruised her with crab apples all those years ago. Now grown up, but just as much trouble.

"My son is now of age, so is to be addressed as 'Lord Vaughan,'" Lady Vaughan corrected her.

"Forgive me, I did not know. Lord Vaughan," she managed as she sat down.

"Where on earth have you been, Flora?" her mother asked, her voice gentle, but her expression saying everything she could not. Flora noted her mother was wearing her finest tea gown.

"I was . . . delayed on the way home due to a . . . cart tipping over and blocking the road." Flora settled on a half-truth. "Please forgive me, Mama, I had to take the trap along the back roads."

"Your daughter drives herself in the trap?" asked Lady Vaughan, her sharp features forming a moue of disapproval.

"Not usually, of course, Arabella dear, but this morning our driver was unwell and Flora had some urgent business to attend to in Hawkshead."

"Forgive me, Mama," Flora repeated as luncheon was finally served. Even though she did all she could to concentrate on the rather vacuous Elizabeth, Archie's sister, next to her, and her talk of the splendors of her wardrobe for the forthcoming Season, she felt "Lord" Archie's apologetic eyes boring into her across the table. Aurelia had been placed next to him and was doing her best to engage him in conversation, but he seemed as distracted as Flora was. As she struggled through the main course of spring lamb, leaving the meat to one side, she comforted herself with the idea of luring Archie down to the stables, then delivering a swift punch to his arrogant aristocratic nose. At last, Alistair pulled back his chair and announced he was retiring to his study to attend to some paperwork.

"Arabella, Elizabeth, and I will adjourn to the drawing room." Rose stood up. "We have much to catch up on, don't we, my dear?"

"Indeed we do," replied Lady Vaughan.

"Aurelia, perhaps you might like to escort Archie around the gardens? The day seems warm enough, as long as you wrap up. Aurelia suffered a dreadful cold a few weeks ago, but then that's what comes of living in the godforsaken north," Rose explained to Lady Vaughan.

Being the only member of the party left without further instructions, Flora rose last and followed them out of the dining room. As she walked through the hallway, she saw that Rose, Lady Vaughan, and Elizabeth had already disappeared into the drawing room, and Aurelia and Archie were gone through the front door to the gardens.

Flora walked slowly and painfully upstairs to her bedroom. Once safely inside, she locked the door and sank gratefully onto her bed.

Dusk was beginning to fall when she was woken by a soft tap-tapping on her bedroom door.

Rolling gingerly off the bed, she sat upright. "Who is it?"

"It's me, Aurelia. Can I come in?"

Flora forced herself to stand and walked stiffly to unlock the door.

"Hello."

"Archie told me what happened earlier. How are you feeling?" Aurelia's eyes were filled with concern. "He was so worried about you and felt absolutely dreadful about it. It was all he could talk about on our walk. He even insisted on writing you a note of apology and I promised that I'd deliver it. Here." Aurelia handed her an envelope.

"Thank you." Flora tucked the letter into her pocket.

"Are you not going to open it?"

"Later."

"Flora, I do understand that the meetings you two have had so far have been . . . unfortunate, but really, Archie is awfully nice. I think you'd like him if you gave him the chance. I do . . . a lot."

Flora saw Aurelia's gaze drift dreamily toward the window.

"Good grief, Aurelia! You're not soft on him already, are you?"

"I . . . no, of course not, but even you must admit he is frightfully handsome. And so accomplished too. He seems to have read every book ever written and spent a year doing the Grand Tour in Europe, so he's very cultured. I felt quite the simpleton during our conversation."

"Archie has had the privilege of a proper education, which, sadly, we females don't seem to be worthy of," Flora countered.

"Well . . ." Aurelia knew that when her sister was in one of her moods, it was pointless trying to argue with her. "It's just the way it is and as there's nothing we can do to change it, we must accept it. Sometimes, I feel you don't like being a woman."

"You're right, maybe I don't. Anyway," Flora continued, her countenance softening as she saw Aurelia's discomfort, "just ignore me, darling, it's not only my body that has been bruised, but my pride as well. I presume our guests have left?"

"Yes, but I hope to see a lot of them during the Season. Their London home is in the neighboring square to Aunt Charlotte's house. And Elizabeth was so kind to me, telling me about all the girls who will be coming out with us. Even Archie said he may come to a couple of the dances this year."

There's that look again, Flora thought, as her sister's voice trailed off into a private reverie.

"Are you coming down for dinner?" Aurelia asked eventually. "I can always tell Mama you have a headache and she'll have Mrs. Hillbeck send up a tray. You're very pale."

"Thank you. I think it's best I stay in bed, I don't feel myself tonight."

"I'll come back and see how you are after dinner. Are you sure you don't want me to tell Mama the truth?"

"No. She'd only fuss. Really, Aurelia, I'm fine."

Once her sister had left the room, Flora put her hand into her pocket and fingered the envelope that lay inside. Drawing it out, she considered whether she should simply tear it up and burn it on the fire, for whatever he had written could hardly matter. Curiosity getting the better of her, she ripped it open, noting the beautiful script, and read the contents.

My dear Miss MacNichol,

I beg your forgiveness for the unfortunate incident earlier today. I had a deal of a task to get my horse under control, and once I did, I rode after you to see if you needed assistance, but could not find you.

I also wish to apologize for my spiteful behavior with the crab apples. Before today's new catastrophe, I had made up my mind to beg your forgiveness retrospectively, and to thank you for not doing what most little girls would have done, and go running in tears to your mama. It saved me a beating.

If there is anything I can do to redeem myself in your eyes, I would like very much to try. Our acquaintance so far has been turbulent, but I hope I may be given a chance in the future to begin afresh. Third time lucky, as they say.

I will see you, I am sure, in London this Season. Until then, I am your humble and apologetic servant,

Archie Vaughan

Flora threw the letter across the room. She watched it float briefly through the air like a distressed butterfly before landing on the floor, and decided Archie Vaughan must be well practiced at writing fine, elegant prose to women. Though she hated to admit it, Aurelia was right. He had a strong physique and chiseled features that the slight dimple in each cheek only enhanced, his wavy dark hair hung carelessly across his brow, and his brown eyes slanted into an easy smile. He was truly, annoyingly handsome.

But his character was a different matter altogether.

"He assumes he will always be forgiven. Well, not this time," she muttered as she walked back across the room and coaxed her stiff body to kneel in front of the cages. The general scuffling from within had alerted her to the fact it was well past her menagerie's suppertime. Reaching for the crate she used to store her seeds and vegetables, she let out a groan of despair.

"And after all that, your food must have fallen out of the trap!"

11

Flora, my dear, I thought we should speak about the coming summer."

"Yes, Mama." Flora stood in her mother's boudoir as Rose sat in front of her triple-mirrored dressing table and clipped on her pearl earrings for dinner.

"Please, sit down."

Flora perched on a blue damask stool and waited for her mother to speak. Rose's face was still as smooth and lovely as it must have been when she was a young debutante, but Flora could see the tightness around her mother's lips and the slight crease of worry between her blond brows.

"As you know, Aurelia and I are leaving for London in a week's time. And your father is taking his annual shooting holiday with his cousins in the Highlands. The question is, what to do with you." Rose paused and looked at Flora's reflection in the mirror. "I am aware that you loathe the city and would not wish to accompany us to London."

You haven't actually asked me, she thought.

"But by the same token," Rose continued, "women are not welcome with the men at the shoot up in Scotland. So, I have spoken to the staff, and your father and I believe it is best for you to stay here at the Hall. What do you say?"

Whatever conflicting emotions floated fast and furiously through her mind, Flora knew there was only one answer her mother wished to hear. "I would be happy to stay, Mama. After all, if I did not, I would worry for the health of my menagerie."

"Quite." A brief expression of relief crossed her mother's face.

"Although, of course, I will miss you, Aurelia, and Papa."

"As we will miss you. But at least the matter is settled. I will inform your father of our decision."

"Yes, Mama. I shall leave you to ready yourself for dinner."

"Thank you."

Flora stood up and walked toward the door. She was just about to open it when she saw her mother had turned around from the mirror to stare at her.

"Flora?"

"Yes, Mama?"

"I love you very much. And I'm sorry."

"What for?"

"I . . ."

Flora watched her mother visibly compose herself.

"Nothing," Rose whispered. "Nothing."

"You look radiant," Flora pronounced a week later, as she stood on the doorstep with Aurelia, ready to wave her sister and their mother off to London.

"Thank you," said Aurelia, giving a slight grimace. "I must confess, this velvet traveling dress feels so heavy and uncomfortable, and the corset is so tight I don't think I shall be able to breathe until I arrive in London and can remove it!"

"Well, it suits you beautifully, and I'm sure you will be the debutante of the Season." Flora hugged her tightly. "Do me proud, won't you?"

"Time to go, Aurelia." Rose appeared behind them on the doorstep. She kissed Flora on both cheeks. "Take care, my dear, and try not to run too wild around the district while we're gone."

"I'll do my best, Mama."

"Good-bye, darling Flora." Aurelia gave her one last embrace, then blew her a kiss as they stepped into the old carriage that would take them to Windermere station, after which they would change at Oxenholme for the London-bound train.

Even to Flora's unworldly eyes, their carriage looked like a relic. She knew it was much to her father's chagrin that they could not afford to buy a motorcar. Aurelia leaned out of the window to wave at her as the horse clopped off down the drive. Flora returned the wave until the carriage had disappeared out of the front gates. Then she went back inside the shadowy house, which seemed to share her sense of abandonment. Her father had left for the Highlands the previous day and as her footsteps echoed through the hall, Flora felt sudden panic at the upcoming two months of near silence.

Upstairs in her room, she took Posy from her cage and stroked her silky ears for comfort, deciding this was practice for her future spinsterhood. She must embrace it.

Bereft of the routine she had adhered to since childhood, Flora had begun to create her own. Up with the lark in the morning, she'd dress hastily, and having dispensed with any idea of a formal breakfast taken alone in the dining room, she'd join Mrs. Hillbeck, Sarah, and Tilly in the kitchen for a cup of tea, fresh bread and jam, and a gossip. Then she'd head out, cheese sandwiches wrapped in wax paper and stowed along with her sketching equipment in a large canvas satchel.

Flora had always thought she knew the countryside around her family home well, but it was only that summer that she truly discovered its miraculous beauty.

She hiked over the hills that surrounded Esthwaite Water, picking up her suffering skirts to scramble over the low dry-stone walls that had divided the farmland for centuries. With the dedication of a practiced naturalist, she cataloged each treasure she came across, such as the small crop of purple saxifrage she found nestled on a crag. Her ears sought out the high cheeps of hawfinches and the trills of waxwings, and her fingers tenderly brushed over the valleys' spiky grass and the rough stones, baking hot from the sun.

On one of the hottest days that June, Flora hiked along the shore of a cool, mirror-smooth tarn in the hope of finding a flower she had only ever set eyes on in her botany books. After hours of searching in the sweltering heat, she finally stumbled across the bright fuchsia-colored heads of the Alpine catchfly, clinging to the mineral-rich rocks. Struck by the contrast of the frilled petals against their hardy home, Flora lay down on the sun-warmed ground to sketch it.

She must have fallen asleep in the drowsy heat, for she found herself waking as the soft fingertips of the setting sun rested on her shoulder. Rousing herself, she looked up through the branches of the Scots pines soaring above, her gaze catching the rare shape of a peregrine falcon perched on a high branch.

Not daring to so much as breathe, she studied its sleek plumage shimmering in the light and its curved beak raised into the breeze. For a moment, neither human nor bird moved. Then with a regal sweep of its wings, the falcon launched into the air, setting the branch aquiver, and soared up into the sunset.

She returned home at dusk, and went immediately to paint the brief sketch she had made of the falcon in full flight.

She spent most evenings poring over her favorite book of flowers by Sarah Bowdich, comparing the blooms she'd collected to the pictures in the book and adding their Latin names to her scrapbook, along with the flower released from the press. She felt irrationally guilty that she was confining something so vibrantly alive to the pages of a book, but at least its beauty was now preserved beyond its natural life span.

She also added a mewling kitten she'd found half drowned beside a tarn to her menagerie. It was tiny enough to sit in the palm of her hand, and Flora reckoned it was only a few days old as its eyes were not yet opened. Somehow, the little animal had managed to drag itself out of what would have been a watery grave. Its determination to survive moved Flora beyond any other creature she'd adopted, and with no one to stop her, the sleek black kitten shared the warmth of her bed.

She named the new addition "Panther" after she found him eyeing Posy hungrily through the grill of her cage, even though the rabbit was five times the kitten's size, and he was soon fully recovered, flexing his tiny sharp claws by climbing the curtains in the bedroom. Once he was weaned, Flora knew she'd have to take him downstairs to the kitchen, or half her menagerie would end up in his stomach.

Aurelia wrote to her once a week, reporting on her adventures in London.

I am glad that the presentation itself is over. My nerves were in shreds as I waited in line to be presented to the King and Queen. In confidence, Flora, Alexandra is far more delicate and beautiful than she appears in her photographs, and the King is uglier and fatter! To my surprise, I've had no shortage of dancing partners at the dances I've attended and two of them have asked to call on me at Aunt Charlotte's. One is a viscount, who Mama tells me owns half of Berkshire, so you can imagine how happy she is! I am not so enamored; he stands at only just above my height—and you know how short I am—and he walks with a limp, due, so I'm told, to having suffered from polio as a child. I feel sympathy for him, but he is definitely no Prince Charming, even though this is no fault of his own.

Talking of "princes," Archie Vaughan arrived as escort to his sister, Elizabeth, at a dance last week. And oh, there is no doubt he is the most handsome man in London. The rest of the debutantes were envious indeed when he asked me to dance, not once, but three times! Aunt Charlotte said it was almost indecent! We talked for a while afterward and he asked after you, puzzled that you weren't with us in London. I explained you hated the town life so had remained at Esthwaite Hall. He said he hoped you had forgiven him. I confess that I might be a little in love with him, even though there's something about him that rather unnerves me.

And that is all my news for now. Mama sends her best. I'm sure you will understand how much she is enjoying being back in the social round. Everyone seems to know her here and she was obviously a very popular debutante before she married Papa. She says she will write soon.

I miss you, my dearest sister.

Aurelia

"My word!" Flora exclaimed in frustration to Panther, who had climbed up her skirts and into her lap as she read the letter. "It would be just my luck to have Archie Vaughan as a brother-in-law."

A few days later, on a hot July afternoon, Flora was sitting in the garden at the table sketching. She had found a wide-brimmed canvas hat of unknown origin abandoned in the boot room, and it now warded off the strong rays of the afternoon sun. Panther was prancing across the lawn, chasing butterflies and looking so adorable that Flora abandoned the flowers she had been sketching and instead sat on the grass to capture his likeness.

She was startled by the sudden sound of footfall behind her. Turning around, she expected to see Tilly home from the weekly market. Instead, a tall shadow passed across her as she looked up into the dark eyes of Archie Vaughan.

"Good afternoon, Miss MacNichol. I do apologize if I disturbed you, but my fist's raw from knocking on the front door, so I came around the back in search of a human being."

"Goodness, I . . ." Flora scrambled to her feet as Panther's fur stood on end and he hissed at the stranger ferociously. "The staff are all out. And, as you know, my family is away," she said abruptly.

"So, you are a veritable orphan in your own home."

"Hardly an orphan," she countered. "I simply don't care for London and chose to stay instead."

"In that way, at least, we share the same opinion. Especially in the mating season, when a new tranche of innocent young females must bat their eyes as coquettishly as possible, in their bid to outdo their rivals for the highest male prize."

"And do you consider yourself a male 'prize,' Lord Vaughan? I hear from my sister you attended a dance last week."

"Quite the contrary," he said. "Despite our pedigree and ancient family name, we are flat broke. You may know my father died in the last Boer War seven years ago and the Vaughan ship had remained unsteered until I came of age a few months ago. However, I assure you I am doing my utmost to stay out of the clutches of any rich heiress I come across."

Flora had not expected such a frank response to her flippant comment.

"May I ask what you're doing here?"

"I'm on my way down from the Highlands. I was there with your father and his party for a few days' shooting. It's a long drive back to London, so I decided I would kill two birds with one stone."

"And who or what are the 'birds,' exactly?"

"Firstly, taking a break from the journey, and secondly, dropping in on the off chance you'd be here and might allow me a few minutes of your company. I wish to apologize in person for what happened in April. And also, perhaps be provided with some refreshment. Although the latter may not be possible, given that there are no staff around at the moment."

"That is the easiest of your requests, Lord Vaughan. I'm quite capable of making tea and I might even stretch to a sandwich too."

"A lady who can make tea and sandwiches! I doubt my sister and my mother have the first clue."

"It's hardly difficult," Flora muttered, standing up. "Will you stay here in the garden while I prepare it?"

"No, I'll come with you and applaud your culinary skills with awe."

"As you please," Flora answered briskly. They headed up the steps to the terrace, and she felt furious with herself that her anger toward him seemed to have dissolved in his barrage of charm and honesty. Determined to hold on to it, Flora increased her pace as they entered the kitchen. Finding the kettle was already full, she placed it on the range to boil, then busied herself at the table with a loaf of bread, butter, and cheese.

"Quite the domesticated country wife, aren't you?" Archie commented, pulling out a chair and sitting down.

"Please don't patronize me, Lord Vaughan. Especially when I'm preparing your food."

"May I beg a favor, Miss MacNichol? As we find ourselves in such informal circumstances, perhaps you could try 'Archie'? And I could try 'Flora'?"

"I certainly don't grant you permission to call me Flora. We are barely acquainted." She slammed the sandwiches onto a plate. "Men around here eat them with the crusts left on. Does that suit you?"

"Good grief, you really are fierce." He smirked as she proffered him the plate as if she'd prefer to throw it. "Ouch!" he cried suddenly, swiping at the small furry menace that had just bitten his ankle. "Your kitten doesn't seem to approve of me either."

Flora suppressed a smile as she swept up Panther into the crook of her arm and turned away to pour the tea.

"Miss MacNichol, is there any way we could start afresh? Given that the first incident with the crab apples was when I was a snot-nosed child of six and the second, a regrettable accident."

"Lord Vaughan"—she rounded on him—"I have no idea why you are here or why you seem to care what I think of you when, from what my sister says, half the young women in London are continually worshipping your attributes. If it's simply because you cannot bear that there is one woman in the world who you cannot seduce, then I am sad for you, but it is simply the way things are. Now, shall we carry the tray onto the terrace?"

"Allow me. And you take him." Archie indicated Panther. "That fierce tiger in kitten's clothes needs to be kept under control in case he attacks me again. You have chosen your pet perfectly, Miss MacNichol." Archie swept up the tea tray and walked toward the door.

Outside on the terrace, the sun shone merrily, in complete contrast to the pall of silence that hung between them. Flora poured the tea and they sat together as Archie devoured the sandwiches with the crusts left on them, knowing she was being intolerably rude. If her mother could see her, Rose would certainly have admonished her severely for her behavior, but she could not bring herself to make polite conversation. Neither, it seemed, could Archie.

"If you'll excuse me," she said eventually, "I must go and collect my sketch pad before it gets damp." She rose from the table, indicating the lawn.

"Of course." He nodded. "And please take that tiger with you."

When she returned, Archie was standing. "Thank you for your hospitality. I am only sad that you seem to have the wrong impression of me and I can't convince you otherwise. I will see you anon, Miss MacNichol."

"I am sure I do not have the wrong impression, but my sister will be very happy to entertain you should you find yourself in these parts again." Flora put her sketch pad down on the table, and Archie's eyes followed it.

"May I take a look?"

"There's nothing worth looking at. They're just rough sketches, I . . ."

But Archie had already opened the pad and was leafing through the charcoal drawings. "Miss MacNichol, you underestimate your talent. Some of these are outstanding. This falcon . . . and that sketch of your black tiger . . ."

"Panther is his name."

"Perfect," he acknowledged. "Well, it's superb. Quite superb. You have a real eye for nature and animals."

"I draw purely for my own pleasure."

"But surely, that's what all the great artists do? The passion comes from within, the need to express oneself in whatever artistic medium one chooses."

"Yes," Flora agreed grudgingly.

"When I was on my tour in Europe, I saw many incredible works of art. Yet so many of their creators lived in poverty for much of their lives—slaves to their muses. It seems there were few who didn't suffer one way or another." Archie's gaze moved from the sketchbook to Flora. "Are you in pain too, Miss MacNichol?"

"What a question! Just because I choose to draw and paint hardly signifies that I suffer from some of form of mental or emotional malady."

"Good. For I wouldn't wish you to suffer. Or be lonely. Surely, rattling around in this old mausoleum all by yourself, you must be?" Archie pressed her.

"I'm not by myself. I have the staff and an entire menagerie of animals to keep me company."

"Your sister mentioned your . . . *collection* of wildlife when last we spoke in London. Apparently, you once befriended a snake."

"A harmless grass snake, yes," Flora conceded, feeling breathless at his sudden hail of questions, which felt rather like the crab apples he'd once thrown at her. "I was not allowed to keep it."

"I think even I would balk at the idea of a snake living under my roof. You are a very unusual woman, Miss MacNichol. I have to admit that you fascinate me."

"I am glad that my oddness keeps you amused."

"Well, I salute you, Miss MacNichol," Archie said after a pause. "You are adept at turning even the most positive comment into a negative. What more can I do to earn your forgiveness? I have tried just about everything, including motoring up and down the country when I could easily have taken the Scotch Express train straight to Edinburgh and back. There," he added, and Flora could see his frustration. "I have told you the truth."

As if drained by his confession, Archie sat down suddenly in a chair. "I left the shoot early to come and see you. But as it's obvious I cannot gain your favor, no matter how hard I try, I will continue on my way, and stop farther down south at a hotel."

Flora surveyed him, her lack of experience with men—especially men as worldly as Archie—hampering her natural instincts. She simply could not understand why he had so inconvenienced himself to apologize to her when apparently he could have any woman in London he wished for.

"I . . . don't know what to say."

"Perhaps you could consider granting me a few days in your company? And during that time, we could talk of all the subjects your sister tells me you are passionate about. As I am too."

"Such as?"

"I'm a keen botanist, Miss MacNichol, and though it's doubtful I have the extensive knowledge that you possess, I like to feel that I am on the nursery slopes of my learning. Though our garden at High Weald does not have the backdrop of raw beauty you have here, it's equally beautiful in its own gentle way. Have you ever been to Kew Gardens?"

"No." Flora brightened at the mention. "But I have always longed to see it. I have read that they collect species from all over the world, as far away as South America."

"Indeed they do, and the new director, Sir David Prain, is inspired. He's been kind enough to lend his assistance to our own gardens. Due to the benevolent climate in the south of England, I have discovered that if sheltered, plants from foreign climes do manage to thrive there. I would enjoy seeing the indigenous flora that must grow plentifully around here too. I am eager to create an unusual collection of plants from all over England—Ouch!"

Panther had climbed Archie's trouser leg and was now purring and preening himself in the valley between his thighs, his pin-sharp claws kneading the cloth of Archie's trousers. Seeing that even her cat had forgiven him, Flora finally relented. "If you feel that I can be of any assistance to your studies, then I suppose I would be happy to show you what I can."

"Thank you," Archie said, and she saw his features relax as he raised a tentative hand to stroke Panther. "I would be most grateful for any expertise you care to impart."

"But where will you stay?"

"I've already taken a room in the local pub in Near Sawrey. And now," he said, rising and offering her the crook of his elbow, the other arm cradling her contented kitten, "will you show me around this beautiful garden?"

Initially, as she began their tour, Flora did her best to test his knowledge, still unsure whether this was another Archie-type ploy to insult and belittle her. But she soon realized that his interest and, indeed, his knowledge were real. There were a number of unusual plants in the flower beds that Archie managed to name without pausing, all apart from one which she told him was called a star flower, or bog star, *Parnassia palustris*.

"I believe it's quite rare and prefers the climate here in the north of England, which is probably why you don't recognize it."

As they wandered along the borders, Archie told her how, as a boy, he'd followed the gardener around like a tame dog. "Sadly, he too died in the Boer War. I came down from Oxford a year ago and with no funds to employ a full staff, I had to educate myself. And found a passion in the process. You should see me at home, in my overalls," he said with a smile. "Next time I come to visit, I'll wear them if you'd like. One should never judge a book by its cover, Miss MacNichol," he chided as he wagged a finger at her.

"But it is your 'cover' that has made you the ladies' favorite in London." Flora looked at him suspiciously.

"Does that stop me having a passion for plants? Or is it more that you thought I was simply a louche cad who spent his time carousing and spending his trust fund?"

Flora lowered her eyes in embarrassment.

"Granted," he continued, seeing her expression, "I am only twenty-one and enjoy the occasional party and the company of pretty women. Sadly, as you also know, the grand old families of England are no longer as rich as they once were and my inheritance came in the form of the ailing High Weald estate, not through an overripe bank account. I want to do what I can to preserve its splendor, outside at least. The walled garden is famous for its beauty. And if that means getting my hands dirty, then so be it."

Flora sat at her desk later that evening and wrote in her journal, her mind whirring with the strange turn of events. Having finished recording every word she could recall their speaking, she stowed the journal in her writing bureau. Unusually, that night Flora lay sleepless, still mulling over the Archie dichotomy she had uncovered today. And the fact that somehow, before he'd taken his leave, he'd persuaded her to take him farther afield tomorrow to see the Langdale Pikes.

"He really is an enigma," she whispered to Panther, his tiny head on the pillow next to her. "And I hate myself for beginning to like him."

12

Good morning, Miss MacNichol," Archie said when they met as agreed in the stable yard. "I've brought us lunch. And don't worry, the sandwiches all have the crusts left on." He hoisted the picnic hamper onto the trap and held out his hand to help her up.

As he climbed up beside her and she took the reins, Flora smiled at his attire. He wore a pair of ancient twill trousers and a roughly sewn checked shirt. On his feet was a pair of thick workman's boots.

"I borrowed them from the publican I'm boarding with in the village," he explained as he saw her eyes on him. "The trousers are a deal too big for me, so I've secured them with a piece of twine. Do I look the part?"

"Indeed you do, Lord Vaughan," she agreed. "A real man of the countryside."

"As we are spending the day being other than we usually are, would it *now* be possible to dispense with formalities? I am simply Archie, the gardener's boy, and you are Flora, the milkmaid."

"Milkmaid! Do I look that low?" She faked offense as she clicked the reins and they trotted off. "Could I not at least be a parlor . . . or even a lady's maid?"

"Ah, but in every story I've read, it is always the milkmaid who is described as the most beautiful. It was not an insult, but a compliment."

Flora concentrated on driving the trap, thankful that her sun hat shielded her face as she felt heat rush to it. It was the first direct compliment on her physical appearance she had ever received from a man and she had no idea how to respond.

The Langdale Valley was cradled between the majestic pikes that swept upward, high into the clouds. They stood, almost biblically parted, to encompass the green of the valley floor, which gently dissipated as the raw rock face asserted itself the higher the eye climbed.

Archie helped Flora down from the cart and they stood and looked upward.

"'In the combinations which they make, towering above each other, or lifting themselves in ridges like the waves of a tumultuous sea . . .'"

"'. . . and in the beauty and variety of their surfaces and colors, they are surpassed by *none*,'" Flora finished for him. "I'm a Lakes girl, I know my Wordsworth." She shrugged at his obvious surprise.

"This is what I love about coming to the mountains," he breathed. "You feel your own insignificance. We are but a pinprick in this vast cosmos."

"Yes, and perhaps that's why those in London seem so full of their own importance."

"They feel masters of their own universe in their man-made cities, whereas out here . . ." Archie didn't finish the sentence, just took in a lungful of fresh air. "Have you ever climbed one of these mountains, Flora?"

"Of course not. I'm a girl. Mama would have a seizure if I suggested it."

"Would you like to? Tomorrow?" Archie grabbed her hand. "It would be an adventure. Which one would it be, do you think? That one?" Letting her hand go, he pointed along the pass. "Or that one maybe?"

"If it's any, of course it should be the highest. And that is Scafell Pike." Flora indicated the tallest one, its peak currently hidden under a halo of cloud. "It's the highest in England, and my father says the view from the summit is unparalleled."

"So, shall we do it?"

"Not in a dress!"

Archie laughed. "Then you must beg or borrow a pair of breeches. Are you game?"

"As long as it's our secret."

"Of course." Archie reached out a hand to tuck a stray wisp of hair back behind Flora's ear. "I shall collect you tomorrow from the front gates at six thirty sharp."

That evening, Flora did something she'd never done before, and entered her father's dressing room. She opened the door tentatively, even though she knew there was no one around to see her—Sarah was at home in the tiny cottage she shared with her mother, and Tilly and Mrs. Hillbeck were tucked away in the kitchen having their nightly gossip. As she stepped over the threshold, she shivered slightly at the sudden drop in temperature. And noticed the room smelled of dust and damp, tinged with a hint of her father's eau de cologne. The room was bathed in evening shadows that slanted across the narrow wooden bed. A clock stood on the nightstand, ticking away the seconds of its owner's absence.

Flora opened the heavy oak doors of the wardrobe, her fingers searching through the rack of trousers and finally settling on a pair of tweed shooting breeches. Realizing she would need socks too, she opened a likely-looking drawer in a mahogany chest, but found it was full of papers. In the corner of it sat a small bundle of cream envelopes tied fast with string. Flora recognized her mother's writing and wondered if they might be love letters from their courting days. Tempted beyond measure to look, as it would perhaps help her understand the mystery behind her parents' marriage, Flora shut the drawer firmly before her traitorous fingers could wander toward them. Finding the socks and adding a thick shirt to the pile over her arm, she walked back toward the door.

Her fingers only skimmed the handle before temptation overrode sense and she headed back to the chest. Clothes discarded on the bed, she opened the drawer and pulled out the pile of letters. After sliding the uppermost one from beneath the string, she read its contents.

Cranhurst House
Kent
13th August 1889

My dear Alistair,

In a week we will be married. I cannot thank you enough for being my knight in shining armor and saving me from disgrace. In return, I swear I will be the most diligent, faithful wife any man could wish for. My father tells me he has already made the transfer and I hope it arrived in your account.

I look forward with pleasure to seeing you and my new home.

With kindest regards,
Rose

Flora read it and reread it, trying to make sense of the word "disgrace." What was it her mother could possibly have done that was so terrible?

"Well, whatever it is, it explains their marriage," she told the empty dressing room. Most likely, her mother had fallen in love with an unsuitable man—that was certainly what happened in many of the books she'd read. Flora wondered who it might have been. Even though her mother never spoke of her growing-up years, Aurelia had recently remarked in her letters how their mother seemed to be known to everyone. Which only underlined the fact that she must have had a past. Flora replaced the letter in its envelope and carefully tucked it back beneath the string before returning the bundle to the drawer. She retrieved the pile of her father's clothes from the bed and left the dressing room.

Flora rose at six the next morning and hastily pulled on her father's breeches, shirt, and socks. Tiptoeing down to the boot room, she borrowed Sarah's stout walking boots—which were rather too small, but would have to do—and a tweed cap of her father's. She left a note for the staff to say she had gone out for the day to collect flowers to paint, and then slipped out of the house. Walking along the drive and through the gates, she saw a brand-new silver Rolls-Royce motorcar parked up on the verge. Archie swung the door open for her and she climbed in.

"Good morning." He smiled at her appearance. "You're looking particularly comely today, Flora the milkmaid. Perfectly attired to be driven in the Silver Ghost."

"At least it's practical," she countered.

"Actually, with that cap on your head, you could be taken more for a boy. Here, put on these motoring goggles to complete the look."

She pulled them over her eyes with a frown. "I am only happy that no one in the area will recognize me."

"Can you imagine what your mother or sister would say if they could see you?" he asked as he started the engine.

"I'd prefer not to. And what on earth are you doing owning a car like this, having told me your family is flat broke? Papa said they cost a king's ransom."

"Sadly, it isn't mine. The owner of a neighboring estate lent it to me in return for the use of a cottage at High Weald. I promised him not to ask any questions as to its purpose. Although admittedly, the poor fellow's wife is currently pregnant with their sixth child in as many years, if you know what I mean."

"I'm sure I don't," she said primly.

"Well, I'm happy to give the car a good run-in through the mountains. I've put a picnic in an old army rucksack that Mr. Turnbull, my very accommodating publican, let me borrow, along with a couple of blankets just in case."

Flora looked out of the window and up to the skies over the pikes in the distance. And frowned at the heaviness of the clouds. "I do hope we haven't picked the only day in weeks when the heavens will open."

"Luckily, it's warm this morning."

"That may be, but my father often says that the temperature drops sharply at higher altitudes. He's climbed most of the pikes over his years here."

"In that case, we'll have to find a barn to park the motorcar in. I've promised Felix on pain of death that I'll return it to him in good nick, and I can't risk having it poured on."

A local farmer kindly agreed to house the Rolls-Royce, Archie glaring at the farmer's wide-eyed children—not to mention the chickens—who looked eager to climb inside.

"Papa said it took him about four hours to reach the summit," Flora commented as they set off toward the valley, walking on the coarse grass.

"Your father's an experienced hiker, I think it will take us a fair bit longer," Archie said, as he dug a map out of his rucksack. "The publican suggested a good path for us to follow. Here." Picking up a stick, he sketched a trail in a patch of dry dirt. "We need to head south toward Esk Hause, then on toward Broad Crag Col." Archie led the way with his map in his hand.

"What are all those tiny white dots high up on the mountainside?" he inquired.

"Sheep. They leave their droppings everywhere underfoot."

"Perhaps we can hitch a ride on one if we become weary. Such useful animals too, providing delicious food for our tables and covering our bodies with their wool."

"I loathe the taste of lamb," Flora stated. "I've already decided I won't offer meat when I run my own household."

"Really? What will you serve instead?"

"Why, vegetables and fish, of course."

"Then I'm not sure I'd want to come and have dinner at your home."

"Suit yourself." Flora shrugged as she marched off ahead of him.

The going was easy for the first couple of hours up the lower slopes of the mountain, and they paused occasionally beside the becks that ran down into the valley, cupping their hands to drink the fresh springwater and splashing their hot faces. They followed the well-trodden paths worn by climbers before them, chatting companionably about everything from favorite books to pieces of music. Then the climb became harder and the chatter ceased as they saved their breath to scramble up and over the jagged rocks that peppered the mountainside.

"I reckon we're a good two-thirds of the way there," said Archie, standing on an outcrop and looking upward. "Come on, race you to the ridge above us."

An hour later, they reached the top of the pike. Breathless and panting, they stood side by side, exhilarated by their achievement. Flora walked slowly around the summit, surveying the magnificent view below them.

"I read in a book last night that on a clear day you can see Scotland, Wales, Ireland, and the Isle of Man," Archie said, appearing next to her. "It's a shame we don't have a photographer to mark the moment. Shall I help you up onto the cairn that marks the pinnacle?"

"Thank you." Archie took her hand and steadied her as she mounted the huge pile of rocks, then let her go as she spread out her arms and looked up to the blue of the sky. "I feel on top of the world!"

"You are—at least in England," he laughed, reaching out his arms as she climbed back down toward him. He took her by the waist and swung her to the ground. Holding her there for a few seconds, he looked at her. "Flora, I do declare that you are simply beautiful when you're happy."

Flora felt the heat rising in her cheeks once more, as a mist suddenly swirled wetly around them and the views disappeared.

"I'm starving," she announced to hide her blushes.

"So am I. How say you we walk downward back into the sun and eat our picnic there? Mr. Turnbull tells me we should head northwest toward Lingmell; the way is well marked with cairns. He says the view onto Wasdale is quite spectacular. We can pause to eat there."

"Then lead the way to our sandwiches," she said, as Archie picked up his rucksack and they moved off the summit.

Twenty minutes later, Flora insisted she could go no farther, so they settled themselves on a flat rock and Archie unpacked their lunch.

"Cheese sandwiches have never tasted more divine," she murmured. "I only wish I'd thought to bring my sketch pad and charcoal with me. I must try to remember this view so I can re-create it on paper." Flora pulled off her cap so that her hair flowed around her shoulders and tipped her face up toward the sun's warmth.

"You have the most wonderful head of hair, I must say," said Archie, reaching for a strand and twirling a ringlet around his finger.

Something inside Flora's body gave a strange little jolt at Archie's intimate touch. "It's as thick and strong as towrope, and my mother has no idea where it comes from," she said. "If you slip and fall on our way, I'll throw you a handful of it and you can use it to haul yourself back up."

Flora gave a smile and turned to find Archie staring at her, a strange expression in his eyes. "What is it?"

"It would be inappropriate to tell you what I was thinking. All I will say is that I find you delightful company in your current euphoric mood."

"Thank you. And I wish to tell you that I have finally forgiven you for almost killing me. Twice."

"Then we are friends?"

For a moment, Archie's face was very close to hers.

"Yes, we are."

As they both reclined on the sun-warmed slab of rock, Flora decided she had never felt so relaxed in the company of another human being, which was quite a turnaround under the circumstances.

"Where do you think your talent for sketching and painting came from?" he asked.

"I've no idea, but I certainly know who it was that inspired me. You can probably see her farmhouse from here."

"And who may this person be?"

"She's a children's writer named Beatrix Potter. When I was seven, she came to Esthwaite Hall with her parents for tea. I was sitting in the garden trying to draw a caterpillar I had just found on a leaf and was comparing it to a slug. She sat down on the grass next to me, admired my caterpillar, and asked if she could show me how to draw it. Then, a week later, an envelope was sent to me through the post. I was so excited: I'd never received anything addressed to me before. And inside, there was a letter from Miss Potter. But it wasn't a normal letter, because it told the story of Cedric the Caterpillar and his friend Simon the Slug, and contained tiny watercolor sketches. It's my most treasured possession."

"I have heard of Miss Potter and her books. She has become famous for them in the past few years."

"Indeed, but when I met her, she was not. And now she lives in Near Sawrey at Hill Top Farm, very close to the public house where you are staying."

"And have you made her acquaintance since she arrived here?"

"No. These days, she's *so* busy and famous that I don't feel I can arrive on her doorstep without being invited."

"Does she live alone?"

"I believe she does, yes."

"Then perhaps she is lonely. Just because she is well-known does not mean she doesn't desire company. Especially from a young woman whom she once inspired."

"Perhaps, but I haven't yet worked up the nerve. She is quite simply my heroine. One day I hope my life will be similar to hers."

"What? An aging spinster, with only animals and plants for company?"

"You mean an independent woman of means who has been able to choose her own destiny?" Flora countered.

"You believe that your destiny is to be alone?"

"As my parents did not see fit for me to be presented at court like my younger sister, I have settled to the thought that I will probably never marry."

"Flora"—Archie reached his hand to hers tentatively—"the fact that you weren't presented does not preclude you falling in love and sharing your life with a man. Perhaps there were reasons . . ."

"Yes. My parents did not have the finances necessary, or the support of Aunt Charlotte, as Aurelia has had."

"That's not quite what I meant. Sometimes, there are . . . circumstances which we may not be fully aware of, which affect others' actions."

"You mean that I am not a beauty like Aurelia is?"

"I certainly did not mean that! You have no idea how brightly you shine. Both outside and in."

"Please, Archie, I understand that you're trying to be kind, but I know why. Now, we must head down the mountain. Can you see the clouds gathering above us? I believe a squall is coming over." Flora stood up, suddenly wishing the conversation had never begun. She felt inexplicably vulnerable, and her mood had altered just as swiftly as the clouds had blacked out the sun.

Fifteen minutes later, both of them were lying facedown against the rough grass and sheep droppings as the heavens opened and the rising wind drove needle-sharp pricks of rain against them.

"Here," said Archie, rifling in his rucksack, "take the edge of the blanket and we can take shelter underneath it."

Flora reached for a corner to pull it over her head. Archie had the other end and they lay there together in the darkness. Their inadequate shield was quickly soaked through.

"Hello," he whispered, and she felt his breath on her cheek.

"Hello."

"Have we met somewhere before? My name's Archie, the farm boy."

"And mine is Flora, the milkmaid." She couldn't help but smile.

"Smells rather of sheep excrement in here, doesn't it?"

"I believe it is the preferred perfume in this part of the world."

"Flora?"

"Yes?"

Then his lips searched for hers, and he kissed her. Small arrows of desire shot straight down from her mouth right through her body, and though she urged her own lips to take heed and detach themselves, they refused to obey. He drew her closer, wrapping his arms and his warmth tightly around her. The kissing seemed to last for a very long time, as Flora's intentions to grow old alone blew away as fast as one of the angry clouds above them. Finally, as the rain ceased, and with huge effort, she drew her face away from his.

"My God, Flora," Archie panted, "what have you done to me? You are miraculous! I adore you . . ."

He reached for her again, but this time Flora pulled away, then yanked off the blanket and sat up dazed from shock and pleasure. Archie appeared too a few seconds later and they sat together in silence.

"My sincere apologies, I'm afraid my feelings got the better of me. I'm sure that you will now add this most recent bad behavior to my list of misdemeanors. Please, Flora, I beg you, don't. I simply couldn't help it. I stand by what I said, and however inappropriate, I adore you. In truth,

I have thought of nothing and no one else since I laid eyes on you back in April."

"I—"

"Hear me out." Archie took her hand in his. "It will be one of the last chances we have to be alone. The reason I escorted Elizabeth to the dance in London was because I was expecting to see you there with your sister. Then I remembered that your father had invited me to join his shooting party in the Highlands and it was the perfect excuse to stop in and see you on the way home. These past three days with you have been . . . sublime. If ever two people fitted like a hand in a glove, it's you and I. Surely, you must feel it too?"

Flora made to stand, but her hand was held fast. "Please believe what I'm telling you," he entreated her. "And I need you to remember every word I've said and look at me and know it's the truth. I have to leave tonight to begin to motor back home, as I've promised my mother I will be back tomorrow. But I swear that I will write to you, and we will see each other again." His gaze was dark but clear as he gripped her hand more tightly. "I want you to trust me. Whatever happens, you must trust me."

Flora turned to him, overwhelmed by this sudden outpouring of feeling. After barely three days together, how *could* she trust him?

She dragged her eyes from his gaze. "We'd better be going or Sarah will wonder where I am."

"Yes, of course." His hand let go of hers like a rope snapping under tension, leaving her oddly bereft.

They trudged down the mountain in silence, their mood as dampened as their sodden clothes.

Finally reaching the motorcar, it was all Flora could do to keep her eyes open, suffering from fatigue and emotional confusion in equal measure. As Archie drove, they sat only a few inches apart, each lost in their own thoughts. Eventually, they drew up at the gates of the Hall and Archie brought the motorcar to a halt.

"Flora, I have to go home and put right a dreadful mistake I now know I have made. But I swear I will. And I beg you, don't dismiss what has happened between us in the last three days. However surreal it may feel to you as time passes, try to remember it *was* real. Will you promise me that?"

Flora stared at him, and took a deep breath. "Yes, I will."

"Good-bye then, darling Flora."

"Good-bye."

Flora got out of the motorcar, slammed the door, and walked rather unsteadily through the gates, feeling as though the earth was not solid beneath her. Arriving in the kitchen, she found Sarah with her feet up on the range, munching on a bit of cake, and Mrs. Hillbeck at the table with Panther nestled in her arms. They both glanced up, startled, before bursting into laughter.

"Miss Flora! Where on earth have you been! And what are you wearing? You look half drowned," Sarah exclaimed as she recovered herself.

"I am," she replied, grateful to them for providing the sense of normality she needed to regain her physical and emotional bearings. Sarah was already rubbing at Flora's hair with a muslin cloth to dry it. "I've just been in the mountains," she said dreamily.

"And it's been right throwing it down," Sarah muttered. "Dearie me, child. You take yourself upstairs and get out of those wet clothes. I'll bring you a tea tray up and fill the bathtub."

"Thank you." Flora walked slowly to the boot room and pulled the soaking walking boots off her sore feet. After hobbling into the hall and up the stairs to her bedroom, she was greeted by a disgruntled scuffle of hungry animals. She removed her sopping clothes and donned her robe, then hurriedly stuffed leaves and seeds through the bars. A wave of exhaustion suddenly overtook her, and she staggered to the bed and lay down.

By the time Sarah arrived upstairs with the tea tray, she saw Miss Flora had fallen fast asleep.

13

Flora spent the following week in bed with a horrible chill. As her fever rose, the entire Archie episode took on a dreamlike quality, and she began to wonder if she'd imagined the whole thing.

When she eventually felt well enough to get out of bed, she walked on legs of jelly downstairs and found a number of letters addressed to her on the silver plate left in the hall for the purpose. She recognized by the writing that two of them were from Aurelia and one was from her mother, but the fourth was written in Archie's elegant script. Sitting on the bottom stair, her hands trembled as she opened the envelope, weak from both her recent illness and fear of what it might contain.

High Weald
Ashford, Kent
5th July 1909

My dearest Flora,

I hope this letter finds you well, although I myself have suffered from a bad chill in the days after our mountain escapade. I wished to tell you that everything I said to you, I meant. I ask you to please bear with me as there is a complex situation that I must endeavor to resolve. It is not of your making—or, for that matter, particularly of mine—but arose simply from my readiness to do the right thing for all whom I love.

I know I speak in riddles, but sadly, plans were set in motion before I saw you and I must now do my best to extricate myself from them, to clear a path forward. I suggest, due to the current sensitivity of the situation, that you burn this letter, as I know how such missives have a habit of falling into the wrong hands. And I would not wish to compromise you.

In the meantime, I entreat you again to trust me, and I remain your friend and ardent admirer,

Archie Vaughan

P.S. Please pass on my best regards to Panther. I hope he is looking after you.

Flora read and reread his words, trying to make sense of them. When they started to dance across the page in front of her, she folded the letter with a sigh and placed it back in its envelope.

To distract herself, Flora reached for the letters from Aurelia. The first one was full of excited gossip.

There are already two betrothals announced and Mama and I have been invited to attend both engagement parties. In truth, there are a number of young men here who seek me out, but none of them have caught my heart. I was disappointed that your nemesis, Archie Vaughan, was apparently unwell and therefore had to cancel his intended visit to London. Now I doubt I will see him before the Season ends and everyone disperses to summer at home or, in some cases, abroad. I confess that returning to Esthwaite might feel a little dull after London, but I am so looking forward to seeing you, my darling sister. You have no idea just how much I have missed you.

" 'Nemesis' . . . hah!" Flora put down the letter and thought how much had changed since she had last seen Aurelia. And then, with a heavy heart, she knew she must acknowledge her sister's feelings for Archie. Aurelia only wished Flora to like him and forgive him. How horrified would she be if she knew the truth?

Flora went up to her bedroom, tucked the letters into the silk pocket at the back of her current journal, and locked that in her writing bureau. She sent up a silent—and rather selfish—prayer that some man—*any* man other than Archie—might capture Aurelia's heart in what little remained of the Season. There were many things she was willing to share with her sister, but she was painfully aware that her newfound passion for Archie Vaughan could never be one of them.

She lay down on the bed and tore open the second letter from Aurelia.

4 Grosvenor Square
London
7th July 1909

Dearest Sister,

It is with a mixture of sadness and great joy that I write to tell you that, after all, I will not be joining you at home as soon as I thought. I have been invited to stay at High Weald by Lady Vaughan! Elizabeth has told me of its beauty and I look forward to seeing the legendary gardens she has described to me. As you can imagine, what is making me most eager to visit is the fact that Archie will be there. I am told he is still suffering from his chill, which is the reason he has not been seen in London and is much missed by all. Mama will return home to Esthwaite alone and I hope you can forgive me for extending my stay down south, but equally, understand the reasons why. I will be home in September and will continue writing in the meantime.

My love to you, my darling sister,
Aurelia

A lurch of pain clutched at Flora's heart. A pain that transcended any blistered feet, fever, or past grief over a lost member of her menagerie. Aurelia was going to stay at High Weald. She would see firsthand the house Archie had described and, even more poignantly, his beloved gardens.

Flora's treacherous mind pictured Aurelia in one of her beautiful dresses, a large sun hat adorned with flowers perched on the top of her blond head, being escorted around the gardens by Archie. As Flora sank back onto her pillows, she thought she might well vomit all over Panther's sleek black fur.

When Sarah knocked on the door an hour later to see what she fancied for lunch, Flora feigned sleep. She doubted she would ever feel hungry again.

Her mother arrived home from London in the first week of August. Flora could see Rose was tense and put it down to her unhappiness at returning home after the bright lights of London. Three days later, her father, who it seemed to Flora was always miserable, returned from the Highlands. Perhaps it was also Aurelia's absence, and the fact that Flora's vivid imagination traveled hourly to dark thoughts of her sister with Archie at High Weald, but the entire household seemed to lie under a pall of gloom.

Now fully recovered from her chill, Flora took up her normal routine, rising early to forage for food for her animals, taking the trap to run errands in Hawkshead, and sketching whatever new treasures she'd found on her travels in the balmy afternoon sun. When she was at home, she heard hushed whispers behind the door of her father's study and the conversation at dinner was even more stilted than usual.

As August gasped its last dying breaths and took summer with it for another year, Rose asked her daughter to come to see her after breakfast. Flora felt a strange sense of relief as she walked toward the morning room and tapped on the door; whatever it was her mother had to tell her, it would be a welcome cloudburst after weeks of pent-up pressure.

"Hello, Mama," she said as she entered.

"Come and sit down, Flora."

Flora sat in the chair her mother indicated. Clear light flowed in from the windows and illuminated the faded colors of the old Mahal carpet underfoot. A fire had been lit in the grate, a sign the seasons were on the turn.

"Flora, over the past few weeks, your father and I have been discussing the future of . . . our family."

"I see."

"I am hoping that what I have to say to you will not come as too much of a shock. Even though you may say little, I'm aware that you note everything."

"Do I?" Flora was surprised at her mother's comment.

"Yes. You are a clever and perceptive young woman."

Flora knew what was coming must be bad, for she could hardly remember such a compliment ever passing her mother's lips before. "Thank you, Mama."

"There is no other way to tell you this, but your father is selling Esthwaite Hall."

Flora's breath caught in her throat and Rose avoided her daughter's eyes as she continued.

"During the past few years, every penny has gone into its maintenance, which is why the household lives so frugally. The fact is, there is simply no more money. And, quite rightly, your father refuses to accumulate debt to fund the necessary repairs. There is a buyer who is prepared to pay a good price and has the money to restore the Hall. Your father has found us a house in the Highlands, by Loch Lee, and this is where we will be moving to in November. I am sorry, Flora. I am aware of how much, out of all of us, you love our home and its surroundings. But there is nothing to be done."

Flora did not—*could* not—speak.

"It is not ideal, I grant you, and . . ." Flora watched her mother swallow hard to keep her composure. "I certainly will find the move difficult, but there it is. As for you, Flora, your father and I feel it would be wrong to take you with us to such an isolated spot, when you are still young and need the company of others. So, I have secured you a position in a household in London, which I think may suit you very well."

For one moment, Flora had a vision of herself blacking the range or peeling the potatoes in a cellar kitchen. "And what is that, Mama?" she finally managed to say, her mouth dry.

"A dear friend of mine is in need of extra schooling for her two daughters. I told her of your proficiency at sketching and painting and also of your knowledge of botany. She has asked me if you would care to join her household and educate her girls in your skills."

"I'm to be a governess?"

"Not in the literal sense, no. The household you are joining is wealthy, and there is a large staff to care for and educate the children. I would see your role as that of a tutor."

"May I ask the name of this friend of yours?"

"Her name is Mrs. Alice Keppel. She is well respected in London society."

Flora nodded, although, living in the wilds of the Lakes as she did, she was not acquainted with the name of *anybody* in London, well respected or not.

"She is a woman who moves in the very highest of circles and it is an honor that she would consider you for such a position." An odd expression passed fleetingly across her mother's face. "Well, there we are. You will be joining the household at the beginning of October."

"And what of Aurelia? Will she move up with you to the Highlands?"

"Aurelia is to live with Aunt Charlotte in London when she returns from Kent. Temporarily, at least. We hope it will not be long before Aurelia is running a household of her own."

Flora's heart missed a beat. "She is to be wed? Who is the man?"

"I am sure your sister will tell you as soon as the engagement is confirmed. Now, Flora, have you any questions?"

"No." What was the point? Her fate was already sealed.

"My dear." Rose reached out a tentative hand to Flora. "I am so very sorry. I only wish things were different for you and me. But they are not and we must simply make the best of it."

"Yes." Flora felt a sudden empathy with her mother, who looked just as downcast as she. "I will . . . adjust to my new circumstances, I'm sure. Do tell Mrs. Keppel . . . tell her I am most grateful."

And before she could disgrace herself by bursting into noisy, desolate sobs, Flora swiftly left the morning room. Upstairs, she locked the door to her bedroom, fell into her bed, pulled the blankets over her head, and wept as quietly as she could.

Everything has gone . . . my home, my sister, my life . . .

Panther had crept under the blankets too and the feel of his soft, warm fur brought on further tears. "And what will happen to you? And Posy, and the rest of my menagerie? I can hardly imagine Mrs. Keppel"—she spat the name out as though it were poison—"wanting an old toad and a rat spoiling her pristine home. I'm to teach children! Good Lord, Panther, I hardly know any, let alone how to educate them. I'm not even sure I like them that much either."

Panther listened patiently, purring in Flora's ear in response.

"How could Mama and Papa do this to me?" Flora threw the covers off and sat upright, gazing at the glorious view of Esthwaite Water beyond the window. Anger had replaced sorrow now and she stood up and paced the room, desperately trying to think up how she could single-handedly save her beloved home. When all lines of possibility were exhausted—there simply *were* none—Flora opened the doors to all her cages. Her menagerie scampered and hopped out of captivity, and crowded around their mistress protectively.

"Oh God." Flora gave a long, deep sigh, gathering them to her. "What on earth am I to do?"

As a mist began to hang over the lake at dawn and dusk fell earlier each evening, Flora spent as much time away from the house as possible. Her father was yet to mention directly to her the planned sale of the Hall, or Flora's imminent move to London. Mealtimes continued just as they always had, and Flora wondered whether her father would actually say good-bye to her when she left in two weeks' time.

The only sign that anything was to change occurred when a number of vans arrived at the front of the house and departed with furniture—whether destined for an auction house or her parents' new abode in Scotland, Flora couldn't say. When she saw the men lifting empty crates into the library, she darted in there and, like a thief, hastily gathered as many of her favorite books as her arms could hold, then scurried upstairs with her haul.

It was haytiming in Esthwaite and its surrounds, and the unusually good weather had the whole village out together, working the fields to bring the hay in before it rained. Flora walked the lanes with her basket, greeting familiar faces she would soon say good-bye to and cutting samples of as many different species of plant as she could find. In London, she imagined there would be a dearth of interesting flora and fauna for her new charges to sketch and draw.

The most pressing problem of all was what to do with her menagerie. If she set them free, none of them would survive in the wild after their years of Esthwaite Hall bed and board. But what else could she do?

And then, awake early one morning, the answer came to her. After breakfast, Flora tied on her best bonnet and walked to the stable to hitch up the pony and trap. "Well," she told Myla as she clicked the reins and they moved off, "she can only say no."

Flora brought the trap to a halt in front of Hill Top Farm and tethered the pony to a post. Then she straightened her dress and bonnet and opened the wooden gate. Walking up the path, she noted the well-tended beds, full of purple autumn crocuses and dahlias. To her left, beyond a green wrought-iron gate, lay a vegetable patch, and she spied large cabbages and the leafy tufts of carrot tops. A wisteria vine climbed the front of the house, and ripening Japanese quinces also cheered its gray walls.

Pausing outside, she knew that the only thing that stood between her and her heroine was the paneled oak door. Her courage almost failing her, she thought about the certain fate of her menagerie if she did not at least try, and she struck the brass knocker. Within seconds, she heard footsteps approaching. The door opened and a pair of bright, inquiring eyes appraised her visitor.

"Hello. How can I help you?"

Flora recognized Miss Potter instantly, and, having expected a maid to answer the door, felt immediately tongue-tied at the sight of her. Her heroine looked rather disheveled, wiping her hands on an apron covered in fruit stains, worn over a plain skirt of gray wool and a simple white blouse.

"You almost certainly won't remember me," she began timidly, "but my name is Flora MacNichol and I live in Esthwaite Hall, not far from here. You came with your parents to tea there once and then wrote me a letter containing a story about a caterpillar and a slug . . ."

"Why yes, of course I remember! My, Miss MacNichol, how you have grown up since. Won't you come inside? I'm just making some blackberry jam and I must watch it as it comes to the boil. It's my first time making it, you see."

"Thank you," Flora said, hardly able to believe that she was being invited in by the famed Miss Potter.

She was greeted by a richly decorated front hall that belied the simple exterior of the house. A grandfather clock ticked by the stairs, and a large oak dresser leaned against the wall, filled with little treasures. Everything was as neat as a pin, not unlike a doll's house, and indeed Flora could almost imagine the mice from Miss Potter's tales scurrying about and wreaking havoc in the cottage. She surreptitiously pinched herself to make sure this was real.

"Oh dear, it's caught at the bottom again," said Miss Potter, rushing to a cooking pot hanging over the open fire, its contents bubbling away rather too merrily. The strong scent of burning sugar pervaded the room. "You must excuse me while I keep stirring. It's usually Mrs. Cannon who does this for me, but I thought I should learn the skill for myself. But pray, do sit down and tell me to what I owe the pleasure of your visit."

"I . . . well, the truth is, I have come to beg a favor, or at least some advice." Flora sat down at the table as requested and heard a disgruntled meow as a large tabby cat removed itself from the chair. Surely this couldn't be Tabitha Twitchit herself?

"Don't mind Tom, he just wants a good fuss. And what exactly would that favor be?"

"I . . . well . . ." Flora cleared her throat. "I have rescued a number of animals, who currently reside in my bedroom at the Hall."

"Just as I did when I was a child!" Miss Potter laughed in delight. "What kind of animals do you have?"

Flora ran through her collection as Miss Potter stirred the jam and listened to her intently. "Yes, I had all of the animals you've described, except for perhaps a toad. Although, maybe I did have one at some point . . . Anyway, you still haven't explained what the favor is?"

"Perhaps you've heard, but Esthwaite Hall is being sold. I am to move to London and work in a household teaching children botany, sketching, and painting. And the truth is, I have no idea what to do with my poor orphaned pets."

"Aha!" Miss Potter lifted the pot off the fire and set it on a corkboard on the table. "The answer is quite simple: They must come and live here at Hill Top with me. I can't say that they will get the attention they are used to, for these days I seem to find myself extraordinarily busy. I write books, you see."

"Yes, Miss Potter, I have every one that you have published so far."

"Do you really? How very kind of you. Well now, as to your problem, I have a large garden shed that is warm and dry and which I use regularly to house wounded birds and the like. Your menagerie would be most welcome to move in. There are plenty of insects in there for your toad. And we keep seeds on hand for our other animals, although I have learned not to feed rabbits hemp seeds anymore—they gave my poor Benjamin rather a funny turn once. You say you have a white rat? I'd have to take care that Tom never gains entry to the shed."

As Miss Potter went through a verbal checklist of how she could safeguard her new arrivals, Flora felt immense relief and gratitude. "I also have a kitten called Panther," she added hopefully.

"I am afraid that may well cause a problem, as my dear Tom has ruled the roost for so long, he may not take kindly to a competitor. Is there anywhere else you can think of that Panther might go?"

"I can think of no option that I truly trust."

"Well, I will ask around and I'm sure we will find someone willing to take him."

"Thank you," Flora said, although her words felt inadequate in the face of Miss Potter's generosity.

"Could I beg your help sieving and pouring the jam into the jars?"

"Of course." Flora stood up immediately as Miss Potter lifted a tray of them onto the table. The two of them stood side by side as they sieved the jam through muslin to rid it of blackberry pips, then began pouring it into the jars.

"It is such a very kindly berry," Miss Potter remarked. "It ripens in the rain, and, as you know, we have rather a lot of that here. So, are you eager to go to London?"

"Not at all. I do not know how I can bear to leave Esthwaite," Flora confessed. "Everything I love is here."

"Well, you must bear it, and bear it you will." Miss Potter scraped the last of the jam out of the pot. "I grew up in London, and there are many beautiful parks and gardens, and, of course, there's the Natural History Museum . . . Why, and Kew Gardens as well! My advice to you, my dear, is to make the most of what you experience there. A change is as good as a rest, so they say."

"I will try, Miss Potter."

"Good." She nodded as they began to place wax discs on the jam and then screw the lids on the jars. "Now, I think we deserve some elderflower cordial for our labors. While I stow these in the pantry to cool down, perhaps you'd be so kind as to pour us both a glass?"

Flora did so, wishing she could express to Miss Potter that her life was everything she desired. Afraid it might sound trite, she simply handed the glass of elderflower cordial to her heroine as they sat down at the table, trying to commit this moment to memory, to comfort her in the uncertain future.

"Do you still sketch, Miss MacNichol? I remember you did when you were younger."

"Yes, but mostly just nature, and the occasional animal."

"What else is there to portray?" Miss Potter chuckled. "And flora and fauna are not fearsome art critics like human beings. So, you are to be a governess of sorts. Is married life not what you wish for? You are certainly comely enough to attract a husband."

"I . . . perhaps. But life has not yet presented me with the opportunity."

"My dear, I am forty-three, and I am still waiting for life to present it to me! And unfortunately broken hearts take many years to mend." A sudden sadness clouded Miss Potter's blue gaze. "Tell me," she continued, "who will be your employer in London?"

"A Mrs. Alice Keppel. I believe the children I will be educating are named Violet and Sonia."

At this, Miss Potter threw back her head and laughed.

"Please, Miss Potter, what is so amusing?"

"Oh, forgive me, I am being childish. But, my dear, surely you must have been forewarned about Mrs. Keppel's . . . connections?"

Not wishing to appear naive, Flora hid her confusion. "I . . . yes."

"Well, indeed, if anything could be worth leaving the beauty of the Lakes for, I could not think of a more interesting household to be part of! Now, I really must get on, for I too have to return to London tomorrow to see my poor ailing mama, and there is a lot still for me to do here before I leave. Please, drop your menagerie here in the next few days. If I am not back, Mr. and Mrs. Cannon, who live in the other wing of the farmhouse, will be happy to care for them. Rest assured they are aware that, in my house at least, the animals come first. Your pets will be cared for like . . . royalty." Miss Potter let out a further chuckle and showed Flora to the front door.

"Good-bye, Miss Potter. I cannot thank you enough for your kindness."

"We Lake and animal lovers must stick together, mustn't we? Good-bye, Miss MacNichol."

14

The few days that remained at her childhood home flew by, and the misery in Flora's heart deepened as she witnessed the family possessions being packed away. She was presented with a large trunk in which to stow away her personal belongings and treasures, which would then go with her parents to Scotland. As she laid out her silk-covered journals—a detailed record of her life here at Esthwaite—to wrap in brown paper, she couldn't help but peer between the covers to read snippets of them, mourning all she was about to lose.

Her parents were so preoccupied that rarely did either throw her a kind word. Even though she had grown used to their manner, her sense of isolation grew apace and she thought she might even be relieved when the day came for her to move to London.

On top of all this, there'd been no word from Archie either, and Flora had decided that whatever he had said about trusting him, the memory of the time they had spent together was best packed away with the rest of her past. Given Aurelia's obvious feelings for him, expressed in the letters she had written to Flora from High Weald, it was the only sensible thing to do. Not that the resolution helped much. She continued to think of him almost every single moment of the day.

Most painful of all was saying good-bye to her beloved animals as she arranged them in Miss Potter's shed and instructed Mrs. Cannon on their needs. The parting was made only slightly more bearable by seeing the delight of Ralph and Betsy, Mrs. Cannon's eldest children, who immediately picked up Maisie and Ethel—the two dormice—and promised they would care for them just as Flora had.

As for Panther, Sarah, who had refused to go up to the Highlands "due to all them mites and ticks," would take him to live at the cozy cottage she shared with her mother in Far Sawrey. At least Flora was relieved that her animals were safe and secure, even if she was not.

On the morning of her departure to London, with a heart as heavy as the great boulder that sat on the shores of Esthwaite Water, Flora went downstairs to greet the Lakeland dawn for the final time.

Outside, the landscape had granted her a last wonderful memory. The autumn skies were lit with streaks of scarlet and purple and as she sat down on the boulder, the air was thick with a low mist. Savoring each trill of the dawn chorus, she took in a deep lungful of the fresh, pure air. "Good-bye," she breathed, closing her eyes like the click of a camera shutter to hold the image indelibly in her mind.

Back in her bedroom, Flora dressed hurriedly for the journey, and shrugging on her traveling cape, she called for Panther. Normally, he would emerge sleepily from under the bedcovers, stretching languidly, his amber eyes indicating irritation at being disturbed. Today, he did not appear, and having searched her bedroom thoroughly, Flora deduced that she must have left her door ajar earlier and Panther had followed her downstairs.

Tilly and Mrs. Hillbeck were already busy in the kitchen.

"Your mother has asked us to pack you a picnic. It's a long journey to London," said Tilly, as she fastened the leather straps on the hamper.

"Have you seen Panther?" she asked them, looking under the table. "I've searched everywhere and I can't find him. I must say good-bye . . ."

"He canna have gone far, Miss Flora, I'm sure, but your mother is waiting for you by the door already. I'll take a look for him, don't you worry," Sarah said, appearing from the pantry.

"Good-bye, Miss Flora, and good luck in that heathen city you're going to. Rather you than me," sniffed Mrs. Hillbeck. "I made you some currant pasties—I know how you love them."

"Thank you, and please promise me that you will look for Panther and write to tell me he's safe?"

"Of course we will, dear. Now, you take care of yourself. We'll miss you," Mrs. Hillbeck added, a tear in her eye.

"I will. Good-bye." Flora took one last desperate glance around the kitchen, then left to join her mother.

"Flora, we must leave now or we shall be late for the train." Her mother stood regally in the hall, her hands tucked into a fur muff against the morning chill. Flora walked toward the door, followed by Sarah carrying the picnic hamper. "Say good-bye to your father. I will see you in the carriage."

To her surprise, her father had come down the stairs to the entrance hall, leaning on his stick more heavily than usual.

"Flora, my dear."

"Yes, Papa?"

"I . . . well, the thing is that . . . I'm jolly sorry about how it all turned out."

"It isn't your fault we've no money to keep the house, Papa."

"No, well . . ." Alistair looked at his feet. "I wasn't referring directly to that, but thank you anyway. I am sure you will write regularly to your mother, and I shall hear of your adventures. I wish you luck in your future. Good-bye, my dear."

"Thank you, Papa. Good-bye."

Flora turned away and felt a sudden deep-seated sadness at the finality of her father's parting words. Stepping into the carriage, she took one last glance at Esthwaite Hall. As they passed through the gates, she wondered if it would be the last time she ever saw it. Or her father.

Once settled in their first-class carriage for the long journey to London, Flora sat quietly, observing how the landscape soon changed from rough hills and valleys to an unfamiliar flatness, and inwardly mourning all she'd so recently lost. In contrast, as the miles slipped past and the train separated its occupants further from their home, Rose's mood began to brighten.

"Perhaps I should tell you a little about the Keppel household."

"Yes, Mama."

Flora only half listened as Rose talked of the beautiful house in Portman Square, the family's high rank in society, and the two girls, Violet and Sonia, who were aged fifteen and nine respectively.

"Of course, Violet is a beauty and Sonia . . . well, poor lamb, let us say she has other qualities to make up for her plainness. She is a rather sweet-natured girl, but it's Violet who's the handful. Then again"—Rose stared out of the window and gave a small smile—"one can hardly blame her, given the life that she's led."

"What life, Mama?"

"Oh"—Rose shook herself visibly—"perhaps it's just that the first child is always indulged."

It was Flora's turn to avert her eyes. But not before she saw a faint blush appear in her mother's cheeks. They both knew that this had not been the case in their own household.

At one o'clock, Rose declared herself hungry and Flora duly opened the picnic hamper. "I do find the food in the dining carriage completely inedible," she added as Flora passed her a napkin and a plate. They both gave a little shriek as a tiny black devil jumped out of the hamper and, after a quick glance at his surroundings, disappeared under his mistress's skirts.

"Good heavens! What on earth is *he* doing here? Flora"—Rose's eyes bored into her—"surely you didn't secrete him in there?"

"Of course not, Mama! *He*"—tears of joy pricked her eyes as she swept Panther up from under her skirts and hugged him to her—"secreted himself."

"What on earth we are going to do with him when we reach London, I really don't know. I'm sure the Keppels will not want animals living in their house, given the company they keep."

"Mama, I understand that Panther may be seen as an inconvenience, but to my knowledge, most children love kittens and it may be that Violet and Sonia do too."

"Well, it's not a good start," Rose sighed. "Not a good start at all."

With Panther fast asleep inside the picnic hamper—it almost seemed as if he understood the game he must play—mother and daughter disembarked from the train at Euston railway station.

"Dear Alice said she'd send her motorcar and driver to greet us. Ah, there is Freed now."

Flora hurried after her mother along the crowded concourse as she walked briskly toward a short man with a neat mustache, wearing a smart dark green coat with shining brass buttons. He took off his cap and gave them a bow. The smell and the relentless noise from both the engines and the crowd were making Flora feel dizzy and overwhelmed. Even Panther let out a fearful yowl of displeasure from the depths of the hamper.

"Good evening, madam, miss, and welcome to London," Freed said, and summoned the porter to assist with their cases. "I trust the journey was comfortable?" he asked politely as Flora and her mother followed him out of the station, the porter trundling behind them with the luggage trolley. An electric brougham was waiting for them, its wooden panels gleaming in the late afternoon sun. They stepped in and settled into the soft leather upholstery as Freed started up the engine with a gentle whir and they set off into the wide streets of London.

Flora peered out at the fashionable men and women strolling down Marylebone Road, and the imposing buildings that seemed to continue forever skyward. A constant plaintive meowing emanated from the hamper, but Flora didn't dare open it to comfort Panther while her mother sat next to her.

The brougham circled a magnificent park, ringed by tall brick houses, and pulled up in front of one of them. Immediately, the door opened and a footman appeared to help them down. They entered the house, and the footman offered to relieve Flora of her picnic hamper.

"No, thank you, sir, I have . . . gifts for the household inside," Flora lied swiftly.

Their capes and hats were taken and they were ushered up a narrow flight of stairs and into a parlor that seemed, on first impression, to be more of a greenhouse than an indoor room, filled as it was with sweet-smelling orchids, lilies, and enormous Malmaisons in cut-glass vases.

Amid the lace-covered cushions on a sofa sat perhaps the most beautiful—and certainly the most finely dressed—woman Flora had ever seen. Her rich auburn hair gleamed in an elaborate tumble of curls, strands of pearls around her neck accentuated her alabaster skin, and a deep neckline revealed the swell of an impressive bosom. Her eyes were of the brightest blue and Flora was transfixed as the woman stood up and came across the lavish room to greet them.

"My dear Rose," she said as she embraced Flora's mother. "Was the journey tiresome? I do hope not."

"No, Alice, it was perfectly comfortable, though both I and Flora are glad to have arrived."

"Of course." Alice Keppel's penetrating gaze then fell on Flora. "So this is the famous Flora. Welcome to my home, my dear. I hope you'll be very happy here. The children are eager to meet you. Nannie told me that little Sonia has spent the day drawing pictures for you. Much to their displeasure, they are now both being bathed and tucked up in bed, so I have promised I shall introduce them to you first thing tomorrow morning."

A pitiful whine came from inside the picnic hamper and a tiny black paw appeared from underneath the lid.

"What on earth do you have in there?" Mrs. Keppel asked as all eyes in the room turned to the hamper.

"It's a . . . kitten," Flora replied, glancing at her mother's horrified face. "Please, Mrs. Keppel, I didn't mean to bring him, but he stowed away."

"Indeed? What a resourceful animal he must be." She let out a peal of laughter. "Let us see this stowaway. I'm sure the children will be utterly delighted."

Flora bent down to release the leather straps of the basket as Rose murmured embarrassed apologies. Ignoring them, Mrs. Keppel bent down too, and as Panther was revealed, she swept him up with a firm and practiced hand.

"What a beauty you are, young man, and mischievous too, I've no doubt. I had a similar cat when I was growing up in Duntreath. I am sure he will make a very welcome addition to the nursery."

As Mrs. Keppel handed a wriggling Panther back to his mistress, Flora could have fallen onto her knees and kissed the woman's feet.

"Now, dinner is at eight, and I have invited some old friends of yours, Rose dear. I will have our housekeeper, Miss Draper, show you to your rooms to change. Flora, I have put you in a room next to your mother. I hope you will like it." Mrs. Keppel reached for Flora's hands and held them tightly. "Welcome."

As they were led up another flight of stairs, Flora wondered if Mrs. Keppel's generous greeting was genuine or just for show. For if it was real, it was the warmest welcome from a stranger she had ever received.

As Rose was about to disappear into her room, a thought struck Flora and she pulled her mother aside.

"Mama, I have nothing suitable to wear for dinner," she whispered as the housekeeper and the upstairs maid hovered behind them.

"You are quite correct," said Rose. "Forgive me, Flora, I should have thought of such a thing, but I was unaware that Mrs. Keppel intended to introduce you to society. I will tell her you are exhausted from the journey and ask one of the servants to bring you up a tray. I will leave the gown I have brought with me behind when I return home tomorrow. It will have to be altered, but I am sure there is a seamstress among the household staff. Mrs. Keppel's wardrobe is vast, as you may imagine."

"Thank you, Mama."

The housekeeper led Flora farther along the long corridor and pushed open the door to a large and richly furnished high-ceilinged bedroom, where a vase of fresh flowers sat on the chest of drawers and soft towels were draped over a washstand.

"Anything you need, miss, just ring the bell for Peggie," said the housekeeper, indicating the maid behind her, who bobbed a curtsy. "She will also take your cat downstairs to the basement to do its . . . business."

"Thank you," Flora said, about to add she was happy to take the cat herself, but the two servants had already left the room. She walked to the window and saw it had grown dark and gas lamps illuminated the square below. Carriages were drawing up in front of other houses, their passengers alighting, attired in gleaming black top hats or wide feather-brimmed ones.

Turning away from the window, she saw Panther had already made himself at home and sat washing himself in the middle of the large brass bed. She climbed on next to him and lay down, staring up at an immaculate ceiling with not a crack or a patch of damp to sully it.

"Goodness, they must be rich if even their 'help' lives in bedrooms like this," Flora murmured, as her eyes closed of their own accord and she dozed off. Later, she jumped at a knock on her door and sat up, disoriented, and struggling to remember where she was.

"Hello, my dear. Did I wake you?" Rose said as she entered the room. She was wearing an emerald-green dress and the family tiara, which usually languished in the strongbox at Esthwaite Hall as there had been so few occasions to wear it. Tonight, Rose seemed to sparkle as brightly as the diamonds that sat atop her head.

"I must be tired from the journey, Mama. I hope Mrs. Keppel isn't offended that I am not coming down to dinner."

"She understands completely. Now, I have brought you something. I thought these might be suitable for you," Rose said as she handed a jewelry box to her daughter.

Flora gasped as she opened the box and saw her mother's pearl necklace and earrings nestled in the velvet. Rose picked up the necklace and fastened it around Flora's neck. Together, they admired Flora's reflection in the mirror.

"It was presented to me by my mother when I made my debut in London," Rose said quietly. "I have held it dear for so long, but now it is time for you to have it." She gently placed a hand on her daughter's shoulder.

"Thank you, Mama." Flora was genuinely touched.

"I do hope you will feel at ease here. Mrs. Keppel seems to have taken to you already."

"I am sure I will. Mrs. Keppel seems awfully nice."

"Yes. Now, I must go down for dinner. Mrs. Keppel says to tell you that she will meet you in the day nursery, which is one floor up, at eight in the morning prompt to introduce you to the children and the rest of the staff. We will say our own good-byes later on. I am catching the train up to the Highlands tomorrow to prepare the new house for your father's arrival." Rose kissed Flora on the top of her head. "Peggie is bringing you up a supper tray. Sleep well, Flora."

"I will, Mama. Good night."

15

Flora awoke the next morning to the unfamiliar sounds of the house and its noisy surrounds. There was a *tap-tap* on her door at seven o'clock and Peggie came in with a breakfast tray and lit a fire in the grate.

Sipping her tea, Flora wondered at the splendor of a household that had servants to wait on the servants. When Peggie had left with Panther firmly tucked under her arm, she put on the best of her meager selection of clothes—a blue linen dress with thistles hand-stitched onto the hem by Sarah. As she was pinning her unruly hair into place, the door opened and Panther and Peggie appeared once more in the room.

"Are you ready, miss? They're waiting for you in the day nursery."

Flora swept up Panther and followed Peggie up yet another set of stairs. Ushered into the room, she saw it had bright white walls and large windows that gave a wonderful view of the park below. Mrs. Keppel was standing by the fireplace, her two daughters beside her. Sonia, the younger of the two, was dressed in a freshly starched white smock and black patent buckled shoes. Her elder sister, Violet, who Mama had told her was fifteen, wore a skirt with what looked like a man's shirt and collar—complete with a tie.

"Now, my dears, say hello to Miss MacNichol."

"How do you do, Miss MacNichol," the two children chorused politely.

"Hello." Flora smiled at them and saw that Violet, despite her strange attire, was already a carbon copy of her mother: all feminine curls and blue eyes. Sonia was darker, narrower, and with a similar complexion to Flora's own. The contrast between the two sisters reminded her immediately of herself and Aurelia.

"What is the cat's name?" Violet pointed at Panther, who sat in the crook of Flora's arm. "Is he safe to hold? His claws look quite vicious and he may well scratch."

"This is Panther, and I assure you he is very tame. But he doesn't take kindly to teasing," Flora added, an inner instinct telling her that Violet had a capricious temperament.

"Might I stroke him?" Sonia approached Panther and cautiously held out a hand.

"Of course you can," Flora replied, handing Panther into her arms and warming to the younger child immediately, as Panther rubbed his head against Sonia's fingers, his eyes slits of contentment.

"Now, Miss MacNichol, may I introduce you to Nannie, and to Mademoiselle Claissac?" Mrs. Keppel said as two women entered the nursery. One was a broad woman in a gray dress and a creaseless apron; the other was a petite, plump blonde who looked at Flora as though she had an unpleasant smell under her nose.

"I am pleased to meet you," said Flora, for some reason feeling she should dip a curtsy to Nannie, sensing that she was the force of nature that obviously ruled the two nursery floors.

"Likewise, Miss MacNichol," she replied in a far softer tone than Flora had expected, with a hint of Scottish burr.

"*Enchantée*," said Mademoiselle Claissac. "You may call me 'Moiselle,'" she added haughtily.

"Moiselle instructs Sonia in the schoolroom," Mrs. Keppel explained. "And Violet attends Miss Wolff's school in South Audley Street."

"And I must not be late, Mama," said Violet, her eyes moving to the clock on the wall. "Vita will be waiting for me outside."

"Of course, my dear. Now, I will leave the three of you to work out the best timetable to accommodate the girls' hour a day with Miss MacNichol."

"Yes, ma'am," answered Nannie, dropping a respectful but awkward curtsy.

Violet sneezed suddenly and her mother turned back toward her with a frown. "I hope you're not catching a cold, Violet dear."

"No, it is almost certainly *that*." Violet pointed at Panther, still snuggled happily in Sonia's arms.

Flora held her breath to see if the kitten would be banished from the nursery but Mrs. Keppel merely shrugged. "I do not believe in these so-called allergies and the best thing you can do in my opinion, darling, is to allow yourself to become accustomed to animal fur."

Flora was beginning to like Mrs. Keppel more and more.

Violet went off to school and Panther was dragged reluctantly from Sonia, who followed Moiselle out of the room for morning lessons. Flora was left alone with Nannie, and the two of them tried to find an hour a day for Flora to instruct the children. Which—in between dancing lessons, gymnastics, and cultural visits to museums and galleries with Moiselle, let alone numerous afternoon social engagements—seemed impossible to fit in.

"Perhaps at six o'clock?" A despairing Flora pointed to a blank hour in the diary.

"Maybe sometimes, Miss MacNichol, but often they are needed downstairs to take tea with . . . a visitor of their mother's."

"Well, we have to start somewhere, or I will never see them."

"I will talk to Moiselle and see if she can spare Sonia for a couple of hours a week in the mornings," Nannie comforted her. "And, of course, you are welcome to join us in the day nursery for lunch and supper, but I daresay you might be eating the latter downstairs very soon. Now." Nannie stood up. "I must get on."

As she'd received no instructions as to what she should do, Flora wandered back downstairs to her bedroom. She sat on the bed, wondering why on earth Mrs. Keppel had invited her to join a household where it was perfectly obvious they didn't need her.

There was a knock on the door and Peggie came in.

"Miss MacNichol, your mother is waiting to see you in Mrs. Keppel's parlor."

"Thank you, Peggie."

Flora walked downstairs to find her mother already in her traveling cape. "Hello, Flora. How are you finding the children?"

"They both seem nice girls, although I have spent only a few minutes with them so far."

"Good, good," she said with a nod. "I am sure you will be happy here, Flora. Mrs. Keppel is a very kind and understanding woman. And you will meet many of the highest in society. I hope you will not let me down."

"I will do my best not to, Mama."

"You have our new address?"

"I do, yes, and I will write often."

"Then I shall rely on you to tell me all the London gossip. I admit to being envious of you; I only wish it was me who was staying here. Goodbye, Flora dear, and I pray this decision was the right one. For all of us."

Rose kissed her daughter on both cheeks, then swept out of the room.

Flora felt tears prick her eyes. She walked across to the window to watch her mother step into the carriage below. Even though it was she who had been sent away from her beloved home, Flora couldn't help but feel it was her mother who was being banished.

"Are you all right, my dear?" Mrs. Keppel had entered the room.

"Yes, thank you." Flora quickly brushed away her tears.

"It must be difficult leaving the Lakes and your family. But please consider this household your new home and all of us as a surrogate family. Now, my dressmaker will call on you tomorrow morning at ten o'clock. We must have a wardrobe made for you before you can be seen, and"—Mrs. Keppel circled Flora like an eagle viewing its prey—"that wonderful head of hair needs a good trim too."

"Really, Mrs. Keppel, I can manage in what I have and my hair was only cut a few weeks ago."

"My dear girl, *you* may be able to manage, but *I* most certainly can't!"

"I thought I might be given a uniform."

"A uniform! Good grief, do you think you are here to be a servant?!" Mrs. Keppel let out a sudden peal of musical laughter. "My dear Flora, the situation becomes more absurd by the second! I think I shall nickname you 'Cinderella,'" she added as she led Flora to the chaise longue and pulled her gently down next to her. "Rest assured, you are not a servant here, but a young friend of the family who is staying as a guest. Just wait until I tell Bertie! He will be most amused. For now, however, until your wardrobe is ready, I must confine you to the upper floors with the children. Which will at least give you an opportunity to become acquainted with them. Sonia is such a sweet thing and Violet . . . well," Mrs. Keppel sighed. "I think she is in need of guidance from an older girl. She is at such a vulnerable and impressionable age."

"I will do my best to help them both, Mrs. Keppel."

"Thank you, my dear. And now I must change. I have guests coming for luncheon."

Flora left Mrs. Keppel's parlor, wondering why on earth this woman would be spending time or money on *her*. She'd arrived believing that she was simply to be a governess of sorts. Now she had no clear indication of what her place was in the household.

Yet, from the little she'd seen, she'd already realized that this was no ordinary home. And Alice Keppel was no ordinary woman.

Flora took up Nannie's offer of lunch and ate with Moiselle and Sonia in the day nursery. Sonia chattered away, glad of fresh company to talk to.

"Moiselle says you might teach me to paint? And about flowers."

"Yes, I'd like to, if we can find time."

"Please find time," Sonia said under her breath as Moiselle stood up to collect pudding from the trolley. "I hate Moiselle and I hate lessons."

"I'll do my best," Flora whispered back.

"Do you have a sister, Miss MacNichol?"

"I do."

"Do you like her?"

"Very much. In fact, I love her."

"Even Nannie says Violet's a bit of a madam. And she's not very nice to me."

"Some sisters aren't, but they love you underneath."

Sonia opened her mouth to make a further comment, then, as Moiselle approached, thought better of it. "I will try and love my sister more," she said gravely.

After lunch, Sonia was taken off by Nannie for a wash and brush-up before being driven to a dancing lesson, so Flora retired to her room to read. Then, feeling in need of some fresh air, she took Panther down the stairs to find a way outside for both of them.

On the ground floor, she had just opened a door in the back passage, the stairs beyond indicating a yard of some kind, when Mr. Rolfe, the butler, caught her arm.

"Where are you going, Miss MacNichol?"

Flora explained her mission and Mr. Rolfe looked positively flustered, his eyes darting to the carriage clock on a side table. "I will call Peggie to collect the kitten and then have her return him to you when he has been outside."

"I thought that I too might take a breath of fresh air."

"That is not possible now. Mrs. Keppel is expecting a guest for tea any moment." Mr. Rolfe called for Peggie, who appeared a few seconds later to take Panther out of Flora's arms.

"Don't worry, miss, I'll take care of him for you. I love cats, I do."

The maid dashed off, and Mr. Rolfe escorted Flora back to the main stairs, glancing constantly toward the front door. As Flora mounted them, she heard a carriage pull up outside. "He's here, Johnson. Open the door, will you?" Mr. Rolfe said to the footman, who leapt to do so.

Wishing she could stay and see who this special guest was, but too frightened to disobey the butler's orders, Flora hurried up the stairs, passing Mrs. Keppel's parlor, from which a strong, flowery perfume emanated. Up in the sanctuary of the floor above, she peered over the banisters, catching the sound of a male voice and heavy footsteps ascending the stairs. Whoever it was had a deep, throaty cough, and a strong whiff of cigar smoke permeated the stairwell. Leaning over farther to try to catch a glimpse of the man, she felt a hand on her shoulder, pulling her back.

"Now, Miss MacNichol, it's best we don't spy on anyone in this house," said Nannie, giving her an amused glance.

A door shut on the floor below and the footsteps receded behind it.

"Mrs. Keppel must never be disturbed when she is entertaining in the afternoon. Do you understand?"

"I do, Nannie."

Flora, red faced with embarrassment, retreated to her bedroom once more.

16

Two weeks later, with the help of Barny, Mrs. Keppel's own lady's maid, Flora drew in her breath as her whalebone corset was tightened and she thought her ribs might crack under the pressure.

"There, it's done."

"But I can't breathe . . ."

"No, none of you ladies can, but look," Barny said, pointing in the mirror. "Now you have a waist. You'll get used to it, Miss MacNichol, all the ladies do. It'll loosen off after a while. It's just new at the moment."

"I can barely move . . . ," Flora muttered as Barny gathered a swath of ice-blue silk and beckoned Flora to step into the middle of it.

"Mrs. Keppel's right about this color suiting your complexion. She's right about everything, mind you," said Barny approvingly as she fastened the tiny seed-pearl buttons at the back of the dress.

"Yes," Flora agreed wholeheartedly. If she was Cinderella, then Mrs. Keppel was without a doubt the fairy godmother of 30 Portman Square. From the scullery maid to the finely dressed guests who appeared almost every night for dinner on the floors below, everyone adored her. She seemed to carry with her an almost magical aura of calm. Never did she have to raise her voice to get what she needed; one word was usually enough.

"She's like a queen," Flora had commented to Nannie, one day last week after returning, starry-eyed, from her first shopping trip with Mrs. Keppel and the girls. They'd visited Morrell's toy shop, where the staff had bowed to her every request.

Nannie, normally so staid, had burst into laughter at Flora's expression. "Aye, that she is, Miss MacNichol, and who's to doubt it?"

Flora had begun to learn the rhythms of the house and the characters who dominated it. Just like Mrs. Keppel herself, the staff who worked for her were, on the whole, charming, and appeared to see it as an honor to be part of the Keppel household. Mr. Rolfe and Mrs. Stacey, the cook, ruled the roost, while Miss Draper, the housekeeper, and Barny had the privileged position of preparing Mrs. Keppel and her private parlor for entertaining, which meant hours of flower arranging, tidying, dressing, and primping.

The little Flora had seen of Mrs. Keppel's husband, "Mr. George," as the staff called him—a gentle giant of a man with a kind face and a soft voice—she had liked. Every night, Sonia would disappear to her father's sitting room to curl up on his knee, whereupon he'd read tales of adventure, which Sonia would repeat to her later.

During the past two weeks, she had spent most of her time on the nursery floor attempting to help Nannie and Moiselle, for want of anything else to do. In the evenings, she and the children huddled around the fire in the day nursery toasting crumpets as Flora told them stories of her childhood at Esthwaite. Violet feigned disinterest, her head buried in a notebook, in which she wrote less often than she chewed the end of her pencil, but Flora knew she listened.

"You drove your own pony and trap?" she confirmed, after Flora had told them about Myla.

"Yes."

"Without a driver? Or a nursemaid or a servant?"

"Yes."

"Oh, how I long for that kind of freedom," Violet breathed, then promptly returned her attention to her notebook.

At least, thought Flora, bringing herself back to the present, she now was in possession of enough clothes to outfit a royal court comfortably, and she hoped Mrs. Keppel would be agreeable to her taking walks in the park across the road, and maybe farther afield in London. After spending so much time inside, Panther wasn't the only one who felt like a caged animal.

"May I dress your hair, Miss MacNichol?"

"Thank you." Flora sat down in front of the dressing-table mirror and Barny began brushing out her long, thick hair with a silver-backed paddle brush.

Although everything else about the household was now reasonably clear in Flora's mind, one mystery remained: the identity of Mrs. Keppel's afternoon guest. Flora always knew when he was due to arrive as the entire household seemed to descend into a state of palpable tension. The first thing that heralded the guest's arrival was the sound of Mabel and Katie polishing the brass rods on the stairs just as Flora rose from her bed at seven in the morning. They would begin at the top of the house and work their way down. At noon, the florist would arrive to fill the parlor with sweet-smelling roses, and after lunch, Barny would disappear into Mrs. Keppel's boudoir to ready her mistress for his arrival.

When the guest arrived, everyone scurried out of sight and a hush fell over the house as the man with the deep-throated cough entered and made his way up the stairs, leaving the smell of stale cigar smoke in his wake. Some evenings, at six o'clock prompt, Violet and Sonia, wearing their most beautiful dresses, would be taken downstairs to Mrs. Keppel's parlor for tea.

On the guest's departure in an enormously grand carriage—Flora had spied the roof of it from the window of her bedroom—it felt as if the household gave a collective sigh of relief, and things would return to normal. Flora longed to glean information from either of the girls on who it was they met behind the firmly shut parlor door, but felt it was rude to pry.

"There, Miss Flora. Do you like it?" Barny stepped back to admire her handiwork.

Flora surveyed the upswept style Barny had achieved, but doubted the combs would be strong enough to hold her hair for longer than a few minutes. Despite herself, she was surprised at the difference fine clothing and tamed hair could make.

"I look . . . different."

"I'd say you look beautiful, miss," Barny said with a smile. "I think you're ready to go down. Mrs. Keppel wants to see you in her parlor."

Flora rose, the bustle on the back of her dress and the tightness across her chest from the corset hampering her progress to the door. "Thank you, Barny," she managed as she walked out onto the landing, just as Sonia was being shepherded down the stairs by Nannie.

"Lawks!"

This was Sonia's new favorite expression, gleaned from Mabel, the parlor maid, when a large black spider had scuttled out of the coal bucket. "You look very pretty, Flora! In fact, I wouldn't recognize you at all."

"Thank you." She chuckled and dipped an awkward curtsy to Sonia.

"Where are you going?"

"Your mama is holding a salon in the drawing room and has invited me."

"Oh, that means lots of ladies standing around drinking tea and eating cakes, doesn't it, Nannie?"

"It does, my love."

"It will be frightfully boring, Flora. Why don't you come to the park and listen to the organ grinder and stroke the monkey and have ice cream with us instead?"

"I wish I could," whispered Flora in Sonia's ear before heading for Mrs. Keppel's parlor.

Mrs. Keppel's face was a picture of satisfaction at Flora's appearance. "My dear, you look quite the refined young lady. So, let us go and greet the guests I have invited to meet you." Mrs. Keppel offered her elbow and they escorted each other down the stairs. "And I have a surprise for you. Your sister is attending."

"Aurelia? How wonderful! I didn't even know she was yet back in London."

"No, well, I think that perhaps she became a little tired of waiting for something that never seemed to happen in Kent." Mrs. Keppel lowered her voice as they entered the drawing room. "Although she insisted on bringing that rather dull friend of hers, Miss Elizabeth Vaughan. I hear she has become engaged to a tea planter, of all things, and will leave for Ceylon soon after her marriage. Do you find her dull, Flora?"

"I . . . don't know her well enough to judge her character, but she's always seemed sweet enough."

"You are so very discreet. It will serve you well in London," Mrs. Keppel answered approvingly as the clock chimed three and a carriage drew up outside. "Now, let us show your sister—and London—just how you have blossomed."

"Flora! Is it really you?" Aurelia said as she entered the drawing room and embraced her. "You look . . . beautiful! And your dress . . ." She took in the expensive lace on the collar and the cuffs and the intricate embroidery on the skirts. "Why, it's exquisite." Leaning closer, she whispered in

Flora's ear. "It seems you too have a sponsor now, dearest. And Mrs. Keppel, of all people; she's one of the most influential women in London."

After greeting an elated Elizabeth, who was smugly showing off her very substantial sapphire engagement ring, Flora led Aurelia away so they could speak in private. "Indeed, Mrs. Keppel has been most awfully kind," she said, indicating a chaise longue. "Shall we sit down? I want to hear all about your summer."

"Then I'd better stay for dinner, and breakfast tomorrow morning," Aurelia sighed, none too happily. Other women were arriving and the sisters watched Mrs. Keppel greet each of them with warmth and interest. "If only Mama could see us now: her two girls sitting among the cream of London society. I think she'd be very proud."

"Well, apart from one shopping trip, this is my first day 'out.' Mrs. Keppel was reluctant to let me be seen until my new wardrobe of clothes had arrived."

"I'm not surprised. She runs the smartest salon in London."

"I must admit, I'm rather confused by this turn of events. I thought I was coming here as a tutor to her girls, but Mrs. Keppel seems to have other ideas."

"If she has chosen to back your launch into society, you could have no one better. Although you must know that there are a few dissenters and some doors that are closed to her, and I'm sure that, living here under her roof, you're already aware of—"

"Flora, my dear girl!" Aunt Charlotte appeared in front of them and Flora stood up, attempting to give her aunt a quick bob of respect, but handicapped by her newly trussed-up state.

"Aunt Charlotte, are you well?"

"Exhausted from the Season, of course. But you, my dear niece, look utterly divine. London must suit you."

"I am only beginning to learn how it all goes here, Aunt."

"It really is quite a miracle that Mrs. Keppel has decided to sweep you up. But then again, I suppose one can understand why. You must come to call on us at Grosvenor Square very soon. Dear Aurelia has been such a delight to have about the house. I will be very sorry when she leaves us to go home to your dear mama and papa. Now then, do excuse me, but I must go and talk with Lady Alington about our little orphan charity."

"You're going back to Scotland?" Flora turned to her sister.

"Yes." Aurelia's eyes clouded suddenly.

"But surely there are dozens of young men desperate to take your hand in marriage?"

"There were, yes, but I'm afraid I turned their attentions down and they have since moved their affections elsewhere. My Berkshire viscount is engaged to a friend of mine. It was announced in the *Times* earlier this week."

"There really was no one who captured your heart?"

"Oh yes, but that was the problem. And should I say, still is."

"What do you mean?" With a sinking heart, Flora already knew.

"Well, when the invitation came to stay with the Vaughans at High Weald, I rather thought that . . . that Archie would propose. He'd been up shooting with Papa in July and I was aware that . . . things had been discussed between them. So I refused the other proposals I'd received, presuming that I'd been invited to Kent so Archie could ask me. But even though I was with him under the same roof for a month, it felt rather as if he was doing his best to avoid me. In fact, I rarely saw him, other than at mealtimes. And oh . . ." Aurelia bit her lip as tears came to her eyes, "Flora, I love him so."

Flora listened, her treacherous heart full of spontaneous relief, but also a gnawing guilt that she might have played a part in her sister's misery.

"I . . . maybe he's simply been waiting for the right moment."

"Darling Flora, it's sweet of you to try and comfort me, but there could not have been more opportunities, had he wished to take them. His mother constantly encouraged him to take me for a walk around the gardens, which really are quite the most exquisite I've ever seen. And all he talked about was his plans to restock them with all sorts of exotic plants I'd never even heard of! Then we'd walk back to the house and he'd disappear to his precious greenhouse and . . ." Aurelia bit her lip again. "In the end I decided I had to return to London."

"Maybe he will realize he misses you and follow you here," Flora suggested flatly. Archie's letter to her was finally beginning to make the most awful sense.

"No. I can no longer live on Aunt Charlotte's generosity, so I must go home."

"Oh, Aurelia, I am so very sorry. Perhaps Archie is just not the marrying kind."

"That is hardly the point. One of the reasons Papa decided to sell Esthwaite Hall was to provide me with a suitable dowry so it could help the Vaughans maintain High Weald, as it would become my family home. You know how Lady Vaughan and Mama were such close childhood friends." Aurelia lowered her voice further, seeing Elizabeth standing only a few yards away. "They planned it between the two of them and that is what Papa was discussing with Archie up in Scotland."

"I see." And Flora *did*, all too clearly.

"I have no choice other than to be packed off to Scotland. It's rather ironic, isn't it?" Aurelia gave her sister a ghost of a smile. "Me returning home as a failure, and you here in London under the patronage of Mrs. Keppel. Not that I begrudge you one bit, of course, darling."

"Aurelia, believe me, I was heartbroken when Mama told me we had to leave Esthwaite. You know how much I loved it. I miss it with every bone in my body. I'd give anything to be back there."

"I know, sister dear," said Aurelia, taking Flora's hand. "Forgive me for my miserable countenance, but if I can't talk to you about this, who can I talk to?"

"Surely, if there was an agreement between him and Papa, Archie must honor it?" Flora frowned.

"And I am quite sure that even if he did, I would no longer wish to marry him. After his quite considerable attentions at the beginning of the Season, he seemed completely distracted when I arrived in Kent. My feeling is that there is someone else who has stolen his heart. But for the life of me, I have no idea who it is." Aurelia gave a deep sigh and Flora wished the floor could swallow her and her duplicitous heart up and take Archie Vaughan with them.

"Now, darling, let us not talk of my problems any longer. Tell me all about life in the Keppel household."

Flora did her best to tell Aurelia of Violet and Sonia and her daily routine, but the betrayal she had been an innocent yet willing party to had reduced her thoughts to sludge. She was all too grateful when Mrs. Keppel came over, wishing to introduce Flora to her friends.

"They are all quite desperate to meet the newest and most beautiful young member of our household." Mrs. Keppel smiled as she took Flora's elbow and proceeded to lead her around the room, showing her off as if she were a personal trophy. And indeed, many of the ladies seemed genuinely agog to meet her. From time to time, she stole a glance at Aurelia, who sat dejectedly on the chaise longue, trying to make conversation with an old woman dressed all in black, who seemed to be as friendless as she.

Eventually, as the guests began to take their leave, Flora excused herself from Countess Torby, who issued her an invitation to the soirée she was holding soon.

"Dame Nellie Melba will be performing for us. She has only just returned from her tour in Australia, my darling, and she is coming straight to Kenwood House," the Countess said in front of the admiring circle around Flora.

Aurelia came over to kiss her good-bye.

"When do you leave for Scotland?"

"At the end of this week. The sooner the better, I believe," Aurelia breathed. "London doesn't take kindly to failure."

"Will you come to visit me here before you go?"

"Of course, and please don't worry about me. Perhaps I will meet a laird up in the Highlands and become mistress of a beautiful estate there." Aurelia gave a weak smile. "It's time for me to forget all about Archie Vaughan. Good-bye, dearest sister."

Once everyone had left and Mabel and the footman had removed the discarded teacups and plates of untouched dainties, Mrs. Keppel ushered Flora to sit in the chair opposite her by the fire.

"Well, Flora, your first foray into London society seems to have been an unqualified success! I think you will find yourself well occupied in the weeks to come. There have been so many invitations issued. Everyone told me how charming they found you."

"Thank you. However, I must not neglect my duties to your daughters."

"My dear girl, can't you see that was a pretext I gave to you and your mother to enable you to come and live under my roof? Of course, having never met you, I wasn't sure how you would . . . *present* . . . so I wished to have a fallback position in place. And then you arrived, so elegant, cultured, and utterly delightful! After this afternoon, a rather splendid dinner later this week, and a far more . . . *intimate* tea party very soon after that, there won't be a household in London that will not wish you to grace it with your presence. You're the talk of the town!"

Flora gazed in complete confusion at this extraordinary woman. "Mrs.

Keppel, for the life of me, I do not understand why anyone in London would wish to invite me to their homes. After all, I was not even presented at court."

"Don't you see, that is what makes you even more fascinating?"

"To be frank, I do not," Flora confessed. "Please don't think me ungrateful, but having accepted my lot in life, to have all suddenly changed about me for no reason I can think of is a little . . . strange."

"My dear, I do understand. One day, all will be explained, but I feel it is not my place to do so. All I ask for now is that you trust me. I shall not steer you wrong. And even though you cannot know it, there are many similarities between us. While I am able to, I wish to help you."

Flora, still none the wiser, could only agree.

That night, she lay down gingerly, relieved to have had the whalebone corset removed. Looking down at her ribs, she counted the tiny purple bruises that had appeared and wondered how the women in Mrs. Keppel's drawing room could suffer the pain every day of their lives.

Removing Panther as he attempted to climb onto her chest, she stroked him.

"I feel I deserve this pain for what I've done. Unless Archie has lied to both of us sisters, and is simply the cad I once thought him. I can only hope I was correct when I told Aurelia he is not the marrying kind," she told him, scratching his velvety ears. "And as for today, I confess I feel rather like Alice falling down the rabbit hole, so I suppose that makes you the Cheshire cat. The question is, Panther darling, why on earth are we here in this house?"

Panther just purred contentedly in response.

17

"Miss Flora, you are to come downstairs immediately to Mrs. Keppel's parlor."

"Why?"

"You have a visitor."

"Really? Is it my sister?"

"No, it is a gentleman."

"What is his name?"

"Forgive me, Miss Flora, I don't know."

Flora followed Peggie down the stairs, holding up her heavy woolen skirts so she did not trip over them. She found Mrs. Keppel standing by the fire with Archie Vaughan.

"Flora dear, isn't it sweet of Lord Vaughan to call on us to inquire whether you are well and happy in your new home? I have tried to assure him that I have not been keeping you in the cellar, feeding you water and dead mice, but he insisted on me proving it to him. And here she is, Lord Vaughan."

Flora could think of many adjectives to describe the reason for Archie's presence here, but the last one she would have used was "sweet."

"Hello, Miss MacNichol."

"Hello, Lord Vaughan."

"You look awfully . . . well."

"I am in good health, thank you. And you?"

"I have recovered from my chill, yes."

Flora evaded his stare, and Mrs. Keppel, like the fairy godmother she was, intervened in the ensuing silence. "Will you take a little sherry, Flora? It will ward off any chill, I'm sure."

"Thank you." Flora accepted the glass and the three of them toasted—to what, she wasn't sure.

"Mrs. Keppel, I see you have expanded your collection of Fabergé ornaments. That is a fine piece," Archie said politely, as he nodded toward a small jeweled egg on the table.

"How kind of you to notice, Lord Vaughan," Mrs. Keppel said. "Now, do please forgive me, but I have to see Mrs. Stacey about the menu for tomorrow evening's dinner and the florist is due at any moment. Please send my best regards to your mama."

"I will, of course."

Mrs. Keppel left the room, but not before she had shot a knowing glance at Flora.

The two of them stood in silence, Flora looking anywhere but at him, yet aware of his gaze resting upon her. In the end, in an agony of whalebone and new shoes, she surrendered.

"Shall we sit down?" Almost collapsing into a chair by the fire, she indicated Archie should sit in the one opposite her. Taking a sip of the warming sherry, she waited for him to speak.

"Forgive me, Miss MacNichol . . . may I call you Flora?"

"No. You may not."

Archie swallowed hard. "No . . . I must explain . . . you don't understand."

"You are wrong, I saw my sister only yesterday. I understand everything."

"I see. May I ask what she told you?"

"That you and my father had agreed Esthwaite Hall should be sold to provide Aurelia with a dowry and High Weald with a much-needed injection of funds on your marriage to her."

Archie removed his gaze from her. "Yes, that is an accurate appraisal of the situation."

"Except, Lord Vaughan, my sister tells me that even though you had ample opportunity at High Weald, you are yet to propose. And Aurelia, having turned down a number of attractive proposals, now finds herself without any alternative other than to retreat to our parents' house in the Scottish Highlands. Their recent move was engendered purely by the fact that our Lakeland home was sold to fund the continuation of your own—and my sister's—future."

"Yes," he replied after a long pause.

"So, Lord Vaughan, please tell me exactly what you are doing sitting in

Mrs. Keppel's parlor with me when you should be rushing to prevent my sister from returning home to the solitary, isolated future which you have condemned her to."

"My God, Flora! Your words could kill a man at twenty paces. Have you ever considered putting them onto paper?"

"I am in no mood for quips, Lord Vaughan. And please desist from calling me Flora."

"I can see that, just as I can see how finely you are dressed and how exquisite you look—"

"*Enough!*" Flora stood up, trembling with rage. "Will you not tell me why you have played, as Panther would with a mouse, with both of us sisters? And on top of that why you swindled my father into selling the home that has been in our family for five generations?"

"Can you not guess?"

"I am struggling to do so, Lord Vaughan."

"Well then, let me tell you something that you *don't* know." Archie stood up and started to pace the room, pausing only to refill his glass from the sherry decanter. "When I first met your sister at Esthwaite, I had decided that it didn't much matter whom I married after all the prospective brides that were marched past me by my mother. I know you are well aware of my reputation and I don't deny it. I have romanced a number of women over the years. In my defense, I should say that it wasn't out of ego, merely out of a desperate need to try to find a partner who might capture my heart. You may think, Miss MacNichol, as many women seem to, that men don't have romantic notions about love the way you do. But I assure you that, in my case at least, you are wrong. I too read Dickens, Austen, and Flaubert . . . and wished to find love."

Flora, who was staring into the fire, took the last gulp of her sherry and remained silent.

"By the time I met your sister, I had, in all honesty, given up hope of finding such a woman. And Mama, as you can imagine, was terribly keen on the idea of Aurelia—her oldest friend's daughter—becoming my intended. She and your own mother had already discussed the possibility and your mother had agreed to talk to your father about selling Esthwaite. You might be aware that she has always loathed the house, seeing it as her punishment for . . . past misdemeanors. The thought of having an excuse to visit her daughter and her oldest friend in Kent any time she pleased, and staying for as long as she wished, I believe more than made up for the inconvenience of moving to the Highlands, a place she knew only too well your papa loves."

"What 'misdemeanors'?" Flora shot back. "You choose to insult my mother's character too?"

"Forgive me, Flora, I am simply trying to explain what has brought us to today. Pray, let me continue."

Flora stared into the fire once more, and gave a slight shrug of acceptance.

"To be blunt, I liked your sister when I saw her in London, found her sweet tempered and pretty, and felt she was someone I could at least live with. So, I agreed with your father on the shooting holiday that I should propose to her and that Esthwaite Hall would be sold."

"Then why on *earth* did you come and visit me on your way back?"

"The truth is, I just . . . don't know." Archie stared at her. "All I can say—and I know it isn't good enough—is that something inside me urged me to. Flora: the little girl I'd pelted with crab apples and then almost killed as I raced on my horse to Esthwaite Hall. Yet who never 'told,' like any other girl would have. And now, all grown up, and so clever and fearless and proud, with the kind of strength in her soul that I have never perceived in a woman before. And yes, beautiful too. Forgive me, Flora, I am a man, after all."

"You are right. That is not a good enough answer," she said eventually.

"You fascinated me," Archie continued. "So much so that I came to see you, despite what I had agreed with your father only a day previously. And all that I had imagined when I thought of the woman I wanted to be my wife appeared before me in those days we spent together. And I realized that what I'd always been searching for had been right under my nose all along."

Flora didn't dare breathe; she simply continued to concentrate on the flames that danced so lightly in the fire, in contrast to the weight of his heavy gaze upon her.

"So, I left Esthwaite, and told you that there was a situation which I must address. But by this time, the wheels were already set in motion and Aurelia arrived a few days later at High Weald. I did my best to avoid her, but I could see that both she and my family were becoming frustrated. Nevertheless, I stuck to my guns, and managed *not* to propose, and eventually she left. I saw her distress, but my resolve and my heart cannot be moved. Because it is *you* that I love."

Archie sat down heavily on the chaise longue. Silence hung over the parlor.

"Will you not respond to my heartfelt declaration, Miss MacNichol?" Archie pleaded.

Flora finally raised her eyes to him and stood up. "Yes, I will. And it is this: You say that everything you have done has been for me. This is *not* true. Everything you have done has been for *you*. For some misguided reason, you believe that I hold the key to your happiness. And, in your quest for it, you have caused the sale of our family home, which I must remind you I loved, forcing my parents to live in exile in Scotland. But more importantly, you have also humiliated my sister in front of London society and broken her heart. I ask you, Lord Vaughan, how could any of this possibly have been for *me*?"

She began to pace as the anger rose inside her. "Can't you see what you have done? In pursuing your own selfish desires, you have destroyed my family!"

"Surely, the pursuit of love is often selfish? I thought . . . I felt that you may reciprocate my feelings."

"You are wrong, but even if I did, I would never put my own feelings above the needs of those I love."

"Then you are the person I have believed you are," he whispered, almost to himself. "And of course, Flora," he said, sighing heavily, "you are right. So, what do you suggest we do?"

"There is no 'we,'" she replied, weary now. "And there never can be. But, if you really wish to prove that you love me, and recover some modicum of integrity, you will go to Aurelia immediately and make your long-overdue proposal of marriage to her. And moreover, you will convince her that you love her."

"That is what you wish me to do?"

"Yes."

"And you cannot admit to any feeling for me?"

"No."

Archie raised his eyes to meet Flora's, and saw nothing but anger in her gaze. "So be it," he said quietly. "If this is what you want, then I will do as you wish."

"It is what I want."

"Then I will take my leave and wish you good luck in the future."

"And I you."

Flora watched him leave the parlor. "I love you too," she whispered desolately to the empty room, as she heard his carriage clatter away from the front door.

18

Thankfully, Mrs. Keppel's plans to launch her into the social whirl of London meant that Flora had little time to dwell on the fact that she had willingly sent Archie back into the arms of her sister.

The following night, Mrs. Keppel's campaign began in earnest. Flora, bedecked in a gown of cobalt-blue duchesse satin with borrowed sapphires placed around her neck, was introduced as the guest of honor at a formal dinner. Over drinks in the drawing room, a sea of faces gathered around her, admiring her poise and beauty and praising Mrs. Keppel for bringing Flora to London.

"I feel it's only right that she should have her own debut. I am simply doing my best to provide it for her." Mrs. Keppel smiled at her guests. Flora had been introduced to them in such a haze of names and titles that her head spun with the effort of trying to remember them all—"Please meet Lady This" and "Lord Someone of That"—so she was relieved to recognize Countess Torby from afternoon tea a few days ago. And, of course, the Alingtons from across the square, whose children were playmates of Sonia and Violet.

Dinner took place in a magnificent dining room on the same floor as the drawing room. Flora was happy to be seated on the left of George Keppel. He turned to her with a smile on his lips beneath his neatly curled mustache.

"Miss MacNichol—Flora—what a pleasure to have you beside me for dinner tonight," he said, helping to alleviate her nerves by pouring ruby-red wine into her glass. "Though it must be a shock coming to live in a city after the beauty of your Lakeland home, I hope you have found much here to stimulate your passions for botany and art. The many galleries we have can teach you more than a book ever could. You must try to entice our girls into a similar passion."

"I will certainly do my best." Flora only half heard Mr. George as Lady Alington across the table from her mentioned that it looked as though "the Vaughan girl has found herself a satisfactory beau. And as for that fly-by-night son of theirs, there have been rumors—"

"Flora? Are you feeling quite well? You have turned rather pale." Mr. George's voice pulled her attention back.

"My apologies, sir, I must be fatigued from the day."

"Of course you are, my dear. I hope that Violet has not been chewing your ear off with her latest idea for a poem."

"She has a strong personality," Flora said carefully. "It is to be admired."

A snort of laughter came from her left. Lady Sarah Wilson's prominent eyes were bright with mirth. "Dear Alice said you had a knack for diplomacy, Miss MacNichol."

She felt out of her depth in these barbed London conversations. "I simply speak from what I have observed, Lady Sarah. How are you enjoying the foie gras?"

There were ten courses—at least seven too many, Flora felt. She had nibbled around the meat, shocked at the number of animals Mrs. Stacey must have roasted, stewed, or curried that day.

When Mr. George finally took the men off for brandy and cigars, Flora followed the women into the drawing room and sipped her coffee quietly as idle gossip passed over her head, mostly about women who had been seen around the city with men who were not their husbands. She listened with a mixture of fascination and horror. Perhaps she was simply naive, but she had presumed that marriage was sacrosanct.

"So, have you any young man in mind for Flora?" Lady Alington asked Mrs. Keppel.

"Perhaps Flora has ideas of her own," her sponsor replied, throwing Flora a piercing glance.

"Oh, and who might the lucky gentleman be?"

"I . . . goodness, I am just arrived in London," Flora replied diplomatically.

"Well, I am sure it won't be long before someone snaps you up, what with Mrs. Keppel's patronage. There are plenty of winter dances at which you'll have the opportunity to cast your eye around. Although most of the decent beaux have already been taken."

Since Archie's enforced departure from her life yesterday, Flora was perfectly happy to return to her original plan and spend the rest of her days alone.

Once everyone had left, Mrs. Keppel kissed her on both cheeks. "Good night, my dear, and may I just say that you acquitted yourself well. I was proud of you tonight. You see, George, I was right about her," she said to her husband as he led her out of the room.

"You were, my dear, but then, when are you ever wrong?" Flora heard him say as they mounted the stairs.

Flora had asked Moiselle and Mrs. Keppel's permission to take Sonia to Kew Gardens for the day. Mr. Rolfe had already arranged for the motorcar to take them there and Flora was tingling with excitement at the thought of being surrounded by nature and studying rare specimens. Even if the diversion she had created was likely to remind her of Archie.

"I *will not* let him spoil it," she told herself firmly.

"Sorry, Miss Flora," Peggie said as she arrived in Flora's room with her breakfast tray, "but Mrs. Keppel wishes you to join her and a guest for tea this afternoon. She says you will have to go to your gardens another day."

"Oh." Flora bit her lip. "Do you know who the guest is?"

"You'll find out soon enough, miss, but I will be attending on you before you join them in Mrs. Keppel's parlor. I will see you here at three o'clock prompt."

"Don't worry," Flora said to Sonia when she saw her in the day nursery and she expressed disappointment at the canceled outing. "I am sure Moiselle wouldn't mind if we went instead to St. James's Park for a walk this morning. We'll have to promise to speak French all the way there and back." Flora winked at her. "How are you this morning, Violet?" she asked, turning to her.

"I am well, thank you. My best friend, Vita, is coming here for lunch after lessons. We have a half day at school."

"I see."

"I shall expect you to be here at one o'clock prompt, Nannie," Violet said.

As she walked from the room, Nannie raised an eyebrow at Violet's imperiousness.

"And I can tell you, Miss Sackville-West is a very strange kettle of fish altogether," Nannie whispered to Flora. "I'm only glad she isn't in my nursery. You should hear the two of them, discussing books and literature like they were proper professors. Takes herself very seriously, does that one. And Violet's right obsessed with her, there's no denying it."

"Then I am eager to meet her."

"Well now, Miss Flora, I'd say that one way and another, you have an interesting day ahead of you."

The walk through St. James's Park with Sonia was just what Flora needed. The October day was bright, if chilly, and the leaves were beginning to turn all shades of amber, burnished gold, and red, dropping to create a vibrant carpet beneath their feet.

"Look." Flora pointed to a rooftop high above them on the edge of the park. "Can you see the swallows gathering? They're preparing to fly south to Africa. Winter is on its way."

"Oh my, Africa!" gasped Sonia, watching the swallows chattering to each other. "That's an awfully long way. What happens if they feel tired when they're flying across the sea?"

"Good question, and the answer is that I really don't know. Perhaps they fly down and hitch a ride on a boat. Look, there's a squirrel. He's probably gathering nuts to store in his house for winter. He'll go to sleep very soon; we won't see him again until the spring."

"I wish I was a squirrel." Sonia wrinkled her small nose. "I'd like to go to sleep for the winter too."

Arriving home just in time for lunch in the day nursery, Flora sat down at the table with the staff and children. Violet barely looked up from her conversation, conducted in intense whispers with her friend, a dark-eyed, sallow-skinned child with short brown hair and a slim torso. If she hadn't known this was a girl, Flora might well have taken her for a boy. She was struck by the odd intimacy between them: Violet touched Vita's hand constantly, and at one point even rested her hand lightly on the other girl's knee.

"Nannie, Vita and I will now retire to my room. Vita wishes to read me her new poems."

"Does she indeed?" Nannie muttered under her breath. "Well, mind you're back down here at three o'clock prompt, for when Miss Vita's nanny arrives to take her home. Your mother has her special guest arriving at four and the house must be quiet. You're to join them at five, Miss Flora," Nannie added as she took Sonia off to wash her face, and Vita and Violet left the room arm in arm behind them.

At three o'clock, Barny entered Flora's room with a dress draped over her arm.

"Mrs. Keppel wishes you to wear this one for tea, so I took it downstairs to give it a freshen-up."

Flora sat down at the dressing table to let Barny tease her hair into ordered rather than wild ringlets, held neatly by sharp-toothed mother-of-pearl combs. Then, subjecting herself to the dreaded whalebone corset, she considered that, despite Mrs. Keppel's overt generosity, she was starting to feel rather like an oversized doll being dressed up on the whim of her owner. Not that there was a lot to do about it without seeming hugely ungrateful. As Barny fastened the cream and blue striped gown, Flora thought that for all of society's insistence that men wished their women to be trussed up, painted, and adorned, she remembered climbing Scafell in her father's breeches. And how it hadn't seemed to matter to Archie one jot . . .

"Miss Flora?"

"Yes?" She dragged herself back from her daydream.

"I was asking whether you can fasten the earrings tighter. Lord help us if one fell off into your teacup this afternoon!"

"Goodness, now, that would be a disaster," she agreed, trying to suppress a smile.

"I'll put a little rose cream on each of your cheeks to give them some color, and you'll be ready to go down when you're called. You just sit quietly with one of your books and Miss Draper will be up for you when they're ready."

"Thank you."

"Good luck, miss."

Flora frowned as Barny left the room, wondering why on earth she needed "luck" to drink a cup of tea with this mystery guest, whom she heard arriving ten minutes later. To while away the time, Flora went to her writing bureau and took out her journal to continue documenting the dreadful conversation with Archie. Even writing it brought her close to tears. Eventually, there was a knock on her door and Miss Draper appeared.

"Mrs. Keppel would like you to join her in the parlor now."

"Very well."

Flora followed Miss Draper downstairs and felt the tense hush of the house that heralded the presence of Mrs. Keppel's special guest.

"Ready?" Miss Draper asked her.

"Yes."

"Very good." She raised her hand to tap on the parlor door and Flora noticed it shook slightly.

"Come," came Mrs. Keppel's voice from within.

"And for pity's sake, don't forget to curtsy when she introduces you," Miss Draper hissed as she grasped the door handle and opened it.

"Flora, my dear." Mrs. Keppel came toward her. "How lovely you look today, doesn't she, Bertie?" She took Flora's hand and led her to a gray-bearded gentleman, whose enormous bulk took up the entire two-seater sofa.

Flora felt a pair of gimlet eyes appraising her as Mrs. Keppel drew her closer until she stood only a foot from him. The room was filled with a cloud of cigar smoke and the gentleman took another puff as he continued to observe her. Flora gave a start as something moved by the gentleman's leg, and she saw that it was a white fox terrier with brown ears that had perked up at her entrance and was now coming to greet her.

"Hello." Flora smiled down at the little dog and instinctively reached to pet it.

"Flora, this is my dearest friend, Bertie. Bertie, may I present Miss Flora MacNichol."

As she had been told to do, Flora gave a deep and—she hoped—graceful curtsy. As she rose as elegantly as she could, she realized this gentleman was very familiar. In the ensuing silence, as the eyes continued to stare at her in a most disturbing manner, Flora finally made the connection. And her knees went weak.

"Didn't I tell you she was a beauty?" Mrs. Keppel broke the silence. "Come, Flora, sit down by me."

She followed Mrs. Keppel to the chaise longue placed opposite the man who was apparently called "Bertie." Flora was only grateful she *could* sit down or she might have fallen to the floor in shock.

Still, the man did not speak, just continued to stare at her.

"I shall ring for some tea. I am sure we could all do with a fresh cup." As Mrs. Keppel pressed a bell to the side of the fireplace, Flora could see that even her sponsor's fabled calm seemed disturbed by the silence. Eventually, Bertie took up his cigar once more, relit it, and puffed on it.

"How are you finding London, Miss MacNichol?" he asked her.

"I am enjoying it very much, thank you . . ." Her voice trailed off as she realized she was not sure how to address him.

"Please, while we are in private, you may call me 'Bertie,' as dear Mrs. George does. We are all friends here. And perhaps you are a little mature to address me as 'Kingy,' like Violet and Sonia." He smiled approvingly then, his blue eyes merry, and the tension in the room lifted a little.

"So," he said, taking another puff on his cigar, "how is your dear mama?"

"I . . . she is well, thank you. Or at least, I believe she is, as I haven't seen her since she left for Scotland."

"Remember, Bertie, that I told you Flora's parents have moved from their house in the Lakes up to the Highlands?" Mrs. Keppel prompted.

"Ah, yes, and a damned fine choice they made. Scotland is without a doubt my favorite part of the British Isles. Especially Balmoral. Have you visited the Highlands, Miss MacNichol?"

"When I was much younger, I went to visit my paternal grandparents and I remember it being very beautiful." Flora struggled to calm herself enough to form coherent sentences. She was surprised by the sound of his voice, his words having an almost Teutonic timbre to them, making him sound rather foreign.

Miss Draper and the footman arrived with tea and a trolley full of sandwiches, cakes, and pastries. A black shadow raced by Miss Draper's feet, and the terrier, who had been remarkably calm until now, launched himself toward it with a series of ear-splitting barks. Without thinking, Flora leapt to her feet and scooped the hissing and spitting cat into her arms.

The terrier's barks were punctuated by a booming laugh. "Caesar, heel!" he commanded, and the dog slunk back to sit down by his master. "Now, who might that be, Miss MacNichol?"

"This is Panther," Flora said, trying to soothe the shuddering cat.

"What a splendid fellow," Bertie said. "How did you come by him?"

"I rescued him from a tarn when he was a kitten, back home in the Lakes."

"Flora, please take Panther outside," Mrs. Keppel said.

"No need on my account, Mrs. George. I love animals, as you know."

Flora duly released Panther into the corridor and firmly shut the door, then sat back down. As Mrs. Keppel poured the tea, she knew she would not be able to touch it for fear her hand would shake so violently that she'd spill it all over her fine dress.

"Miss MacNichol, it strikes me that you have a very cunning and clever comrade-in-arms in Mrs. George here. For"—Bertie took a puff on his cigar, smiling fondly at Mrs. Keppel—"I can tell you truthfully that I never thought I'd see the day that—"

What the day was, Flora would never know, because inhaling the cigar smoke prompted an enormous bout of coughing and choking. His already ruddy complexion became beetroot red, his eyes streaming as his chest struggled to take in enough breath. Mrs. Keppel poured a glass of water and squeezed next to him on the sofa as she put the glass to his lips, forcing him to sip it.

"Damn you, woman! I don't need water, I need brandy!" He pulled a large paisley handkerchief from his topcoat and, pushing the water away so it spilled all over Mrs. Keppel's skirts, proceeded to blow his nose loudly.

"Bertie, you really are going to have to give up the cigars," Mrs. Keppel chided as she rose and crossed to the decanter sitting on the sideboard. "You know that every doctor you see says the same. Those things will be the death of you, they truly will." She handed him the brandy, which he drank in one gulp before holding the glass out for another.

"Nonsense! It's simply the damned British weather, with its interminable damp. Remember how well I was at Biarritz?"

"Bertie, you know that's not true. Only the last time we were there, you—"

"Enough!" he roared, then swiftly downed the second brandy. That done, his gaze fell once more on Flora. "Can you see what I have to put up with, Miss MacNichol? I am treated like a child in the nursery."

"You are treated as though you are loved," Mrs. Keppel countered firmly.

Flora waited for a further explosion, but as Mrs. Keppel sat down next to him and took his hand in hers, he nodded placidly.

"I know, my dear. But it does rather feel that everyone is out to spoil my fun these days."

"Everyone is out to make sure that none of us have to endure the pain of losing you."

"Enough of all that." He waved a hand toward Mrs. Keppel as though swatting a fly. "I am hardly giving a good first impression to Miss MacNichol. So, tell me about yourself. What pursuits do you enjoy?"

"The countryside," Flora replied, as it was the first thing that came into her head. "Of course," she added hastily, "it is all I have known, and I may have loved city life just as much if I had been brought up here. I am learning that London is a very beautiful place."

"No need to apologize, Miss MacNichol. If fate had been kinder, I too would have chosen the country. Tell me, do you ride?"

"I do," replied Flora, simply unable to address him as "Bertie." "Although I confess, I would be at a loss on Rotten Row. I have learned to ride on rough terrain and am not at all graceful in the saddle."

"Ah, those were the days!" He clapped his hands together like a child. "When I was a young man, there was nothing I liked better than galloping across the Scottish moors. What other pursuits make your heart race, Miss MacNichol?"

"I wish I could tell you that it was poetry, or sewing, or that I could play the piano perfectly, but the truth is all I love tends to be out in the open air. Animals, for example . . ."

"I couldn't agree more!" He gestured fondly to the dog wagging its tail at his feet. "And as for the arts . . . well, in my position, I must tolerate and applaud them. Yet you cannot imagine the interminable nights I've sat at the opera, or at plays that I am meant to find some spiritual or psychological meaning in, or at recitals of poetry that I cannot understand a word of—"

"Bertie! You do yourself an injustice," Mrs. Keppel butted in. "You are extremely well-read."

"Only because I have to be. It is part of my job." He winked at Flora.

"I do love painting animals, although I don't seem to be able to capture humans. They seem far more . . . complicated." Flora hoped the answer would placate them both.

"Well said!" Bertie slapped his mountain of a thigh.

"Bertie, your carriage is waiting downstairs. You know that you have an engagement tonight and—"

"Yes, I am fully aware." He rolled his eyes at Flora in unspoken companionship. "Miss MacNichol, Mrs. George is right. I must leave to serve the nation and the Queen."

Flora rose immediately and was about to perform another deep curtsy when he beckoned her toward him.

"Come here, my dear."

She walked the few paces and stood in front of him. And was astonished as he took her hands in his, his fingers heavy with rings of cabochon rubies and gold crests.

"It has been a pleasure to make your acquaintance, Miss MacNichol. It only serves to remind me that Mrs. George is always right in her instincts. Now, come and help me up, woman, will you?"

He rose from the sofa with Mrs. Keppel's assistance. And, even though Flora was tall herself, he towered over her. "I do so hope that we will be able to enjoy more time together in the future. Especially in the country. At Duntreath perhaps?" His gaze fell on Mrs. Keppel, who nodded.

"Of course."

"Now, Miss MacNichol—Flora—I must take my leave. Good-bye, my dear."

"Good-bye."

"Come, Bertie, I will escort you downstairs."

With that, Mrs. Keppel, the terrier, and the King of the United Kingdom of Britain and Ireland and of the British Dominions beyond the Seas, Defender of the Faith and Emperor of India, left the parlor.

19

Did you meet Kingy?" Sonia, ready for bed with curl papers in her hair, stopped her on the nursery landing two hours later.

"Yes, I did."

"Don't you think he's sweet? Even if he looks quite frightening and fat, he's really a very nice gentleman."

"I quite agree," Flora laughed, kissing Sonia on the top of her head. "Good night."

"Flora?"

"Yes?"

"Please will you come and tell me one of your stories? They're so much more interesting than the picture books Nannie reads me."

"I will tomorrow."

"That's what grown-ups always say." Sonia pouted as Nannie loomed over her charge, ready to sweep her upstairs.

"I promise, Sonia. Now good night, and sweet dreams." Flora, in need of distraction from the overwhelming afternoon, continued into the day nursery to find Violet curled up in a chair by the fire reading a book.

"Am I disturbing you?" Flora asked quietly. Violet jumped and looked over the top of her book.

"It would be rude to say you were."

"Then I will leave."

"No." Violet indicated the chair opposite her.

"Are you sure?"

"Yes, I am," Violet said with purpose.

Flora walked across the room and sat down. "What are you reading?"

"Keats. Vita gave it to me as a belated birthday present."

"That was generous of her. I must confess, I wouldn't know good poetry from bad."

"It is only my observation, of course, but certainly with the Romantic poets such as Keats, it doesn't matter how well one has been versed in literature. It matters more how one has been versed in love."

"I am not sure what you mean, Violet," Flora replied, although she was almost certain she did.

"Well, before I met Vita and she explained poetry to me, I found it very dull too," Violet said, gazing into the fire. "But now, I read the words he wrote, and I can see that it is a universal expression of love for those who cannot express it for themselves. Do you see?"

"I believe I do, Violet. Pray, continue."

"Well, the very fact that Vita gave me this anthology indicates that she wishes me to read the words that she herself feels unable to say."

"You mean you believe that she loves you?"

"As I love her." Violet's direct blue gaze—so like her mother's—challenged Flora. "Do you think that's wrong?"

After a day of trying to consider what she said before she spoke, Flora answered honestly.

"There are many forms of love, Violet. One can love a parent in one way, a sibling in another, a lover, a friend, an animal . . . each in different ways."

Flora watched Violet's face as everything it contained seemed to soften and a veil fell from her eyes.

"Yes, yes! But, Flora, how can we possibly choose whom we love when society dictates it?"

"Well, even though outwardly we must do as society dictates, the feelings we hold inside us may contradict that completely."

Violet was silent for a moment, but then she smiled and for the first time since Flora had set eyes on her, she looked happy.

"You understand!" Violet closed her book, stood up, and walked toward Flora. "I wasn't sure exactly what it was Mama saw in you at first, but now I know and I am glad you're here. You've been in love too. Good night, Flora."

As Violet left, Barny appeared at the door. "Excuse me, Miss Flora, Mrs. Keppel wonders if you would care to join her in her boudoir before she goes out to dinner."

Flora rose and followed Barny to the other end of the corridor, where Mr. and Mrs. Keppel had their private suite of rooms.

"Flora, do come in and take a seat by me." Mrs. Keppel sat at her dressing table like an empress.

"Thank you," Flora said, sitting down on the edge of a velvet-covered chair and admiring Mrs. Keppel's loose auburn hair, which cascaded down past her creamy shoulders in natural curls. She was dressed in a Chantilly lace dressing gown and corset beneath, her bosom spilling ebulliently over the top of it. Flora thought she had never seen Mrs. Keppel looking more beautiful.

"I want to tell you that Bertie was very taken with you today."

"And I with him," Flora answered carefully.

"Well, he is not what he once was," Mrs. Keppel said, noting her tone. "He is ill and yet will do nothing to remedy his situation. Nevertheless, he is a kind and wise man and extremely dear to me."

"Yes, Mrs. Keppel."

"Barny, would you kindly leave us for a few minutes?"

"Yes, ma'am." Barny, who had been hovering behind her mistress waiting for the signal to start dressing her hair, departed and Mrs. Keppel turned to face Flora.

"My dear." She reached for Flora's hands and squeezed them tight. "I wasn't sure whether introducing you to Bertie was wise, but you simply could not have acquitted yourself any better."

"Couldn't I? I was awfully nervous."

"You were simply yourself and, as the King commented to me when he left, as natural as a wild Scottish flower that grows among the gorse."

"I am . . . glad I won his approval."

"Oh, Flora," Mrs. Keppel sighed deeply. "You cannot know how much. And how grateful I am to *you* for being . . . just who you are. He warned me not to spoil you, to turn you into another society lady, to make sure your pure nature isn't ruined by being here in the city. He's very much hoping to spend time with you again. However, as you have not been officially presented, I'd prefer—and so would he—that we keep today's meeting and any future interaction between the two of you a secret."

"Yes, although both Sonia and Violet know I saw him."

"Why, of course they do!" Mrs. Keppel chuckled. "I do not speak of those within these walls. One of the reasons Bertie loves to pay calls here to Portman Square is the complete discretion and privacy he finds, which is so lacking in the rest of his life. Do you see, Flora?"

"I do, Mrs. Keppel."

"Good. Then I am sure that you and Bertie can look forward to getting to know each other better in the future."

"Yes, I would like that. I . . ."

"What is it, my dear?"

"I was just wondering whether Mr. George was . . . included in the secret of the King's visits here." Flora felt her face flushing red at her insinuation.

"Why, of course he is! Bertie and he are great friends and they shoot together often when the King comes to stay at Duntreath in the autumn."

Feeling like an imbecile for asking, Flora blushed even redder.

"Within this house, we keep no secrets from each other. Now, I must call Barny in as we are to leave for dinner at Marlborough House in thirty minutes." Mrs. Keppel rang the bell on her dressing table. "The prime minister is joining us tonight, which means we will spend the evening discussing Kaiser Wilhelm's latest antics."

Flora wondered at this woman who dropped famous names as if they were stones from cherries. "I hope you enjoy it."

"Thank you, I am sure I won't. I have just remembered that tomorrow you are to visit your sister, Aurelia, and your aunt at her house in Grosvenor Square. I am otherwise engaged, but Freed will drive you there and back."

"Thank you."

"And now, my dear, my congratulations once more on your conduct at tea this afternoon. I am certain it will not be your last meeting with Bertie."

"Sister, dear!"

Flora was greeted with an enormous hug at the door of Aunt Charlotte's drawing room. As they walked inside, Aurelia closed it behind them. "I've asked Aunt Charlotte if we can have some privacy, as I'm in urgent need of your advice." She ushered Flora to the sofa and sat down next to her. Flora thought how different her sister looked from the last time she'd seen her. Her lovely eyes were sparkling with life and her complexion was glowing. And Flora knew exactly what the reason must be.

Please, God, don't let me show my pain . . .

"I asked you here because since we last met, I have had a visitor."

"Really? And who might that have been?"

"Archie Vaughan!" she exclaimed. "He called on me two days ago, just as I was putting the finishing touches to my packing. I am due to leave for Scotland the day after tomorrow, you see. You can imagine how surprised I was to see him."

"Goodness!" Flora feigned shock. "I can."

"Of course, I'd presumed that he had simply come to say good-bye to me out of politeness. He came in here, closing the door behind him, then immediately took my hands in his and told me he'd made a terrible mistake! You could have knocked me over with a feather."

"Indeed, I am sure I could have."

"I asked him what kind of 'mistake' he meant, and he explained how the responsibility of marriage had suddenly frightened him, that perhaps he simply wasn't the marrying kind—just as you said!—and that he feared he would let me down as a husband, which was why he did not propose to me when I was at High Weald."

"I see."

"He told me it was only after I left High Weald that he'd realized how much he'd missed me." At this, Aurelia's gaze drifted off as she relived the moment.

"Oh my, how . . . romantic."

"And when his mother informed him I was ready to leave London to journey up to Scotland any day, he said he knew he must come after me and stop me. And that is exactly what he did."

"So he has proposed?"

"Yes! Oh, Flora, he asked if I could ever forgive him for making such a terrible error of judgment, and immediately went down on one knee and offered me the most dazzling emerald engagement ring."

"And what was your reply?"

"Well—and this is where I hope you will be proud of me—I said that because of the sudden turn of events, I needed to take a few days to think about it. And that is why I asked you to come to see me. You are so sensible in matters of the heart, dear Flora. What do you think I should do?"

Flora swallowed any personal thoughts she might have on the subject. "Perhaps the first question to ask is why you did not accept his proposal immediately. What held you back?"

"Why, Flora, I told you only a few days ago that I would refuse any further proposal, although that was perhaps because I was protecting myself and my pride. And also, I am still not sure that he loves me as I love him."

"Has he said he loves you?"

"Yes . . . or at least, he said his life would be empty without me."

"Well then, there we are!" Flora forced a bright smile. "It amounts to the same thing, whichever words Archie chose to use."

"Does it?" Aurelia looked at her beseechingly. "Perhaps I expect too much and have too many romantic notions, but his initial hesitation makes me feel—despite the reasons he gave me—that he had reservations."

"Which he has now resolved, and which had nothing to do with you."

"I asked him if there was someone else who had captured his heart. He swore that there was not."

Flora's heartbeat quickened. "Then surely everything he has told you is enough for you to accept his proposal?"

"Yes, but you know that I had other suitors earlier in the Season and they were ardent in their pursuit of me." Aurelia stood up and began pacing the small drawing room. "I was showered with flowers and love notes, and even though I did not want *them*, I was certainly convinced they wanted me. With Archie, I feel rather as if *I* am the ardent suitor, chasing a man who has always seemed . . . indifferent to me."

"But even from my limited experience of men, I know that many of them approach love in a very different way to women. Some are overtly romantic, but many are not. Look at our father," Flora said, grasping for an example. "Even though it is obvious he adores Mama, he is not and never has been openly romantic with her."

"Do you really think he adores her?" Aurelia paused in her pacing. "I've always rather wondered. And I certainly don't want a marriage like that."

Flora realized she had lost ground by using her parents' distant union as an example. "Perhaps it's simply that men are taught that they mustn't show emotion. And Archie Vaughan is just one of those men."

Aurelia stared at her sister, a hint of suspicion in her eyes. "I know you have never liked him, or trusted him for that matter. I am rather surprised you seem eager to defend him in this."

"My feelings about him are irrelevant. I am only trying to be pragmatic and as honest with you as I can be. You've asked for my opinion, and I have given it. He has seen the error of his ways and wishes to marry you. I doubt you could ask for more, especially given the alternative . . ."

"I know. Up until Archie's proposal, I felt I might die of misery at the thought of being banished up to Scotland with Mama and Papa."

"Then, you have your answer."

"Yes, except I could not bear it if I thought Archie didn't really love me and was simply marrying me to take my dowry and save his family home."

"Dearest Aurelia, I think Lord Vaughan has proved all too successfully that he has a mind of his own, and cannot be forced to do anything he doesn't wish to."

"You really think I should say yes?"

Flora told the biggest lie so far.

"I do."

"And despite your negative feelings toward him, you will agree to be my chief bridesmaid and dance at my wedding?"

"Of course."

"Then . . ."—the cloud lifted from Aurelia's face—"you have convinced me. I will tell him I shall accept his proposal when he comes to visit me tomorrow afternoon. Thank you, my darling sister, I do not know what I would do without you. Now, the decision is made, let us call for some tea. I feel positively weak from the stress."

An hour later Flora allowed Freed to hand her into the brougham, exhausted from the tension of the deception. She had done what was right in persuading Aurelia to accept Archie's proposal. Yet doubt gnawed at her all the way home to Portman Square. All Aurelia wished for was to have her love for Archie returned by him.

Flora knew it was the one thing he could never give her.

"I presume you are already aware of the notice in this morning's *Times*?" Mrs. Keppel passed the newspaper to her and Flora read its substance.

"Yes, Aurelia told me of Lord Vaughan's proposal."

"And you are happy they are to marry before Christmas? It's an unusually short engagement."

"Perhaps they both feel as though they have wasted precious time. I am very happy for both of them, they love each other dearly."

Mrs. Keppel's eyes slanted knowingly. "Then I am happy too, and will send a note of congratulation to them from the household forthwith."

"As I will send mine."

"By coincidence, there is a letter arrived for you by hand from the Vaughans' London household this morning. I told Mr. Rolfe that I would give it to you personally."

"Thank you." As calmly as she could, Flora took the letter from Mrs. Keppel's delicate white hand.

Mrs. Keppel watched her fingering the envelope. "My dear Flora, I am at home this afternoon and not receiving any visitors if, having read the letter, you wish to join me later for tea."

"I . . . thank you." Flora left the parlor and hurried upstairs to her bedroom. Closing the door firmly, she sat down on her bed and stared at the letter. Just the sight of his writing made tears burn at the back of her eyes. Tearing it open, her fingers trembled as she unfolded the paper.

18 Berkeley Square
Mayfair
19th October 1909

I have done as you requested, even though I know it is wrong for all three of us. Now it is agreed, I have suggested we marry as soon as possible.

Despite it all, I love you.

Archie

"Ah, Flora, I was expecting you."

"Were you?" Flora hovered at the door of Mrs. Keppel's parlor later that afternoon.

"Of course," she said matter-of-factly. "Close the door behind you. Your tea is already here, so we will not be disturbed."

Flora did so and walked slowly toward Mrs. Keppel, in an agony of indecision. She'd never been one to confide in others before, but today . . .

"Do sit down, my dear, and warm yourself by the fire." Mrs. Keppel handed Flora a cup of tea and she sipped it gratefully. "Now, we can sit here and take tea and gossip, or we can talk about the real reason that you appear before me now. Which would you prefer?"

"I . . . do not know."

"Love is so very confusing, is it not? And you, like me, prefer to keep your own counsel. My darling Bertie always tells me that knowledge is power and that however tempting it is to give away that power to another in return for comfort, it is unwise to do so. And *both* of us have chosen not to do so."

"Yes." Flora was amazed at her insight.

"So, Flora, you have been privy to *my* secret. Everyone in London believes they understand the relationship between myself and the King, and criticizes it. But their malicious gossip and their wish to discredit me blinds them to the simple fact that I love him. An outsider might claim that my relationship with him is just a sham to further my own ambition, just as they might say that your rejection of Lord Vaughan's attentions was cruel. But I know your true motivation stems from love for your dear sister."

"Mrs. Keppel, what are you saying? I . . . no one has the least idea of any relationship between myself and Lord Vaughan . . ."

"I am aware of that, and I doubt there is anyone in London who has guessed the situation, other than myself. I saw your faces after you met here a few days ago. And the . . . predicament was written all over both of them. Your secret is safe with me. Please, Flora, trust me and let it out before you drive yourself mad."

Eventually, Flora did so. And as Mrs. Keppel poured her a glass of sherry and offered her a clean lace handkerchief, and she spoke of all that had happened between them, there was no doubt she felt lighter.

"You will not be the first or the last to send the man you love into the arms of another because you feel it is what should be done," Mrs. Keppel said. "I once had a very similar situation before I was married to dear George, or met Bertie. You have acted correctly for the noblest of reasons, and now you must move on."

"I know. And that is the hard part."

"Well, the best way to do that is to keep yourself distracted, and I am more than happy to provide you with the opportunity." Mrs. Keppel smiled. "There are a number of dances coming up, and I can assure you that before you attend your sister's wedding, we will have garnered you at least two proposals."

"Thank you, but I am not interested in any suitors at present."

"That is because you have not met them yet." Mrs. Keppel's eyes gleamed. "We shall begin with a dance at Devonshire House, and then there is a rather grand ball out at Blenheim, which is such a trek, but I feel we should make it and—"

"Mrs. Keppel?"

"Yes, my dear?"

"Why are you doing all this for me?"

She glanced away into the fire, then looked back at Flora. "Because I feel you're the child we never had."

Star

October 2007

Ceanothus
(California lilac—Rhamnaceae family)

20

I felt a hand patting me repeatedly on the shoulder and I brought myself back to the present. I looked up to see the closing credits of *Superman* on the screen, and Rory standing by me.

"*Superman II* now?"

I looked down at my watch and saw it was past five thirty in the afternoon. "No." I shook my head. "I think that's enough for one day. Want to see the pheasant?" I asked Rory to distract him.

He nodded eagerly and I roused myself from the chair and the past, knowing that this wasn't the moment to start analyzing what I'd read and whether it had any bearing on my own existence. In the kitchen, Orlando was sorting through the delivery from the farm shop.

"Major brownie points for your thorough plucking of the pheasant," he said. "You'll be relieved to know that I've just retrieved the shot that ended its life, so we'll have no broken teeth tomorrow." He held up a small saucer, in the center of which were three pieces of lead shot.

Rory immediately picked up a piece and studied it. "Poor bird."

"Ah, yes, but lucky us tomorrow. Miss Star, this is for tonight's feast."

I saw a gorgeous blood-red steak fillet lying on the marble slab in front of him.

"I know no one else who can do justice to its perfection. If you don't mind, I prefer to eat at eight sharp in the evening. It gives a good three hours to digest the food before one sleeps," said Orlando, glancing at the clock.

"Then I'd better get on."

"While you're doing that, I shall take this little chap off for a game of chess. Loser does the washing up after supper."

"But you always win, Uncle Lando," Rory complained as they trooped out of the kitchen.

I prepared the meat and the vegetables, then sat down, inhaling the scent of cooking and enjoying the wonderful warmth of the kitchen. Mulling over what I'd read, I realized that the figurine Pa had given me must be Flora's adored cat, rather than an actual panther as I'd presumed. And then I thought about Flora, who Pa Salt had indicated was something to me. There were definitely similarities between us—namely our shared interest in botany and our love for nature. But then, millions of people also enjoyed these pursuits, and from what I'd read, it was far more likely to be Aurelia whom I was connected to. After all, it seemed that she was the one who would marry into the Vaughan family.

The worst thing was, I wanted so badly to find a link, something that would bond me inextricably to High Weald, and allow me to be a part of this extraordinary family, two members of which in particular I was growing fonder of by the day.

Once we had eaten the fillet, and Orlando pronounced it "heroic," I took Rory upstairs for a bath, unsure of the rules for such things. I let him take the lead, as he unhooked his hearing aids and placed them carefully on a shelf.

"Shall I leave?" I asked as he stepped into the full bubble city I had run for him. But he shook his head.

"Talk to me. Tell me a story about your family, Star."

So I sat on the old-fashioned wooden toilet cover and, relying heavily on mime and facial expressions when my signing fell short, gave Rory the most potted version of my childhood at Atlantis I could manage, throwing in a few stories of me and CeCe getting into trouble.

"Naughty sisters!" Rory giggled, as he stepped out of the bath and into the towel I held out to him. His green eyes grew serious then. "I want a sister or brother too. Sounds fun."

I helped him put on his pajamas and handed him his hearing aids. He fitted them snugly back onto each ear, then wrapped his arms around my shoulders and gave me a kiss on my cheek. "Will you be my sister, Star?"

"Course I will," I said as we walked along the corridor to his bedroom.

A few minutes later, Orlando appeared in the doorway, hovering uncertainly. "Ablutions completed?"

"Yes. Good night, angel," I said, giving Rory a kiss.

"Good night, Star."

After breakfast the next day, I browned off the pheasant legs in a large cast-iron pot before adding berries, herbs, and some red wine, which I hoped would simmer down to create a luscious sauce. Then I wrapped the breasts in bacon and set them aside for baking later. Rory sat painting at the kitchen table and we worked peacefully together as I began rolling out the pastry for a fruit pie. I'd watched CeCe paint hundreds of times, but her art tended to be very precise, whereas Rory mixed the watercolors to the shade he required, then sloshed them on with abandon. As I put the pie into the range, I saw he'd produced an autumnal landscape that I wouldn't be able to replicate if I had months to do so.

"Amazing," I said as he signed his name on the painting, and I noticed how his hand formed the letters clumsily, in direct contrast to his flowing brushstrokes.

"I like painting."

"We all like things we're good at," I said with a smile.

Orlando had gone out earlier that morning. He hadn't said where, but I had the feeling he was not looking forward to it. He arrived back with Mouse in tow just as I was mashing the potatoes.

"Look." Rory indicated his painting. "For Star."

Orlando dutifully praised it while Mouse merely swept a cursory glance over it.

"What say you I fetch the bottle of Vacqueyras I've decanted to complement Star's pheasant?" Orlando said to no one in particular, as he headed to the pantry to retrieve the wine.

"Did you read my transcription?" Mouse asked me abruptly.

"Yes, I did, thank you." I indicated the neat pile of paper beside the telephone.

"Find it informative?"

"Very."

"I'd like to see that figurine if you have it."

"Actually, I didn't bring it with me after all," I lied, hoping my face wasn't turning red, as it usually did when I told an untruth.

"That's a shame. Orlando thinks it's a Fabergé."

"I'll have another look for it before I leave."

"You do that."

The telephone rang and Mouse reached for the receiver.

"Hi, Marguerite. Yes, everything's fine here. He's fine too, aren't you, Rory?"

"Yes!" Rory shouted so his mother could hear. "Fine."

"What time are you due back?"

I busied myself at the range so as not to look as though I was listening.

"I see. Well, I certainly can't do it, but I'll ask Orlando and Star if they can. Orlando?"

"Yes?" He'd appeared from the pantry with the wine.

"Marguerite's been asked to stay on longer in France. She wants to know if you and Star can spare a few more days here to look after Rory."

"Sadly, that is an impossibility. I have two major auctions coming up in London, which I must attend. What about you, Mouse?"

"Hardly. You know what I have on at the farm at the moment. Besides, Rory's on half term and . . ."

My eyes fell on Rory, who was sitting in the middle of the two brothers, turning his head from side to side as they conducted their verbal tennis match. And probably feeling of little more importance than the metaphoric ball they were batting between them.

"I'll do it," I said suddenly. "I mean, if you can manage without me at the shop, Orlando."

"I can think about it, certainly."

Rory patted Orlando's hands and signed vigorously. "Yes, please let Star stay! Good food!" There was a momentary silence as the brothers' dual gazes fell on me.

"Given the dearth of customers in the bookshop, she probably has nothing more taxing to do than dust," said Mouse.

My hackles rose at this comment, but I fought to control myself. I could see Orlando was doing the same.

"Of course, the most important thing is that Rory is happy," he said eventually.

"Right then, did you hear any of that, Marguerite? Star will stay on and Rory's happy with the arrangement," Mouse said into the receiver. "I'll be around to keep an eye out. Let us know what time you're back on Wednesday, will you? Okay, bye now."

"Food's ready," I said to Orlando, who had poured a glass of wine for all of us.

"Wonderful. We'll eat in here, shall we? And I . . . *we*"—Orlando glanced at his brother—"are awfully grateful for your offer."

"No problem," I replied as I turned back to the range.

After the lunch, which—even though I say so myself—was something of a triumph, given I had never tackled pheasant before, Orlando was taken off to Ashford in Mouse's Land Rover to catch the London train. The *froideur* between the brothers was obvious, and I presumed it was to do with their earlier meeting, and the conversation with Marguerite.

Mouse had said he would return to say good night to Rory, but the clock passed eight and there was no sign of him. I dragged Rory away from his *Superman* movie, bathed him, and put him to bed.

Back in my own room, I searched in my rucksack for Pa Salt's letter and the black cat. I studied the little creature carefully, remembering Flora's vivid descriptions of Panther.

"Is this you?" I asked the ether, and, receiving no reply, stowed it away again. If it was a Fabergé, as Mouse had suggested, I knew it was of great value. Perhaps Mrs. Keppel, who had also delighted in Fabergé's creations, had given the cat to Flora as a gift . . .

There was only one way to find out, and that was to show the Sewer Rat . . . *Mouse*, I corrected myself. My own pet name of his pet name could not under any circumstances slip out.

I went to the bathroom and dipped myself as fast as I could in the bath full of bubbles I'd recently poured for Rory, having learned last night that the hot water tank only ran to one tubful a day. Then I hurried to the bedroom to put on my layers before going downstairs.

I was hovering by the front door, wondering if I should lock up for the night, when a figure appeared out of the gloom behind me, making me cry out in shock.

"Only me," said Mouse. "I let myself in through the back door while you were upstairs. I just wanted to give you these." He held out two enormous brass keys on a ring.

"Thanks."

"And thank you for doing this. It's obvious Rory has taken to you already. Marguerite says she'll call tomorrow. It's most unlike her to agree to stay on. Something must be up," he muttered. "She normally works locally, so that she can at least get home for Rory in the evening. But it seems her fame has spread. Anyway, you'll need some supplies to keep you going for the next few days. If you can write me a list, I'll swing by tomorrow morning for it. It'll be early, though."

"No problem," I replied. "Would you mind if I use the telephone to let my sister know I won't be back tonight? My mobile doesn't work here."

"Feel free. And if you're desperate to send an e-mail, you can come to my place. Turn right at the gate and cross the lane to the other side. There's a sign for 'Home Farm' a few hundred yards along on your left. It may not be grand, but at least it has Wi-Fi."

"I should be fine."

"And if you did manage to find that figurine, I really would like to see it. There are a number of holes in our family's past that I'm keen to fill in."

"I'll have another hunt through my bag."

"I hope you find it eventually. Good night, then."

"Good night."

I let him out of the door and then locked it firmly. Then I went to the kitchen, picked up the telephone, and dialed CeCe's number.

"Hi, it's me."

"Sia! Where are you? And why are you calling from a strange number?"

I explained as best I could, and there was a long pause.

"So, this family is not just paying you a pittance to work long hours in a bookshop, but they're now also using you as an unpaid nanny and chef?"

"Orlando said I'd still get my wages, and Marguerite will pay me extra on top too."

"The problem with you is that you're too softhearted."

"It was an emergency, and I was the only one who could help. And I really don't mind. I love it here," I replied honestly.

"You just make sure they pay you what you're owed. I miss you, Sia. This apartment is far too big for just one person."

"I'll be home soon, and if you need me, I'll be on this number."

"I'll skip the last class at college on Wednesday so we can have dinner together. I feel I've hardly seen you in the past few weeks."

"I know, I'm sorry. Sleep well, Cee."

"I'll try. Bye."

The call was ended abruptly at the other end and I sighed as I made my way into the drawing room to make sure the fire was not likely to set us alight in the night—another golden rule of Pa's. I switched off the lights and made my way up to bed. Checking on Rory, who was blissfully asleep, I thanked the heavens that I had been granted two more nights in this wonderful, wonderful house.

21

I was up early the next morning, woken by Rory, who pounced on me in bed and said he was hungry. By the time Mouse arrived in the kitchen to collect my shopping list, we were sitting down to breakfast.

"Something smells good," Mouse said, to my amazement. It was rare to hear him utter a positive comment.

"Would you like some? It's only eggy bread."

"I haven't had that since I was a child. Yes, if it's not too much trouble."

"There's fresh coffee in the pot on the table," I indicated.

Rory patted Mouse's arm and signed to him. "Can I come out on the tractor?"

"What?" Mouse had barely glanced up to look at him.

"Rory wants to know if he can come out on your tractor," I said as I put down the plate in front of him with slightly more force than necessary.

"God, no," he said as he began to devour the eggy bread with a hunger that had been noticeably lacking the past couple of times I'd cooked for him. "This is so good, I love nursery food. Right." He swigged his coffee back, stood up, and grabbed the list from the table. "I'll be back to drop this off when I can."

And with that, he was out of the door.

"No tractor?" Rory looked up at me with a plaintive expression that tore at my heart.

"Not today, Rory, no. But how about you get dressed, and then you can have a cycle on that bike of yours?"

Rory cycled to the orchard and there we collected as many apples and damsons as we could carry. The ancient trees were in desperate need of pruning, but I knew it would have to wait until late winter.

"We'll never eat all this," Rory signed as we trundled the fruit back in a squeaky wheelbarrow I'd found.

"No, but they'll taste good in pies and jam."

"You *make* jam?"

"Yes," I laughed at his surprise, realizing he must have grown up believing that most things he ate came from an invisible supermarket fairy.

I spent the afternoon making pies, and Rory asked for his habitual *Superman* movie. Having put in the DVD for him, I went back to the kitchen to make a cup of tea and check the progress of the pastry in the range. My fingers itched to reorganize the pantry and cupboards, but I desisted, knowing it wasn't my place to do so.

I looked at the clock and saw it was nearing six, and time for Rory's supper. Given there was no sign of the promised shopping, I went to see what I could find.

I was just taking the last pie out of the oven when the back door opened and Mouse appeared with two plastic bags full of shopping.

"There you are," he said as he dumped them on the kitchen table. "Are you planning a party here?" He pointed at the pies.

"Just using up the windfall from the orchard."

He took out a beer from one of the bags and opened it. "Want one?" he offered.

"No thanks."

"Rory okay?"

"Fine," I said, as I dived into the shopping bags and pulled out some sausages. I tipped them onto a baking tray and put them in the oven to cook. "I'm making homemade chips," I added as I opened a bag of potatoes and fetched a peeler from the drawer. "I hope Rory likes them."

"Given that he and Marguerite live mostly on eggs and cans of baked beans, I'm sure he'll be fine. As would I, if there's enough."

I smiled a secret smile at his sudden enthusiasm.

"Of course." I indicated the big bag of potatoes. "I'll go and tell Rory you're here." I made toward the door.

"Just before you do . . ." His tone held me back, and I turned to see his face suddenly somber. "I want to ask you truthfully whether you have that Fabergé figurine here with you. Either you really haven't, or you simply don't want to show it to me. I understand why you may not feel you can trust me," he continued. "After all, I've hardly been very welcoming. I wouldn't worry, Star, everyone thinks I'm a shit. And they're not wrong. I am."

So now we were back to self-pity. And if he expected me to contradict him, he was mistaken.

"Anyway," he continued in the face of my silence, "how about we make a deal? I'll tell you the rest of what I've found out about our family history, and you show me the cat. Because if it *is* a Fabergé, I've got a good idea of who gave it to Flora MacNichol."

"I—"

"Mouse!" Rory arrived in the kitchen and the moment was gone.

Over supper, Mouse was definitely cheerier than I'd seen him before; whether he was doing his best to lull me into a false sense of security before snapping back into his usual morose self, or it was the homemade chips that had done it, I had no idea. But I was happy for Rory that Mouse was at least making an effort to engage him. I suggested they play a game of tic-tac-toe, which Rory had never heard of. After I'd shown him how to play, he took to it with gusto, shouting with happiness every time his crosses won. I knew Mouse was letting him win, and that too was an improvement.

"Time for bed," Mouse said suddenly.

I looked up at the clock and saw it was only just after seven, but Rory had already stood up, like a rookie soldier who had just been given his marching orders by a sergeant major.

"I'll take you upstairs for a bath," I said, holding out my hand to him.

"Night, Mouse," Rory said.

"Night, Rory."

After I filled the bath, Rory splashed around, then lay back and closed his eyes as I shampooed his hair. He plunged himself under the water, then emerged and opened his eyes.

"Star?"

"Yes?"

His hands came up out of the water to sign. "Don't think Mouse likes me very much."

"I think he does, but he's rubbish at this." I indicated our hands.

"Not hard. We will teach him."

"Yes," I said, and held out the towel in front of me so he could step out and maintain his modesty. I helped him put on his pajamas and took him along the corridor to his room.

"Now, do you want me to read you a story, or am I too bad at it?" I teased, tickling him gently.

"You're much better than Mouse, so yes please."

Rory turned before I did to see Mouse standing in the doorway, and I was grateful he didn't understand the language our hands spoke.

"Want me to tuck you in, Rory?" Mouse asked.

"Yes please," he said dutifully.

"Night night." I kissed Rory on the forehead and left the room.

"You're very good with him," Mouse said later, entering the kitchen as I was just finishing the washing up. Of all the modern conveniences I wished for at High Weald, the first would have been a dishwasher.

"Thank you."

"I presume you've worked with deaf kids before?"

"No, never."

"Then how . . . ?"

I explained to him briefly how I'd come to learn to sign. He took a beer out of the fridge and cracked it open.

"It's interesting that you and Rory have met and bonded, as you're certainly a woman of few words. He doesn't miss the absence of them as a hearing person would. You don't give much away, do you?"

Neither do you, I thought.

"You live with your sister, is that right?"

So he remembered. "Yes."

"Boyfriend? Significant other?"

"No." *Not that it's any of your business.* "You?" I rounded on him.

"I'm fully aware no one would have me, and that's fine."

I wasn't going to be goaded into a response. In the silence, I stowed away the plates and cutlery.

"As a matter of fact," he said eventually, revealing—as everyone did after a long silence—more information than he'd originally intended, "I was married once."

"Oh."

"She seemed to think I was okay."

Again I said nothing.

"But then . . ."

I continued my silence.

"She died."

I knew I was beaten. There was no way I could not reply to *that* statement.

"I'm sorry." I turned around to see him standing awkwardly by the table.

"So was I. But that's life . . . and death, isn't it?"

"Yes, it is," I said, thinking of Pa Salt.

There was a slight pause before he glanced at the clock on the wall and said, "I should go. I have three months' worth of outstanding accounts to tackle. Thanks for supper."

Leaving his half-drunk beer on the table, Mouse left through the back door.

That night, I couldn't sleep. I felt dreadful about his abrupt departure, which I knew had been engendered by my cold response after he told me his wife had died. However rude he usually was, he had confessed an emotional confidence. And I had given him an unemotional platitude in reply.

In essence, I had allowed myself to sink to *his* level.

Eventually, exhausted from being exhausted, I staggered up with the sunrise at half past six, put on my layers, and went down to the kitchen.

Then I did the only thing that I knew would calm me—I baked a cake.

After breakfast, I asked Rory if he could take me to Mouse's farmhouse, to which he nodded eagerly.

"I was thinking that maybe we could take this cake to him as a present," I said.

"Yes." Rory gave me a thumbs-up. "Mouse is lonely."

With Rory on his bike and the cake nestled in a tin between my palms, we headed up the drive and from there across the lane. Rory led me along the narrow grass verge and I inhaled the evocative and unmistakable scent of deep autumn in England: the rich smell of fermentation as the countryside discarded the remnants of another summer, ready to renew again in spring.

"Here." Rory pointed to a sign, which led us to an overgrown driveway. He hared off as I followed more sedately with the cake. Finally, the farmhouse came into view—a sturdy red-brick building without any of the embellishments of its neighbor across the road. If High Weald was aristocratic, Home Farm was workmanlike and cozy.

In the center of the farmhouse stood a large door—once painted a cheery red, but now a peeling, faded version of its old self. Growing along the front of the house were lavender bushes that were way past their best and needed replacing, but their calm scent still filled the air. Rory raced around the side of the house and headed straight for the back door.

"Can you knock?" I indicated, and he thumped it, enjoying the vibrations. There was no response.

"Knock again," I suggested.

"Always open. Go in?"

"Okay."

Feeling like a guilty trespasser, I followed Rory inside and found myself in a kitchen that was a miniature version of the one we had just left. Except this one was even more chaotic, the pine table almost invisible under used coffee cups, newspapers, and what looked like account ledgers with receipts and bills spilling out from their pages. The breeze from the door closing behind us sent a couple fluttering to the floor. Putting down the cake, I stooped down to pick them up, just as Mouse entered the kitchen from the inside door.

He stared at the receipts in my hand and frowned.

"They were on the floor," I said wanly, as I put them back on the table. "We brought you a present. Rory, give Mouse the tin."

"Star baked it," he signed. "For you."

"It's lemon drizzle cake," I added.

Mouse stared at the tin as if it might contain a bomb. "Thanks."

"It's okay."

As we stood there uncomfortably, I shivered in the chill of the room. The range was not turned on, and the coziness promised by the exterior of the house was clearly not present inside.

"Everything all right?" Mouse said.

"Fine."

"Good. Well, if you'll excuse me, I have to get on."

"Okay." Rory and I retraced our footsteps to the back door. I paused with my hand on the doorknob, deciding I had to be the bigger person. "We're having shepherd's pie for supper, if you want to join us." Then I opened the back door and released us into the relative warmth of the freezing October day.

Rory and I spent the afternoon playing endless games of tic-tac-toe.

When he grew bored with that, I taught him how to play battleships. I wasn't quite sure if he'd grasped the concept; instead of putting a cross for his ship in the specific square, he drew the ships instead, which at least whiled away the time as he insisted on making each miniature picture perfect, rubbing it out when it wasn't.

Having switched on his cherished *Superman* DVD, I yawned as I put the kettle on to boil. Not just from my lack of sleep last night, but from my first experience of entertaining a child nonstop.

I thought back to Atlantis, and what we girls used to do to amuse ourselves during the holidays, marveling at how Ma had coped with six of us, each at different stages of our development. I realized I couldn't remember ever being bored—I'd always had CeCe and the rest of my sisters. As an only child, Rory had no one to play with. And if there'd ever been a tiny part of me that had felt resentful about being in the middle of our huge female nest, and the lack of one-on-one attention, I now felt blessed.

Having assembled the shepherd's pie, I left it in the range to finish cooking, then went upstairs to make Rory's bed and my own. Sitting down on mine, my fingers stiff from the bitter cold, I retrieved the box containing Panther. As the lemon drizzle cake didn't seem to have mended the rift, and I still felt guilty for letting anger replace empathy last night, I slid it into my back jean pocket and went downstairs, knowing it was the one thing I could offer Mouse that might redeem me.

Seven o'clock, then eight o'clock came and went. I bathed Rory, then tucked him into bed, and walked back down the stairs to clear away supper. I was just about to switch off the kitchen lights and sit in front of the fire to read when the back door opened.

"Sorry I'm late. I got held up," said Mouse. "Any shepherd's pie left?"

"Yes." I went to the pantry to retrieve it, then put it in the range. "It'll take a few minutes to warm up." Not sure what to do with myself, I hovered by the kitchen table for a moment.

"I could murder a beer. Do you want some wine?" he asked.

"Okay."

Mouse fetched the drinks. "Cheers." He clinked his beer can against my glass as we sat down.

"Thanks for the cake by the way. I had some for lunch, it was fantastic. I also came to tell you that I won't be around tomorrow. I'm off to London to tackle Orlando about selling the shop."

"It'll break his heart," I said, aghast. "It's his life."

"Do you think I don't know that?" he snapped. "But we can't go on like this. As I said to you—and him too—the business can be run online. The money from the sale of the building can at least clear the debts we've accrued. And I have to buy some new machinery to keep the farm going. I understand your sentiments, but I'm afraid life is cruel, Star, and that's the way it is."

"I know," I said as I bit my lip to stem the tears that were threatening to form.

"Sadly, one of us brothers has to live in reality, and to be frank, if I don't do something now, we're in danger of the bank declaring the business bankrupt and seizing the shop as an asset against our debt. Which would mean they'd sell it for a tenth of what it's actually worth, and we'd see precious little of the funds that would be left over from the sale."

"Yes, I understand. But you must see what a loss it is. It's a legacy—"

"Legacy?" he said with a derisive snort. "This family has never had much luck—or perhaps I should say *sense*—when it comes to money. We've only held on to High Weald by the skin of our teeth. Not that it's my concern but I know that Marguerite is in it up to her neck too."

"Oh dear," I said lamely, and rose to retrieve the shepherd's pie, uncertain of what else to say.

"Anyway, not your problem, I know. Other than the fact you may have to look for another job in the next few months. Just our luck there's a downturn in commercial property because of the world economic situation. It never rains but it pours, as they say."

"Don't worry about me, it's Orlando who will suffer."

"You're very fond of him, aren't you?"

"Yes, very."

"As he is of you. There aren't many people who can deal with his eccentricities. These days he'd probably be diagnosed with some syndrome or other—OCD and the like—and that's aside from his determination to live his life as a throwback to a hundred years ago." He shook his head. "When we were little, it was always Orlando who had our mother's attention. He was her darling; she homeschooled him from the age of nine because his asthma was so severe. The two of them would be holed up in the library, reading their precious Dickens. He's never had to live in reality. As he always says, the past was a much more civilized and gentle time."

"Apart from the continual horrific wars," I said. "And the lack of antibiotics or any health care for the poor."

He looked at me, startled, then gave me the present of a sudden laugh. "True. Not to mention the debtors' prisons."

"Orlando wouldn't do so well in one of those."

"No Sancerre and starched shirts in the poorhouse."

We shared a wry smile as I placed his plate down in front of him, thinking how different these two brothers were, rather like CeCe and me.

"A lot of people—not just Orlando—want to glamorize the past. I certainly do," he muttered with feeling as he picked up his fork to eat.

"How old was your wife when she died?" I asked cautiously, feeling I should broach the subject and try my best to atone for my behavior last night.

"Twenty-nine. We were very happy."

"My sister lost her fiancé in a sailing accident a couple of months ago, only just after our father died. As you say, life is cruel." I was forcing the words out, saying far more than I normally did, in penance.

"I'm sorry for your sister. I wouldn't wish it on anyone to lose their partner and their father in quick succession. It happened to me too," he sighed. "Harking back to the past again, have you any theories about how you could possibly be connected to this family?"

"None."

"What? You mean you haven't spent the past three days at High Weald searching through the drawers to find a connection?"

"No, I . . ."

I felt a guilty heat rise to my cheeks. Mouse was so difficult to read, I had no idea whether he was teasing or rebuking.

"I certainly would have done if I were you," he said. "Let's face it, if you had found a connection, you could have stood to inherit what you may have thought was a significant amount of money. As it stands, we can include you in the bankruptcy petition."

"I haven't searched the house, and I'm not poor," I added defiantly.

"Well, lucky old you. And for the record, Star, I was teasing you."

"Oh." I hated that he'd read my mind.

"Please, I know my sense of humor is confusing, but I promise I was joking. Defense mechanism, *n'est-ce pas*? To keep people at bay. We all have one. Look at you. You're very hard to read . . . Occasionally I feel I know what you're thinking from the expression in those blue eyes of yours . . . but most of the time, I haven't got a clue."

I immediately looked away from him, and he gave a chuckle before taking another sip of his beer. "Anyway, I was rather hoping that while you were here, you'd find something that I haven't seen for a long, long time."

"What is that?"

"As you've already gathered, Flora MacNichol was a prolific diarist for much of her life. Her journals—forty or fifty of them—sat on a bookshelf in the study at Home Farm for years. My father found them in a trunk in the attic when he was cleaning out the house after his parents died. That's how he knew of the . . . anomaly he told me about when he was dying."

"What 'anomaly'?"

"It was to do with the inheritance when High Weald was divided in the forties. Putting it simply, he felt our line—i.e., the Forbeses—had been cheated out of what was rightfully ours."

"I see."

"Naturally, when I came to research our family history, I pulled them down and started working through them. But I've come to a grinding halt—all her journals from 1910 onward are missing. Star, I know that there were far more than there are now on that bookshelf. They used to take up two shelves and now it's less than one." He shrugged. "The problem is, those missing years may contain the proof of my father's theory. Not that I can do anything about it now, but I'd like to know for sure, one way or the other."

"I understand," I said.

"By the way, have you found your figurine?"

"I have." I decided there was little point in lying further.

"Thought you would. Can I see it?"

I dug into my jean pocket and drew out the box. "Here." I passed it across the table to him.

He opened the little box solemnly, then reached into the top pocket of his shirt for a pair of reading glasses and studied the figurine carefully.

"Well, well," he muttered, then drew the glasses off his nose. "Can I borrow this for a week or so?"

"Why?"

"I want to have it authenticated."

"I'm not sure . . ."

"Don't you trust me, Star?"

"Yes, I mean . . ."

"Either you do or you don't," he said with a smile. "So, Asterope, Star . . . it seems we are playing a game of cat—"

"And Mouse." With that, we both laughed and it broke the tension between us. "You can take the figurine, if you swear to return it. It's very precious to me," I said.

"I promise. Oh, and by the way, Marguerite called and said she won't be back until late tomorrow evening."

"That's okay. I'll stay until Thursday morning and go straight to work in London."

"Thanks. Right," he said, as he took a gulp of his beer, "I'm afraid I must go. I have to get the accounts together tonight to show Orlando everything he doesn't want to see tomorrow."

"Treat him gently, won't you?" I begged.

"Orlando or this?" he joked as he stowed the box in the pocket of his Barbour. "I'll do my best." He stood up and walked to the back door. "But sometimes the truth hurts." He paused. "I've enjoyed tonight. Thank you."

"That's okay."

"We'll talk soon. Good night, Star."

"Good night."

22

The following day, a woman arrived at the back door and announced she was there to collect Rory for his riding lesson. I grilled my charge on whether this was normal, but the warm hug and kiss he gave her proved she wasn't there to kidnap him. He returned red cheeked from cold and exhilaration, and as we sat together at the kitchen table I asked him to paint a picture of himself for me. He told me not to look while he painted, so I made him a couple of batches of brownies—one for the freezer, and one to eat now.

I watched his copper-colored head studiously bent over the picture, and felt a wave of protective love for this little boy who had somehow managed to creep inside my heart. Who knew what the future held for him, given what Mouse had told me. Would High Weald still be his when he was old enough to preside over it? The good news was, he hardly seemed aware of adult troubles and had an optimistic, open nature that people were drawn to.

He trusts in humanity . . .

"For you, Star." Rory nudged me as he proudly handed me the painting.

I took it from him and studied it. And found a lump in my throat. Rory had painted a picture of the two of us together in the garden: him holding my hand as I bent over to study some flowers. He had managed to catch the way that I stood, how my hair fell across my cheeks, and even the long fingers that currently held the picture.

"Rory, it's wonderful. Thank you."

"Love you, Star. Come back soon."

"I will treasure it forever," I told him, as I did my best to pull myself together. "Now, how about a brownie and some *Superman*?"

He gave me an eager thumbs-up, and we walked hand in hand toward the sitting room.

After the last bedtime story, I packed my luggage, ready to leave early the following day, hoping that Marguerite wouldn't mind giving me a lift to the station so I could be on time at the bookshop. I tried not to think of the conversation that had almost certainly ensued between the two brothers during the course of today. As I walked back downstairs, I touched the banister and tried to ingrain its solid beauty in my memory to last me until next time I was here.

I saw the lights of a car flash up the drive at ten o'clock. The front door slammed a few seconds later and I went to greet the current chatelaine of High Weald.

"Darling Star." Marguerite flung her arms around me. "Is Rory okay? Thank you so much for being here with him. Mouse tells me you've been wonderful. Is there anything to eat? I'm starving," she managed all in one breath.

"Yes, Rory's fine. Fast asleep but excited to see you. And yes, there's something keeping warm in the range."

"Great. God, I need a glass of wine. You?" Marguerite said as she headed for the fridge in the pantry.

"No thank you."

She proceeded to pour herself a hefty glass of wine and immediately slugged back a mouthful. "I feel as though I've been on the road all day. The chateau is in the middle of nowhere. And then, of course, the plane was delayed."

Despite Marguerite's protestations, she looked amazing. There was a light in her eyes and a flush to her skin that told me that wherever she had been and however long it had taken her to return, she was happy.

"How is it going in France?"

"Wonderful," Marguerite replied dreamily. "Oh, and the painting as well." She gave a soft laugh.

"Rory's talented too. He must get it from you."

"I doubt that." Marguerite raised her eyebrows. "His art is in a completely different league. His gift has come from someone else," she added as an afterthought. "You know Mouse went to see Orlando at the bookshop today?" She dug in her voluminous leather handbag and pulled out a packet of Gitanes. "Smoke?"

"Thanks." I took one from the packet and she lit it for me. It was a long time since I'd smoked a French cigarette. "Mouse said last night he was going to London."

"Orlando is distraught, of course." Marguerite took a deep drag of her cigarette and flicked ash into a hapless cactus pot that sat on the kitchen windowsill. "Apparently, he refused point-blank to even look at the accounts."

"I'm looking forward to tomorrow then," I muttered under my breath as I loaded some coq au vin onto a plate.

"To be honest, I'm very glad you're going to be with him. And so is Mouse. He swung me up from Gatwick on his way back from London. Even though it's unlikely that Orlando will do anything stupid, one just never knows. Dear me, money really is the root of all evil, isn't it?"

"Yes," I agreed, as I put the plate in front of her, then made myself some chamomile tea and sat down.

"Star, you are a hero, really. This looks scrumptious. What a delight to arrive home and have a cooked meal put in front of me." She forked up some chicken and gave me an amused look across the table. "When the bookshop is eventually sold, you'll be out of a job. You wouldn't consider coming here and helping me out domestically and with Rory?"

I could see she was half joking, but I shrugged. "Maybe."

"Of course, you're overqualified completely—please don't be insulted by the suggestion. It's just that it's so difficult to find someone I trust to take care of Rory, and Mouse eulogized over how well the two of you got on. And Hélène, who owns the chateau, has offered me another room to paint. I'd love to take the offer. It's an amazing place, and I just adore it there."

I sat in silence, knowing Marguerite had no idea that she was offering me my dream. To live there at High Weald, taking care of Rory, the house, and the gardens, and being able to cook every day for this unusual and fascinating household. I knew I had to seize the moment before Marguerite's brain flitted on to something, or *someone*, else.

"Seriously, I'd be happy to help you anytime. I love it here," I said. "And Rory."

"Really?" Marguerite cocked an eyebrow. "Goodness, do you mean it? I couldn't pay you very much, as I'm sure you already realize, but you'd get bed and board . . . I'd have to ask Orlando, but perhaps we could even share you between us? If he agrees, it would mean I could accept that commission. Hélène is eager for me to start as soon as possible . . ." Her voice trailed off and I could see the excitement of possibility in her eyes.

"I wouldn't want to let Orlando down, of course, or have him feel I'm deserting him. Especially now. But he doesn't really need me all the time."

"Orlando will want what's best for Rory, I'm sure. And besides"—Marguerite's eyes twinkled—"he mentioned that you might be related to us."

"I can't see how. Not yet, anyway," I qualified.

"Well, you've certainly managed to find a way into all of our hearts since you arrived, Star. I can't wait to find out how you fit in. Mouse must have told you how messy the Vaughan/Forbes family tree was. And still is." She stopped suddenly and gave a huge yawn, her sensual, full lips opening and then closing. There was nothing delicate about her, but her attractiveness lay in her overlarge features and the strength they implied.

"Time for bed," she said, standing up.

"I'll lock up," I offered.

"Would you really? Wonderful."

"Would it be all right for you to drop me at the station in the morning? I have to catch the eight o'clock to London."

"Mouse said he'd take you. I think he wants to brief you about Orlando. Good night, Star, and thank you again."

I was up early the next morning so I could prepare breakfast for Marguerite and Rory before I left.

I wrote a note to tell Marguerite that the sausages, bacon, and pancakes were keeping warm in the range, and directed her to the four pies that sat at the bottom of the freezer. Mouse tapped on the back door and I picked up my luggage and followed him to the car.

"Did you see Marguerite last night when she got in?" he asked me as we set off along the drive.

"Yes."

"So she must have told you that Orlando didn't take the news well."

"She did."

"Listen, Star, if there's any way you can make him see sense, I'd be very grateful. I tried to explain that the bank would step in anyway if we didn't sell the bookshop ourselves, but he literally put his hands over his ears and stormed upstairs. And then locked himself in his bedroom."

"Like a child having a tantrum."

"Exactly. Orlando may come across as sweet and gentle, but I don't know anyone more stubborn when it comes to hard decisions he doesn't want to make. The bottom line is, we have no choice. He must realize that."

"I'll do my best, but I doubt he'll listen to me."

"It's worth a shot at least. He likes you and trusts you. Have a go, anyway."

"I'll try," I said, as we approached the station.

"Could you give me a call to let me know how he is? He wasn't answering either his mobile or the landline last night."

"I will," I promised, as I got out of the Land Rover. "Thanks for the lift."

"It's the least I could do. And when you're at High Weald again, I'll tell you about the next installment of Flora's journals," he called through the window. "Get ready to be amazed. Bye, Star." And then a wide smile hit his lips and spread slowly up to his eyes, lighting up his handsome face. "Take care."

I gave him a small wave and headed into the station.

Arriving at Kensington Church Street, I was filled with trepidation as I unlocked the door to the bookshop. Not only because I had no idea what I'd find inside, but also due to the endless texts and voice mails from CeCe I'd received as my mobile had found a signal on the train. I'd been so wrapped up in High Weald, I'd completely forgotten to call and let her know I was staying on a further night. Her last message had read:

Star, if I dont here from you by morning, I'm calling the police to regester you as missing. Were are you?!

I felt dreadful, and had left her equal amounts of apologetic texts and voice mails, telling her that I was fine and I'd see her at the apartment later this evening.

I was comforted to see that nothing in the bookshop had changed, and as Orlando was never normally there when I arrived, I busied myself with my usual routine. However, when he still hadn't appeared by eleven o'clock, I began to worry. I looked to the door at the back of the shop that led to the staircase and the space above, which I'd never entered but could only presume was where Orlando lived. Of course he might be up there conducting one of his auctions . . . But as he hadn't appeared through the door yet with his cake, dismay ran through me. I knew Orlando's routine was sacrosanct.

I spent the next half hour pacing up and down, oscillating between looking through the window onto the street and hesitating to listen for the door at the back of the shop.

By noon, I was beside myself, and decided I had no choice but to see if he was upstairs. When I opened the door, it creaked at my touch, betraying my movements. I crept up the steep staircase and arrived on a small landing to find three doors in front of me. I knocked tentatively on the door to my right.

"Orlando? It's Star. Are you there?"

There was no reply, so I grasped the handle and pushed it open to find myself in a tiny kitchen containing an ancient sink, a Baby Belling oven, and a fridge whose shape was now back in vogue from fifty years ago—this was almost certainly the original version. Retreating, I performed the same routine at the next door and found an equally antique bathroom with a hideous linoleum floor, reminding me of the apartment CeCe and I had lived in before we'd moved. How Orlando managed to look so fastidiously well groomed given the facilities he had at his disposal was a mystery to me.

I turned to the last door and knocked again. "Orlando," I said, louder this time. "It's me, Star. Please, if you're in there, let me know. I'm worried about you. Everyone is," I added plaintively.

Still nothing. I tried the handle, but this time it resisted my pressure. It was obviously locked. There was a sudden thump from inside, as if a heavy book had fallen onto the floor. A bolt of fear went through me. *What if he hasn't taken his medication?*

I went at the door with more urgency. "Please, I know you're in there, Orlando. Are you okay?"

"Go away," came a muffled voice.

I felt a rush of relief. If he was well enough to be rude, I didn't need to worry.

"Okay, I will," I called through the door. "But I'm in the shop if you want to talk." I went back down the stairs, restoked the fire, and walked outside to text Mouse and let him know that, at the very least, Orlando was alive, if still refusing to come out.

At one o'clock, the time I hoped he would appear to fill his permanently demanding stomach, there was no trip of footsteps down the stairs. Grabbing my purse and keys, I left the bookshop, locking the door behind me, and headed for the shops along the road. If there was one thing that might smoke Orlando out, it was the smell of food.

Twenty minutes later, having returned with my ingredients, I went up to the tiny kitchen. The lack of utensils proved a problem, but I found one small saucepan in which I sweated off shallots and garlic for a sauce, then added cream, herbs, and a dash of brandy. There was also a misshapen frying pan for the two filets mignons, to which I also added mushrooms and halved beef tomatoes. Once everything was under control, I left the kitchen and walked across the landing, noting with pleasure that it was filled with the tempting smells of garlic and meat juices.

I knocked on Orlando's door. "Lunch is ready," I called through it gaily. "I'm plating it up now and taking it downstairs. Perhaps you could bring the wine—it's chilling in the fridge." Then I arranged the steaks and their accompaniments on our plates, and stood at the top of the staircase.

"Don't be too long now, nothing worse than a lukewarm filet mignon," I said, then walked carefully down the stairs with my bait. Approximately three minutes passed before I heard his tread on the stairs. And a sad, disheveled Orlando lookalike appeared in the doorway, holding a bottle of Sancerre and two wineglasses. His hair was awry, and the shadow of unshaven stubble crossed his chin. He was wearing the paisley dressing gown I'd seen at High Weald, and his peacock-blue embroidered slippers.

"Is the door locked?" he asked me as he glanced at it anxiously.

"Of course. It's lunchtime," I replied calmly.

He shuffled forward, and for the first time in my life, I saw for myself the cliché of someone aging years overnight.

"I hope you like the steak. It's as rare as you can get, and the sauce on the side is herb," I encouraged, sounding even to myself like a nurse speaking to a child.

"Thank you, Star," he mumbled as he set down the Sancerre and two glasses. Then he levered himself into the chair as though his bones ached.

Giving a huge sigh, he garnered the energy to reach for the bottle and pour a generous measure into each glass.

"To you," he toasted. "At least I have one friend and ally."

I watched him slug back the contents of the glass and immediately refill it, and wondered anxiously what a drunken Orlando would be like.

"Eat up," I urged.

It was the only time in our short history that I put my knife and fork together before he did. He ate like an ailing patient, cutting the fillet into minuscule bites and then chewing each one endlessly.

"The food is perfect, as you know very well, Star. It's me that isn't . . ." His voice petered out as he put another tiny piece of steak into his mouth. Swallowing, he took a vast gulp of wine and gave me the shadow of a smile as he put his cutlery down. "Today, even food defeats me. You've heard from my brother, I presume."

"Yes."

"How can he? I mean . . . the cruelty! This"—he swept his arms around the bookshop—"is my world. My only world."

"I know."

"He says we will be bankrupt, or, more accurately, the bank will rupture all we have unless we sell. Can you believe it?"

"Sadly, yes, I can."

"But how? This . . . *bank* person can't presume to steal what is ours? Surely my brother is exaggerating?"

The expression on his face was so heartbreaking I had to swallow hard before I could answer him. "I'm afraid not. Apparently, there are debts—"

"Yes, but they are nothing compared to the price this building would raise if they sold it. They must realize they have surety."

"I think the problem is that the banks are not in particularly good shape either. They're"—I knew I had to choose my words carefully—"nervous too. The world economic situation isn't that healthy just now."

"Are you telling me that the sale of Arthur Morston Books—not to mention my *soul*—is going to solve their crisis? Goodness, Star, I expected more of you than this. I thought you were on my side."

"I am, Orlando, truly. But sometimes life just doesn't work out like you want it to. It's horrible, but true. Life just isn't fair. And from what I gather, it's the farm as well that is suffering."

"What?!" Orlando's pale complexion turned from pink to red to purple. "Is that what he told you?"

"Yes. He needs to buy new machinery to give the farm a chance of earning its keep."

I wondered then if Orlando would actually explode with rage. His sweet features were contorted into such anger and derision it was hard to think how a physical body could control that amount of emotion.

"HA! Ha ha ha! And did he perchance tell you why the farm has fallen on hard times?"

"No."

"So he didn't mention the fact that he rarely came out of his bedroom for the first three years after Annie died? That he let the entire acreage go to rack and ruin because he was unable to get up, drag himself downstairs, and speak to the farm manager, who waited for him so many days and weeks with the unpaid bills? Until all the suppliers refused to provide the basics of what any farm needs, and the manager had no choice but to resign? Animals died under my brother's watch, Miss Star, through malnutrition and negligence. Not to mention the crops that were left to fester for years until even they could no longer find the will to live . . . Let me tell you now, this situation is almost completely of my brother's making. Not mine."

"Surely," I said eventually, for once venturing into the silence as Orlando topped up his wineglass, "you understand why?"

"Of course I do. He had lost the love of his life. I am not unsympathetic to such a plight. But"—his face darkened once more—"there are things that *you* don't know, and I am not at liberty to tell you, that are—in my book at least—unforgivable. There comes a point in every human being's life when one must forget one's own tragedy and step up to the mark for those who need you. My brother wallowed in self-pity for years and that's the truth. We all did our best to show him love and support, but even the softest and most understanding of hearts can harden when one watches a person intent on destroying himself."

Orlando stood up then, hands shrouded in his robe pockets, and began to pace.

"I can assure you, Miss Star, that his family supported him in every way possible. As you well know, people choose to become a victim or a hero. He chose the first option. And now, because of that, I . . . and *this*"—he indicated the room again as dust motes floated like tiny angels around him in the weak October sunlight—"are the sacrificial lambs."

With that, he sank to the floor and wept.

"God, what a mess . . . ," I heard him mutter to himself in a high voice. "We are all a mess. Every single one of us."

Kneeling down beside him, I tentatively put my arms around his shoulders. He resisted at first, then nestled into my embrace, and I rocked him like I would a small child.

"You don't understand what this means to me. You don't understand . . ."

"Orlando, I do. And if I was able to, I'd let you stay here forever. I promise."

"You're a good person, Star. You're on my side, aren't you?"

His agonized eyes looked up at me.

"Of course I am. And when you are calmer, perhaps I can tell you of some ideas I've had."

"Really? I'll do anything, anything . . ."

Of course, I *had* some ideas, but they were rational ones that took the circumstances into consideration, and I doubted they would appeal to Orlando.

"Well, I'm all ears." He pulled away from me and scrambled to standing, looking as if I were about to offer him the golden fleece. "How about I go upstairs and ablute? I'm currently *déshabillé* and I revolt even myself," he admitted, looking down at his state of dress. He went toward the plates, but I shook my head.

"Today is unusual and I will clear up."

"So be it." He walked toward the back door, then turned in afterthought. "Thank you for everything, Miss Star. I knew you'd be the one person I could rely on. And when I come back down, I'll tell you a secret too."

Then he stood there and giggled just as Rory did.

"What?" I couldn't help but ask.

"I know where they are." Orlando grinned, then turned and disappeared through the door.

I waited until I heard him reach the top of the stairs, then went to clear away the remnants of our lunch and followed him up, feeling that another bridge had been crossed by the fact he'd allowed me into his private enclave. As I washed up the plates in the tiny sink, I mulled over his parting words. I almost certainly knew what Orlando was talking about—it could only be Flora MacNichol's journals. I felt torn in two by the warring brothers.

Back downstairs, I turned the CLOSED sign to OPEN, as it was well past two o'clock, then stood in the center of the room, studying the bookcases. For I *knew* I'd seen a set of books—covered in brown silk—as I'd taken another off the shelf next to them. I also knew Orlando and his playful mind. Where better to camouflage what he'd taken from Home Farm than in a place that contained thousands of the same?

My eyes scanned the shelves, and then I closed them, trying to place the exact book I'd pulled off the shelf and the location of it . . .

And there it was. As clear as a virtual file pulled from my memory bank.

"*Orlando*," I muttered, walking toward the English section and casting my eyes to three rows from the bottom. There they were on the shelf marked "British Fiction, 1900–1950."

Bending down, I pulled out a slim volume, opening it at the first page.

The Journal of Flora MacNichol

1910

I snapped the book shut and replaced it on the shelf as I heard heavy footfall on the stairs. Orlando was taking the steps faster than usual, and I was only just by the fire, stoking it, before he slammed into the room.

"Feel better now?" I asked him calmly as I added some more coal.

There was a pause that went on for so long I had to turn and see why. His face was purple again, and his arms were crossed as he advanced toward me.

"I'll beg you not to patronize me further. Given that you had calmed me, I just took a call from my brother. He stated that you have agreed to take a job as a housekeeper-cum-nanny at High Weald."

"I—"

"Don't lie to me, Star! Did you or did you not agree to the proposition that was put to you?"

"Marguerite was desperate because she has an ongoing commission and so I said that I would—"

"Abandon me and turn your coat to work with the enemy?!"

"I said I would go there sometimes and help Marguerite by looking after Rory! That's all. She said she would ask you if you'd mind if she borrowed me occasionally when the shop wasn't busy. This has nothing to do with Mouse."

"Good God, woman! It has *everything* to do with my brother. He does all her dirty work, including calling me just now on the pretext of making sure I was okay. And then announcing that you would be needed at High Weald from the weekend."

"Orlando, I really have no idea what you're talking about."

"No, I'm sure you don't. And there I was, thinking you were on my side . . ."

"I am, Orlando. Really."

"No you're not. Can't you see it suits him? But it doesn't suit *me*!"

He paused and took some deep and much-needed breaths.

"I'm sorry," I said helplessly.

"And I'm more so," he said as he stared at me, anger gone and an expression in his eyes that I couldn't quite decipher. "Well, off you go."

"Off I go where?"

"Trip home to whatever rabbit hutch you live in and pack your bags for High Weald. Marguerite and Mouse need you."

"Please, I'm your employee, my loyalty lies with you. I love it here . . ."

"Sorry, but if you expect me to fight for you after your betrayal, I won't."

He gave a theatrical shrug, closed his arms tighter across his chest, and turned away from me like a sulky little boy.

"I won't go to High Weald. I want to stay here."

"And I am dismissing you."

"That's not fair!"

"As you said yourself only today, Star, life isn't fair."

"Yes, but—"

"Star, it has been blindingly obvious since the moment I made the mistake of taking you into the hornet's nest that you fell in love at first sight with High Weald and the more garrulous members of my family. Who am I to hold you from them? It's a siren call, dear girl, and you have fallen for it, hook, line, and sinker. Fly away, but expect to get stung."

If his words weren't so painful, I would have laughed at the Edwardian melodrama of the situation. Tears threatened behind my eyes.

"Okay," I said, walking past him to my luggage and rucksack. "Good-bye, Orlando. I'm so sorry."

I continued to the door in silence and had just laid my hand on the knob when he spoke again.

"At least Rory will benefit from your tender attentions. I'm glad of that. Good-bye, Miss Star."

I pulled open the door and walked out into the foggy street, the sky already darkening. My feet carried me automatically across the road toward the bus stop. The bus stop where I'd first set eyes on Arthur Morston Books.

I stood by it, looking back toward the shop, and there in the shadows, behind the maps laid out in the window, I saw the shape of a man standing watching me.

I turned my head, unable to bear Orlando's silent derision.

23

Thankfully, the apartment was empty when I arrived home. Dumping my luggage in our shared bedroom that felt even more suffocating after spending the past five nights alone, I went to take a long shower. As the piping-hot water poured over my body, I let not only my tears but my voice flow and I howled, wondering how on earth, in the space of twenty-four hours, I'd managed to mess it all up.

I stepped out and wrapped myself in a fluffy white towel, and I knew the answer. I'd been greedy. And selfish. Like a woman who had fallen passionately in love, I hadn't seen the ramifications of my actions, being far too hungry for my prey.

Which, as Orlando had so succinctly put it, was High Weald. And its occupants . . .

Of course, I should never have said that I'd take any employment that I'd been offered there, especially under the recent circumstances. No, I should have said I would speak to Orlando—who, after all, was the person who had originally introduced me to the wonderland—before I could agree to anything.

But I hadn't. And here I was, once more unemployed. Because if I went to High Weald now—the hornet's nest, as Orlando had described it—the best friend I had ever made in my life would see me as a traitor. And I just couldn't bear the thought of that.

As I emptied my rucksack to find my hairbrush, with a sinking heart I saw that the brass keys to the bookshop were still tucked into the inside pocket. I remembered that glorious moment only a few weeks ago when Orlando had pressed the keys into my hand with a smile, and quickly dismissed it from my memory. I decided defiantly he could either fetch them himself or I would drop them off if I was in the area. But I certainly wouldn't go out of my way to return them.

I padded downstairs to make myself a cup of tea and found the normally pristine kitchen in chaos. Five days' worth of plates had been dumped into the sink—even though a dishwasher sat below the worktop next to it. The floor was covered with crumbs and splashes, and when I looked for a tea bag in the caddy to put in a mug that I'd rinsed out, I found it was empty.

"Christ, CeCe!" I murmured angrily, searching desperately through the cupboards to satisfy my craving. In the end, I dunked an herbal tea bag into the boiling water and, leaving the kitchen as it was, went outside onto my terrace. Luckily, most things on it were either in hibernation or not in need of water, due to the heavy dew. I noted the camellia needed to come in before it suffered from frostbite, but given its size and weight, I felt too weak to drag it, so tonight it would have to do with a dustbin bag placed over its delicate flowers.

Retreating indoors, and deciding that, as it was gone six o'clock, it was okay to have a glass of wine, I poured myself one and sat in the center of one of the enormous cream sofas. As I looked around me at the perfect, sterile space—the complete opposite of everything High Weald represented—more tears filled my eyes.

For I knew that I belonged in neither world—not here in the one my sister had created, which contained little or nothing of me, nor at High Weald.

I was in bed when I heard the crash of the front door a couple of hours later. I'd left CeCe a note written in big letters on the fridge so she would see it. I'd said I'd come down with a horrible cold and had gone to sleep in the spare room so I didn't infect her. As expected, having heard her call out for me as she arrived, I traced her footsteps aurally into the kitchen, where she'd normally find me. There was a pause as I pictured her reading the note, then the sound of her climbing the stairs. There was a knock on the door.

"Star? You okay? Can I come in?"

"Yes," I croaked pathetically.

The door opened and the shadow of CeCe appeared in the chink of light.

"Don't come too close. I'm in a horrible state." I coughed as throatily as I could manage.

"Poor you. Can I get you anything?"

"No. Taken drugs."

"If you need me in the night, you know where I am."

"I do."

"Try and sleep. Maybe now you're home, you'll feel better."

"Yes. Thanks, Cee."

Through my half-opened left eye, I could see she was still hovering at the door, watching me.

"Missed you," she said.

"Missed you too."

The door closed, and I realized that was another lie I'd uttered today. I rolled over and begged the heavens for sleep. And thank God, He eventually answered my prayer.

I awoke the following morning, feeling as drugged up as I'd told CeCe I was last night. Stumbling out of bed, I saw a note pushed under the door.

Left for collige. Call if you need me. Love u. Cee.

I walked down the stairs and noted the kitchen had been tidied and looked as pristine as it usually did, which made me feel guilty for lying to her last night. I switched on the kettle, then remembered we'd run out of tea bags.

Wandering into the sitting room, I peered through the glass at a day that appeared considerably brighter than the one before it.

As I stared out of the window my thoughts flew unbidden to High Weald and I wondered if Rory was awake yet, and what he would have for breakfast now that I was no longer there to make it for him. *Come on, Star, he's with his mother, he's happy . . .*

And yet—maybe it was vanity rather than instinct—I *felt* him missing me.

No.

"That is not your life. They are not your family. Rory is not your child," I told myself out loud.

I walked upstairs and for want of anything to fill the emptiness, I adopted Orlando's policy of routine and took another shower, after which

I dressed and went downstairs to sit at the desk. Today, I told myself, I would try to begin my novel. Do something for *me*, to start forging my own destiny. So I picked up my notebook and pen and began to write.

A few hours later, I came to and saw that a fiery dusk was already descending. Putting down my pen and massaging the fingers that had clenched it so tightly, I stood up to get a glass of water. I looked at my mobile and saw there were a number of texts and two voice mails, which I studiously ignored, until both curiosity and fear that something had happened to Orlando—or perhaps Rory—melted my resolve.

"Hi, Star, it's Mouse here. I don't know whether Orlando passed on the message, but Marguerite is off to France this weekend. She said you might be willing to take care of Rory and the house while she's gone. Can you get back to me as soon as possible? The landline at High Weald isn't working—something to do with an unpaid bill—so she asked me to call you. Thanks."

The next message was from Shanthi, asking how and where I was, and saying that it would be great to meet up soon. The mellow sound of her voice comforted me, and I made a mental note to call her back and arrange a day and time. I checked my text messages and saw two more from an obviously desperate Mouse. With Orlando currently off the scene, the job of taking care of Rory would inevitably fall to him. I was about to put the mobile down when Mouse rang again. This time, I decided I must answer it.

"Star, thank God. I was wondering if I had the wrong number. I tried calling Orlando, but he isn't picking up either."

"No, he wouldn't be."

"Did you get my voice mail and my texts earlier?"

"Yes, I did."

"And can you come to High Weald next week?"

"No, I'm afraid I can't."

"Right." There was a pause on the line. "Can I ask you why not? Marguerite said you seemed pretty keen on the idea of working for her sometimes."

"Yes, but only with Orlando's agreement. And he didn't agree."

"Surely he can spare you for a few days for the sake of his nephew?"

"Yes, he can. He sacked me yesterday after your call to him. He called me a traitor," I added abruptly.

"God." Mouse gave a long sigh at the other end of the line. "I'm sorry, Star. This isn't your mess at all, and we shouldn't have involved you in it. I wasn't thinking before I called him . . ."

"Yes, well, that's the way things are."

"And you won't consider coming here, even for the weekend?"

"Sorry, but I can't. Orlando has been so kind to me. I don't want to betray that kindness."

"No, I see that. Ah, well . . . you're probably better off out of our crazy family anyway. Rory will be devastated—we're all getting bored with his eulogies about you."

"Send him my love."

"I will, of course. And maybe, when the dust has settled, you might change your mind."

"I don't think so. Sorry."

"Okay. I'll leave you alone. Just one thing, though. Can you give me your address so that I can at least send you on what you're owed for taking care of Rory last week?"

"It really doesn't matter. I was happy to do it."

"It certainly matters to me, so if you wouldn't mind . . ."

I gave him our address and he said he would put a check in the post.

"Right, well then, my troubled relatives and I will leave you in peace. Perhaps Orlando will calm down and go down on bended knee to beg you to come back."

"I doubt it. You told me how stubborn he is, and I've hurt him deeply."

"No, Star, I have. This is all my fault. Anyway, good luck with finding some other employment, and keep in touch. Bye now."

"Bye."

The line went dead. And despite my firm stance, it felt like the ending of a beautiful love affair. With a house, a family, and what may or may not have been my *own* past. I swallowed hard to prevent the tears, then went to the kitchen to prepare supper for CeCe and myself. Just the two of us once more.

As I sliced the vegetables for a stir fry far more aggressively than was needed, I realized that, on every level, I was back to square one. While I was waiting for CeCe to arrive, I only hoped that my feigning illness would dissuade her from a delayed attack of the sulks over my forgetting to tell her I was staying on at High Weald. I then texted Shanthi—I had to start somewhere with a life of my own—and invited her over for a cup of coffee at her convenience. She texted back immediately and said she'd be delighted to pop in at four tomorrow. I was at least happy that this gave me a great excuse to bake a cake—something other than lemon drizzle, I thought morosely as I heard the front door open and close.

"Hi, Sia, how are you feeling?"

"Much better, thank you."

She frowned as she studied my face. "You look very pale still."

"I'm always pale, Cee," I chuckled. "Promise, I'm fine. How are you?"

"Oh, okay, sort of," she said, and I knew she wasn't. "Want a beer?" she asked me as she went to the fridge to reach for one.

"No thanks."

"How was nursery-maiding?" she said, coming to sit down opposite me.

"Fine, thanks. Rory's a sweetie."

"Will you be going again?"

"No. It was a one-off."

"I'm glad. Goodness, Star, you have a first-class degree in English literature, speak two languages fluently, and are the most intelligent person I know. You've got to stop selling yourself short."

It was CeCe's oft-repeated refrain and I really wasn't interested in pursuing it.

"What about you? What's up?"

"How did you know something was?" CeCe came over and folded her arms around me. "Thank God I've got you," she sighed heavily.

"So what is it?"

"It's hard to explain, but it's like being back at school, with all the other students bonding and me feeling like I just don't fit in. Actually, it's worse than school, because I don't have you there. I try not to mind, but I really thought that a group of artists would be different. But they're not. And it hurts, Sia, it really does."

"Of course it does."

"The tutors criticize my work nonstop. I mean, I know that's what they're paid to do, but the odd compliment wouldn't go amiss occasionally. At the moment, I feel completely demoralized and on the verge of jacking it all in."

"But I thought the whole point was the show at the end of the year? That the college shipped in eminent art critics and collectors to see your work? Surely, however tough it is at the moment, you can't give up on that?"

"I don't want to, Sia, but Pa always said that life is too short to be miserable."

"He also said we must never give up," I cautioned. It struck me that we sisters could adapt Pa's many words of wisdom however we saw fit now that he was gone.

"Yes." CeCe bit her lip and I was surprised to see the beginnings of tears in her eyes. "I really miss him. Thought I'd cope, but there's a hole, you know?"

"I do," I said softly. "Cee, you haven't been there long. Why don't you give it more time and see how it goes?"

"I'll do my best, but I'm struggling, Sia, I really am. Especially with you away so much."

"Well, I'm back now."

CeCe went up to take a shower and I began to add the ingredients of the stir fry to a wok. And thought that perhaps *both* of us were destined to be outsiders—two lone wolves with no one else but each other. However much I had recently tried to escape, history and literature were peppered with stories of unmarried sisters who had sought comfort from each other. Maybe I needed to surrender and accept my fate.

We ate dinner together, and for the first time in a while, CeCe's presence comforted rather than irritated me. And as she showed me photos on her phone of her latest paintings from college, which I genuinely thought were the best I'd seen her produce for a long time, I thought how a change of perception and acceptance might alter everything.

We went to bed early that night, both of us exhausted for very different reasons.

Perhaps we're more similar than I care to believe, I thought as I stared up at the moon through the window. We were both afraid of the cruel world outside our comfortable nest.

24

For reasons probably to do with the old chestnut called pride, I had not told CeCe I'd been sacked from my job. So, the next day, I got up with her, knowing she left half an hour before me, and went through the usual morning routine.

"Have a good day," CeCe called as she left.

"You too." I waved as I pretended to slurp my coffee down in a hurry.

Once the door was closed, I trawled through my cookbooks to find a cake recipe to make for Shanthi. I decided to plump for something typically English—a malt loaf—but with some added spice as a nod to her heritage. Then I went out to the supermarket to buy the ingredients and some tea bags.

The doorbell rang at exactly four, and I pressed the buzzer so Shanthi could enter the building. The fact that someone had taken the trouble to visit me warmed my heart. As she emerged from the lift, I was waiting for her on the doorstep.

"Star!" She threw her arms around me and hugged me to her. "It's been too long."

"Yes, it has. Come in."

"Wow!" she said as she surveyed the enormous sitting room. "What a place. You didn't tell me you were a trust-fund kid."

"I'm not really. My sister bought this. I'm just a tenant."

"Lucky you," she said with a smile as she sat down.

"Tea? Coffee?"

"Actually, I'm going to have water. Or any herbal blend you might have lurking in the depths of your cupboards. I'm on a fast, you see."

I looked at the malt loaf, plump and fresh, just waiting to be devoured, and sighed.

"So, how have you been, *ma petite étoile*?"

"You speak French?"

"No," she said with a laugh, "that's about the only phrase I know, and it happens to contain your name."

"I'm well," I said as I took over the tray with her tea, the malt loaf, and a pat of fresh butter to spread on it. Orlando's afternoon cake habit had stuck and I would have some anyway.

"What have you been up to?"

"I've been working in a bookshop."

"Which one?"

"Oh, one that you'd never have heard of. It sells rare books and we don't get many customers."

"But you're enjoying it?"

"I love it. Or at least I did."

"You're not working there anymore?"

"No. I was asked to leave."

"Star, I'm so sorry. What happened?"

I debated whether to tell her. After all, I hadn't even managed to tell CeCe yet. But then, Shanthi had a way of drawing me out. And if I was honest, that was why I'd been so eager to see her. I needed to talk to someone.

"It's a long story."

"Then I'm all ears," she said, as she watched me munching on a slice of spicy malt loaf. "Okay," she added, "I surrender. That cake looks absolutely delicious."

After I'd cut her a slice, I began to tell her of my odyssey into the Vaughan/Forbes family, Shanthi only occasionally interrupting to double-check she'd got the facts right, until I was at the denouement of my sorry story.

"So, there we are." I shrugged. "Once again, I'm unemployed."

"They sound absolutely fascinating," Shanthi breathed. "I always think these old English families have such character."

"You could say that, yes."

"And you might somehow be related to them?"

"If I am, I shall never find out now. I doubt I'll hear from any of them again."

"I absolutely think you will, and very soon. Especially one particular person."

"Orlando?" I asked her eagerly.

"No, Star. Not Orlando. But if you can't see who it might be, then I'm not going to tell you. And . . . it also sounds as though they're hiding something."

"Does it?"

"Yes. Something just doesn't make sense. The house sounds amazing, though," she added.

"It was. I loved being there. Even though my sister told me they were using me and I was worth more . . . I like being domestic and looking after people. Do you think that's wrong?"

"You mean in the days of all of us females having to be career women and smash our way through the glass ceiling?"

"Yes."

"I don't think it's wrong at all, Star."

"Well, I like the simple things. I love cooking, and gardening, and keeping a nice home . . . and I loved taking care of Rory. It made me happy."

"Then that's what you must aim for, Star. Of course, you'd need one further ingredient to make the magic happen."

"What is that?"

"Don't you know what it is?"

I looked at her and I did. "Yes, it's love."

"Exactly. Which, as you know, can come in many different shapes and forms; it doesn't have to be the traditional man/woman scenario. Look at me: I have a pretty continuous stream of lovers of both sexes."

I blushed, despite myself. Shanthi studied my reaction with a smile on her lips.

"Do you find talking about sex uncomfortable, Star?"

"I . . . no . . . I mean . . ."

"Then you won't mind me asking—because I've been dying to since I met you—whether you prefer men or women? Or, like me, both?"

I stared at her, horrified, wishing that the squashy sofa cushions could swallow me up, or that some natural disaster would occur now so I wouldn't have to face these questions.

"I'm straight," I mumbled eventually. "That is, I like men."

"Really?" Shanthi nodded sagely. "Then I was wrong. Don't worry, I shall cross you off my list of possible conquests." She laughed gently.

"Yes," I muttered, knowing my face was bright red. "More tea?"

Whether she wanted it or not, I was going to put the kettle on. Anything to get away from her interrogative gaze.

"You're so beautiful, Star, yet you seem totally unaware of it. The physical self isn't shameful, you know. It's a gift from the gods, and it's free. You're young and lovely. You should enjoy the pleasure your body can bring you."

I stood in the kitchen, unable to return to the sofa and have those eyes upon me. For I simply could not continue this conversation. I asked then—no, *begged*—for divine intervention in whatever shape or form. And to my astonishment, a few seconds later, it came with the sound of the buzzer.

Not caring if the person standing outside the door was an ax murderer or, more likely, CeCe, who would often ring to save her having to root through her bag for the key card, I picked up the receiver.

"Hello?"

"Star? It's me, Mouse. I was just passing, and thought that rather than posting your check, I'd hand it to you in person."

"Oh."

"Perhaps you can come downstairs and collect it. There doesn't seem to be a post box outside."

He was right, the developers had forgotten to install one, and the doorman was always conspicuously absent whenever I walked into the lobby. After an agony of indecision, my fear of further chat with Shanthi eventually won.

"Come up," I said. "It's the third floor, the door directly opposite the lift."

"Thanks."

"Sorry," I said as I wandered over to the sofas and hovered uncomfortably. "A friend decided to pop in."

"I must be going anyway," she said, standing up.

I walked her to the door, unable to hide my relief at her swift exit.

"It was lovely to see you, Star. I'm sorry if I embarrassed you."

"It's fine." I could hear the whir of the ascending lift and realized I'd have to introduce them to each other.

"Well, good-bye, my little Star." Shanthi put her arms around me and clasped me to her generous chest. Which was how Mouse found us as the lift doors opened.

"Sorry," he said, as Shanthi released me. "Not interrupting anything, am I?"

"Not at all," Shanthi said with a pleasant smile, "I'm just on my way out. Star is all yours." She walked past us both and stepped into the lift. "What's your name by the way?" she asked him as she pressed the button to take her down.

"Mouse."

"Ha! Told you, Star." Shanthi gave a thumbs-up from behind his back before the doors closed, and I heard her throaty laugh echoing through the building as the lift descended.

"What was the joke?" he inquired as I led him into the apartment. "I didn't get it."

"Don't worry, nor did I," I said with feeling.

"She looked like an interesting character. Friend of yours?"

"Yes. Can I offer you a cup of tea or coffee?"

"You don't have a beer, do you?"

"I do, yes."

"This place is amazing," Mouse commented, as he strode to the windows, where the lights of London were twinkling in the deepening dusk beneath us. "Now I know for certain that you're not a gold-digger who's after High Weald. Who needs that moldering heap when you have this."

"It's my sister that owns it," I explained for the second time that day.

"Well," he said as I handed him the beer, "here's to rich relatives. Wish I had some lying about," he added as he took a slug and I led him to sit down on the sofa. He eyed the malt loaf hungrily. "May I? I haven't eaten all day."

"Of course." I cut him a slice and smothered it in butter.

"This is absolutely delicious, as is everything you cook. You have a real gift."

"Thank you," I mumbled, wondering meanly where this charm offensive was leading, and what it was he wanted. Because nobody just "passed" our front door. In fact, one needed a map and compass to find the entrance.

"Before I forget, here you go." He pulled an envelope from the pocket of his Barbour. "I hope you think that's enough. I also added two weeks' wages for the bookshop to it."

"You didn't need to, really," I said, fully aware of his current financial plight. "How's Orlando?"

"Belligerent and noncommunicative . . . which is the reason I came up to London. I hadn't heard from him since I called him about you. Obviously I was concerned. The shop was locked when I arrived this afternoon. But luckily I have another set of keys. He's still holed up in that bedroom of his and wouldn't let me in there. The only way I could get him to speak to me was by threatening to call the police and break the door down to see if he was still alive."

"Nothing's changed then."

"No. I also went to see a commercial property agent to start the process of putting the building on the market. Hopefully, if the bank sees we're making moves to sell, and they'll be repaid what we owe, they'll hold off grabbing it themselves for the time being."

"Did you tell Orlando that?"

"God, no, I thought he might throw himself out of his attic window if I did. It's such a shame he won't have you back. He's just sitting there, brooding all day and night. Well, he'll get over it eventually. We all have to from losing things we love."

"But it can take some time. Can't it?" I said, wondering if the remark would hit home. "After all, it's only been a few days."

"Point taken," Mouse responded, and, from the expression on his face, I could see he was deciding whether to take offense or not. Frankly, I didn't care if he did.

"You're right," he said after a long pause. "Now, listen, Star, there's another reason I've come to see you, and it's got nothing to do with me or my family. It's about you."

"Me?"

"Yes. After all, the reason you first entered the bookshop was to find out more about your own past. And now we've all messed your life around, through no fault of your own, might I add. So I thought it was only fair to come here and offer to tell you what more I know about Flora MacNichol. And at least explain to you where I believe that cat came from originally."

"I see."

"It's at Sotheby's, by the way. I dropped it off earlier today. They'll give me a call once they've made their inquiries, but they're pretty sure it is a Fabergé. And I should tell you that, if it's authenticated, it's worth a fortune. Even a tiny figurine like 'Panther' can go at auction for hundreds of thousands."

"Really?" I was amazed.

"Yes, really. It seems like you may well have just realized your own inheritance. Now . . ." Mouse pulled a number of slim silk-covered volumes out of another of his capacious pockets. I saw they were identical to the ones I'd found on the shelf in the bookshop. "This one"—he tapped it with his fingertips—"continues from where my transcription left off. One way and another, I haven't had time to do the same with this, but I have read it. Star, do you want me to tell you more? Put it this way, it's an absolutely fascinating story. With what one might call a dramatic denouement."

I hesitated. Yesterday, and this morning, I'd made such an effort to put the last few weeks behind me and march on determinedly into a future of my own making. Was being dragged back again to High Weald and its long-dead residents a good thing? If a connection *was* established between us, I would be inextricably linked to them for the rest of my life. And I was no longer sure that I wanted that.

"Okay then," I said eventually, knowing that I'd kick myself if I refused.

"It might take some time, though. Flora's writing is quite difficult to decipher, so I'll read it out to you, as I'm used to her hand now. We won't be disturbed, will we?" he asked, opening the journal.

"Not for a while, anyway."

"Good. Then I'll begin."

FLORA

London

December 1909

25

The Keppels had not been invited to attend the wedding of Archie and Aurelia, which was being held at High Weald, the Vaughan seat in Kent. This omission had surprised Flora, given that they seemed so popular in London. Mrs. Keppel herself had taken it in good part.

"Frankly, we hardly know the Vaughans," she said with an airy wave of her hand. "They tend to stick to the country set."

Flora accepted her explanation, although she knew that Mrs. Keppel had a country residence in Kent and was presumably a part of the "set."

A motorcar had kindly been put at Flora's disposal for the weekend of the wedding. Sitting in the backseat as Freed drove her out of London, she wondered how she could face the next forty-eight hours. She had dreamed up dozens of plans to make it impossible to attend the wedding—from standing at the top of the stairs and trying to pluck up the courage to throw herself down so she could plead a broken leg, to standing in the park as the chill November wind and rain cascaded over her, wishing for pneumonia. It seemed that, physically at least, she was indestructible. So here she was, on her way to her sister's wedding to Archie Vaughan, the man she loved.

And the thing that made it worse was the fact that she would have to see High Weald and Archie's beloved gardens, which he'd described to her with so much passion in the summer. Yet she could not let herself forget that it was *she* who had set the events in motion.

Flora remembered her mother's face, so animated at the engagement party that Aunt Charlotte had hosted for the happy couple at her London house. There was a genuine sense of relief that the sacrifice of Esthwaite Hall had been worth it. Her parents were already in situ at High Weald, ready for the wedding celebrations.

There were eight bridesmaids in all—although Elizabeth, Archie's sister, would be absent. She had sailed for Ceylon with her new husband in November, and an heir to the tea plantation was already on its way.

In forty-eight hours, it will all be over and I will be traveling home, Flora thought determinedly as suburbia disappeared and plowed fields and bare winter hedgerows began to appear on either side of the road.

An hour later, Flora spotted a number of tall, fragile chimneys peeking through the skeletons of the trees. As the motorcar turned into the drive, a ravishing old red-brick building appeared in front of her.

"I do not want to love this house," Flora said to herself as she gazed at the mellow façade. The charmingly uneven windows had partially surrendered to their age, the hinges and frames crooked and bowed in places, like elderly people. Even though the day was icy cold, the sun was shining, setting the frost on the perfectly clipped box hedges aglitter. It was like the entrance to fairyland.

"We're here, Miss MacNichol," said Freed, who then duly walked to the back door of the motorcar and opened it for her.

Flora stepped out and gazed at the large arched oak doors with the trepidation of a prisoner about to enter a jail. The doors opened as she walked across the gravel and Aurelia appeared through them.

"Darling! You're here. I do hope the journey wasn't too tiring."

"It was barely two hours, it's so close to London."

"Yet a world away, don't you think? And so much gentler than the surroundings of Esthwaite. Now," she said, tucking Flora's arm in hers, "as there's much to do and so many people arriving, I thought we ought to pretend we aren't here just for a while, so I can have you all to myself."

They entered a low-ceilinged hall, where a fire burned brightly in the grate, spreading its warmth across the well-worn stone floor.

"Come up with me and we'll hide in my room," said Aurelia with a giggle, pulling her sister up a wide wooden staircase, bedecked with heavy Tudor carvings. Aurelia led her along a corridor and opened a door at the end of it, revealing a small room containing two single brass beds. Its walls had the same rich oak paneling that gave the rest of the house a comforting warmth, even in the chill winter light that streamed through the narrow windows.

"This is where I will sleep tonight. I was hoping you would stay here too in the other bed."

"Of course I'll stay here, if you wish me to," Flora answered.

"Thank you. It all feels rather overwhelming, as you can imagine. And I've hardly seen Archie since we arrived. Both of us have been so busy . . ."

Flora saw her sister's expression darken for a few seconds, then Aurelia recovered herself and smiled brightly.

"So firstly, do tell me everything you've been up to in London. From what I hear, you've been quite the social butterfly."

Flora gave Aurelia a brief history of the endless dances, dinner parties, and soirées she'd attended over the past two months.

"Yes, yes"—Aurelia flicked the detail away with her hand—"but what I *really* want to hear about is Freddie Soames."

"Oh yes, Freddie." Flora rolled her eyes. "He's a leading light on the London social circuit."

"I know *that*, but I want to hear about the two of you."

"There is no 'the two of us.'"

"Really, Flora, I may be tucked away in the country, but even I've heard the gossip."

"He is nothing to me, really, Aurelia."

"I think you are being coy. London is awash with how he is courting you. Everyone is saying he is about to propose."

"London can say what it likes."

"Flora, he's a viscount, no less! And will one day be an earl!"

"That's as may be. But I will never marry for a title, you know that."

"Not even for vast tracts of fertile Hampshire land and a tiara? You do know he's coming tomorrow? He's a distant cousin to the Vaughans—once removed, whatever that means."

"I didn't know. But then, I've thrown all his letters on the fire."

"Flora! Almost every woman who came out with me only married their current husband because they couldn't have Freddie. Not only is he rich, but he's devilishly handsome to boot. And there he is, at your feet!"

The devil is an apt comparison, thought Flora with a sigh.

"He refused the wedding invitation when we first sent it out," Aurelia continued. "Then, when he heard you were my chief bridesmaid, he wrote to Lady Vaughan to accept. Are you sure you're not a little in love with him?"

"Absolutely."

"Oh, well, I am disappointed. I was hoping you were in the midst of a full-scale love affair and I'd be the first to know all the details."

"There are simply no details to report."

"Well, could you pretend? At least for tomorrow."

"No," said Flora with a laugh. "Now, may I see your wedding dress?"

That evening, much to Flora's relief, the groom had been banished from the house and was staying with the Sackville-Wests at Knole, situated not far from High Weald. Supper was provided for the bridal party in the long dining room, where hundreds of candles had been lit in the chandeliers. Flora had already met the other bridesmaids in London, and as socially adept as she had become on such occasions, her mind disengaged as she did her best to make small talk.

Her mother looked happier than she'd ever seen her, and even her father seemed jovial tonight. His favorite daughter had netted the fish that he'd been so eager to catch for her; he had sacrificed their family home to ensure it.

She was glad when the bride-to-be announced she was retiring and took Flora upstairs with her.

"This is my last night of sleeping alone," Aurelia said as she sat in front of her dressing table and Flora helped her to comb out her long blond hair.

"Really? I thought that once one was married, one was able to sleep alone as often as one wants," Flora commented dryly. "Certainly Mr. and Mrs. Keppel sleep separately."

"One can hardly question *that*."

"What do you mean?" Flora knew very well but wanted to hear it from her sister's lips.

"Well, can you imagine being poor Mr. Keppel? Everyone in London knows about Alice and the King. You must too, surely?"

"Certainly they are close friends, yes." Flora's face betrayed nothing.

"You can't be so naive as to believe that they are merely friends? Everybody knows that—"

"Everybody knows what they want to know. I live under their roof every day, and I have seen nothing inappropriate about the relationship. Besides, how could Mr. George possibly condone what you are implying? He is a man of great pride and integrity, and Mrs. Keppel adores him."

"If you say so."

"I do. And like Mrs. Keppel, I couldn't give a fig for tittle-tattle. It's like mist, with no substance, that swiftly drifts on."

"Well, Mrs. Keppel and the King's 'mist' hangs over London like a fog." Their eyes met in the mirror and Aurelia's expression softened. "Let us forget imperfect marriages and concentrate on one that I hope will be as perfect as I can make it." She stood up from the stool and walked toward the bed. Flora pulled back the blankets and helped her into it.

"Good night." Flora kissed her gently on the forehead, then got into her own bed and turned out the lamp.

"Flora?" Aurelia's voice sounded small in the vast darkness of the room.

"Yes?"

"Do you think . . . it will hurt?"

Flora's heart lurched at the thought of the intimacy her sister was alluding to. She paused before she replied. "To be truthful, I don't know. But I believe that God is good, and wouldn't make us suffer to show a man our love. Or to give him children."

"I have heard stories."

"That is just gossip again."

"I want to please him."

"I am sure you will. Just try not to be afraid. I hear that is the key."

"Do you?"

"Yes."

"Thank you. Good night again, dear sister. I love you."

"And I you." Both women closed their eyes and went to sleep, dreaming of being embraced by the same man.

"I am ready. How do I look?"

Flora looked at her sister, the cream lace of her gown delicate against her peachy skin, the Vaughan tiara sparkling atop her golden curls. "Absolutely radiant." Flora smiled and handed her a spray of deep red roses.

"Thank you, darling sister. So," Aurelia breathed, "it is time to go."

"Yes. Papa is waiting for you at the foot of the stairs."

"Wish me luck." Aurelia reached out for Flora's hand and squeezed it.

"Good luck, my darling."

Aurelia walked toward the door of the bedroom, then turned back. "It was you alone who convinced me to make this day possible. And I will never forget it."

As she left the room, Flora glanced back at her reflection in the mirror and saw the pain and guilt that were written across her face.

The old church on the estate was packed to the brim with four hundred guests, as the bride, her father, and the bridesmaids walked into the small lobby at the back.

"Flora," whispered Aurelia, as her long train was carefully arranged behind her, "is he there? Can you look?"

Flora walked to the door that separated them from the congregation and opened it a few inches to peek out. A pair of dark eyes swiveled to meet hers from where he was standing at the front of the church. Swiftly closing the door again, she turned to her sister and nodded. "Yes, he's there."

Signals were given, and the organ began to play the wedding march. The door swung back and Flora followed her father and her sister down the aisle. Flora listened to the vows, shivering in her thin ivory silk dress as she watched her sister become Archie's wife in the eyes of God. When the bride and groom emerged from the vestry, having signed the register, Flora forced herself to meet Archie's stare as he passed her with Aurelia on his arm. She took up her place to walk behind them out of the church and into the frosty winter day.

Despite herself, Flora could not help but appreciate the sheer beauty of her sister's wedding breakfast. Being only three weeks from Christmas, the great hall at High Weald was decorated with flickering candles, and sprigs of holly and mistletoe hung from the beamed ceiling, baked from the heat of the enormous fireplace. Apparently, so one of the guests told her, Henry VIII had once romanced Anne Boleyn in this very hall. Rather than champagne, speeches had been toasted with mulled wine, and mince pies had been provided instead of trifle.

Flora felt drugged from the heat and the vast amounts of food and wine. She was grateful when Archie stood up and announced a break in proceedings while the orchestra set up for the evening's dance. She took the opportunity to leave for some much-needed fresh air. Collecting her velvet cape, she walked out into the early evening chill. Darkness had well and truly fallen, and the wide terrace and the magnificent walled garden beneath it twinkled with lanterns that had been placed along its many borders. Flora only wished she were seeing it in high summer, rather than adorned by artificial light. She made her way down the steps, pulling her cape about her more closely as she wandered the length of the gardens, the noise of the feast receding in the distance. She paused as she reached a high brick wall in front of her, her breath crystallizing in the cold air.

"It's rather beautiful, isn't it?"

Flora jumped and turned to see a shadowy figure standing beside an enormous yew tree. The voice caused her heart to lurch.

"Yes."

"How are you, Flora?" the voice came out of the darkness.

"I am well. You?"

"I am married. I did as you asked me to."

"Thank you."

"I love you," he whispered.

Flora stood rooted to the spot.

"Will you not answer me? I just said I love you."

"Your statement does not deserve an answer. You married my sister only a few hours ago."

"Only at your behest."

"For God's sake! Are you trying to punish me?"

"Perhaps, yes."

"Then please, if you love me as you say you do, stop this. Whatever was between us for those few days is gone."

"If you believe that, then you are deluding yourself. It can never be gone."

"Enough!" Flora turned to make her way back to the house. As she did so, a hand whipped out and grabbed her upper arm, pulling her closer. Unable to cry out for fear of attracting attention, Flora found herself in Archie's arms. And his lips descended upon hers.

"My God, Flora, how I have ached to do this again . . ."

For far longer than she wished to admit, Flora abandoned herself to the sheer joy of being in his arms with his mouth on hers. Eventually, some modicum of sense entered her brain, and with huge effort, she struggled out of his grasp.

"What have we done!" she whispered. "Please, let me go."

"Forgive me, Flora. I saw you walking into the gardens from the terrace, and remembered all that we talked about when I was with you at Esthwaite and . . . you mustn't blame yourself."

"Let us pray that Aurelia never has to forgive us," she said with a shudder. "I beg you, make my sister happy." Without waiting for a reply, Flora stumbled back along the path toward the house.

Archie stood in the shadows of the ancient yew tree and watched his love run away from him.

26

Flora ran up the stairs and into her room. Slamming the door, her breath coming in short, sharp bursts, she sat down on the bed, trying to still her heartbeat.

"God forgive me," she muttered, too aghast and ashamed at what had happened to even allow herself the comfort of tears. Almost immediately, there was a knock on her door. Shrugging off her cape, she opened it.

"Where have you been?"

"I . . ." Flora thought she might faint at the sight of Aurelia, looking unusually tense and cross.

"Well, never mind where. I've been waiting for you to come and help me out of my dress and into my evening gown!"

"Oh my, of course! I must have dozed off . . ."

"Please, can you hurry, Flora? I must meet Archie at the doors of the great hall at seven and it is almost half past six now."

Still apologizing profusely, Flora followed Aurelia along the corridor and into an impressively large room dominated by an enormous canopied four-poster bed. It was made from solid dark wood, and Flora quickly averted her eyes from it, trying not to think of its imminent purpose. A fire had already been lit to warm the room for the bridal couple, and its light danced across the heavy tapestries that adorned the walls.

Flora fumbled with the seed-pearl buttons at the back of Aurelia's gown and prayed her numb fingers might drop off from frostbite—it was no less than she deserved.

"And of course, all through the wedding breakfast, everyone noticed how Freddie Soames's eyes never left you," Aurelia chattered on as Flora helped her into a dusky rose-colored evening gown. "It's obvious he's completely smitten. Mama says that he is almost twenty-five and has to take a bride soon. Would you say yes if he proposed?"

"I've never given it a thought."

"Flora, for all your time in Mrs. Keppel's household, you really are very naive when it comes to men. Now, I think I should let my hair fall loose at the back. What do you think?"

"I think it would look wonderful." Flora only hoped that Aurelia would not notice the deep blush of guilt spreading like a rash up her neck.

"Can you fetch Jenkins? Apparently she is to be my permanent lady's maid—a wedding gift from Archie's mother. I'm not sure that I like her much, but she is awfully good with hair. Then you must go and make yourself beautiful. I am sure Freddie will be asking for many dances with you tonight."

Flora went in search of Jenkins, then tended to her own toilette. Not that she cared to fix her appearance for tonight. Despite her protestations to Aurelia, it was true that Freddie Soames had pursued her relentlessly for the past two months. Even though most women in London society gushed over his handsome looks, Flora thought him an arrogant, louche bore, who had seemed on all occasions she'd met him to be in his cups. If he possessed a brain, she had not yet been privy to its machinations.

However, he did seem to be smitten by her, and London society would not be surprised if an engagement was announced . . .

Entering the great hall a few minutes later, she saw the tables had been removed and the chairs pushed back to allow room for dancing.

"Pray silence for the bride and groom! Lord and Lady Vaughan."

Flora watched Archie lead Aurelia onto the dance floor to a round of applause. He wrapped an arm around his wife's waist for the traditional first dance as the orchestra struck up. The floor began to fill with other couples and the room, heady with the scent of rich perfumes, became a swirling rainbow of beautiful gowns.

"May I have the honor of the first dance?"

Flora jumped as she felt a heavy arm on her shoulder. She looked up into the glazed eyes of Freddie Soames.

"Good evening, Lord Soames."

"S'pose you're feeling your lot is always to be the bridesmaid and never the bride, eh, Miss MacNichol?" He pulled her up and led her unsteadily onto the dance floor. "Must say, rather like that dress of yours," he whispered into her ear.

"Thank you." Flora turned her head aside, the stench of alcohol on his breath making her queasy.

"You haven't been avoiding me, have you? Every time I've come to search you out, you seem to have vanished."

"I'm chief bridesmaid, I've been attending to my sister."

"Of course you have. So it wasn't you I saw in the garden with the groom when I came looking for you earlier on?"

"No . . ." Flora gulped in shock and fought to keep her composure. "I was upstairs with Aurelia helping her change."

"Really? Well, well, could have sworn it was you, but whoever the lady in question was, it doesn't bode well for your sister's marriage."

"Don't say such things! Archie and Aurelia are devoted to each other! You must be mistaken."

"There was no mistake, but you can trust that the secret is safe with me," he added as the dance came to an end. "No wonder you have been so elusive in the past few weeks, Miss MacNichol."

"You couldn't be more wrong."

"Then prove it by saying you'll marry me." Freddie nuzzled his face into her hair as the orchestra began to play another waltz. "Otherwise, I may not believe you."

Flora swallowed hard, glancing at Archie and Aurelia, and then at Freddie's smug, self-satisfied expression. He had *seen* her, and they both knew it. Her heart was racing, and if she'd had doubts up to now about her course of action, she had to let them go. This was her just punishment and she had to accept it.

"Yes, I will."

"What?! You'll marry me?" Freddie stumbled briefly, before righting himself.

"Yes."

"Well, well, I have to admit, I didn't expect *that*."

"Really, if you were teasing me, please say so and—"

"No, I wasn't," he said quickly. "I presumed I would have to continue to be patient with you." Freddie abruptly stopped dancing then, causing a pile-up around them. He lifted a finger to her cheek and stroked it as Flora did her best not to shudder. "You really are a most enigmatic young lady, Miss MacNichol. I never quite know what you're thinking. You are sure you are serious about accepting my proposal?"

"Yes. Utterly."

"And dare I ask if this decision is purely because you have feelings for me?"

"What other reason could there be?"

"None, of course," he laughed. "Well. I haven't got a ring here to give you." Freddie suddenly appeared nervous and uncertain.

"Will we dance or will we move to the side?" Flora felt conspicuous standing in the middle of the floor.

"We will dance. I relish the fact that we are discussing our union as we glide around to the music of Strauss. You must, of course, meet my parents; they already know of my intentions toward you."

"And are they happy?"

"They are intrigued, as the whole of London has been since you arrived here. I hope very much that you will approve of what will be your new home. It is a vast estate."

"I have heard."

"And does that frighten you?"

"I am not frightened of much, my lord."

"I can see that. And that is what excites me. The question is, will you ever be tamed?"

"I wouldn't have thought a 'tame' woman would excite you."

Freddie threw back his head and laughed. "My God, you will present me with a challenge. But one that I long to overcome."

Flora felt his fingers tighten on her waist, squeezing her flesh.

"We shall announce our engagement as soon as we can. We could almost announce it now, given that most of London is here in this room."

"Yes, we should." Flora wanted no means of possible escape after tonight.

Freddie stared at her. "Are you serious, Miss MacNichol? You would be comfortable with me announcing our betrothal now?"

"Of course. Whether it is now or tomorrow or next week, it makes no difference. You have asked me to be your wife, and I have accepted."

"Then so be it."

In perfect accord, the orchestra came to the end of the waltz. Freddie led her through the crowd and spoke to the conductor. Pulling her next to him, he called for attention. "My lords, ladies, and gentlemen,

I have an announcement to make. On the occasion of her sister's marriage to Lord Vaughan, Miss Flora MacNichol has agreed to be my wife."

There was a palpable intake of breath from the onlookers as Freddie kissed her hand, then a round of applause. Immediately, Aurelia walked toward them. "I knew it!" she said delightedly.

"So, we will look forward to seeing you at Selbourne Park for a spring wedding," said Freddie, having beckoned a servant to bring him a glass of champagne. "To my betrothed!" Freddie lifted his glass in a toast as the assembled company scurried to search for a glass they could raise too.

Archie, dragged forward by Aurelia, appeared in front of them. Flora caught the look in his eye, before he turned to his own wedding guests. "This has been a wonderful evening, only enhanced by my dear sister-in-law's news. To Freddie and Flora!"

"To Freddie and Flora!" chorused the guests.

As Archie signaled for the orchestra to continue, Flora was surrounded by well-wishers, which included her mother and father.

"Goodness," said Rose as she kissed Flora. "This was something I never expected. Mrs. Keppel was right: It was an excellent idea to send you to her in London. Now you are to be a viscountess. My dear Flora, it is no less than you deserve."

They embraced and when Rose pulled away, Flora saw her eyes were full of tears.

"Please don't cry, Mama."

"Forgive me, I underestimated you. I hope that one day you'll forgive me."

"Forgive you for what, Mama?"

"Nothing," Rose replied quickly. "Just know that tonight, I am as proud of you as any mother could be."

Now even her mother was talking to her in riddles, but Flora was too overwhelmed to try to unravel them. "Thank you, Mama."

Her father followed suit and embraced her quickly, as always embarrassed by any overt show of affection. "Good show, Flora, my dear, good show."

Next in line to congratulate her was Archie.

"Congratulations, sister-in-law."

"Thank you," Flora said, her heart in her throat.

Without another glance, Archie walked away from her.

"So, you return to me an engaged woman?" Mrs. Keppel embraced Flora as she walked into her parlor the next day.

"I do."

"And are you happy? After all, Viscount Soames is the current catch of London."

"I am very happy."

"Set the tray down there," Mrs. Keppel ordered Mabel, before turning to Flora. "Draw your chair closer to the fire and tell me all about Freddie's proposal. Was it desperately romantic?"

"I suppose it was, yes. He asked me as we were dancing."

"At your sister's wedding! Oh, Flora, I am so very happy for you."

"My parents send you all their love and thanks."

"It is a shame that we won't see them over Christmas. As you know, we are going to Crichel. Have you decided whether you will join us there yet? I know your sister has invited you to stay at High Weald."

"I would very much like to come to Crichel, Mrs. Keppel. I mentioned the idea to Freddie, and he tells me his own family estate is quite close by in the New Forest."

"It is indeed, yes. Perhaps Freddie and his father can join the men for the Boxing Day shoot and I can introduce you to his mother, the Countess. Well then, that is settled, and the Alingtons will be thrilled to have you as their guest."

"Thank you, I shall be delighted."

Mrs. Keppel regarded her. "For an engaged girl, you do not look as you should."

"How should I look?"

"Happy. And yes, I admit to having been surprised when I heard about it. I was aware Viscount Soames was fond of you, but—"

"I am happy," Flora interrupted. "Very. And I wish to thank you for all you have done to make this situation possible."

"My sweet girl, none of this would have happened without you being simply *you*. So, you will be meeting Freddie's parents?"

"I believe something is being arranged."

"Despite their impeccable pedigree, and a name that stretches far back into British history, they are . . . unusual. The Earl is very outspoken in the House of Lords. And I'm terribly fond of Daphne. She's quite a character, as you will discover. With a rather racy past." She raised her teacup to Flora with a smile. "I presume you will be staying here until the wedding?"

"Mama did not indicate otherwise."

"Then I must write to her seeing if we can hold the engagement party here for you. I am sure that all of our friends will wish to attend."

Flora watched as Mrs. Keppel's face lit up at the thought, and wondered if, in her future role as a viscountess, she would ever take delight in the organization of social events. Somehow, she doubted it.

"Would you excuse me, Mrs. Keppel? It was an extremely late night yesterday, and I am feeling quite tired out from all the excitement."

"Of course. Are your parents putting the announcement in the *Times* or shall I?"

"It wasn't discussed."

"Then I shall include the matter in my letter to your mother. We will see you at dinner. I am sure that George and our other guests will wish to congratulate you in person."

Flora left the room and walked wearily up the stairs to her bedroom. Engagement announcements, more parties . . . she simply wanted it all over and done with. She hadn't even been presented at court, and to boot she didn't have a dowry—her parents couldn't afford it. How was she to be a viscountess?

"Panther has been wondering where you are."

Violet appeared like a ghost on the shadowy gaslit landing, the cat tucked up in her arms.

"Thank you for looking after him, Violet."

"That's all right, he seems to like me. Mama says you're engaged to Viscount Soames?"

"Yes."

"I must admit, I am surprised."

"Why?"

"I don't mean to be rude about the man you wish to marry, but every time I have met him here, he seems to have been drunk. And if you speak to him, he really is quite stupid. And you're not."

"That's very sweet of you to say, but I can assure you that it's the right thing for me to do."

"Because you are frightened of becoming an old maid?"

"No, because I want to marry Freddie."

"Well then, good luck, but you won't catch me bending to society's rules." Violet passed Panther to his mistress and stalked up to the night nursery floor.

"No, Violet, I'm sure I won't," Flora sighed as she watched the girl leave, then closed her bedroom door. She stood there for a while stroking her purring cat, feeling despair wash over her.

What was done was done. She had absolutely no right to follow her heart any longer.

Flora left London with the Keppels on Christmas Eve, arriving a few hours later at Crichel House in Dorset, a vast Georgian pile of pale beige stone, rendering Esthwaite cottage sized by comparison. An enormous Christmas tree sat resplendent in the hall, the candles being lit by the maids as dusk fell.

"Goodness, I shall need a map to find my bedroom later," Flora commented to Mrs. Keppel as the assembled party of thirty people gathered for drinks in the gracious drawing room before dinner.

"My dear, if you think this is a large house, wait until you see Selbourne Park!"

Christmas Day dawned and the entire party walked to the church, which conveniently—and rather oddly, thought Flora—stood in the garden. After that, an extravagant round of present-giving ensued. The women, Flora noticed, were all receiving beautifully crafted brooches or miniatures of animals, flowers, and trees. Made, Mrs. Keppel informed her, by Fabergé.

"And this one is for you," Mrs. Keppel said as she presented her with a gorgeously wrapped box. "It's from your friend Bertie," she whispered. "He wishes you a very merry Christmas. Open it."

Flora did so, and found a small, sleek black onyx cat, with amber eyes that, as she looked closer, she saw were fashioned from tiny semiprecious stones.

"It's Panther!" Flora cried, as she read his name engraved on the metal stand. "And I adore it!"

"He had it made especially for you," Mrs. Keppel added as Flora stroked the figurine.

On Boxing Day, Freddie and his parents arrived. Father and son went immediately to join the guns on the estate, while Mrs. Keppel took Flora and the Countess into the morning room to get to know each other.

"Come and sit by me, my dear. And please, call me Daphne, as I hope to call you Flora."

"Of course," Flora said, squeezing in next to the much larger woman on the small sofa.

"I shall find a maid to bring us some refreshment," said Mrs. Keppel, leaving the room.

"Ah, dear Alice," commented Daphne, "so discreet and accommodating. Now, my dear, you can imagine my relief that Freddie has finally chosen a bride. I am sure you are aware of his high-spirited temperament, but I know you will be able to tame him. He needed an unusual woman, and with your exotic past, I feel you fit the bill well."

"I . . . thank you."

"We ourselves are an unusual family, but then again what family isn't behind closed doors?" The Countess winked at her. "Of course, the Earl had to be persuaded, but he's settled to it now. After all, one could not ask for better breeding stock, could one?" She gave a buttery laugh and patted Flora on the knee. "You are indeed an attractive young woman," the Countess continued as she studied Flora through glasses that hung on a chain around her thick neck. Flora could see the heavy layer of powder on the woman's face, and the bright cheek and lip color she wore made her think of a character in one of Sheridan's Georgian farces. "Before we leave tomorrow, we must arrange a date for you to visit Selbourne; perhaps the third weekend in January? I do find the month so dismal, don't you?"

Over dinner that evening, she and Daphne discussed dates for the wedding.

"Well, Mama," said Freddie, pressing his thigh against Flora's under the table. "In my book, it can't come soon enough."

"Do you have any preference, Flora dear?"

"June?" suggested Flora neutrally.

"Personally, I always feel that June weddings are rather vulgar and May is so much fresher," countered Daphne. "Shall we agree on the second Friday? It will time nicely with the start of the Season."

"As you wish, Daphne." Flora lowered her eyes.

"Then that is settled! I will send the invitations to be printed at Mr. Smythson's shop on Bond Street. They will, of course, not be sent out until six weeks before, but everyone who needs to know will be told far sooner. Do you think cream vellum or white?"

"Not long now, dear girl," Freddie whispered to her as he rose to join the men for brandy and cigars. "I am impatient for our wedding night. Where would you like to go for our honeymoon? I have friends in Venice, or perhaps the south of France? In fact, dash it all, we will plan a tour and be away for the entire summer!"

Just as with his mother, any thoughts Flora might have had on the subject had been elegantly railroaded. This was a family that was obviously used to having its own way. However, as she walked the long corridors of Crichel to her bedroom, Flora was only relieved that she was not at High Weald, having to suffer the sight of Archie and Aurelia, newly returned from their honeymoon.

27

January in the city passed in a veil of sleet, snow, and sludge—the ugly relations of the pristine sheets of white that covered the screes and fells of the Lake District. Flora had little time to ponder her past or her future. Her days were filled with making arrangements and decisions for her forthcoming nuptials—or, more accurately, agreeing to whatever it was that her mother-in-law-to-be suggested. And when she wasn't poring over menus, guest lists, and seating plans, she was with the dressmaker for fittings, not only for her wedding dress, but for her trousseau. Mrs. Keppel had written to her parents offering to pay for Flora's new wardrobe as a wedding gift. When both Flora and her mother had protested at this generosity, Mrs. Keppel had waved it away with a flick of her wrist.

"It is the least you deserve given the circumstances. Rest assured, it will not be troubling my own coffers. We can hardly have our new viscountess looking shabby, now, can we?" She smiled as Miss Draper adjusted a hat with outrageously long ostrich feathers on Flora's perplexed head. "We are transforming you from Cinderella into the princess you truly are."

Flora had gone down to Hampshire to visit Selbourne Park in January and felt quite overwhelmed at the sheer scale of it. It seemed to her the size of Buckingham Palace, but, as the Countess had pointed out, Selbourne was far older than "that recently built" royal residence. As Flora was ushered inside the vast marble-floored entrance hall with attentive flunkies on either side of her, she wondered how on earth she would ever learn to command the legions of staff.

"You're not to worry, Flora," Daphne said as they entered a drawing room the size of two tennis courts. "I will not be deserting you for some years yet. You are undoubtedly a bright young thing, and will learn just as I did when I married Algernon."

Dinner that evening was a tense affair, with the Earl grumbling into his turtle soup about the most recent ruckus in the House of Lords, and Freddie's hands reaching for her under the table like a lecherous octopus. At least Flora had warmed more to Daphne. The Countess was now well into middle age, but Flora tried to imagine the tempestuous young belle she must have been when, as rumor had it, she had run off to Gretna Green with an "unsuitable man." The family had dragged her back to Hampshire kicking and screaming and married her off to the Earl.

A plate of *panachée* jelly was set in front of each diner and Flora watched as Algernon spooned it into his dour mouth.

"If that damned Asquith brings that bill to pass—"

"Oh hush, Algy, not at the table!" cried Daphne, before turning to Flora and giving her a weary sigh. "Let us turn to more palatable topics. The invitation list is coming along nicely, although I'm sorry to say your grandparents have regretfully declined their invitation—"

"My grandparents?" Flora, so accustomed to her small family, had almost forgotten she had any.

"Yes, your mother's people, the Beauchamps."

"If I had my way," Freddie whispered to Flora, his hand rubbing up and down her skirts, "we'd run away tonight."

On a dreary February morning at Portman Square, just two days after her twentieth birthday, which was celebrated with a grand dinner, there was a knock on her bedroom door and Miss Draper entered. "Miss Flora, Mrs. Keppel is waiting for you in her parlor."

Flora made her way downstairs as she'd been bidden.

"My dear Flora, I feel we have hardly seen each other in the past few weeks." Mrs. Keppel turned to greet her. Flora noticed she looked pale and her expression was strained beneath the bright smile of welcome.

"I have been much caught up in the process of getting married."

"I fear it is far more exhausting than marriage itself. Do sit down, and tell me how all the arrangements are going."

Flora dutifully repeated the facts and figures of the event and Mrs. Keppel nodded approvingly.

"It will be without doubt the event of the Season. And I shall be as proud as any mother as you walk down the aisle toward your intended.

Now, Flora, I have something to put to you: I was wondering if it might be possible to drag you away for a few days next month to Biarritz? Violet, Sonia, and I take an annual trip there and stay at Mr. Cassel's Villa Eugénie. The King is also in residence in the town at the Hôtel du Palais. I think it would be restorative for you after such a long London winter. The sea air would put some color in your cheeks before your wedding."

"Thank you, but I doubt the Countess would be happy if I took a holiday only a few weeks before the wedding. I could not in all faith leave her when there is so much to be done."

"Oh, she loves doing it. Besides, I have already secured her blessing. And Freddie's."

"I see." Not for the first time, Flora felt that her life was not her own and she must bow to whatever her patron wished her to do. "Then, as it is decided, I would be happy to come."

"Wonderful! That is settled then. I am sure that Violet and Sonia will be very happy. You know how they both adore you. And Bertie too, will be happy. Poor thing, I do worry so about him. He has been under such dreadful pressure from his government and his health continues to plague him. I . . ."

Flora saw a shimmer of tears well in Mrs. Keppel's eyes. Never before had she seen vulnerability in them.

"I worry for him," she finished. Composing herself, she managed a weak smile. "It has been a long, cold winter this year and we are all feeling as gray as the sky outside. But spring is coming, and I just know you will love Biarritz. So now, tell me about Freddie."

As Mrs. Keppel had promised, Daphne sent Flora off to Biarritz with her blessing.

"Of course you must go," she had said on her last visit to Portman Square. "Some sea air and good company can only make you bloom for your wedding day. And who knows? We may have to alter the seating plan to accommodate a further guest. We'll be needing quite a large seat." Daphne had chuckled at her own private joke.

Freddie too had advocated the trip. "One must always bow to a higher cause," he'd said as he'd kissed her hand, ready to depart with his parents after dinner at Lord and Lady Darlington's. "On the thirteenth of May, you will be mine. All mine," he'd added, with a lingering glance at her bodice.

Flora helped the girls pack for their journey. They were leaving a few days early to stay for a week in Paris first. She would join them later at the Villa Eugénie, where they would be guests of Sir Ernest Cassel, who was a regular visitor to Mrs. Keppel and—so Nannie had informed her—chief financial adviser to the King himself.

The Keppel girls had a large trunk each, plus assorted baskets, to fill with their wardrobes and possessions. It looked as if they were leaving for six months rather than one.

"Do you think Panther could hide in my basket the way he hid in yours when you left to come to London?" asked Violet.

"I think it would have to be his decision. Perhaps you should leave the lid open tonight and see what happens?"

"Yes." Violet sank onto her bed, her face a picture of melancholy. "I'd like to take something I love with me at least."

"You will have Nannie, your sister, and your mother, Violet. Surely you love them?"

"Of course I do, but they're family. They're not . . . *mine*." Violet's shoulders began to shake and tears rolled silently down her cheeks.

"What on earth is the matter?" Flora went to sit beside her.

"Nothing . . . everything . . . Oh, Flora! I love her so . . ."

"Who?"

"Mitya, of course! But Rosamund wants her too, and while I am away she will do her best to steal her from me. I can hardly bear it!"

More tears followed as Flora searched her memory for who this "Mitya" could be. She certainly empathized with Violet's distress.

"Does Mitya love you back?"

"Of course she does! Except she doesn't realize it yet."

"Perhaps your being away will help. Sometimes it does."

"Do you think so?" Violet looked up at her, naked desperation in her eyes.

"Yes, I do."

"Because, you see, I can never be happy without her."

"I understand, Violet."

"I know you do, and I am glad that you are coming to Biarritz."

As Flora slipped into bed that night, she put two and two together and realized that "Mitya" was Violet's pet name for Vita Sackville-West, the sallow-faced girl who had come for lunch. Flora reflected on Violet's obsession with her friend. She knew that crushes on other girls were relatively common, but Violet was fifteen and Vita two years older. She wondered if anyone else in the busy household was aware of it. Mrs. Keppel was almost certainly far too preoccupied with her own circumstances to have noticed and Flora pondered if she should mention it to Nannie. But it was hardly the kind of thing one could discuss with a middle-aged Scottish spinster.

The following day, Flora watched a motor truck being loaded up in front of the house. Studded wardrobe trunks standing almost as tall as she, dozens of hat and shoe boxes, and a traveling jewel case were packed into the truck, to depart for Victoria station. A palace courier was standing quietly in the front hall, his hands crossed in front of his uniform. He straightened as Mrs. Keppel and the girls appeared, ready to leave for the station and the boat train to Dover.

"Dearest Flora, we will see you in Biarritz. Moiselle will accompany you and keep you safe."

"Yes, Mrs. Keppel. I hope you have a wonderful time." She could see her patron was tingling with excitement.

"Thank you. Now come on, girls, we mustn't delay the train."

"Good-bye, Flora, see you next week," said Sonia, looking utterly charming in her new pink traveling coat. "I am sad I can't show you our very own private carriage that has proper chairs and tables in it and everything. They treat Mama like the Queen of England in France, you know."

A week later, Flora and Moiselle also arrived in Biarritz. It had been a long journey across the Channel to Calais and down by train to the southwest of France. Flora felt utterly exhausted.

"Bienvenue à Biarritz, mesdemoiselles!"

"Merci, monsieur," said Moiselle to the footman who had helped them

off the train and onto the platform. As they exited the station, Flora grimaced at the heavy gray sky that threatened rain. In all the paintings and photographs she'd seen, the sun was always shining in the south of France. Today, it felt like England.

"It is not far to the Villa Eugénie," said the footman as he assisted them into the backseat of a magnificent Rolls-Royce, before seating himself in the front next to the driver. Flora gazed out of the window and felt exhilarated by the thought of seeing the Atlantic Ocean. Rarely had she been out to the seaside, certainly not since she had been a small child. They drove through the sedate town; the wide promenades were quiet, perhaps due to the inclement weather, and she admired the tamarisk trees and hydrangeas that grew outside the chic cream and pink houses. Flora arched her neck to catch glimpses of the seafront, where the foaming waves crashed down on the sand.

The Rolls-Royce left the cobbled streets of the town center and, shortly afterward, turned into the driveway of a large villa. The footman helped them out of the motorcar, and they were greeted by a butler as they moved up the steps to the grand white doors.

Feeling rather like an animal who had been transported from one zoo to another, Flora followed Moiselle across a vast palatial hall and up a wide flight of stairs. The only sound she could hear was that of shoes echoing on the tiled steps. Just as a maid was opening the door to her room, a small pair of arms wound themselves around her waist.

"Flora! You're here!"

"Yes, I am." Flora smiled as she turned around to be greeted by Sonia's delighted expression.

"I am so glad," Sonia said as she followed Flora and the maid into the bedroom. The windows were open and the sea air at least smelled fresh and cleansing. Sonia jumped on the bed as the maid began unpacking Flora's trunk. "It has been so dull since we arrived in France. Kingy has not been well, you see. Mama has been caring for him."

"Oh? What is wrong with him?"

"Mama says he caught a chill when he was in Paris and since he arrived two nights ago, we haven't seen him or Mama once and have been stuck here by ourselves." Sonia lay down on the large bed, its headboard a washed blue silk with gilded acorns atop each corner. "This has a very nice mattress," she remarked. "Can I sleep with you tonight?"

"If Nannie will let you, of course you can."

"Nannie is so worried about Mama being worried about Kingy that I think she would let us go all day without even washing our hands!"

At this remark, Flora knew that the King must be seriously ill. "This is a beautiful house, isn't it?" Flora joined Sonia on the bed as the maid closed the door.

"I suppose so, but it's rained a lot since we've been here, and everyone seems rather gloomy."

"Well, I'm excited to be in France. I've never been here before."

"It's not really much different," said the nine-year-old expert. "They just speak a different language and eat strange things like snails for supper."

Nannie arrived in search of her charge and Sonia left the room. Flora lay back on the bed and felt her eyelids drooping.

She was awoken by a sharp tap-tapping at the door.

"*Entrez*," she said as she sat up.

"Mademoiselle Flora, I left you for as long as we could."

It was Moiselle. "Thank you, I . . . what time is it?"

"Past three o'clock. Madame Keppel has asked if you would join her at the Hôtel du Palais at five. I wanted to give you enough time to change."

"Will it be for dinner?"

"She didn't say, but the King will almost certainly be joining you. I will send the maid up to help you dress."

"Thank you."

As Flora closed the window and hastened to get ready, her stomach churned at the thought of dinner with the King. She hadn't seen him since they'd taken tea together in October.

After being pushed and pulled into an emerald-green tea gown, she was ushered into the motorcar and driven to the Hôtel du Palais, which overlooked the sea. With its opulent red-and-white frontage and tall windows, it looked every bit the palace of its name. She was greeted at the entrance by a smartly dressed man.

"Miss MacNichol?"

"Yes."

"I am Sir Arthur Davidson, equerry to the King, and I will escort you up to his rooms."

Flora was led swiftly through the palatial entrance hall and upstairs in a lift. They stepped out into a wide, sumptuously carpeted corridor and walked toward a uniformed butler who was standing outside a set of double doors.

"Please tell Mrs. Keppel that Miss MacNichol is here," said her escort.

The butler nodded and disappeared inside. Flora waited silently, not sure how one should converse with an equerry of the King.

"Flora, my dear!" Mrs. Keppel appeared through the double doors and gave her a spontaneous hug. "Come in, come in," she said, closing the door on the equerry and leading Flora into an exquisitely furnished sitting room with long windows that gave a wonderful view of the ocean. "The King is sleeping at the moment, but will be up in time for dinner. He wishes to eat here in our private dining room. I must warn you that he is not at all well. I . . ."

At that Mrs. Keppel's words were drowned out by a dreadful, deep coughing sound from the next room.

"Come and sit down and we shall take a glass of sherry each. I, for one, would certainly enjoy it."

Mrs. Keppel went to the array of decanters arranged on the sideboard and poured them each a glass. As she handed Flora hers, Mrs. Keppel's hands shook and Flora noticed there were dark rings under her eyes.

"How sick is the King?" Flora ventured nervously.

"He took a chill in Paris and for the last two days has had a terrible attack of bronchitis. Dr. Reid, his physician, and I have been nursing him, but thank goodness, Nurse Fletcher has now arrived from England; she has cared for him before." Mrs. Keppel swiftly drained her glass.

"Is he getting better?"

"He is at least getting no worse, though, of course, the silly man refuses to help himself. He still insists on continuing with his routine rather than staying in bed, but at least we have managed to confine him to these rooms." Another bone-wracking cough emanated from next door and Flora too took a large gulp of her sherry.

"Are you sure it's appropriate for me to be here if he is so sick?"

"My dear, as I said, the King refuses to surrender to his illness and I doubt he has dined alone a single night of his life. The Marquis de Soveral, the Portuguese ambassador, is also joining us, but, of course, the King would hardly be content with just the two of us and his doctor present at table. When I said you had arrived here earlier today, he was most eager that you join us."

"Then I am honored."

"At least he has not been smoking those confounded cigars; Dr. Reid is convinced they are the cause of his bronchial problems. No doubt the moment he is recovered, he will begin again. But what can one do? He is the King after all."

Flora wanted to ask why, if the King was so sick, the Queen was not in attendance on her husband, but felt it was inappropriate to do so.

"You must be weary if you have not slept for the past two nights," Flora said.

"Indeed I am; I sat with him throughout the night, sponging him down as his fever was so high. To be honest, Flora, there were moments when I feared for his life. But now that Nurse Fletcher has arrived, he is in safe hands." There was yet another attack of coughing from next door. "Excuse me, Flora, I must go to him."

For the following fifteen minutes, the doors to the suite opened and closed as steaming bowls and strange-smelling poultices made their way through to the King. Flora secreted herself in the farthest corner by the drawing room window, trying to make herself invisible.

Eventually, as the light was fading across the sea and the sun illuminated the clouds in a splendor of reds and oranges, Mrs. Keppel and Dr. Reid appeared, deep in conversation.

"The question is, should we alert the Queen?" Dr. Reid asked.

"The King has already stated that he does not want to alarm his wife," snapped Mrs. Keppel. "Besides, she abhors Biarritz."

"That may be, but it would be most tragic if . . ." Dr. Reid wrung his hands in agitation. "Of course, he should be in a hospital, but he will not hear of it."

"I should think not. Can you imagine the furor if the newspapers hear of this?"

"Madam, there are already a number of reporters downstairs, asking why the King is not taking his usual walks along the promenade and leaving the hotel to dine. I doubt we can keep them at bay for much longer."

"Then what are we to do?"

"I will sit up with him tonight and monitor him hour by hour, but if his breathing does not seem easier by morning . . . whether the King wishes his wife and the rest of the world to know of his indisposition or not, we must contact the palace."

A knock at the door made them both turn around. Flora stood up to answer it.

"Flora, my dear, I had forgotten you were here." A faint blush rose to Mrs. Keppel's cheeks as she realized their conversation had been overheard.

The equerry stepped into the suite. "The maids are here to lay the King's table for dinner."

"Yes, yes, let them in," Mrs. Keppel sighed, throwing a despairing glance at Flora. "He still insists that he rise to dine with us in here tonight."

Mrs. Keppel left for her own room to ready herself for dinner and Dr. Reid disappeared into the King's bedroom. Flora watched the dining table being laid by the three maids, the gold-rimmed china plates and the heavy silver cutlery carefully nudged into place at precise angles to the crystal wineglasses, before the maids removed themselves as quietly as they had arrived.

Flora was only thankful that the coughing from next door seemed to have abated; perhaps the King was finally sleeping. As the door to the bedroom opened, Flora turned anxiously, expecting Dr. Reid. Instead, the King himself appeared in the room, fully dressed and breathing heavily.

"Your Majesty." Flora hastily drew herself to standing and swept a deep and embarrassed curtsy. She felt the King's eyes upon her, squinting across the vast drawing room.

"Well, bless my soul! If it isn't little Miss Flora MacNichol," he panted.

"Yes, Your Majesty."

"Come and help me to a chair, will you? I've escaped while my jailors are busy in the bathroom, no doubt preparing some ghastly, foul-smelling poultice or injection."

Flora walked toward him, listening to his irregular breathing and praying that he didn't breathe his last with her. He held out his elbow to her and she took it shyly.

"Where would you like to sit?" she asked as they progressed slowly and painfully across the room, the effort of walking rendering him speechless and only able to point to his preferred chair. It took all of Flora's strength to support him as he sat down heavily, and she watched him fight a further coughing fit. His eyes watered and his breathing increased apace.

"Shall I call for Dr. Reid, Your Majesty?"

"No!" he hissed. "Just pour me some brandy!"

Flora walked to the tray of decanters, only wishing the King *would* have a coughing fit and alert the doctor to his escape from the bedroom. Following the fat pointed finger with a nod, she picked up one of the decanters, poured a small glass, and turned toward him.

"More!"

Doing as instructed and filling it to the brim, Flora took the brandy back to him and watched as he took it and downed it in one.

"Another," he whispered, and Flora had no choice but to repeat the exercise.

"Now," the King said, passing the empty glass to her, "that's what I call medicine. Shh." He put a shaking finger to his lips as Flora replaced the glass on the tray. "Sit." He pointed to the chair closest to him and she did so.

"So, Miss MacNichol, Flora . . . I approve of that name. Scottish, you know."

"Yes, Your Majesty."

"It is odd, is it not?"

"What is, Your Majesty?"

There was a long pause before the King was able to continue speaking.

"That you and I find ourselves alone together. On an occasion where I might not see the sun tomorrow morning."

"Please, Your Majesty, do not say such a thing!"

"I . . ."

Flora watched the vast man struggle for air and saw tears filling his eyes.

"I have made many mistakes."

"I am sure you have not."

"I have . . . I have . . ."

Another lengthy pause ensued.

"I am only human, you see. And I have loved . . ."

Flora decided the best thing to do was to avert her eyes as the King's staccato soliloquy continued.

". . . *women*," he managed finally. "You are to be married soon?"

"Yes, I am."

"A viscount, I hear?" He smiled suddenly.

"Yes, Your Majesty, Freddie Soames."

"And . . . you love him?"

"I believe I will grow to do so, yes."

At this, the King began to chuckle, then, realizing it was not possible given his condition, he brought his mirth under control.

"You have spirit, like me. Come here."

Flora went toward him and took his outstretched hand, hearing the deathly rattle in his chest.

"Wasn't sure, you see."

"About what, Your Majesty?"

"When Mrs. George suggested it. Clever woman, Mrs. George . . . always right."

At that moment, the bedroom door opened and Dr. Reid walked in, followed by a nurse.

"We thought we had left you to sleep, Your Majesty." Dr. Reid's eyes fell accusingly on Flora. "You know it is by far the best medicine."

"So you tell me," rasped the King. "But so is . . . good company." The King then winked at Flora before the attack of coughing he had been suppressing could no longer be prevented.

Water and more steam were brought to him and Mrs. Keppel appeared, looking refreshed and calm in a blue velvet evening gown.

"Mrs. George, where on earth have you been?"

"Really, Bertie, you should be in bed," she chided.

"Where is Soveral? He's late to dine. And I am . . . starving."

Flora left the hotel suite two hours later to take the short journey back to the Villa Eugénie. The dinner she had just endured—and "endured" was the only word for it—had been one of agonizing tension. The King's guests had listened to his increasingly labored breathing, pretending all was normal, yet fearing he was about to collapse as his convulsive cough overtook him. The King had eaten what Flora would label a substantial dinner for at least two people, and also—despite the disapproving looks of some of his guests—drunk a considerable amount of red wine.

"I will stay here with him," Mrs. Keppel had told Flora. "Send my love to the girls and tell them I will see them when Kingy is better."

They had said their good-byes, then Flora was escorted downstairs to the waiting Rolls-Royce. Leaning her head back on the plump leather seat, she felt completely mentally and physically drained by the events of the day.

28

Flora didn't see Mrs. Keppel for the following three days, so she and the children amused themselves by going out for bracing walks along the promenade, then returning to the Villa Eugénie for lunch. When the sun came out, they spent time sketching and painting the unusual plants that grew in the villa's gardens.

Having shown little interest in her painting up to now, Violet had attached herself to Flora. And indeed, her delicate watercolors showed genuine ability. But both sisters were unsettled, wondering why their familiar Biarritz routine had been disturbed. Flora could not enlighten them, having been told point-blank by Mrs. Keppel to mention nothing about the severity of the King's condition.

"Why aren't we going out for picnics with Mama and Kingy? It's so dull just staying here at the villa, and I haven't even worn any of my new dresses yet," Sonia complained.

"Because the weather has been so wet and Kingy doesn't wish to catch a cold."

"But it's sunny today, Flora, and we haven't seen Mama for days now. She must be bored too."

"I am sure we will see her very soon, and Kingy too," Flora replied with a certainty she didn't feel.

That evening after an early supper, Nannie took Sonia upstairs for a bath and Violet sat with Flora, scribbling away in the notebook she always carried with her.

"Flora?"

"Yes?"

"Kingy is very ill, isn't he? Will he die?"

"Goodness, no, he just has a bad cold. Everyone is simply being cautious because he is the king."

"I know you're lying. But it doesn't matter." Violet turned to her notebook, chewing the end of her pencil.

"What are you writing?"

"Poetry, although I am quite dreadful compared to Vita. I believe she will be a writer one day. She seems to be having such a wonderful time in London preparing for the Season, I daresay she doesn't even think of me at all."

"I'm sure that's not true," Flora reassured Violet, seeing the darkness in her eyes which always preceded her black moods.

"It is. She is so beautiful, like an untamed Thoroughbred . . . wild and unfettered. But, of course, life—and men—will tame her."

"Perhaps life tames us all, Violet. Perhaps it has to."

"Why? Why must we women marry someone who is chosen for us by others? Things are changing, Flora! Just look at what the suffragettes are doing for women's rights! Surely it could be different? And marriage itself . . ." Violet shuddered. "I cannot understand how two people who hardly know each other are meant to spend the rest of their lives together. And do . . . that unspeakable thing, despite being complete strangers."

"I'm sure you will understand all that when you get older, Violet."

"No, I won't," she said simply. "People keep saying that, but I don't like men. It's like asking a cat and a dog to live and sleep together. We share nothing in common. Look at Mama and Papa."

"Come now! From what I have seen, your parents are quite happy together. And great friends."

"Then tell me why, at this moment, my father stays in London at the office, while Mama is here nursing a sick King?"

"Perhaps it's too much to ask your spouse to provide everything you need."

"I disagree. Vita fulfills me on every level. I would never become bored with her."

"Then you are lucky to have found such a friend."

"She is far more than my friend. She is my . . . everything. I don't expect you to understand, or anyone for that matter." Violet stood up abruptly. "I'm going to bed. Good night, Flora."

Mrs. Keppel appeared at the Villa Eugénie early the following morning. They crossed each other on the stairs as Flora was on her way down to breakfast.

"How is the King?" Flora whispered.

"Thank God, he has turned the corner. His fever is down, and for the first time, he slept peacefully last night."

"That is wonderful news."

"It is indeed. And this morning, he insists on joining friends for luncheon, so I must prepare myself. It has been a long few days, and to be blunt, I feel quite exhausted. Are the girls upstairs in their room?"

"Yes."

"Then I will go and reassure them. No doubt Bertie will wish life to resume as normal now he believes he is well again. And for the world to know that he is too. He even lit up one of his hateful cigars this morning."

After that, life *did* return to normal. Flora helped dress the girls for outings with their mother and the King every day.

"It's awfully strange, Flora, as there are so many nice places we could sit and eat, yet Kingy insists we take our picnic on the side of the road!" said Sonia, as she returned from one such outing and ripped her straw hat from her head.

"It's because he likes everyone in France to see him and bow and scrape in front of him," replied Violet cynically. "Perhaps he thinks it upsets the French king."

"Well, I don't know about that," said Sonia, "but really, he does look awfully old. And really quite ill."

"You could say the same thing about Caesar. That dog stinks to high heaven," complained Violet, brushing dog hair off her skirts.

The following day, Flora was presented with a letter, handed to her by the butler.

High Weald
Ashford, Kent
England
14th March 1910

Dearest Flora,

I know that you are currently with Mrs. Keppel, and Mr. Rolfe at

Portman Square kindly gave me your address in Biarritz. For, dearest sister, I wish you to be the first to know that you will be an aunt before the year is out! Yes, I am expecting a child! I confess, I am terrified, and feeling quite dreadful, which my physician tells me is usual for the early stages of pregnancy.

Darling Flora, I long to see you and I ask if it might be possible for you to come and stay here for a while, when you return to England? Mama is unable to travel down from the Highlands to be with me, as Papa has taken a fall on his bad leg and broken his ankle. Much of my day here is spent alone, as I currently feel too unwell to go out. I am lonely, dear sister. I know your wedding comes soon, so I would not keep you from the arrangements, but perhaps you could spare at least a few days? Please write as soon as you can, and tell me when I can look forward to your visit.

Your loving sister,
Aurelia

Flora, reading it over breakfast, felt as sick as her sister professed to be. The material proof of Aurelia and Archie's coupling was enough to make her rise from the table and take herself off to her room.

The very thought of staying at High Weald was anathema.

"Stop being so selfish!" she reprimanded herself as she paced back and forth. "Aurelia needs you, and you must go to her."

Sitting down at the desk, Flora drew out her writing paper and ink pen.

Villa Eugénie
Biarritz
France
19th March 1910

My dearest sister,

My happiness for you knows no bounds. I am due back in England in just over a week. Despite the ongoing wedding plans, of course I will spare the time to visit you. I will come to you directly once I have arrived in England.

Your loving sister,
Flora

Flora's last night at the Villa Eugénie coincided with the King's first visit to the household. When she arrived downstairs, the drawing room was already full of guests, many of them speaking in fast, indecipherable French. Mrs. Keppel was holding court, a tiara glittering amid her lush auburn curls. Surveying her, Flora realized that this *was* Mrs. Keppel's court. For a month a year—away from England—she was the queen she so wanted to be.

The King's arrival was heralded by Caesar, the fox terrier, trotting before him through the double doors, followed by the usual whiff of pungent cigar smoke. The attention in the room immediately left Mrs. Keppel and focused on its new occupant. Flora was relieved to see the King was at least able to breathe, yet his eyes were still rheumy and his complexion pallid.

"I hear you're leaving tomorrow." A gentleman, whose resemblance to the King was disconcerting, appeared by her side. From his gray beard and mustache down to his considerable girth, he could have been his double.

"Yes."

"The King seems much recovered from his ailment, does he not?"

"He does, yes," said Flora, wishing the gentleman would introduce himself, as she had drawn a blank on his name. "Thank goodness."

"I heard from the King that you were a great comfort during his illness."

"I do not think so, sir, I—"

"The King thinks otherwise. And all of us thank you."

"Forgive me, sir," Flora surrendered, "but I'm not sure we have ever been formally introduced."

"My name is Ernest Cassel, and you are currently a guest under my roof." He smiled at her, laughter in his eyes.

"I must apologize, sir, I have seen so many new faces in the past few months . . ."

"There is no need to do so. The good news is, I know who *you* are. Allow me to hand you my card. There might come a point in the future when you need to contact me. I am not only your host at the Villa Eugénie, but also a close friend and adviser to both the King and Mrs. Keppel. Now, shall I escort you into dinner?"

It was only later, when the King and his entourage were leaving, that he finally sought her out. She smiled at him as she rose from her curtsy.

"I am glad to see you looking so well tonight, Your Majesty."

"Thank you, Miss MacNichol. We will see each other when I return to London, God willing. Good-bye, my dear." Then the King kissed her hand and, with a smile, departed.

Flora arrived at High Weald two days later. Aurelia met her at the door and ushered her into the drawing room for a restorative tea.

"So, tell me all about the King. I can hardly believe you have met him!"

"He was well and jovial, as he always is," Flora replied.

"Of course, it cannot be the first time that you have met him. Given Mrs. Keppel's . . . position in his life."

"There's no doubt that they are extremely close friends."

"I understand if Mrs. Keppel has sworn you to secrecy."

"She really hasn't."

"Arabella says she even wields power with the government! Flora, forgive me, I forget that you are such an innocent and trust only in the better nature of humans and animals. Anyway, I shall compromise your discretion no longer, and instead tell you of everything that has been happening here since we last met."

Flora listened to her sister's fond chatter about Archie's care for her condition, and loathed herself for how duplicitous her soul really was.

"It is hard to believe that I shall soon have a child to keep me occupied. Everyone here prays it's a boy. Whereas I hope it is a girl. And healthy, of course."

"So Archie is happy about the baby?"

"Oh yes, and I think I have even managed to put a smile on Arabella's face. You know, I do sometimes wonder why Mama was so friendly with her." Aurelia lowered her voice. "Perhaps she was nicer back then. Or maybe it's the fact that she lost Archie's father in the war. But she really isn't a very warm person."

"I am afraid I can't comment as she's never spoken more than a couple of sentences to me. You poor thing, it must be difficult living under the same roof as her."

"At least she too is away at present, so we have the house and each other to ourselves. Also, I have some news! Even though Mama cannot come just now because of Papa's broken ankle, she wrote to tell me that Sarah's mother died a few months ago, and suggested I should write to her and ask her if she would come to live here permanently to be my personal maid and help me through my pregnancy and the birth. To my joy, she wrote back immediately and said she could think of nothing she'd like more. So, tomorrow Sarah arrives at High Weald and I will feel at least that I have one person on my side in this household."

"How wonderful! But you say Archie has been attentive to you?"

"Oh, he is, when his head isn't in a botanical book or peering at a plant in his hothouse. Sadly, he's gone to London as he has business to attend to there. He said he will be back at some point next week. Depending on when you are leaving, I doubt you will see him, which is a shame."

"Yes." Flora felt her emotions rise in relief and then fall traitorously in disappointment. "At least it means you're all mine."

"I know you have never really taken to him, Flora, but he is a good man, and kind to me."

"Then that is all that matters."

"Yes. Now, forgive me, Flora, but I think I must go and rest."

"Of course. May I help you to your room?" she asked, holding a decidedly green Aurelia by the elbow as she rose.

"Please do, yes. And I am always better in the afternoon."

Flora walked upstairs with Aurelia. As she called for her maid and asked for the tea, Flora pulled wide the sheet and blanket on the enormous canopied bed in which Aurelia—and, no doubt, Archie—slept.

"Thank you," Aurelia said as Flora helped her up onto the mattress. "I am told this nausea will pass very soon. And it helps so enormously that you are here."

Flora sat in the chair close by until her sister's eyes closed and she fell asleep. She tiptoed out and went to her own room to freshen up, but felt herself drawn to the window, where she could see the sun illuminating the garden. Even though she knew pregnant women could feel ill in the first two or three months, Aurelia was now over that time, at almost four months. Flora only prayed all was well.

The comforting bulk of Sarah arrived the next day, looking overwhelmed and red faced after the long journey from Esthwaite, but overjoyed to see her two girls.

"Mama has said she will come down for the birth, but Sarah is a godsend," Aurelia said as she joined Flora in the dining room for dinner that evening. "She seems very pleased with her new lady's maid uniform, although it will have to be let out. I do hope the other staff won't bully or look down on her. They seem to think that everybody born in the north is inferior, including me." She gave a small, false laugh.

"Don't be silly, Aurelia darling. I'm sure that you are imagining it."

"And I am sure that I am not. Even my own husband calls me a mouse and tells me I mustn't allow the servants or Arabella to order me around so. Perhaps I am not cut out to run a household."

"Being sweet and gentle hardly precludes authority, or, in fact, respect. You are simply feeling vulnerable because of your condition, that is all."

"And again, I say I am not. It's very odd because—forgive me for saying this—at home you seemed to be the shadow, whereas here in this house it's *me*. How things have changed in the past year."

"But you are happy with Archie?"

"Of course. You know how I adore him, but now, because I am with child, he does not visit me any longer. And . . ." Aurelia sighed. "It is difficult to explain, but that is the only time when I feel I possess him fully. You will understand soon enough what I mean when you marry Freddie."

"Yes. I am sure I will," Flora replied, repressing the usual shudder. "And if you believe you have problems with your household, you should see my future home. I am only too glad to let the Countess continue running it, for I will barely know where to begin."

"My sister, the Viscountess . . ." Aurelia shook her head. "Who would have believed it?"

"Who indeed?"

Flora was relieved that Sarah had brought with her some much-needed fresh Lakeland air, both metaphorically and physically. And in her capable, caring hands, over the following days, Aurelia brightened considerably.

"I never thought I'd see the day when I had my girls back. One married and expecting a child, and the other about to be . . . almost royalty!" Sarah exclaimed as she tucked Aurelia up in bed for her afternoon nap. "I always liked Lord Vaughan, I did, such a pleasant gentleman. Do you remember,

Miss Flora, when he came to visit you at Esthwaite last summer and you got half drowned climbing Scafell?"

Flora's blood froze in her veins at Sarah's remark. She had not uttered a word to Aurelia—or anyone else for that matter—of where she'd been that day when she'd appeared back in the kitchen at Esthwaite, soaking wet.

"And you in your pa's breeks and cap! I'd never seen owt like it! Me and Mrs. Hillbeck laughed and laughed at the sight of you."

"Archie came to visit you at Esthwaite last summer?" Aurelia looked at her sister, puzzled.

"Yes." Flora recovered her composure. "He was on his way back from shooting in Scotland and decided to drop in. I'm sure I told you, darling."

"If you did, I don't remember it." Aurelia's lips were set tightly. "You climbed Scafell together?"

"That they did, and she went to sleep before I'd even drawn her bath that night," Sarah cackled. "In them funny clothes, looking like a man, and her going to be a viscountess in a few weeks' time!"

"You definitely didn't tell me *that*," said Aurelia.

"No. I was embarrassed, as you can imagine. Sarah is right, I did return home in rather a state, but Archie wished to see the mountains, and I had no choice but to show him. Now, are you all settled? We will leave you in peace." Flora went over to the bed and kissed her sister on the cheek. "Rest well, and I'll be in my room reading." Before the slightest look could betray her, Flora headed for the door.

Safely in her own room, she put her head in her hands, breathing heavily and pacing across the wooden floor. Now she wished that Archie *were* here, so she could talk to him about what had just happened. No doubt Sarah knew the publican in the village who had lent Archie his clothes for the journey, or perhaps someone had seen her step into Archie's motorcar at the gates—it was a small community. It hardly mattered how Sarah knew she'd been with Archie that day. What mattered was explaining *why* she hadn't ever told Aurelia about it.

At dinner that night, Aurelia made no mention of Sarah's revelation. Neither did she ask for further details when Flora escorted her upstairs to bed and kissed her good night. Yet—and perhaps it was her imagination—she had felt a coolness in her sister's manner.

Flora did not sleep well that night. One way and another, she was grateful when a letter arrived for her from the Countess, asking her if she could spare a few days to travel to Selbourne and discuss wedding plans.

Aurelia hardly murmured when Flora asked if she would mind if she took her leave to go to Hampshire.

"Of course you must. And I am feeling much better already." Aurelia looked at Sarah fondly, as she tidied the room. "And Archie will be home soon."

"I am leaving early tomorrow morning, so I may not see you before I depart. But I will be back in three days, I promise."

"Thank you. Now Sarah is with me, all will be well. Do send my love to the Countess and Freddie." Aurelia gave her a tight smile, then rolled over in preparation for sleep.

Flora left, knowing without a doubt that her sister was suspicious. Entering her room, she went straight to her writing desk, and drew out a sheet of writing paper and her ink pen.

High Weald
Ashford, Kent
2nd April 1910

Aurelia knows of your visit to the Lakes. Sarah, our old maid, who has come to High Weald to take care of her, told her of it. Please do your utmost to reassure her that nothing inappropriate took place. I am frightened for my sister's state of mind and do not wish to compromise her health. She has never been strong. You are to be a father and the safe delivery of your child is of the greatest importance.

F.

29

At last!" Freddie said as he greeted her in the hall of Selbourne Park and kissed her hand. "I was beginning to wonder if you had deserted me and England's shores for good. How was Biarritz? And the King? The gossip in London goes that his condition has been far more serious than his subjects have been told."

"Oh, he was quite well when I left," Flora was able to answer almost truthfully. "He had a cold, that was all."

"Good, good. Mama is hoping he might attend our nuptials. He's been sent an invitation. Did he mention it when you saw him?" Freddie offered her his elbow and they walked through to the vast drawing room.

"No, his private secretary organizes his diary, so even if he *was* attending, he might not know. Is your mother here?"

"Not at present, no. She is out visiting one of her charities in Winchester. And Papa is up in London. So, my dearest Flora, we are quite alone." Freddie's hands snaked around her waist and pulled her closer. His lips came down onto hers and his tongue forced her mouth open.

"Please, Freddie!" Flora struggled to free herself. "The servants might appear at any moment."

"So what if they do? Doubtless they have seen much worse," he chuckled as he tried to kiss her again.

"No! I can't. We are not yet married."

"As you wish." Freddie relaxed his grip on her, his mouth forming into a pout. "I cannot see what difference a ring and an entry in a church register make. I hope you will not withhold your passion from me after that."

"Of course not. We will be joined in the presence of God." She lowered her eyes chastely.

"Well, damn it," he said. "I am eager for that moment. Now, seeing as you will allow me no closer than a leper until we are wed, I shall ring for some tea and you will tell me in full of your adventures in France."

Flora was relieved when the Countess appeared an hour later. Trying to keep Freddie's hands off her was akin to being constantly pawed by a ravenous tiger. After luncheon, Freddie departed to—as he put it—blow off some energy on his horse, while she and Daphne settled down to the details of the wedding.

Taking her glasses off her nose, Daphne smiled at her. "I suppose you are thinking how ridiculous this all is, my dear. And if you aren't, I certainly am. But, of course, one must do the conventional thing. How is young Violet Keppel?" she asked, changing the subject.

"She is well, and both of the girls are very much looking forward to being bridesmaids."

"Such an odd girl, I've always thought . . . Lady Sackville, a dear friend of mine, was telling me only last week that Violet seems to have a strange fixation on her daughter, Vita. What do you think?"

"I only know they are friends."

"Whatever the case, Victoria has refused to entertain Mrs. Keppel at Knole. Which rather surprises me, given her own mother's scandalous past. But then it's often those who have been cast out of their own glass house who seem the most eager to cast the first stone at others. Victoria certainly doesn't approve of the Keppel girls' being part of your train. I had a deal of a job to convince Algernon it was the right thing to do. He doesn't like going with the times—rather an old fuddy-duddy, bless his heart. Well now," the Countess said, patting Flora's hand. "I think it's time for a sherry, don't you?"

Later, Flora stood at one of the floor-to-ceiling bedroom windows, surveying the enormous gardens in front of her. Beyond the yew hedge was a deer park and she could see the animals moving like shadows against the twilight. The outsized proportions of everything in the house made her feel like a tiny doll taken out of her toy house and transplanted into a human one.

She then thought of High Weald, which, though large, had a cozy and warm atmosphere. She hoped Archie would receive her letter before he left London.

If he didn't, and Aurelia confronted him and he confessed, everything she had done to separate her life from him and her sister would be in vain.

After three days with Freddie—the most time she had ever spent with him—Flora had learned his concentration was nonexistent: He would often ask her a question, and by the time she had begun her answer, his gaze had wandered off and he had lost interest entirely. One day, just to test him, Flora had started to tell him of her childhood, and when she saw his mind wandering, had recited a nursery rhyme instead. He hadn't even noticed.

Flora had decided she should not waste her energy in conversation with him. His favorite pastime beyond all others was drinking. When he was drunk, she knew she could stand on her head on the dining table with her bloomers showing and he wouldn't notice. On the last night of her stay, he invited his group of louche friends to join them for dinner. Flora became the butt of many lewd jokes as they sat at table, all of them already half-cut.

Daphne caught her on the stairs as Flora was retiring from the raucous drinking games, boorish laughter drifting up from the drawing room.

"My dear, I confess that my son's behavior tonight has not been what either of us would wish for. But believe me when I tell you that this is his last gasp. He understands his future responsibilities to both you and Selbourne, and will adhere to them."

"Of course." Flora lowered her eyes in deference. The Countess's hand reached for hers.

"Just remember, marriage is not the end of a woman's life. In a way, it is the beginning. And as long as one provides an heir and is discreet, it can become more than enjoyable. Just look to your patron and learn. Good night, my dear." Daphne squeezed Flora's hand and wandered off to her own suite of rooms.

It was with relief and trepidation that Flora returned to High Weald.

"Aurelia is currently sleeping. She has not been at all well since you left," Arabella, returned from London, informed her as they met in the entrance hall. "That new maid of hers insists on feeding her all kinds of nefarious concoctions, which I am sure can't be helping her."

"I have taken Sarah's remedies since I was a baby, and I have always found them to be helpful," Flora replied defensively.

"I'm sure. Now, Cissons will see you up to your room."

"Thank you."

"I don't think Cook has prepared anything for you, Miss MacNichol, but I am sure she can rustle up some soup if necessary," said the housekeeper as she escorted Flora to her room.

"I'm not hungry at present, thank you."

Flora waited a few minutes, then walked along the corridor to Aurelia's bedroom. She opened the door, wincing as the heavy wood creaked. The room was dark, but as her eyes adjusted to the dimness, she saw Sarah dozing in a chair by the window. Leaving the room and feeling a sudden need for fresh air, she turned tail and went downstairs.

As she stepped outside, her nose picked up the first scent of spring. Daffodils lined the verges, reminding her of Esthwaite, and as she stepped down into the walled garden, she saw with delight that it was waking up from its long winter sleep.

Thankfully, the garden was deserted, although Flora had given herself a serious talking-to on the way here and felt calm about encountering Archie. Whatever had been could never be referred to again. Archie was now not only her brother-in-law, but soon to be the father of her niece or nephew. And Flora herself would be married within a few weeks. They were family now and could not avoid spending time together. She was determined for their relationship to be platonic, because that was all it could ever be.

And when I see him, I will say so, she told herself as she walked along the pathways. Flora could see how Archie had planned the walled garden with nectar-heavy flowers to attract as many bees as possible, and they hummed fat and contented above the pink hellebores and white viburnums. The air felt vibrant and alive, as if the garden were as pregnant as her sister. Flora only hoped she would have the chance to see it when it gave birth in the summer, to what she imagined could only be a fragrant profusion of color.

"Flora." A voice behind her made her jump.

"Archie," she said as she turned to face him. "Why do you always seem to creep up on me?"

"Because your attention is always focused elsewhere. I received your letter in London."

"Thank goodness. I was concerned it would fall into the wrong hands.

I wanted to warn you in case Aurelia mentioned our . . . meeting at Esthwaite to you."

"Thank you. I returned yesterday and she hasn't said anything about it so far."

"Then let us hope it is forgotten. She does not look well."

"No, she doesn't. But you do, Flora. Shall we walk?"

Flora acquiesced and the two of them took off along the paths. As Archie talked of his future plans for the gardens, Flora had to keep reminding herself of her earlier promise, that she could and would be friends with her brother-in-law.

"So how are you?" Archie halted suddenly below the magnificent yew tree. Flora could see the tiny light-green stems of rebirth at the tips of the branches, and tried to shake the memory of the last time she had stood beneath it.

"I am well. I have just been down to Selbourne to see Freddie."

"And all goes according to plan?"

There was a moment's hesitation before Flora nodded, which Archie caught immediately.

"Of all people, surely you can speak truthfully to me? Despite Freddie being labeled the catch of London, it's simply a fiscal and physical illusion. As I am sure you will be aware by now, the real Freddie is a barking-mad drunk. Personally, I think he may have fallen out of the cradle and banged his head as a baby."

"He is certainly . . . different, yes." Flora suppressed a smile.

"What a state we all find ourselves in. Believe me, it is not just my own selfishness that makes me say this, but I wish with all my heart you were not marrying him, for your own sake."

"It is what it is. I do like his mother, though."

"It is not her you will be sharing a bed with at night. But there we are."

"How dare you speak to me that way!" Flora felt a blush spreading up her neck and into her cheeks.

"Forgive me. I cannot help myself, just the thought of you with *him* . . . God, Flora, you must understand how I feel, surely? I have missed you so these past few months."

"Do *not* say another word to me. I mean it." She turned and began to walk away, but he caught her hand before she could escape. His touch sent involuntary shivers up Flora's spine, but she pushed them down. "Let me go, Archie," she muttered. "I really must return to Aurelia. Your *wife*."

"Yes, of course." He gave a deep sigh, then a small nod of acceptance, and dropped her hand. "I will see you at dinner."

She headed straight upstairs to see if Aurelia had yet woken, but Sarah barred her way at the bedroom door, putting a finger to her lips.

"She is upset today, poor mite, complaining of a bad headache. She has told me to tell you to leave her be, but I'm sure she will want you to look in on her later."

Flora went to her room to dress for dinner, feeling horribly uncomfortable that Aurelia was denying her access. She mulled over all the times that she had sat by her bedside in the past, whenever Aurelia had been unwell, and felt a knot of worry settle in her stomach. Once she was dressed, she went down to join Arabella and Archie in the drawing room.

"It seems your wife is indisposed again," Arabella murmured over her glass of sherry. "I do hope this phase passes soon. When I was having you, dear, I carried on as normal. Modern girls are so different."

"Perhaps it's simply that *people* are all different, Mama," countered Archie. "I am sure that Aurelia does not wish to feel so rotten."

"It's almost certainly a girl she's having. All my contemporaries that had one were as sick as mongrel dogs during their pregnancy."

"Well, I for one would love a daughter," Archie said. "I am sure they are easier than boys."

"Easier, perhaps, but not as useful. Shall we go into the dining room?"

As the three of them sat together at the far end of the long table in the oak-paneled dining room, Flora thought how ironic it was to be facing Archie with his mother sitting in between them, conscious that she had taken her sister's place. Just as the soup was about to be served, the door opened and Aurelia appeared.

"Forgive me for my late arrival, but the rest has obviously done me good, for I feel much recovered."

As Aurelia sat next to her husband and the maid hastily laid another place, Flora saw how pale she looked. Yet her blue eyes were shining with a strange intensity.

"Are you sure you are well enough to sit up at table, my darling?" Archie asked her, laying a hand on her shoulder.

"Why, of course. In fact, I feel positively ravenous!" she giggled, her tone high-pitched and false. Flora was pleased to see that Archie could not have been more attentive, even cutting up the beef for her and, to Arabella's obvious disapproval, feeding her small morsels.

"We mustn't let you fade away, my darling. You really are dreadfully thin."

"I shall remind you of that when I am the size of a house in a few months' time."

As the evening progressed, and Flora saw some color return to her sister's cheeks, she let herself relax.

"So, tell me, how was your future home? From all I have heard, it is quite magnificent." Aurelia looked askance at her sister.

"It is indeed. And no doubt will be a challenge to me."

"Marriage is a challenge we all must face."

"Yes."

"And Freddie seems so devoted to you already. That's all a wife can ask for really, isn't it?" Aurelia turned to Archie and beamed at him.

Flora watched quietly as Aurelia's untouched trifle was cleared away and Arabella suggested they move through to the drawing room for coffee.

"Would you mind if I retired now? I am feeling so very much better, but I don't wish to overdo it. Perhaps you would accompany me upstairs, Flora?"

"Of course." Flora rose as Aurelia bade her husband good night and they left the room together.

Aurelia was silent on the way upstairs. Sarah bustled along the corridor toward them as Aurelia opened the door to her bedroom.

"Shall I help you into your nightgown, Miss Aurelia?"

"No thank you, Sarah. I am sure that Flora can help me tonight. You go to bed."

"Anything you need, you know where I am. Sleep well, miss."

"Isn't it funny, the way she still calls me 'miss'? Even though I am a married woman—and, in fact, a 'lady' for some months now," Aurelia commented as she shut the bedroom door firmly behind them.

"Shall I help you unbutton your gown?"

"Thank you." Aurelia sat down on the stool in front of the dressing table, and Flora stood behind her, regarding her sister's reflection in the mirror.

"It is interesting, isn't it, how things can be so very different from how one perceives them?"

"How do you mean?" Flora asked nervously as she began to undo the buttons on Aurelia's gown.

"For example, the fact that I was convinced you and Archie loathed the sight of each other. But then I discover that you had, in fact, spent three whole days together at Esthwaite when I was in London last summer."

"As I said, Archie was simply on his way down from Scotland and thought he'd call in." Flora forced her hands to continue, popping the buttons through one by one.

"Yes." Aurelia stood up so that Flora could remove her dress from her shoulders. "That is what you told me a few days ago, and what I believed," she said, as Flora began to loosen the stays on her sister's corset. "Until I began to think."

"About what?"

"Oh, this and that. Pass me my nightgown, sister dear. It is chilly in here."

Numbly, Flora picked up the silken nightgown that had been laid out on the bed and Aurelia put her arms in the air to enable the gown free passage over her body and the tiny bump that protruded from her stomach.

"It was something that Freddie said to me on my wedding night, just after he'd announced your betrothal," Aurelia continued.

"And what was that?" Flora pulled back the covers so Aurelia could slip into bed.

"He kissed me and wished me congratulations on my own marriage, and I returned the compliment on his forthcoming nuptials to you. He then laughed and whispered that we had both better take care of our respective husband and wife in future, as they seemed to be extremely fond of each other. I, of course, corrected him, saying he couldn't be more wrong and that, if anything, I had worried about the fact my sister and my husband had disliked each other since they were children. 'Oh, but you're wrong,' he whispered as he led me out on the dance floor. And I was, wasn't I, Flora?"

Two pink spots of color had appeared high on Aurelia's pale cheeks and her eyes glinted as she lay back on the pillows.

"Aurelia, I hardly think so. Freddie was very drunk that night."

"That's what I thought at the time, and I forgot all about it. Until I discovered Archie's visit to the Lake District."

"Forgive me for not telling you about it. It was simply an oversight, I—"

"Hardly an oversight, sister dear. When I saw you in London shortly afterward, and questioned you on Archie's state of mind, I asked you why you thought he hadn't proposed. You said you had no idea, and yet you had spent three days in his company just a few weeks previously. If anyone could have known his thoughts, it would have been you."

"We didn't discuss it . . . truly, all we talked of was plants—"

"Yes!" Aurelia gave a tight little smile. "A shared interest in botany. But even if his future intentions toward me were not spoken of, you must understand why it strikes me as odd that you never mentioned my husband's visit once."

"Yes . . . yes, in retrospect, I do. But I had just arrived in London, and was rather overwhelmed. Forgive me, Aurelia. It truly was an oversight."

"Perhaps, even given what Freddie had said to me the night of my wedding, I could have continued to overlook it. Sadly, it has played on my mind. So, today, while Sarah thought I was sleeping and I knew Archie was outside in the gardens, I went to his dressing room. And look what I found, stuffed into the pocket of the coat that he'd returned from London in yesterday."

Aurelia reached under the pillow, pulled out a letter, and handed it to Flora.

"I believe that is your writing, sister dear?"

Flora read it swiftly—it was the letter she'd written to Archie, warning him that Aurelia knew of their time together in Esthwaite.

"That isn't evidence of anything! I was simply worried that you might view it as such. Which is exactly what you have done."

"Please, don't patronize me!" Aurelia's voice shook with latent fury. "This letter alone indicates an obvious intimacy, a relationship between the two of you, of which I had no idea. And if that wasn't enough, as I stood reading it in the light from the bedroom window, I saw you together in the garden. Flora, my husband was holding your hand."

"I . . ." Flora shook her head; she had no more words with which to defend herself. "Forgive me, sister dear. I can only swear to you that, even though the evidence is damning, nothing . . . untoward has ever taken place between Archie and me."

"And there was me believing the two of you couldn't stand each other." Aurelia gave a grim chuckle. "Well, many a wise poet has said that there is a thin line between love and hate. It seems that stands true for the state of affairs between my husband and my sister. Good God, you must both have laughed at my stupidity!"

"Never! All I ever wanted Archie to do was to marry you."

"Out of pity!" Aurelia spat at her. Flora took a step back from the bed. "Perhaps, he wanted to marry you all along, but you begged him not to after you'd seen me so distraught in London. Well, sister *dear*? Did you arrange it with him to assuage your own guilt?"

Her words hung in the air. Flora stood, turned to stone by her sister's venom and the truth of her words.

"I see." Aurelia nodded, the first flicker of tears visible in her eyes. "Well, I do not thank you for it. For you have bound me to a life of misery, married to a man I love who cannot ever love me. And now I am having his child and there is no escape for either of us. Flora, what have you done to me? And what did I ever do to you to deserve this cruelty?" Aurelia shook her head desolately. "I would rather I were dead."

Her voice broke as she began to cry. When Flora moved to comfort her, Aurelia swiped at her aggressively.

"Please, Aurelia, I say again that I meant for none of this to happen. I would do anything rather than see you hurt. I will . . . go away, even though there is nothing between Archie and me . . ."

"My husband was holding your hand in the garden this very afternoon!" she hissed through her tears. "Don't you dare continue to tell me lies! You treat me like a little girl when I am a married woman about to have a child of my own! And do you know the worst thing? It's not the relationship you have had with my husband—whatever it consists of—it's the fact that I have always trusted you more than any other person on this earth! I believed you loved me, that you had my best interests at heart. I've looked up to you since the day I was born. I have not only lost a husband—if I ever had him in the first place—but also my beloved sister."

"Please, Aurelia, think of your condition," Flora begged, seeing that she was becoming hysterical.

"Were you thinking of my 'condition' when you held my husband's hand in the garden today?"

"*He* took my hand, I could not stop him—"

"Don't blame him! I watched you stand there for far longer than you needed to, looking into his eyes like a lovesick girl."

Flora turned and walked toward the stool by the dressing table, feeling she would collapse if she didn't sit down. For a long time, a silence divided the two sisters.

"Not for the life of me did I ever mean to hurt you, Aurelia. I take full responsibility for my disgraceful behavior and I will never forgive myself for it."

"And nor should you! The question is, what on earth do I do now?"

"I can understand your hurt and pain, but I swear to you that Archie cares for you deeply."

"But his true passion is for you. Perhaps we should share him, just as your patron shares the King with his long-suffering Queen! Perhaps you could be his mistress, while I simply give birth to his babies, would that suit you?"

Flora stood up, her whole body trembling. "I will leave tomorrow morning. Even though you cannot believe me, I know that you and Archie can have a happy and successful marriage. I will tell him—"

"You will do no such thing! At the very least, you will grant me the promise that you will never again speak to my husband or contact him in any way. If we are to have any chance of a future together, he must not know of this conversation. I will say you have been called away to London."

"You will not attend my wedding?"

"No. I will say that my pregnancy has rendered me indisposed. And take scant comfort from the fact that you will almost certainly be as miserable as I, in a marriage to a man you cannot love, and who is frankly unlovable."

"Are you saying you wish never to set eyes on me again?"

"Never. You are no longer my sister," Aurelia answered tightly.

There was another silence as Flora stood up. "Is there nothing I can say or do to make penance?"

"No. Now, please leave. Good-bye, Flora."

"I will think of you every day for the rest of my life, and never forgive myself for how I have hurt you. Good-bye, darling Aurelia."

Flora, her eyes welling with tears she felt too guilty to shed, took one last glance at her sister to store it in her memory forever, and left the room.

30

"Goodness! I didn't expect you back so soon, Miss Flora," commented Nannie as Flora entered the day nursery at Portman Square.

"I have fittings to attend for my dress and my trousseau," she lied in reply.

"I reckon you're missing the bright lights of London, aren't you? And there was you always waxing lyrical about the countryside. A right city girl you've become," Nannie laughed.

"Are Mrs. Keppel and the girls here?"

"No, they haven't returned from France yet. They're due back next week." She paused and scrutinized Flora's demeanor. "Are you all right, miss? You look a bit out of sorts."

"Yes, I am quite well, thank you," she said, and left the nursery feeling she would never be "all right" again.

In the next few days, Flora was relieved that the house was quiet so she could endure her wretchedness alone. She took herself off for long walks in the fast-burgeoning parks of London, hoping that nature would comfort her. But all it did was remind her of Archie, and then, by immediate default, of Aurelia. As she walked determinedly, desperate to exhaust herself so she might fall into a mind-numbing sleep, the pain of losing the person she loved most in the world tore into her. She could not rest; neither could she eat. Her guilt knew no bounds, and as she prepared herself for a wedding to a man who repulsed her, Flora saw a life sentence of misery as a just punishment.

Almost three weeks before the wedding, Mrs. Keppel and the girls returned from France.

"My dear, you have grown so thin!" Mrs. Keppel exclaimed as they took tea together in the parlor. "It must be the stress of your forthcoming marriage. I remember losing two inches off my waistline before I married George."

"How is the King?" Flora changed the subject.

"He is much recovered since you saw him, but under the most dreadful pressure from his government, who are determined to embroil him—no, to *blackmail* him—into agreeing to constitutional changes he does not agree with. I am glad he has been abroad and at least distanced from it all. There is no doubt the pressure has affected his health, let alone his state of mind. He is not strong, as you saw in Biarritz. I feel desperately sorry for him, poor thing. He is a far better king—and man—than he has been given credit for."

Flora walked from the parlor later, thinking that Mrs. Keppel did not look herself either. And wondered what secrets *she* held.

In the next two weeks, as the dreaded day grew closer, Flora was thankful to be kept busy. She had attended the last fitting at Worth, along with the seven bridesmaids, having explained to Daphne that Aurelia felt unable to attend on her, due to her pregnant state. Violet had overheard this conversation and sought her out at home later.

"Flora, I am so sorry to hear that *votre soeur* is unable to be your maid of honor."

Violet's new habit of peppering her speech with snippets of French irritated the entire household and Flora gave a wry smile.

"Thank you."

"I'd just like to say that, as I am now the eldest of your attendants, if you would like me to take the role of your maid of honor, I would be honored to do so."

"That really is kind of you, Violet, and I am sure I will be in need of your help. I tried on the tiara I will wear at the wedding, and goodness knows how I will stand its weight," Flora said, touched by her offer.

Violet sat down on Flora's bed and surveyed her as she prepared for dinner downstairs.

"Flora?"

"Yes, Violet?"

"Can I be truthful with you?"

"That depends."

"Well, don't think I'm being rude, but you look perfectly *misérable* at present. Are you not looking forward to being married?"

"Of course I am, but like any girl, I am nervous."

"Do you love Freddie?"

Something about Violet's bluntness deserved an honest reply. "I . . . don't know him well enough to love him. But I am sure I will in time."

"I think I shall simply refuse to get married. I would far prefer to remain a spinster than have to marry someone I don't love. Everyone says to me that I'll change, but I know I won't. Not like Vita . . ." Violet's expression darkened. "She is such a turncoat."

"What do you mean?"

"She makes her debut this summer and all she can talk of is her new gowns and the young men who are already calling on her at Knole. And after all she said to me . . ."

"People do change, Violet. Sometimes the world just can't be as we wish it to."

"When I was younger, I believed in fairy tales, did you?"

"Every child does."

"Maybe it's been different for me: I grew up with a mother who wears a tiara and spends her holidays with the King of England. I have always been treated like a princess. Why should I grow up and believe differently? I just . . ."—Violet sighed and stretched dramatically—"want to be with the one I love. Is that wrong?"

"No." Flora swallowed hard. "Or at least, it's not wrong to *want* it. Whether it actually happens is a different story."

"And not a fairy tale." Violet sat up and swung her legs off the bed.

"Maybe not everyone deserves a happy ending," Flora replied, mostly to herself.

"Well." Violet stood up and walked across to the door. "I do."

With that, she left the room, and Flora thought back to the girl she had once been at Esthwaite, who had believed in fairy tales too.

On a rainy day at the beginning of May, Flora was called to Mrs. Keppel's parlor.

"Please leave us," Mrs. Keppel snapped at the parlor maid. "We do not wish to be disturbed."

A startled Mabel scurried from the room and Flora wondered what had happened. She had never seen Mrs. Keppel be anything other than polite to her staff.

"Please, sit down."

Flora did so and Mrs. Keppel walked to the fire, took the poker from its stand, and attacked the burning embers viciously. "It is cold in here, even though it is already May, don't you think? And the King, so I am told, has caught another chill. Yet, guess where he dines tonight? At the Keyser woman's home! He goes to play bridge with *her* when he is newly returned to London. What he sees in her, God only knows. Forgive me, Flora," Mrs. Keppel said, sitting down. "Perhaps it is inappropriate to talk to you of my concerns, but who else can it be?"

Flora had no idea who "the Keyser woman" was, but guessed that perhaps Mrs. Keppel was not the only one of the King's female "companions." "Can I pour you a sherry?" she offered lamely.

"Perhaps a brandy will be better. Like the King, I am quite chilled. Normally, of course, he leaves straight from France for his Mediterranean cruise. But given the current political crisis, he has had to return home sooner, or those who are eager to will criticize his absence. And where is his wife? She has left him behind and is cruising the Greek isles! Is there no woman who truly cares for the poor man?"

Flora handed her the requested brandy and Mrs. Keppel put a shaking hand around it. "Thank you, my dear. Forgive me for not being myself."

"I hardly think your concern for the King's well-being is in need of forgiveness."

"So many in this town have had an ax to grind against me for my relationship with Bertie, but none of it was out of selfishness. It's simply because I love the man. Is that a crime?"

"I don't believe so, no."

"Yes, he has made mistakes," Mrs. Keppel continued, setting down the glass, "but when one is told by one's mother that one is not fit to walk on the very earth that his father trod, and then his rightful place as king is denied him because she simply did not trust him to take her place, what kind of legacy does that give any child, let alone the Prince of Wales? What was he to do for all these years as he sat idle, waiting to take up his natural role? And all because of her blind love for his 'perfect' father. Let me tell you, Flora, no human being is perfect. Bertie has suffered so much from her constant disdain of him."

Flora was shocked at Mrs. Keppel's diatribe. She had been born under the reign of Queen Victoria, the most powerful sovereign in Christendom, the very *essence* of motherhood, with her enormous family and her loving husband. What Mrs. Keppel was saying was in such contrast to Flora's own Madonna-like image of the old queen, she could not take it in.

"And now, having spent every ounce of himself proving to the world that he *could* be a good king, he is simply exhausted, and his health is failing fast. Flora"—Mrs. Keppel grabbed her hand, the cold fingers squeezing her own—"I fear for his life. I really do."

"Surely there are many who watch over him and care for him at the Palace?"

"You would be surprised. Bertie is surrounded by weak men and women who will only do his bidding, who live to please him or whoever holds the seat of power. To be close to a sovereign is to learn that, despite the numerous people who seem to care, it is truly the loneliest position on earth."

Flora only caught a glimpse of Mrs. Keppel through the nursery window the following evening as she left the house, the feathers on her large velvet hat positively shuddering with each agitated step. Violet joined her at the window, Panther in her arms.

"Mama has been very odd lately. Is Kingy unwell again?"

Flora kept her tone light. "I am sure everything is quite all right."

Flora did not see Mrs. Keppel at all the following day; she was either out or keeping to her private rooms. She could only hope that the King was not suffering another attack of the bronchitis he had endured in Biarritz.

The next morning, as she was walking downstairs with Sonia to enjoy the glorious May sunshine and sketch the burgeoning delphiniums in the park opposite, she met Mrs. Keppel in the entrance hall.

"How is he?" she whispered as they went together to the front door.

"Dr. Reid says he is extremely unwell. He is being administered oxygen and has requested I go to him. The Queen is still not home." She stepped into the brougham and Sonia and Flora continued on their way across to the park.

At five thirty, Flora saw the brougham draw up to the house and Mrs.

Keppel emerge. Later, she walked downstairs to dinner, but found only Mr. George at the table. He greeted her with a weary smile as she sat down.

"I'm afraid Mrs. Keppel is indisposed tonight, and is eating in her room," he said. "I presume you have heard that the King is unwell?"

"I have, yes."

"They have posted an announcement outside Buckingham Palace, saying that 'His Majesty's condition causes some anxiety.' My wife was with him there today, and confirms the King is seriously ill. Thank God, the Queen is returned from her cruise and is at the Palace now."

"All we can do is pray," Flora said eventually.

"Yes." Mr. George nodded sadly. "That is exactly what my wife said to me earlier tonight."

"Miss Flora, are you awake?"

Flora jumped into consciousness, having no idea what time it was. "What is it?" she asked as she saw Barny standing in the half-light at her door.

"It's Mrs. Keppel, she's hysterical. If you could go to see her . . ."

"Of course. Where is she?"

"In her boudoir. See if you can calm her."

In fact, Flora hadn't needed to be told where Mrs. Keppel was, for the pitiful sobbing emanating from behind the door would have led her there anyway. Feeling it was rather pointless to knock, she did so a couple of times for the sake of politeness, then opened it.

Mrs. Keppel was pacing the room in her nightgown and silken robe. Her thick auburn hair fell wildly about her shoulders, mirroring her current state of mind.

"What is it? Is it the King?"

"No." Mrs. Keppel paused to see who was asking, registered Flora, and continued as she closed the door behind her. "It's the Queen! Last night, she arrived home, having been away from Bertie all these weeks when he has been so ill, and she had me banished from the Palace! Now I am not allowed to see him in his dying hour! How can this be? How can it be?"

Mrs. Keppel sank into a silken huddle on the rug and sobbed. Flora walked toward her and knelt down beside her. Eventually, Mrs. Keppel calmed herself enough to speak again.

"Flora, I love him. And he loves me! And needs me! I know he wants me there!" Mrs. Keppel fumbled in her robe pocket, drew out a letter, and unfolded it. "See," she said, stabbing at it with her index finger, "you read it."

Duly, Flora took the sheet of paper from her trembling hands.

My dear Mrs. George,

Should I be taken very seriously ill I hope you will come and cheer me up but should there be no chance of my recovery you will I hope still come and see me—so that I may say farewell and thank you for all your kindness and friendship since it has been my good fortune to know you. I feel convinced that all those who have any affection for me will carry out the wishes which I have expressed in these lines.

"I see," said Flora quietly.

"What should I do?"

"Well," she said slowly. "I think that he is the king, and you are his subject. And . . . this letter decrees that he wishes you to go to him."

"But can I show it to the Queen? His wife? Would it be an unseemly thing to do, to use this to beg to be in the presence of a man who has only a few hours left on earth, so that I may say good-bye? I just . . . want to say . . . good-bye."

If ever Flora had felt the weight of the world on her shoulders, she felt it now. It wasn't her place to tell the King's mistress whether she should run to him on his deathbed, ignoring the displeasure of the Queen. She could only put herself in the position of a woman who loved a man and wanted to see him before he died.

"I think," Flora said, taking a deep breath, "that I would go to the Palace. Yes, I would," she reiterated. "Merely because, even if you cannot gain entry to see the King, you will always know that you tried to do as your sovereign requested. Yes." Flora looked Mrs. Keppel in the eyes. "That is what I would do."

"My dissenters inside the Palace will hate me all the more for it."

"Perhaps. But he will not."

"God knows what will become of me when he is gone . . . I dare not think."

"He is not gone yet."

"My dearest Flora." Mrs. Keppel lifted her shaking arms toward her. "You are a joy to me. And to the King." She took Flora into her arms and held her. "I will send him your love."

"Please do. I am extremely fond of him."

"As he is of you." Mrs. Keppel wiped her tears away and picked herself up off the floor. "I will go to the Palace, and if they do not let me see my love, then so be it. But at least I have tried. Thank you, Flora. Can you send in Barny to me to help me dress? I must not wear black"—she shuddered—"but some gay color that will cheer him."

"Of course. Good luck." Flora left the room.

For the rest of the day, the residents of 30 Portman Square held vigil, waiting for Mrs. Keppel to return home. Nannie arrived with regular bulletins as to the King's health, passed on from Mrs. Stacey, who took the gossip on the street from the tradespeople who called at the kitchen door with the household deliveries.

Sonia came to sit by Flora in the day nursery.

"Do you think Kingy's off to heaven today? All the servants are saying he's going to die."

"If he does, I am sure he will go to heaven," said Flora. "He is a very good man."

"I know some people are scared of him, but he always played games with me. He used to race bits of toast down his trouser leg for me, getting butter everywhere. And he is kind, even though I don't much like his dog, so I think that Kingy will grow wings and go and live on a cloud with God. After all, *He* is a king too."

"Yes, He is," said Flora, as Sonia nestled into her and sucked her thumb.

Dusk was descending when Flora finally heard the brougham return to the front of the house beneath the window, then saw a figure being half carried out of it. She raced to the top of the stairs and leaned over the banister, straining her ears to hear Mrs. Keppel's voice. All she heard was silence.

"Mr. and Mrs. Keppel are taking supper in their rooms, Miss Flora. I'll bring you up a tray to yours," said Mrs. Stacey, who Flora saw was wearing black. *Or maybe she always has and I never noticed*, Flora thought.

At midnight, she still lay awake and listened to the nearby church bells chime midnight, sounding like a death knell. Shortly toward one o'clock, she heard bells tolling mournfully from all over London.

"He's gone, God bless him, God bless the King," said Nannie, greeting Flora as she arrived on the nursery floor the following morning. "The girls are inconsolable. Perhaps you'd come and see them?"

"Of course." Flora walked in and found them huddled together in an armchair with Panther sprawled across their laps.

"Oh, Flora, Kingy has died in the night! Isn't it awful?" cried Sonia.

"Yes, it's terribly sad."

"What will Mama do now? We will never go to Biarritz again, and she will never be a queen," said Violet.

"Kingy will always be a king, and your mother will always be a queen," Flora said gently as she gathered them to her and they leaned into her embrace.

"There are thousands gathering outside the Palace, but a lot's outside our doorstep too," said Nannie, who was by the window, peering onto the street below. "They want her to say something, but what can she say? Mrs. Keppel was the people's queen, you see, but of course, she's not here."

"Where is she?" asked Flora.

"Gone with Mr. George to stay at the Jameses' in Grafton Street," Nannie said quietly. "We are to follow soon. You stay with the children and I'm going to pack." Flora nodded.

"I want to see Mama," Sonia sobbed into Flora's shoulder. "Why has she gone with Papa and left us?"

"People who are sad often want to be left in peace."

"Then why can't we just draw the blinds in our home and be sad here?"

"Maybe that's quite hard to do with lots of people making noise outside, darling," she said, stroking Sonia's hair.

Violet pulled away from Flora and stood up. "Why have they gone to the Jameses'? It is the most dreadful house and they are the most dreadful people." Violet's lips tightened as she looked down onto the crowd outside the front door. "Why are people so nosy? Why can't they just leave us alone?"

"They too are mourning and want to be close to those who were close to Kingy."

"I wish I could join all the people outside the Palace . . . just be invisible and mourn him."

"Well, you are all who you are, and there isn't a lot to be done. Now, Nannie is packing, and you must both be big and brave as Kingy would have wished you to be."

"We will try, but we are not grown-ups yet, Flora—merely *enfants*," Violet said haughtily, sweeping out of the day nursery.

Flora duly followed her to find Nannie.

"Do you know if there is any directive for me? Am I to join you?"

"Mrs. Keppel didn't mention you, Miss Flora. My instruction was only to take the children and Moiselle to Grafton Street."

"I see."

"Well, you are to be married in a week's time. Maybe she thought you would go to stay with your sister or your fiancé's family?"

"Yes, of course."

"This is the end of an era, Miss Flora." Nannie shook her head and sighed heavily. "After today, nothing will ever be the same for any of us."

Flora waved the girls a tearful good-bye from the entrance hall as she watched them being bundled into the brougham with Nannie and Moiselle, the reporters and the public held back by policemen. Mr. Rolfe closed the door of the car and Flora thought how like vultures the onlookers appeared in their black mourning clothes. As she walked upstairs, she wondered if she would ever see any of the Keppels again.

Back in her room, the house eerily quiet, Flora wrote a telegram to Freddie to ask whether it was convenient for her to arrive at Selbourne tomorrow, then handed it to Mr. Rolfe to send. She knew there would be no refuge at High Weald.

After packing her clothes in her cases, she went again to the window, and saw that the crowd was beginning to disperse. And as night fell, the street grew silent—*Silent as a grave*, she thought. She tried not to feel hurt or abandoned. After all, as Nannie had said, Mrs. Keppel had almost certainly presumed Flora had at least two sanctuaries to go to, if she had thought at all in the midst of her enormous grief.

Flora opened the window in her room and sat on the sill with Panther in her arms, looking up at the clear night sky.

"Good-bye, darling King. And Godspeed," she said to the stars above her.

31

"A visitor for you, Miss Flora," said Peggie as she entered Flora's bedroom.

"Who is it?"

"The Countess of Winchester. I've put her in the drawing room downstairs and given her tea."

"Thank you."

Flora was relieved that the Countess had responded to her telegram only a day after she had sent it, though surprised that Daphne had come to see her in person. She walked downstairs and opened the drawing room door to see Daphne sitting on the chaise longue, wearing a sumptuous dark velvet gown, black sapphires glittering on a band in her graying hair.

"Dearest Flora, I am so very sorry for your loss." Daphne stood up and took Flora in her arms.

"It is hardly my loss, rather the country's, and the world's."

"Well, we have all lost," said Daphne. Taking the natural role of hostess, she invited Flora to sit down. "'Tis all so tragic, is it not? And the timing simply couldn't be worse."

"Perhaps no time is good to lose the King of England."

"Of course, but now the wedding simply cannot take place next week. Any form of celebration will be seen as a slight against the King."

"I understand that it will have to be postponed."

"Yes, I am sure you do. Especially under the . . . circumstances."

Flora didn't quite understand her obviously barbed comment but continued regardless. "I assume you received my telegram. The Keppels have left the house and I feel it is not right for me to stay here either. I was hoping I could come and stay at Selbourne until Freddie and I are married."

"Surely you can stay at your sister's house in Kent?"

"That would not be . . . convenient."

"Really?" Daphne scrutinized her. "I thought that dear Aurelia relied on your company."

"She does, yes, we have always been close . . ." Flora grasped for a suitable explanation but was at a loss. "I cannot stay there and that is that."

"I see."

Silence hung about the room.

"My dear," Daphne sighed eventually. "Given how things are now with the King passing on, I must inform you that the wedding can't ever take place. I am sure you understand."

Flora looked at Daphne in total confusion. "It is canceled?"

"Yes."

"I . . . can you tell me why?"

Daphne took a long time to gather her thoughts before she spoke. "May I pour you some tea?"

"No thank you. I beg you to tell me why my marriage to Freddie won't happen. I understand the need for postponement, but—"

"Because of who you *are*, my dear. Surely you can see that, at a time when everyone is feeling for the Queen and her dreadful loss, it would be totally inappropriate?"

"Oh," said Flora, the penny finally dropping, "because of Mrs. Keppel."

"Yes, that too."

"I understand."

"I am not quite sure you do, my dear, but for my part, all I can say is that I am grieved at this unexpected turn of events. I believed that you could give Freddie the stability he needed, and was looking forward to welcoming you into our household. But given the altered circumstances, my husband cannot now advocate any union between you and his heir. As you know, women can only do what their husbands tell them. There now, please don't be aggrieved, my dear. It is simply the way things have turned out, and no fault of yours."

Flora said nothing, feeling like a leaf blown in the wind, completely powerless to control her own destiny.

"Perhaps you can return to Scotland, to stay with your parents, if you can't go to your sister's house?" Daphne suggested.

"Perhaps I can, yes."

"Well then, I doubt there is more to say. You can be assured that Freddie is devastated, as all of us are, but no doubt he will recover, as will you." Daphne stood up and walked toward the door. "Good-bye, my dear, and God bless."

Flora remained frozen in her seat for a while after Daphne had left. She felt numb . . . there was neither relief at her sudden release, nor fear as to where she would go from here. In this house, her life seemed to have begun and then ended.

"Or maybe it has ended and begun," she muttered, trying to rouse herself from her grief over the King, the Keppels' abrupt departure, and the shock at her future's coming to a sudden halt.

Dusk began to fall—a dusk that the King would never see. The streets outside were deathly silent, as if the whole of the city were tucked away inside their homes mourning the passing of their monarch. She leaned back in the chair, and a tear dripped down Flora's cheek as she remembered him in this house, his great presence and zest for life. She must have dozed off, as the clanging of the doorbell jolted her awake and she opened her eyes to see that it was dark. Searching in the blackness for the door of the drawing room, she opened it slightly and listened at the crack.

She heard Mrs. Stacey and Peggie mounting the stairs.

"Go and see if Miss Flora's in her room, and I'll put on the drawing room lights. It would be useful to know when she intends to leave—Mr. George sent round a messenger earlier, asking me to mothball the house until they have decided what to do. I've sent the footman up to the attic for the dust sheets."

"If I was her, I'd be leaving London as soon as I could. Out of respect for the Queen if nothing else."

"I'm still not sure she even knows," Mrs. Stacey replied.

"Well, if she don't, she ought to know; the rest of London seems to," hissed Peggie.

"Get on with you! See if she's up there, and I'll light the lamps."

Flora backed away from the door as Mrs. Stacey entered, giving a little squeal of shock as she saw Flora standing in front of her in the dark.

"Goodness, Miss Flora! You didn't half give me a fright."

"My apologies," Flora said as Mrs. Stacey began to light the lamps.

"You have a visitor," she said. "I'll send him up and also get Mabel to come and restoke the fire. There's a right chill in here."

"Who is it?"

"Sir Ernest Cassel, Miss Flora."

Mrs. Stacey left the room and Flora went to the large gilt mirror that hung over the fireplace to tidy her hair. She wondered what on earth Sir Ernest was doing visiting her and, for that matter, what Peggie had meant about leaving London out of respect for the Queen. And deducing that she must be tainted by her association with Mrs. Keppel . . .

"Good evening, my dear Miss MacNichol."

Sir Ernest Cassel entered the room and came over to her to kiss her hand. She could see that his eyes were red rimmed, his skin pale.

"Please, Sir Ernest, do sit down."

"Thank you. I am sorry to intrude on your grief; it is indeed a terrible day for all of us who knew and loved the King. And, of course, for his subjects. He would be amazed and gratified by the outpouring of sentiment from his beloved empire. They are still standing vigil by the thousands outside Buckingham Palace. And this a king who thought he could never follow in his mother's—or his father's—footsteps. I . . . well . . ." He swallowed hard. "It is a fitting tribute."

"May I ask why you have come, sir? Mrs. Keppel is no longer in residence."

"I am aware of that. I called in on her in Grafton Street to offer my personal condolences to her and her family. She was indisposed, and dear Sonia told me that her mama is quite mad with grief and will not even see her own daughters."

"She loved him so very much."

"I believe so, yes. And also, being blunt, Miss MacNichol, perhaps she cries for herself. Her 'reign' is over too, along with the King's."

"It is a very difficult time for her."

"And for her daughters. Although, knowing her as I do, I am sure that Mrs. Keppel will bounce back, but it is only right that she take a low profile now."

"Do you by any chance know if she managed to gain an audience with the King before he died?"

"Yes. I was there. And the whole episode was most unfortunate. When she saw the King, Mrs. Keppel became completely hysterical. The Queen had to ask for her to be removed from the room. It was not the dignified performance we have come to know from her, but then," Sir Ernest sighed, "what *is* dignified about death? So, while I was at Grafton Street, I asked if I could see you, and was most surprised to find that you had been left behind here. You seem to have been positively abandoned."

"Oh, I am sure it was not on purpose. As you said, Mrs. Keppel has become quite mad with grief. At worst it was an oversight and at best it was due to the fact she knew I would find sanctuary at my sister's house, or my fiancé's."

"I admire your loyalty, but I can assure you that everything Mrs. Keppel has ever done in her life has been carefully thought through. Perhaps you understand why she felt it important to disassociate herself from you at this moment?"

"No." Flora gave a grim chuckle. "Although you are not the first to visit me here today. The Countess of Winchester, mother of my fiancé, Viscount Soames, arrived this afternoon to tell me that my wedding next week wasn't only postponed due to the King's death, but canceled. Forever."

"Then the King was a wise man indeed, for he foresaw this."

"Did he? Was that because of my association with Mrs. Keppel?"

"Partly, yes, but not wholly."

"Sir Ernest." She stood up and warmed her hands by the fire, her frustration and exhaustion and grief getting the better of her. "Ever since I was called to come to London seven months ago to reside under this roof, I have felt that I am an innocent pawn in a game that everyone knows the rules of, except me. Forgive me for my bluntness, but I *entreat* you to tell me why I was brought to London in the first place. I was a nineteen-year-old girl from a good but hardly aristocratic family, whose parents had not even the funds for their eldest daughter to make her debut. Then I suddenly find myself with Mrs. Keppel as my sponsor in the highest echelons of society, taking tea with the King himself! And having a viscount propose to me, which meant that one day I would become a countess, married to an earl and presiding over one of the greatest estates in the whole of England."

Out of breath from emotion, Flora paused and turned to look directly at him. "And now, the King is dead, Mrs. Keppel has left me behind here, and I am no longer to be married. Sincerely, I understand neither of these abrupt changes of fortune, and it is maddening! I have felt constantly that everyone else knows something that I don't. I—"

"Miss MacNichol, I can see quite clearly now why you describe yourself as an innocent pawn. Like others, I presumed you knew. Please, let me pour us both a brandy."

"Really, I do not drink brandy."

"Think of it as medicinal. You are going to need it."

Sir Ernest rose and went to the tray of decanters as Flora, embarrassed by her show of emotion, did her best to regain her composure.

"Here, drink it, my dear, it will warm you."

"Please, Sir Ernest, I never wished to come to London originally, and in retrospect, I am ecstatic to be released from a marriage to a man I could never have begun to love. So do not fear you will upset my sensibilities further. The very fact you are here with me tonight, on the night of the death of our King, only confirms that you must have the answers I need."

"Forgive me, for on this night of all nights, you bring my emotion to the surface. Last year, the King told me he was uncertain about Mrs. Keppel's idea of bringing you to live with her in London. But then, of course, he grew fond of you, and, just as Mrs. Keppel intended, fonder of *her* for introducing you into his life, especially at a moment when his days were numbered. And he knew it, oh, how he knew it. Just after you had been with him in Biarritz, he sent for me and asked me to make provision for you on the event of his death. He asked me to give this to you." Sir Ernest opened his briefcase and removed a slim envelope, which he handed to her.

As she took it, she saw it was addressed to her in an erratic spiky hand.

"Also, when I visited the King last night, he had asked me to bring some money with me—a large sum—and it was to come in notes. I went to see him, and put the amount by his bedside. He nodded and thanked me, and said he hoped to be able to pass on the money to where it was needed. Sadly, only shortly afterward, he slipped into a coma. One of his advisers returned the envelope to me, feeling it was inappropriate for such a large amount of cash to be sitting by the King's bedside. It was almost ten thousand pounds. I knew who the money was intended for. And here I am." He reached into his briefcase once again and brought out a parcel wrapped in brown paper, which he placed into Flora's shaking hands.

"You cannot mean the money was for me? I hardly knew the King. I only met him twice—"

"My dear young lady, I am truly surprised Mrs. Keppel never told you. And I wish I wasn't the one whose duty it is to tell you now." Sir Ernest downed the rest of the brandy as Flora watched impatiently.

"Miss MacNichol—Flora . . ."

"Yes?"

"You are his daughter."

Flora knew she would remember that short sentence for the rest of her life. As she stared out into the night, she began to wonder why she had never contemplated the thought before. Yet, she knew that even if she *had* considered it, she would have dismissed it as absurd. Now, as she looked down at the envelopes on her lap, and then at the man who had been the King's closest adviser sitting opposite her, everything made perfect sense.

Perhaps in some untouchable part of her psyche she *had* known, but because the idea was so untenable, she had never allowed it to come to the surface.

The mistress and the illegitimate child . . .

Deciding brandy was definitely in order, Flora took a gulp from the tumbler she had ignored earlier. "Forgive me, sir, it is quite a shock. And surely, there is no proof that this is so?"

"It is known by all concerned to be the truth. And, most importantly, by your father. Your *real* father," he corrected himself. "You can understand that, after the King's liaison with your mother, there could be no acknowledgment of her . . . predicament. Your mother agreed to marry immediately and to move away from London."

"Which is why my grandparents would not set eyes on me, or attend my wedding . . ."

"It is also why you did not have a debut. How could you possibly be presented at court to the Queen, who would almost certainly know who you were?"

"I could not, sir, I agree. And my father—that is, my mother's husband—now I understand why he could hardly look at me. He must have known."

"I am sure you are correct in your assumption. If you were to study your parents' marriage certificate and your birth certificate, you would find that there is a three-month . . . inaccuracy in the dates."

Flora thought back to the letter she had found in her father's chest of drawers.

"Yes. And I also know that money changed hands. I believe my . . . *step*father was paid to marry my mother. Did he . . . did the King love my mother?"

"Forgive me, I cannot comment, but he was certainly most fond of you."

"Mrs. Keppel knew of the relationship between my mother and the King?"

"They made their debuts together. They were friends."

"The whole of London has known who I was," she whispered. "And I have not."

"At least, under Mrs. Keppel's patronage, your fortunes rose."

"I too was part of the King's 'alternative' court . . ."

"And it was a court that made the King very happy."

"Why did Mrs. Keppel bring me to London?"

"Again, I can't say for certain whether she wished to introduce you to your father for *your* sake or his. Or, in fact, to benefit herself and thereby gain the King's patronage. However, things turned out as they did and the King told me on a number of occasions how much he enjoyed your company. And indeed, he saw many ways in which the two of you were alike. Your appearance in his life gave him great joy, Miss MacNichol. If he had lived longer, I am sure your relationship would have become closer."

"And through this, I became something to be coveted by others because they knew I was the King's daughter. And recently accepted by him, even if illegitimate . . . ," Flora mused quietly. "That is why Freddie thought to marry me. The Countess kept speaking of my 'good stock' and even talked of the possibility of the King's attendance at our wedding . . ."

"It perhaps had a bearing on events, yes. But, of course, now the King is dead, and the Queen lives—"

"And the illusion that was created with Mrs. Keppel's magic wand has disappeared like a dream. Well . . ." Flora allowed herself a ghost of a smile. "Whatever has been and whatever may come, I am glad that I at least spent some time with him."

"He was proud of you, Miss MacNichol, but had to be so in secret. I hope you understand."

"I do."

"And now, as you have alluded to, there is a new era dawning; the old court is at an end, and we who served it are washed away and must endeavor to survive the future. I, on behalf of the King, hope the contents of that envelope will enable you to do so. And I suggest that you have no false pride about using it. He saw you as a free spirit, an innocent untainted by all he had to deal with from birth. Whatever your future may be, use his legacy wisely. So, will you go to stay at your sister's?"

"I cannot."

"The doors are already closed to you there?"

"Yes." Flora decided not to elaborate.

"Please remember that the position you find yourself in is through no fault of your own. You must feel no guilt. The machinations around you are not of your making. It is a simple accident of birth. That has been your curse and, I sincerely hope, your recent pleasure."

"It was indeed a pleasure to become acquainted with the King."

"And now, Miss MacNichol, I must take my leave. As you can imagine, I have much to do, but I know you were uppermost in the King's thoughts when he was close to death."

"Thank you for sparing the time to come and see me." Flora rose, and Ernest Cassel followed suit.

"Don't thank me. I feel quite dreadful that I must now leave you here alone in this house."

"No, Sir Ernest, I *do* thank you for it. For better or worse, you have given me the answers I've been searching for ever since I arrived in London. Now that I know, it is possible for me to move forward."

"And I will always be at your service. If you wish me to help invest your inheritance, do not hesitate to contact me. And may I say that the grace with which you have taken what I have had to tell you tonight marks you out as a great princess. And as your father's daughter. Good night, Miss MacNichol."

Ernest Cassel gave a slight bow, then swept out of the room at great speed, which Flora instinctively knew was to hide his own emotion. With Panther at her heels, she walked sedately upstairs to her room, as if it were any other day. Someone had lit the gas lamps and she lay down on the bed, studying the hefty envelope. A strange sense of calm had overtaken her; what she had just been told was no more surreal than the events of the past seven months. Now everything fitted together like a completed jigsaw puzzle.

She slept then, nature taking pity on her and allowing her shocked mind to rest. She woke in the early hours just before dawn. And, with Panther purring by her side, she opened the first envelope.

26th April 1909

My dear Flora,

(I do commend your mother on your name—you are aware I have always been partial to Scotland.)

As you will know by now if you are reading this I am your blood father. If you doubt this, as I can assure you I did before Mrs. Keppel suggested that I meet you, then doubt it no longer. My dear girl you even have my nose! In this I sympathize with you, for it is unattractive but sits on your face nobly. There is much that I recognize of myself in you and to be blunt Flora, I was not particularly wishing to, although the facts of your conception are undeniable: I can confirm that your mother was untouched by another when we began our brief liaison.

Firstly you must forgive me for my behavior toward her and, subsequently, you. I hope you are able to understand the situation I was placed in. No more needs to be said about that other than that I was glad when I heard your mother had been safely married.

Ernest Cassel will have seen you and handed this to you, along with an amount that I hope will secure your future. I beg you to only count yourself lucky that you do not lead the life of your half brothers and sisters. It is my hope that at least one of my children can live a life unfettered by protocol and the demands of a royal position. Live your life in the freedom of anonymity as I wished to have had the chance to live mine. And above all, be true to yourself.

So now, my dear Flora, I wish you happiness, fulfillment, and love. And I am saddened that I have not had longer to get to know you better.

Remember the short moments we shared.

And I beg you please burn this letter for all concerned.

The letter was signed in Edward's script, with the royal seal.

Flora then opened the heavy envelope, already suspecting what it would contain. Out fluttered hundreds of notes—the value of which she would count later.

Flora stuffed the money back into the envelope, and the letter into the silken pocket at the back of her journal. Then she rose from her bed and rang the bell for Peggie, asking her to tell Freed she would need him to drive her to Euston station shortly.

After boarding the train and settling herself in a carriage, she peered through the window as it left the station. Panther meowed in his basket and as there was no one else in the carriage with her, she took him into her arms.

"Don't cry, my darling," she murmured. "We're going home."

STAR

October 2007

Rubus fruticosus
(blackberry—Rosaceae family)

32

So, there we are. It's quite a story, isn't it?"

Mouse's voice had a soothing resonance to it, and I'd closed my eyes, forgetting where I was as he transported me back almost one hundred years ago. Flora's rich, descriptive language—the kind that Orlando adored and continued to use himself—only enhanced the picture I'd created in my mind.

Flora's real father . . . a king. But that wasn't the point. I swallowed the lump in my throat at the emotion she had felt and so poignantly described in her journal. And wondered how I would feel if the same thing ever happened to me.

"Star? Hello?"

I did my best to focus on the figure sitting on the sofa opposite me. "This . . . story. Do you think it's true? I mean, he was the King of England . . ."

"It absolutely could be true. Edward was renowned for having a number of mistresses at any particular time in his reign. I've checked out the historical facts, and I've found one recorded pregnancy apparently attributed to Edward VII. And given the level of contraception, or lack of it, at the time, I'd reckon it would be a miracle if there weren't more that went unrecorded."

"How awful for the Queen. It amazes me that Mrs. Keppel was such a pillar of society."

"Certainly in the upper classes here in England, monogamy only became a prerequisite of marriage comparatively recently. In Flora's day, arranged marriages between the great families of England were just that: a business deal. Once an heir was on the scene, both men and women were allowed the freedom to take lovers as long as they were discreet."

"Are you a historian?"

"I studied architecture at university. But interestingly, humanity's needs and wants have a lot to do with the buildings they live in. Secret passages that led from one boudoir to another, for example . . ." Mouse studied my expression. "You're looking prim, Star. Are you prim?"

"I have morals," I answered as calmly as I could. This was not the question to ask me after my earlier conversation with Shanthi.

"Fair enough. So, does it excite you that you may be related to our British royal family? After all, your father left you a Fabergé cat as a clue, which Flora states in her journal was given to her by Edward VII."

"Not really," I admitted.

"Perhaps if you were English, it would. I know any number of people who would be falling over themselves to prove a royal connection. We Brits tend to be the most appalling bunch of snobs and social climbers. I'm sure it's far more egalitarian in Switzerland."

"It is. I'm more interested to know what happened to Flora after she ran home to the Lake District."

"Well, all I can tell you is—"

I heard the key in the lock then, and immediately stood up.

"Your sister?"

"Yes."

"I must be off anyway."

Mouse was standing as CeCe entered the room.

"God, Sia, I had a shit day—"

She stopped short as she saw Mouse by the sofa.

"Hello, I'm Mouse," he said.

"CeCe, Star's sister."

"Pleased to meet you," he offered as CeCe brushed past him on her way to the kitchen. "Right, I guess I'll be off."

I followed Mouse to the door.

"Here. Keep them." He pressed Flora's journals into my hands. "You might want to reread them. And also"—he leaned his head down to whisper in my ear—"take a look inside the silk lining of the back cover."

"Thank you," I said, honored that he trusted me enough to take care of what, in essence, was an important English historical archive.

"Sia? Have you made any supper? I'm starving!" came a shout from the kitchen.

"You'd better go," he said. "Bye, Star." Then he bent down and gave me a light peck on the cheek.

"Bye," I said, and slammed the door on him as soon as he was through it, my cheek burning where he'd kissed me.

I was up before CeCe the next morning, and when she came down, I made her a plate of honey on toast as a peace offering, knowing it was one of her favorites.

"Got to run," she said when she'd finished it. "See you later."

I went upstairs to retrieve the journals. Ever since Mouse had left last night, I'd been desperate to read them. I decided that I wouldn't dwell on how rude CeCe had been to him, or the fact that she hadn't even asked me who he was.

Opening the back of each journal in turn, I soon found what I was looking for. I gently pulled out the frail sheet of paper hidden in the silk pocket at the back of the journal. Unfolding it carefully, I read the letter that the King of England had written to Flora, his illegitimate daughter. And marveled at how it had remained a secret for almost one hundred years. Replacing it, I then read through the final pages of the journal, doing my best to decipher the writing. And I pondered on the possibility that I was somehow related to the highest in this land. But I also knew Pa Salt well enough to be aware there would be twists and turns on my road to discovery. And something told me that the journey wasn't over yet.

The problem was, I couldn't make it alone. And there were only two people on the planet who could help me, one of whom was now out of bounds. And the other . . . well, I really didn't know about Mouse at all.

Then I realized I could have handed him the keys to the bookshop when I saw him last night. I had to return them, and break the last link I had to Orlando and the magical world of Arthur Morston Books. I also needed—and felt I deserved—a reference. I penned a letter to Orlando, and decided that if the shop was shut, I would drop it with the keys through the letter box. Besides, I needed to get out of this apartment, otherwise I'd brood on what Shanthi had said to me last night.

As I got on the bus, I pondered that it hadn't been her query over my sexuality that had destabilized me. After all, on my travels with CeCe, people we'd met had presumed we were a couple; we hardly looked like sisters—her dark butterscotch skin and diminutive stature in contrast to my height and pale complexion. And we showed obvious natural physical affection with each other. It wasn't even that Shanthi had made it clear she found me attractive . . . it was what *else* she'd said that had destabilized me. Her laser-beam perception had struck to the heart of my deepest problem.

Stepping off the bus, I walked to the door of the bookshop, praying that Orlando would still be barricaded in upstairs so I could drop the letter and keys through the letter box and run. I pushed the front door and found it was open. My stomach turned at the thought of facing him.

Thankfully, there was no sign of him in the shop, so I dropped the keys and letter onto the table, and retraced my footsteps to the door. About to leave, I stopped short, thinking how irresponsible it was to place a set of keys to a shop chock-full of rare books out in open sight. I picked them up again, and took them to the hidden alcove at the back of the shop. I put them in a drawer, and decided I'd text Orlando to let him know where I'd left them.

Turning to make a hasty retreat, I saw the door that led upstairs was ajar. And a highly polished black brogue enclosing a foot lay at a strange angle on the floor beyond it. I stifled a scream, then, taking a deep breath, pushed the door open as far as it would go.

And there was Orlando, lying in the tiny lobby that led to the stairs, his head resting on the bottom step, the three o'clock cake still grasped in his hand.

"Oh my God!"

I bent down and heard his shallow breathing and saw a bloody gash in the middle of his forehead.

"Orlando, it's Star. Can you hear me?"

There was no response, and as I sat there and dug out my mobile, I dialed 999 and told the woman at the other end what had happened as succinctly as I could. She asked me then if the injured party had any medical conditions, and I suddenly remembered.

"Yes, he has epilepsy."

"Right. An ambulance will be with you shortly." Then she talked me through how I should put Orlando in the recovery position. I did my best to follow her instructions. Orlando might have been thin, but there was a whole six feet of him trapped in a tiny space at the bottom of a staircase. Thankfully, a few minutes later, I heard a siren approaching and looked up to see a blue light flashing outside the shop window.

"He's over here." I waved to the paramedics as they came in. "I can't wake him . . ."

"Don't worry, miss, we'll sort him," said one of the paramedics, as I stood up to give them room to get to their patient.

As they checked him over, attaching a probe to his finger to monitor his stats, I dialed Mouse's number. It went to voice mail, and I explained as calmly as I could what had happened.

"He's coming round, miss. He's taken a nasty bump to his head, so we're going to take him on the van to get him checked out at hospital. Want to hop on?"

As they lifted Orlando onto the waiting stretcher, I grabbed the keys to the shop back from the drawer, locked up behind me, and followed the paramedics to the ambulance.

A few hours later, Orlando was sitting up in bed, looking dazed and pale, but at least he was conscious. A doctor had explained to me that Orlando had had an epileptic seizure and had almost certainly tripped on the stairs, knocking himself out.

"He has a concussion from the thump he took, but his brain scan came back normal. We'll keep him in for observation overnight, and he should be well enough to be allowed home tomorrow."

"Sorry," came a croaky voice from the bed.

"Orlando, you don't have to apologize."

"You've been wonderful to me, and now you've saved my life." A small tear rolled down his cheek. "Eternally grateful, Miss Star, eternally grateful."

He slept then and I went outside for some fresh air, and texted CeCe to tell her that my employer had had an accident, and that I might be home late as I was with him at the hospital. Just as I was preparing to go back inside, my mobile rang.

"Star, apologies. I've been out on that damned tractor all day, and there's never any bloody signal here," Mouse said, his voice tense. "I'm at Ashford station now. I'll see you in an hour or so. How is he?"

"Feeling pretty sorry for himself, but okay."

"I'll guarantee you that he hasn't been taking his medication properly.

Perhaps it was in protest against me selling the bookshop. I wouldn't put it past him."

"I don't think Orlando would knowingly put his life at risk, Mouse."

"You don't know him like I do. Anyway, thank God you found him when you did."

"I'm going back inside now. See you later." I snapped my mobile off and walked back through the hospital doors.

Orlando was moved to a private room on a ward, and once he was settled and the nurses had completed their checks, I was allowed to see him.

"He's all yours," one of the nurses muttered as she passed me on the way out.

"What have you been up to, Orlando?" I asked him as I sat down.

"Who, me? I simply asked if they had any Earl Grey rather than the dishwater they pretend is tea. And there's no cake, apparently."

"It's way past three o'clock."

"I suppose it is," he replied, surveying the blackness outside the window. "My stomach must have lost two hours in the day due to my . . . incident. It is obviously suffering from jet lag."

"Probably."

"I thought you'd gone home and deserted me," Orlando added.

"I had to make some calls. Mouse is on his way here to see you."

"Then I shall inform the nurses that I do not wish him to be allowed entry."

"Orlando, he's your brother!"

"Well, he needn't bother on my account. But I'm sure you'll be glad to see him."

I remained silent. Even though Orlando was behaving like a spoiled child, I was secretly pleased that he seemed to be back to his old self.

"I do apologize, Miss Star," he said eventually. "I am aware that this entire situation has nothing to do with you. And that my words to you the other day were cruel and unnecessary. The truth is, I've missed your company. In fact, today I was just on my way upstairs to telephone you, beg your forgiveness, and ask you if you'd return to work. Unless, that is, you've taken the job at High Weald."

"No, I haven't."

"You've found other employment already?"

"No. My loyalty lies with you."

"Even though, in my despair, I acted hastily and dismissed you?"

"Yes."

"Well, there's a thing." Orlando managed a weak smile. "So, will you come back to the bookshop? Or at least return for the time it takes to man the book 'ship' until it is well and truly sunk?"

"Yes. I've missed it—and you."

"Well, well, have you really? Goodness, Miss Star, how kind of you to say so. You are a veritable angel of mercy to all of us. And, of course . . ."

He paused, and closed his eyes for so long I worried that he'd lost consciousness again.

"Yes, Orlando?" I prompted him.

His eyes flickered open. "I understand that it would be selfish of me to keep you to myself. When others—specifically Rory—need you. I have decided that I must put his happiness before my own, and share you." He closed his eyes again, and lifted a weary hand. "You have my blessing to go to High Weald whenever it is deemed necessary."

There was a brief knock on the door and the nurse appeared.

"I have your brother here to see you, Mr. Forbes."

"Let him in. He just wants to see that you're okay," I said before Orlando could open his mouth to resist. He stared at me, then nodded like an obedient child. If he'd been surprised at my firm reprimand, he wasn't the only one.

"Hello, old chap. How are you feeling?"

Mouse entered the room and walked toward us. He looked exhausted—far worse than his brother in the hospital bed.

"No better for seeing you," Orlando replied tersely, and turned his head away to look out of the window.

"He's on the mend then." Mouse gave me a wry look.

"Yes," I said, standing up to offer him the chair.

"Really, don't leave on my brother's account," Orlando remarked acidly.

"I really should be going."

"Of course," Mouse said.

"Behave yourself, or at least try to." I smiled as I kissed Orlando on the forehead, avoiding the bandage taped to his wound. I picked up my rucksack and walked toward the door. "Let me know how the patient is," I said to Mouse.

"I will. And thanks yet again, Star. You're a hero."

During supper with CeCe later that evening, my mobile rang.

"Excuse me, I just need to take this." I stood up, feeling CeCe's eyes boring into my back, and walked onto the terrace.

"Hi, Star," said Mouse. "Just reporting in. If all goes well, Orlando should be discharged tomorrow. But the doctor was wary of him being alone for the next few days, given the head injury and his epilepsy. He might be more prone to fitting, especially since—as I suspected—Orlando admitted he had 'forgotten' to take his medication recently. The upshot is, whether he likes it or not, I'm going to have to take him back to Kent with me."

"Do you need me to come down and help? Orlando agreed it was okay."

"Star, if you would, that would be fantastic. Marguerite leaves again for France next Sunday and Orlando's made it patently clear he won't stay at Home Farm with me, so you'll have both Rory and Orlando with you at High Weald. Text me the time of the train you're getting on, and I'll come to the station to pick you up."

"Okay, will do. Bye." I ended the call and went back to the table.

"What does that family want of you now?" CeCe demanded.

"I have to go down to High Weald again. My boss is recovering there and he needs my help."

"You mean he needs you as an unpaid nurse," CeCe snorted. "Goodness, Sia, you're paid peanuts, and let's face it, you're only shop staff, after all."

"I've told you, I love the house and the family. It's no hardship." I piled up the empty plates on the table and carried them to the sink. "Can we leave it be? I'm going, and that's that."

"You know what, Sia?" CeCe said after a pause. "You've changed since you met that family. You really have."

33

Maybe I had—*changed*, that was. And like with any addiction, be it narcotics or a person, I'd been given a green light to return to High Weald, and every single reason not to had flown from my mind like smoke on a breeze. My mobile rang as I was clearing away breakfast the next day and I saw it was Orlando.

"Hello. How are you feeling?" I asked him.

"I am at least out of confinement, but have been unceremoniously carted down to the arctic conditions of High Weald. Against my will, I might add. I am perfectly well and able to take care of myself, and I resent being treated like a three-year-old child."

"I'm sure that Mouse was only following doctor's orders."

"The only bright spot on the horizon is that I hear tell you are joining us soon. At least I'll have some decent food to look forward to in the desert of my misery."

"I am, yes."

"Thank God. Really, I have no idea how poor Rory survives. I wouldn't be surprised if he was suffering from malnutrition and scurvy. Kent is known as the Garden of England, yet we live on toast and baked beans. I shall call the farm shop and order in supplies forthwith, and we shall eat like kings when you arrive. Also, I was wondering if I could request a favor?"

"What is it?"

"Could you pass by the bookshop and pick up my laptop? I believe it currently resides on my bed upstairs. I have a couple of clients who are searching for a Trollope and a Fitzgerald to present to their loved ones for Christmas. I'm sure there's Internet in Tenterden, and needs must when the devil drives."

"Mouse has Internet at Home Farm," I reminded him.

"I am aware of that, Miss Star, as it is technically my family home too. But given the circumstances, I would not darken his doorstep if I were on the verge of death, let alone for the sale of a book."

"Yes, I can go," I said, ignoring his comment.

"Thank you, and I shall look forward to seeing you."

"Bye, Orlando."

I took a bus up to Kensington High Street and, on the way to the bookshop, bought myself three thick woolen jumpers, some bed socks, and a hot water bottle as ballast against the cold.

Arriving at the bookshop, I headed up the stairs and swung open the door to Orlando's bedroom. There were books piled on every available inch of surface. A stack of them were masquerading as a bedside table, and a lamp stood precariously on top of *Robinson Crusoe*. The laptop sat in the middle of the bed, on top of the faded eiderdown and surrounded by even more books, to the point where I wondered how Orlando found space to sleep at night.

I carried the laptop downstairs, thinking there was little doubt about the love of Orlando's life. And what an accommodating love it was: at the turn of a page, he could be transported anywhere he wished to escape to, away from the drudgery of reality.

I walked through the shop, then a thought struck me and I hovered by the "British Fiction, 1900–1950" section. With a jolt, I saw that that particular patch of shelf was now empty, only a fine line of dust visible on the wood where Flora MacNichol's journals had sat. As I left the shop, I wondered if Orlando had moved them elsewhere or if he had something else in mind for them.

The journey down to High Weald was now a familiar one and I did not panic when I arrived at Ashford and couldn't see Mouse's car waiting for me. He turned up eventually, gave me a curt "hi," and we sped out of the station at breakneck speed.

"Glad you're here. It's not been fun playing nursemaid to my brother. I know you're fond of him, but God, he can be difficult when he wants to be. He's still refusing to speak to me."

"He'll get over it eventually, I'm sure."

"He may have to do it faster than that. I had a call from the owners of the shop next door to Arthur Morston Books. They sell Far Eastern antiquities, and apparently, business is booming, what with the Russians buying up properties in London. They've made an offer on the shop. It's a good one, and the agent thinks he can push them up farther with the threat of putting it on the open market."

"But what about the books? Where would they go? Never mind Orlando," I said.

"God knows," Mouse said grimly. "I hadn't expected to think about things like this so soon. But given the difficult market, we have to consider the offer."

"Will there be any money left over for Orlando to find an alternative home for him and his books?"

"Once the shop is sold and the debt paid off, the rest of the funds will be shared between the two of us. In fact, given Orlando has hundreds of thousands of pounds' worth of stock in that shop, we won't come out of it too badly at all. There'll be plenty for him to take out a lease on another premises if that's what he wants to do."

"Good."

"To be fair, this situation isn't just down to Orlando. It's also due to my mismanagement of the farm. Anyway," Mouse sighed, "many a slip, as they say, and we'll just have to wait and see how serious our bidder is. Right." He swung the car into High Weald's drive. "I hope you don't mind me dumping you and running, but I've got a million things to do at home tonight."

"No problem." I got out of the Land Rover and Mouse went to retrieve my luggage from the back.

"Could you have Rory ready for school at eight thirty tomorrow morning? It's only half a mile away, in what is rather grandly called High Weald village. Do you drive, Star?"

"Yes. I took my test in Switzerland eight years ago."

"Great. It would help a lot if you were mobile and could drive Marguerite's Fiat. I'll put you on the insurance."

"Okay." I gulped, thinking how rusty I'd be, besides having to drive on the left-hand side of the road.

Mouse drove off and I lugged my luggage to the front door, which opened immediately to reveal a welcome party.

"Star!" Rory threw himself into my arms, nearly knocking me backward off the step.

"Salvation is at hand! Thank the heavens," said Orlando from behind him, taking my luggage and putting it by the bottom of the stairs. Then he led us toward the kitchen, where the table was loaded with provisions he'd ordered in from the farm shop. I gave an inward sigh at the way Orlando spent money—despite their economic crisis, it seemed the Forbes family had never learned to economize.

"I didn't know quite what you'd want, so I bought everything I could think of. I must say that we were rather hoping for leg of lamb tonight. In fact, Rory and I have already picked the rosemary. Did you know that once you grow a bush in your garden, it's awfully bad luck to ever cut it down?" he said as he took a piece and put it under his nose like a fake mustache, causing Rory to giggle. "I remember this rosemary bush being here when I was a young pipsqueak like you. Now, Miss Star, what can we do to help?"

We sat down to eat two hours later and afterward played a game of Scrabble, which Orlando won by a mile.

"Uncle Lando is so clever," signed Rory, as I led him upstairs. "He said Mouse was making him sell his bookshop."

"Maybe. Now, let's get you into bed, and I'll send Orlando up to read you a story."

"Good night, Star, I'm glad you came back."

"So am I. Night, Rory."

"Morning," Mouse said as Rory and I got into the Land Rover. I chanced a glance at him as we drove away from the house and thought again how strained he looked.

"Pay attention to where we're going, will you, Star? If you have a practice in the Fiat, I can't see why you couldn't drive Rory to school from now on."

I concentrated on the route he took, which must have been less than seven minutes in duration but involved a number of left and right turns. We pulled up in front of a charming old schoolhouse, set next to a green in the center of the village.

"Star, come in with me," Rory signed, and pulled me down from my seat.

We walked in through the gate and joined the mothers shepherding their children through the playground. As everyone hung their coats on pegs, Rory reached out for a hug from me.

"Come to get me later?" he asked as a little girl came to offer her hand to Rory.

"Come on, Rory," the girl said to him. "We're going to be late."

With a last wave, Rory was off down the corridor.

"Okay?" Mouse asked me as I stepped into the car.

"Yes. Rory's obviously happy there."

"For now, at least. The school has been phenomenal with him, but whether he can continue in mainstream education as he gets older is another thing altogether," he said as we set off back down the country lanes. "Think you can manage to collect him tonight? I've got a meeting at half past three."

"I'll have a practice in the drive this afternoon."

"The keys are in the pot by the telephone. Call me if there's a problem."

I hopped out at the top of the drive and he zoomed off without another word.

In the kitchen, Orlando was sitting at the table. "There's some wonderful bacon in the fridge and some locally picked mushrooms. I do so love mushrooms," he said, giving me a sideways glance.

"How are you feeling?" I asked as I gathered his requested ingredients from the pantry and the fridge.

"As fit as a flea, or a fiddle. Though for the life of me, I cannot understand how a fiddle can be 'fit.' The fiddle player, granted. What are you doing today?"

"Giving myself a driving lesson in the Fiat. I have to pick Rory up from school at three thirty."

"Perfect! Then perhaps you could incorporate me into your plans. I need to visit Tenterden, a quality little town nearby. It has the most wonderful bookshop, where my mother used to take me as a child . . ." Orlando's voice trailed off as his current situation entered his thought process. "Anyway," he said quickly, "I am sure that they will have somewhere with broadband, and the delicatessen makes the best smoked salmon mousse I've ever tasted."

So, having coaxed the Fiat's reluctant engine to life, and completed a couple of practice runs up and down the drive to get to grips with a gear stick that resembled a large black lollipop, my equally nervous passenger and I set off for Tenterden. Orlando's directions were as unreliable as the car I was driving, and we bumped, screeched, and stalled our way along the narrow country lanes. By the time we reached Tenterden, my nerves were in shreds. I managed to find a parking space adjacent to the village green, its fast-shedding trees protecting a row of well-tended clapboard houses.

"I can assure you that the harrowing journey we have just taken will be well worth the effort," Orlando pronounced as he strode across the green and I followed him, feeling as though I had indeed been transported to a much gentler time. A church tower overlooked the old timber-framed buildings, and people chatted outside the colorful shops, or sat on the benches on the green.

He stopped abruptly outside a café, complete with mullioned toffee-shop windows, then held the door open for me to step inside. A woman looked up from serving a customer, and a wide smile appeared on her face.

"Master Orlando! How lovely to see you in here."

"And you, dear Mrs. Meadows. How is life treating you these days?"

"Times are tough for us independent shops. You'll have seen what's happened next door." She indicated to the left with her thumb.

"No, we approached from the other direction. What is it?"

"Mr. Meadows has had to close the bookshop. The two rents were killing us. And the café is the premises that's making money."

Orlando looked as if he had been punched in the stomach. "The bookshop is closed?"

"Yes, two months ago now, but so far, we haven't managed to find anyone to take over the lease. Will you be staying for your lunch?"

"We will indeed," Orlando said. "What is it today?"

"Chicken pie and mash."

"Then we'll take two of those, Mrs. Meadows, if you please. With two glasses of—"

"Sancerre," Mrs. Meadows answered for him. "You look as scrawny as always, Master Orlando. That young lady of yours not feeding you?" She nodded at me and smiled.

"I can assure you, she feeds me as well as you used to. Come, Miss Star."

We sat down at a knotted pine table and Orlando slumped onto his wooden chair, shaking his head. "I am grieving. Yet another part of my former life has disappeared. Meadows's Bookshop was a shining beacon of peace and tranquillity lighting up my childhood memories. And now it has gone."

Having eaten our chicken pies, which were indeed delicious, Orlando asked Mrs. Meadows if "the establishment possesses broadband." She duly took Orlando and his laptop to an office in the back.

In the meantime, I went to explore Tenterden, savoring the town's unique Englishness, with its quaint houses and shops set along narrow paved streets. I peered through the window of a toy shop, strewn with fake cobwebs, plastic spiders, and broomsticks. As it was Halloween the day after tomorrow, I decided it would be fun for Rory to celebrate it, as my sisters and I had always done at Atlantis. Pa Salt had told us that the Seven Sisters of the Pleiades were nearing their highest point in the sky at Halloween, so it had always felt like our very own holiday. When he was home, he'd take us up into his observatory and, one by one, let each of us look through the telescope at the star cluster. It was always me who had a problem finding *my* star—Asterope. It didn't seem to shine as brightly as my other sisters' stars.

"But you have *two* stars to your name, darling. They're just so close together that they look like one. See?"

And Pa Salt had lifted me up again. And I *had* seen.

"Perhaps I'm your twin star," CeCe had piped up.

"No, CeCe, you have your own star," Pa had told her gently. "And it's very close by."

Having collected a Harry Potter costume for Rory, I bought a witch's cloak and hat for me, and a wizard outfit for Orlando. At least I knew I'd have no problem persuading *him* to dress up. I then paused in front of a pair of mouse ears, whiskers, and a long tail. And, chuckling to myself, put them by the till too. I walked back along the high street with my bulging bag, then paused to buy a pumpkin.

"Good God! Let a woman loose among shops and she'll bankrupt her family in the blink of an eye." Orlando was standing out on the street.

"I bought some supplies for Halloween."

"High Weald is already awash with ghosts of the past, but I suppose it can always do with a few more. Now, just look at this." He pointed to the shop next door to the delicatessen, its bay window dominated by a large TO LET sign. "So sad," he sighed. "So very, very sad."

By Halloween, I'd become used to the Fiat's eccentricities. I dropped Rory at school, telling him there'd be a surprise waiting for him at High Weald later. On the way home, I carried on a few yards farther and turned left into Home Farm. *He can only say no*, I thought as I marched to the back door and knocked.

"It's open," came a shout from inside.

Mouse was sitting at the table, his head bent over his accounts ledger.

"Hello, Star," he said, giving me his first smile in days. "How are you?"

"Good, thanks."

"As a matter of fact, so am I. I've had some news. I'll put the kettle on." He stood up and filled an old iron kettle and put it on the range to boil. "Our London neighbors have upped the offer on the bookshop and want to proceed as soon as possible. There's even a chance the money could be in the bank by Christmas."

"Oh."

"You don't sound very pleased."

"I'm just thinking of Orlando, that's all."

"Better this than both of us ending up homeless and penniless. And now there really will be enough for Orlando to lease a local bookshop, and even buy a small house of his own if that's what he wants to do."

"I came here to ask you to join us tonight at High Weald. It's Halloween and we're all dressing up."

"Good idea," he said, surprising me with his positive response. "My God, Star, I'm so relieved. You have no idea just how bad things have been financially."

"Can I ask you not to mention it to Orlando this evening? I'd like Rory to have a nice time."

"Okay. How is he?"

"He's good."

"And you? You look well too. That sweater suits you. The color matches your eyes. By the way, you haven't come across those journals at High Weald yet, have you?" he asked suddenly.

"No, sorry," I said, only half lying. They had disappeared again, after all. And not from High Weald.

"Well, who knows where they've gone? It's just a shame that I can't confirm what my father told me before he died. But maybe the past is best left in the past. Have you heard from Marguerite?"

"She called last night, yes. She said the work was going well."

"And I'm sure it's not just the lure of murals, money, and wine straight from the cave that have sent her running back to France. My guess would be that she's met someone."

"Really?"

"I haven't seen her so energized in years. It's amazing what love can do, isn't it? It lights you up from the inside." He gave a small, sad smile. "Have you ever been in love, Star?"

"No," I replied honestly.

"That's a shame."

"Right." I stood up abruptly. The intimate turn this conversation was taking was making me uncomfortable. "I'll see you tonight for supper at seven o'clock prompt. By the way," I said as I walked toward the back door, "we have a costume for you too."

Once Rory was home from school, we lit the pumpkin and placed it by the front door. Then we both put on our costumes.

"I've never played 'Halloween' before," Rory announced excitedly. "Marguerite said it was an American idea and we shouldn't celebrate it."

"I don't think it matters where the idea has come from, as long as it's a good one. And it's always fun to dress up."

We made our way down the stairs to show off Rory's Harry Potter costume to Orlando, who was already in the kitchen, replete with cloak, hat, and long white beard. I decided he could have a second career as a double for Dumbledore.

"You look positively malevolent," commented Orlando as he took in my witch's costume.

"Star is a white witch, so she's good." Rory hugged me.

Just as he said that, Mouse arrived through the door and Orlando frowned at me in disapproval.

"You didn't tell me *he* was joining us," he said in a stage whisper that could plainly be heard by his brother.

"Does Mouse have a costume?" Rory asked.

"Of course. Here." I produced the bag from a cupboard and handed it to him. He looked inside it and frowned.

"Really, Star, this isn't my thing."

"For Rory?" I whispered to him. "Maybe just the ears." I took them out of the bag and proffered them to him.

"You can be a real mouse now!" Rory shouted, delighted at the idea. "I'll help you."

I continued to stir the pumpkin soup, not daring to look if Mouse was giving in to Rory's heavy persuasion.

"How are you, Orlando?" asked Mouse as he headed into the pantry. There was no reply, so he returned with a bottle of beer and some wine and offered me a glass. I looked up at him and suppressed a chuckle at the ears Rory had placed haphazardly on his head, and reached to straighten one that had been bent.

"Suits you," I said with a smile.

"Thanks," he muttered as he turned back to the table.

Despite the tension between the brothers, Rory's excitement was infectious. We ate the soup, then I produced "ghost burgers" and "spider potatoes," which I'd fashioned from mash and then deep-fried. After pudding, I went to the drawer and pulled out a DVD of the Harry Potter film I'd bought in town.

"Shall we go and watch it?" I asked the three of them.

"Not *Superman*?" Rory signed.

"No, but I think you will like this," I encouraged. "Would you go and switch it on, Dumbledore?"

"Of course. I've been trying to persuade Rory to let me read the book to him for the past year." Orlando stood up, twirling his wand. "Come, Harry, let me lead you to Hogwarts and all its glories."

"I must go." Mouse took off his ears and laid them on the table. "Thanks for tonight, Star. Rory loved it."

"I'm glad."

"You're so good with him, you really are."

Then he walked over to me and, after a pause, gave me a sudden tight hug. I looked up at him and saw the expression in his eyes as his head descended toward mine. And then, as if he'd changed his mind, he planted a deep kiss on my forehead. "Good night."

"Night," I said as he released me, went to the kitchen door, and left.

Even though the first Harry Potter film was one of my all-time favorites, I hardly saw it, my mind spinning back time and again to the moment Mouse had reached for my lips.

"Come on, young man, it's way past your bedtime." I heaved my reluctant Harry Potter off the sofa as the credits rolled on the screen.

"No story tonight, old chap, it's late," said Orlando. "Sleep tight and don't let the bedbugs bite."

After I'd kissed Rory good night, I wandered back downstairs, intending to clear up the kitchen.

"Where are you going now?" Orlando brandished his wand at me as I picked up the used mugs of hot chocolate from the drawing room. "You never stop, do you? Please, Miss Star, sit down. I feel we've hardly talked in days."

"Okay." I sat down in the armchair by the fire, mirroring our usual seating at the bookshop. "What would you like to talk about?"

"You."

"Oh," I said, having braced myself for another outpouring of misery over the sale of the bookshop.

"Yes, Miss Star, *you*," he repeated. "It strikes me that you've done rather a lot for this family, and especially for me and Rory. Therefore I feel I should give you something in return."

"Really, Orlando, that's not necessary. I—"

"It's certainly not financial recompense, but in my view, it's something far more important."

"Really?"

"Yes. Really. You see, Miss Star, I haven't forgotten why you sought out Arthur Morston Books in the first place: you were sent by your father on a quest to find out about your true heritage."

"Yes."

"I was wary at the start, of course—as anyone would be when a stranger announces a connection to one's family. Especially a family with such a complex history as ours. You asked me who Flora MacNichol was, and I told you that she was the sister of our great-grandmother—in other words, our great-great-aunt, which is indeed true. But not the *whole* truth."

"I see."

"I very much doubt that you do. And nor does anyone else, apart from me. Because, Miss Star, during those dreadful years of sickness as a child, all I could do was read to escape."

"Mouse told me."

"I'm sure he did, yes. But even he could not know that on my voracious voyage through the bookshelves of Home Farm, I read everything there was. Including Flora MacNichol's journals." Orlando paused dramatically. "*All* of them."

"Right." I decided to play along with Orlando's little game. "And you know that some are missing? Mouse has been looking for them to help him research the family history. Do you know where they are?"

"Of course I do."

"Then why haven't you told him?"

"In truth, I didn't feel he was doing the research out of best intentions. Miss Star, you must understand that my brother has been a very bitter and troubled man since his wife—and our father—died. I felt that putting the information the journals hold at his disposal would have provided even more fodder for his internal fire. I can assure you that it has been difficult to get a civil word out of him, so mired in his own sorrow has he been. He has not been in his right mind."

"And why would the journals have made it worse?"

"I'm sure that Mouse has already informed you that he was given certain . . . information by our father before he died. Mouse became obsessed with discovering the truth about his past. Simply because he had no future to cling on to. Do you understand?"

"I do. But what has this got to do with me?"

"Well now . . ." Orlando reached down for a canvas bag tucked by the side of his chair. He delved inside it and pulled out a pile of familiar silk-covered notebooks. "Do you know what these are?"

"Flora MacNichol's journals."

"Indeed, indeed." Orlando nodded. "I had, of course, retrieved them from Home Farm a while back and hidden them among the thousands of books in the shop. As you know, it would take a month of Sundays to find them there," he added gleefully.

I decided to give him his moment and refrain from telling him I'd already found them.

"So, Miss Star, here they are. Flora MacNichol's life between the years 1910 and 1944. They contain written proof of the deception that took place in our family, the ramifications of which have resonated down through the years. And, one could also say, contributed heavily to where all three of us find ourselves today."

I sat silently, presuming he meant Mouse, Marguerite, and himself.

"So, given that you have been so very noble in your actions toward the blighted Forbeses, I feel that it is only fair that I continue to steer you in the right direction, from where my brother left off."

"Okay, thank you."

"Now, where exactly have you got to with Mouse?"

"Flora finding out who her father really was. And running away from London to go home."

"Then I suggest I pick up the story from there. Forgive me if I do not read every word—we have over thirty years to cover." He indicated the pile of slim volumes. "Some of it is exceedingly dull, but rest assured, it builds up to a quite magnificent climax. So, let us begin. You are quite right that Flora ran 'home' to the Lakes that day. She managed to find her way to Near Sawrey and threw herself on the mercy of Beatrix Potter, who took her in and gave her shelter. Then, a few months later, she used the bequest from her father to buy a small farm nearby. And for the following nine years, lived as a virtual recluse, tending her animals and her land."

"She was still so young—only in her twenties," I whispered.

"Now, now, patience, Miss Star. I've just told you that things perk up for her." Orlando picked up the first journal and flicked through its pages, then put it down and rifled through the pile to find another. "Now, we are in the Lakes, in February of 1919, on a bitingly cold, snowy morning . . ."

FLORA

Near Sawrey, The Lake District

February 1919

34

Flora cleared a narrow path through the snow from her front door; a thankless task, as she could tell from the heavy skies that another load would drop on her handiwork at any moment. Nevertheless, she needed to get out of the cottage and walk down the lane to see Beatrix, who had recently suffered from an attack of bronchitis. It was pointless taking Giselle, her Northumbrian-bred pony, who should have been used to the conditions, but whinnied if the snow passed above her shins and then stubbornly refused to budge.

Dressed in the thick tweed breeches she had fashioned for herself—so much more practical than skirts—and heavy boots, she picked up her basket of supplies and set off down the icy slope to a lane hidden underneath the heaps of snow.

She paused, as she always did, at the sight of the windows of Esthwaite Hall glinting at her from across the lake. A lake so heavily frozen that she reckoned she could don a pair of skates and be across it in a few minutes. The weather this year had been the worst she could remember in her nine years here. To her sadness, she had lost a number of sheep, as had every farmer in the district.

She could see Castle Cottage in the distance, the house that Beatrix had moved to since her marriage to dear William Heelis, her gentle solicitor husband. It was Beatrix who had told her Wynbrigg Farm was up for sale and suggested she buy it. Flora had painstakingly renovated the cottage and restocked the farm.

Beatrix was not as young as she used to be, even though she continued to deny it and could still be found on top of the fells in search of either sheep or a new species of wildflower that did not yet grow in her garden. Many of the plants ended up in Flora's own borders if Beatrix gave her a cutting.

On that fateful evening in 1910 when she had fled from London, only knowing that she must return to her beloved Lakes, Beatrix had saved her. Many in the village thought the author a strange and bad-tempered old stick, but Flora had seen and felt the kindness her heart contained.

She was Flora's closest—in fact only—friend. She adored her.

And loneliness was a small price to pay for independence, Flora thought as she stomped through the knee-deep snow. And at least she had been hit far less hard than most by the Great War—the armistice only declared last November—for she'd had no one close to lose. Although it would be a lie to suggest she had not thought constantly about those she still loved. Archie Vaughan haunted her dreams and nightmares, despite her determination not to think of him in her waking hours.

But at least her farm kept her busy, and the war had made it imperative she learn the art of self-sufficiency. The dairy had run short on milk, pumping what her few cows could produce for the boys in France, so Flora had bought a goat to provide her own. The local carthorses had been requisitioned for the war, and she had only been able to keep Giselle, the pony. Vegetables became scarce too, so Flora had started her own vegetable patch and raised chickens for their eggs. Despite her hunger, she had never been tempted to wring any of their necks. She had not eaten a single slice of meat since returning to the Lakes.

Sometimes, Flora thought back to those grand dinners at Portman Square—the gross abundance of food and animal flesh—and thanked God she now had the means to run her own household, however meager the menu.

"Are you alive?" she asked the freezing-cold air, an image of Archie forming in her mind. In truth, the agony of not knowing was intolerable. Beatrix, to whom Flora had poured out the whole sorry story when she'd first arrived here all those years ago, had begged her to contact her sister to let her know where she was—and to ask after both of them. "War changes everything," Beatrix had said, but Flora knew that nothing could ever change her dreadful betrayal. Or Aurelia's expression when she had told Flora she never wished to see her again.

Occasionally, she heard news of her parents through local gossip and it was with deep sadness that she had heard her father had died two years ago. She had written a letter to her mother in Scotland, but had never sent it. The bitterness Flora harbored toward Rose, following her abandonment after the King's death, had rendered her incapable of communication. She had heard recently that Rose had left the Highlands and gone abroad—no one seemed to know where.

Winter was always the hardest time of year for her, for she could not exhaust herself with physical work to banish the dark thoughts that crowded in. She would be glad when spring arrived and her days became busy once more. Panting from her exertion through the snow, Flora arrived at Castle Cottage and knocked on the door. As always, she was greeted first by Beatrix's two Pekingese dogs.

"Flora dear, do come in," Beatrix said, as a flood of warm air enveloped her. "I was just baking a cake with my last egg. You might as well be the one to enjoy it, as William has gone through the snow to his office in Hawkshead. Now, don't be afraid of trying this one, Mrs. Rogerson helped me with it."

"How kind of you. And see, I have brought you some fresh eggs." Flora took off her gloves and placed the three eggs carefully on the table. "Are you better, dear Beatrix?"

"Much, thank you. It was a nasty chill. And these days, it does go to my chest so."

"I also brought you some camphor," she said, taking it from her basket. "And a jar of last year's honey from my hives." She sat down at the kitchen table as Beatrix cut her a piece of the sponge cake, the mean top and bottom more than compensated for by the amount of jam in the center. As she put the slice to her lips, savoring the smell, a sudden thought struck her.

"What date is it?" she asked.

"Why, it is the sixteenth of February."

"Goodness!" Flora sat back and chuckled. "Would you believe that it is my birthday today? And you have offered me cake!"

"My dear! Then I couldn't have decided to bake it for any better purpose." Beatrix sat down and squeezed her hand. "Happy birthday, Flora."

"Thank you."

"So remind me, how old are you today?"

"I am . . ."—Flora had to think about it for a few seconds—"twenty-nine."

"Still so very young. Just over half my age," Beatrix said. "I always think of you as older. Please take that as a compliment, if you can."

"Oh, I do. I feel as though I have lived a very long time."

"Well, you know me to be a woman of the earth, but even I occasionally need to return to civilization in London, and I wonder sometimes if you should too. Especially as the war is now over."

"I am happy enough," commented Flora, feeling a hint of irritation.

"I know you are, dear, but William and I were saying only the other night that we worry for you. You are still young and beautiful—"

"Please, Beatrix, there is no need to flatter me."

"I do not. Flatter you, that is. I merely point out the facts. Will you not think of contacting your family? Perhaps suggest a visit to them down south to lay the ghost to rest?"

"You know we have talked of this before, and the answer is still no. Aurelia does not wish to ever see me again. What could I bring to her life except a painful reminder of the past?"

"What about love, Flora?"

Flora stared at Beatrix in confusion. She didn't understand why her friend was talking of such a thing; Beatrix was not normally sentimental. She bolted down the rest of the cake and stood up. "I must get back now. Thank you for your kind wishes, but I assure you I am well and happy. Good-bye."

Beatrix watched her young friend leave the kitchen, and as she saw her march off through the snow down the lane, the loneliness and isolation Flora lived in continued to trouble her deeply.

Four months later, on a sunny day in June, a tear-stained Flora opened the front door of the cottage to Beatrix's repeated knocking.

"Goodness!" Beatrix took in her distraught expression. "What on earth has happened?"

"It's Panther! He went to sleep as normal on my bed last night, but then this morning, he didn't . . . wake up."

"Oh, my dear," Beatrix said as she stepped inside and closed the door. "I am so terribly sorry."

"I loved him so much! He was the only link I had with the past, you see. In fact, he was *all* I had . . ."

"There, there." Beatrix led Flora into the kitchen, sat her down, and set the kettle to boil on the range. "He lived a good long life."

"He was only ten. I've heard many cats can live to be much older." Flora lowered her head as her shoulders heaved in silent sobs.

"Well, the time he lived was healthy and happy. And we both know there's nothing worse than watching an old animal suffer a drawn-out, painful death."

"But it was so sudden! I don't understand."

"No one does, except our Lord above." Beatrix poured the water into a teapot. "Where is he now?"

"Still on my bed. He looks so comfortable there, I don't want to move him."

"You will have to be practical, Flora. Panther needs to be buried. Shall I help you?"

"Yes . . ." Flora's eyes filled with further tears. "Forgive me for being sentimental. You know I have lost many animals in my time, but Panther was special."

"Of course he was. Some animals just are."

"Would it be ridiculous to say how alone I feel now without him?"

"Not at all." Beatrix put a cup of tea in front of her. "I'm sure you must have a box out in your store cupboard. Why don't I fetch it and go upstairs and put dear Panther inside it? I'll bring him down and you can say good-bye before I close it. Then we can go outside to decide whereabouts in the garden you would like to put his grave."

"Thank you." Flora offered her a wan smile as she left the room.

Having buried Panther, and done her best to console a devastated Flora, Beatrix left Wynbrigg Farm and walked back along the lane to Castle Cottage. Opening a drawer in her writing bureau, she took out the letter she had received some days ago and reread it. Its contents made her weep, a rarity these days in the wake of the Great War, during which so much tragedy had occurred. As they ate supper, she discussed the situation with William, her husband.

"I went to see Flora this morning to put the idea to her, but I did not feel the timing was appropriate. She was distraught about losing her cat."

William tapped out his pipe thoughtfully. "From what you have just told me, I think it makes your suggestion even more valid. And I would be inclined to simply present her with a fait accompli. She can only say no."

"Perhaps you're right. Thank you, my dear."

A week later, a still-desolate Flora saw Beatrix striding up the path again, holding a large bundle in her arms.

"Good morning, Flora," Beatrix said as she stepped inside the cottage. "Your garden borders are looking wonderful, especially the Star of Persia—an excellent addition."

"Thank you," Flora replied. Although since Panther had gone, she hadn't cared much about anything. "What . . . is *that*?"

Beatrix removed the blanket that had shielded the contents. "This, my dear, is a baby."

"Goodness." Flora walked toward Beatrix and peered more closely at the tiny face, its eyes closed fast in slumber. "And what exactly is it doing here with you?"

"It's a 'he' and he is two weeks old. You know that I am a patron of the local hospital and this little mite was brought in a few hours after he was born. A neighbor heard his cries from the homestead next to her up on Black Fell. Sadly, she found the mother had passed away after the birth, but this little thing was bellowing as loud as you like between her legs. The cord that attaches mothers to babies had not yet been broken. She cut it with a bread knife, sent her husband for the undertaker, and brought the baby down the fell to the hospital. May I sit down? He is heavier than he looks. Such a strong little thing, aren't you?" Beatrix cooed to the bundle affectionately.

Flora led Beatrix into the kitchen and pulled out a chair for her, marveling at this new, maternal side to her friend.

"Where is the father of this baby?"

"Well now, it's a tragic tale. The father was a shepherd, sent out to France to fight three years ago. His last leave was in August, and soon after he returned to the front, he perished in the trenches during the Battle of Épehy. And this only a few short weeks before the armistice. His body was never sent home." Beatrix shook her head, sadness etched on her features. "And now, neither of them are here to see their son. I can only pray they are joined in heaven, God rest their souls."

"Does the baby not have relatives?"

"None that the neighbor knew of. All she could tell the hospital staff was that the mother came from Keswick and her name was Jane. When I arrived at the hospital for my monthly visit, I was told of the baby and his tragic fate. I went to visit him, and even though he was unwell at the time, I admit to being quite taken with him and his plight."

"He looks very well now."

They both watched as the baby stirred, his tiny rosebud lips forming a pout of disapproval, before emitting a sucking noise. "Soon he will wake and need feeding. There in my basket you will find a bottle. Would you warm it? I am instructed babies don't like it cold."

"Is it human milk?" Flora asked, fascinated, as she found the bottle in the basket and began warming it in a pan of water on the range.

"All the babies are weaned on watered-down animal milk, though I am told that cow's milk sometimes gives them colic, in which case they are fed goat's milk instead."

"Yes . . ." Flora hesitated. "Why is the baby here with you? Are you and William thinking of adopting him?"

"Goodness me, no! However much I mourn that I will never be a mother, I accept that it would be unfair to take in a baby now. Flora, my dear, perhaps you forget that I am fifty-two years of age, old enough to be this little one's grandmother. What a thought," Beatrix chuckled. "William and I will almost certainly be dead when he comes of age."

"So you are simply minding him for the day?"

"Yes." The baby began to stir in earnest, his tiny arms appearing from beneath the blanket as he stretched himself. "On my visits to the hospital," Beatrix continued, "I see many sick babies and young children, but this little one is a fighter. Despite the traumatic circumstances of his birth, the nurses have told me he has recovered completely. Would you mind if you took him for a while? My arms are aching dreadfully."

"I . . . I've never held a baby before, I don't want to drop him or harm him . . ."

"You won't. We were both babies once, and despite, I am sure, our inept but well-meaning mothers, we managed to survive. Here. I'll get the bottle." Beatrix lifted the baby into Flora's arms.

The solidity of him startled Flora; he looked so tiny and yet, as every part of him began to move in different directions and he mewed just like Panther for food, his sheer determination to be alive brought a tear to her eye.

"I've tested the bottle on my hand to make sure it's not so hot that it will burn him, or so cold that it will frighten him off," said Beatrix as she handed it to her.

"What do I do with it?" Flora asked as the baby, perhaps smelling the milk so near and yet so far, began to wail loudly.

"Why, put it in his mouth, of course!"

Flora teased the teat between the rosebud lips, which had perversely clamped together. "He's not taking it."

"Then drop a little milk onto his lips. Flora, I've seen you nurse enough lambs and encourage them to drink. Simply employ the same technique."

Flora did so, and after a tense few seconds, she finally managed to wedge the bottle into his mouth and he began to suck. Both women breathed a sigh of relief as peace reigned once more in the kitchen.

"What will become of him?" Flora asked after a while.

"Who knows? Now he is well, he can't stay at the hospital. They have written to me to ask me to inquire for him locally, but if no home can be found for him, he will be sent to an orphanage in Liverpool." Beatrix shuddered. "I have heard it is the most dreadful place. And then, when he is old enough, he will be found some form of employment in a cotton mill if he's lucky, or the coal mines if he's not."

"And that is really the best this innocent child can hope for?" A horrified Flora looked down at the baby's calm expression of contentment.

"Sadly, yes. Perhaps the best thing would have been for him to be taken with his mother. There is little hope of a future, as the number of foundlings grows apace every month. Many women are struggling without any means of support for their children since their husbands have not returned from France."

"Surely we have seen enough of wasted human life?"

"Waste breeds waste, dear girl. The entire world is trying to recover from its near destruction. Forgive me for saying so, but tucked up here in front of our well-fed fires, it is very easy to become dislocated from what is happening beyond us. When I journey to London, I see the desperation of the maimed soldiers begging on street corners, the poverty that is this dreadful war's own epilogue."

"He's finished, he's falling asleep." Flora put the bottle onto the table. "Beatrix, why have you brought this baby here?"

"Because I wanted you to see him."

"Is that all?"

"Mostly yes. Also . . ."

"What?"

"Sometimes I worry that you have closed yourself off from the outside world."

"Maybe that is what I wish for. Like you, I prefer animals to people."

"That is not true, Flora, and you know it. My main source of happiness *is* another human being. If it were not for my husband, my life would be very empty indeed."

"Here." Flora handed Beatrix the sleeping baby. "He is fed."

"For now." Beatrix took him back into her own arms, then stood up. "Will you hand me my basket?"

Flora did so and watched as Beatrix wrapped the blanket around the baby in preparation to leave. "Thank you for bringing him here," she said as they walked out of the door and down the front path. "What is his name?" Flora asked as she opened the gate.

"He is known as 'Teddy,' because all the nurses want to cuddle him." Beatrix smiled sadly. "Good-bye, Flora."

Later that evening, Flora sat down to write her journal, but found it impossible to concentrate. The baby's huge eyes and their uninhibited gaze haunted her. In the end, she gave up and paced around her immaculate drawing room. Everything was in its place, exactly where she had put it. No one ever came to disturb the safe, calm order she had created for herself.

She made herself a cup of Ovaltine, which Nannie had always advocated before bedtime for Violet and Sonia.

Violet . . . dear Violet, so passionate and still controlled by her overwhelming love for her friend Vita Sackville-West. She knew that Vita had married a few years ago, but Beatrix had recently brought mutterings of gossip from London about a renewed relationship between the two women. Flora, as always, closed her ears to talk of her past life, but even so, she had gleaned enough to understand that the love between the two childhood friends had blossomed into something deeper.

Flora sighed at the thought that if anyone should be the subject of the newest outrageous liaison in London, it should be Violet, truly her mother's daughter. She had been schooled for it—and learned through her upbringing that notoriety was normal.

Whereas, *she* had run away . . .

Upstairs in bed, she listened to an owl hoot—the only creature still up and awake as the long, dead hours of the night passed. Loneliness fell on her like a dark cloak as she returned downstairs and to her writing bureau. She took a key from one of the drawers to unlock the small pigeonhole, and put her hand in the secret compartment. She retrieved a journal and opened it, her fingers reaching into the silken pocket on the inside of the back cover. And drew out the letter her father—Edward—had sent to her via Sir Ernest Cassel.

Live your life in the freedom of anonymity as I would have wished to have had the chance to live mine. And, above all, be true to yourself . . .

She gazed for a while at the signature. "Edward . . ."

"Teddy," she said suddenly.

And then Flora MacNichol laughed for the first time in as long as she could remember.

"Of course," she said. "Of course."

35

Baby Teddy moved in with Flora two days later and they both did their best—and at times, their worst—to get used to each other. Flora's approach was to view him as an orphaned lamb who needed warmth, love, and, most of all, milk. Yet she was baffled that she could clear any form of animal dung without a care, but felt a wave of nausea pass over her while changing his full napkin.

Teddy was by no means a contented baby; as if he were a puppy that had lost its mother, she would lay him down in his makeshift cradle—a drawer filled with blankets placed close to the range—after his last bottle of milk. Then she would prepare for bed, creeping up the stairs, sliding between the sheets, and closing her eyes in relief. But only a few minutes later, the wailing would begin.

She'd try to ignore it, after instructions from Beatrix that babies needed "training like animals," but Teddy did not seem inclined to play by the rules. As the decibels rose and his cries reverberated around the thick stone walls of the farmhouse, Flora knew it was a war of attrition, and Teddy always won.

The only time he seemed at peace was when he was nestled next to her in bed. And finally, even though she knew she was making a rod for her own back, but so physically, mentally, and emotionally exhausted she'd stopped caring, she let him sleep next to her at night.

After that, some modicum of peace descended on the cottage. Even so, the farm suffered from lack of attention, culminating in her employing a youth from the village to do the basic work she no longer had time for. And despite her carefully contrived routine's being disrupted beyond repair, the fact that another beating heart lay in her arms every night helped her own frozen heart begin to thaw.

With the summer sun out, she began to take Teddy for walks, fashioning a sling from a length of cotton that she wrapped around both of them—the rough paths and rocky terrain being unsuitable for a perambulator. She ignored the curious glances of the villagers—she could imagine the local gossip and chuckled at what they must think. And as the days passed, she began to feel the sense of peace and fulfillment she had thought would elude her forever. That was, until one hot day in July when she had a visitor.

Having just put Teddy down for his afternoon nap, she busied herself in the garden, the carefully planted borders so neglected over the past month they were crying as loudly for her attention as Teddy did. As she went about unwinding the bindweed from the lupines, sweating in the strong afternoon sun, she thought how nature, left even for a short time to its own devices, would immediately regain control.

"Hello, Flora."

Her hands—filled with earth and weed—froze where they were.

"My name is Archie Vaughan. Do you remember me?"

I really must be suffering the effects of the sun, she thought. Did she remember him? The man who had haunted her for the past nine years? It was the most absurd question her lonely mind had ever conjured up.

"May I please come in?"

She turned around to end this ridiculous hallucination, but as she gazed at the figure standing patiently behind the gate, then shook her head and blinked a number of times, the image refused to disappear.

"Ridiculous!" she shouted out loud.

"What is 'ridiculous'?" the hallucination answered.

"You are," she said as she picked herself up and marched toward the gate, having read enough books to know that when one was dehydrated, the imagined oasis disappeared as one approached it.

"Am I?"

She was now staring over the gate, close enough to smell the familiar scent of him and even the lightest wisp of breath on her cheek. "Please go away!" she ordered in desperation.

"Flora, please . . . it's me, Archie. Don't you remember?"

Then the mirage reached out a hand and a finger touched her cheek, bringing with it sensations that could not *possibly* be a dream.

His touch seemed to drain every last drop of blood from her veins, and she staggered, reaching for the gate to steady herself as her head spun.

"Good God, Flora . . ."

And suddenly, the ground was reaching up to her, and she collapsed on the path.

"Forgive me," she heard vaguely as she felt a cool breeze wafting across her face. "I should have sent a telegram and warned you I was coming. But I was afraid that you would make sure you were out."

The soft voice made her open her eyes, and she saw what looked like a beige calico fan passing back and forth in front of them. As her eyes focused, she realized it was her sun hat, and beyond that was a face: thinner than she remembered, almost gaunt, with a lightning streak of gray hair growing from his temple. His eyes no longer shone clear, but were those of a haunted man.

"Can you stand? I need to get you out of the sun."

"Yes." Leaning heavily upon him, he helped her up and inside the house. She pointed him in the direction of the kitchen.

"Surely you need to lie down?"

"Goodness, no!" she said, feeling as fey and silly as any heroine in a penny romance. "Can you bring me water from the pitcher in the pantry?"

He did so, and she gulped it back thirstily, his grave eyes never leaving her. She had a sudden vision of what he must see: a woman whose face was sprinkled with lines, fashioned from grief, loneliness, and the harsh weather of the Lakes. Her hair was unkempt as usual, spilling from its knot, and her body enclosed in a filthy, roughly sewn smock. Cotton breeches covered with grass stains and wooden clogs completed the ensemble. In short, she looked a fright.

"You look so beautiful," Archie murmured. "The years have served you well."

She gave a snort of laughter, thinking that perhaps the strong sun had blinded *his* vision. Thankfully, her faculties were returning and gathering reluctantly like an exhausted army to her command.

"What are you doing here?" she asked him sharply. "How did you find me?"

"I shall answer the latter question first, and tell you that your family have known of your whereabouts for years. You won't be surprised to learn that your presence here was reported almost instantly to your mother by Stanley, the old stable hand at Esthwaite Hall. And, oblivious to the drama that had recently unfolded between her two daughters, Rose wrote to Aurelia."

"I see."

"You will understand that, in order for our marriage to survive, it was best for all three of us to let sleeping dogs lie and refrain from contact. However, Aurelia watched over you, from a distance."

"I am surprised indeed."

"It is a truism that time can heal, Flora. And all of us have realized during the past few years how little time we may have left." Archie's eyes darkened.

"Yes."

There was a silence as both of them stared into the distance, memories gathering thick and fast.

"I am here because Aurelia wanted to make amends," Archie continued eventually.

"But it is *we* who are the guilty party."

"Agreed, but it was Aurelia who banished you from her life. When our child was born a month ago, her first thought was to write to you. She felt it was time."

"A new baby? How many do you have now?"

"Just the one. I . . ."

Flora heard the catch in Archie's voice and read the expression on his face. And then she knew.

"No," she whispered.

"Aurelia died three weeks ago, ten days after she gave birth. I am so very sorry, Flora. You know she was never strong, and the pregnancy took a fatal toll on her health."

She closed her eyes as tears sprang to them. Her beautiful, sweet-natured sister no longer breathed. She would never again look into those clear blue eyes, so full of hope and laughter. Even in her self-imposed exile, she had always felt her sister there. The finality of it horrified her. And she berated herself for all the wasted years.

"Oh God . . . oh God . . . ," she muttered. "I can hardly bear it. Did we . . . contribute? I would gladly have given my own life in her place, you must know that."

"Above anyone, I know it, Flora. You sacrificed your own happiness for hers. And truthfully, when we first married, it was . . . difficult. Especially as we struggled to have the one thing we needed to bond us—a child. Aurelia lost our first baby, then went on to suffer more miscarriages. Soon after that, the Great War came. I joined the Royal Flying Corps and was away from High Weald for most of the last three and a half years. We continued to try for a child, but to no avail. The doctor warned us that it would be pertinent for Aurelia's health to refrain, but she would have none of it. And last autumn, she found herself with child once more. We . . . I"—he corrected himself—"have a daughter."

"I . . . oh, Archie . . ." Flora dug out a filthy handkerchief from her pocket and blew into it.

"I am so very sad I am here because of this terrible news. But Aurelia insisted upon it."

"Insisted on what?"

"That I come here in person, to give you this. It was her last request before she died." He took an envelope from his jacket pocket and handed it to her. Just the sight of the familiar script made Flora's head swim.

"Do you know what it contains?"

"I . . . might have an idea, yes."

She fingered the envelope, her hands shaking as terror surged up inside her, thinking of the damning words it might contain. Then she felt a warm hand touch hers. "Don't be frightened. I told you that she wanted to make amends. Will you open it now?"

"Excuse me." Flora stood up and walked from the kitchen across the entrance hall and into the drawing room. She sat down in an armchair and split the wax seal.

High Weald
Ashford, Kent
16th June 1919

My dearest sister,

There is so much I wish to say, but as you know, I am not an accomplished wordsmith like you. And I grow weaker by the day, so forgive me for the relative brevity of this missive.

I have missed you sorely, my darling sister. There has not been a day when I have not thought of you. At first, yes, I hated you, but recently, I have begun to berate myself for the actions my jealous nature induced in me nine years ago. There has been so much time wasted, which can now never be recovered.

Therefore, as I watch my darling daughter lying peacefully in her crib next to me, unaware that she will never know her mother as she grows, I must try to put things right. Flora, I do not want my child to be brought up without a mother. However much Archie will love Louise, he can never bring her the tenderness of feminine arms, or a listening ear to guide and nurture her as she grows into womanhood.

Dear Sarah will stay on, of course, to care for Louise's basic needs, but she is getting old. And we both understand that her education and views on the world are narrow, through no fault of her own.

This brings me to the favor I must ask of you: when I inquired of my spies in Esthwaite recently as to your well-being, they told me that you live alone. If this is still the case, and you would be willing to come out of your isolation, I beg you to consider moving to High Weald to bring up my daughter as your own child.

I am certain you will love her with every shred of your beautiful heart. And also, comfort my poor husband in his grief. Flora, you cannot know what he went through during the war, and now to be faced with the loss of his wife, and to bring up our daughter alone, is more than I can bear for him.

Please, at least consider the possibility of such an arrangement, and allow me to have my immortal soul cleansed of my selfish error. You have suffered for long enough. You may find this letter surprising, but I have realized over time that we cannot help who we love. And Archie has confessed to much of the blame for what happened back then. He told me how he pursued you and misled you about the arrangement already made between himself and Father when in Scotland.

My darling Flora, I am exhausted and can write little more. But believe me when I say there has been so much suffering in the world of late, and my fervent last wish is to relieve those I love of further pain in the future. And to hope they find happiness.

I will pray that you can find it in your heart to understand and forgive me. And if it suits you to do so, bring up my daughter in her home, with love and compassion.

All my best love, dear sister.

Pray for me also.

Aurelia

Flora gazed out of the window, her senses numbed by the extraordinary letter. The generosity it contained was somehow worse than the recriminations she felt she deserved.

"Flora? Are you all right?" came a voice from the door.

"She asked *me* for forgiveness," she whispered. "Oh God, Archie, she shouldn't have done that. It was we who caused *her* pain."

"Yes, although much of the blame rests firmly on my shoulders. I was blinded by my love for you."

"How could she find it in her heart to be so forgiving? I doubt I could find it in my own if I were in her shoes. And," she said, pausing to steady herself, "I can never tell her now that it wasn't just your marriage that forced me to run away and live here alone."

"Really?"

Flora hesitated, and then, deciding there should be no further secrets, went to her writing bureau. She retrieved the letter from the silk pocket of the journal of 1910 and handed it to Archie. "It was this too."

She watched him as he read it, occasionally raising an eyebrow in surprise. "Well," he said, as he handed it back to her. "Well, well."

"Did you know? I believe the whole of London was aware at the time."

"To be truthful, I had heard rumblings of your . . . connection with a certain family, but I had never given them much credence. Besides, when the old king died, and George V took the throne, any gossip about the old court disappeared into his coffin with him, as the courtiers scrambled for prominence in the new regime. So . . ." A glimmer of a smile appeared on his face for the first time. "Should I now call you 'Princess Flora'? Good God, I hardly know what to say, although it explains many things."

"There is nothing *to* say, but now you can understand why I left London immediately. The world was weeping for the Queen, and just like Mrs. Keppel, I was an unwanted reminder of her husband's misdemeanors."

"But *unlike* Mrs. Keppel, you were to blame for none of them," Archie countered. "And whereas you have had the dignity to stay removed from society, she has returned to London and continues to thrive. As for her daughter, she is currently in the limelight of notoriety. Violet and Vita ran away to France together after the armistice, Vita leaving her husband and two children behind. The gossip is all over London; they even say Violet encouraged her to do so. The Keppel family has no shame, whereas you have behaved with dignity and grace, like the princess you are."

"Hardly." She managed a smile then too, as she looked down at her attire.

"Those qualities come from inside, Flora. Now, I must ask how you feel about Aurelia's last wishes."

"Archie, I cannot begin to process what I feel. And besides—"

As if on cue, a loud wail emanated from upstairs.

"What is that noise?" Archie frowned.

"Excuse me," she said as she rose. "Teddy needs feeding."

As Flora walked upstairs to collect what she knew would be a sweaty, smelly, and endlessly noisy bundle, she allowed herself a chuckle. Even though it was true that her life over the past nine years had been stagnant, it would now be her turn to give Archie Vaughan a surprise. *And what a surprise it is*, she thought, as she walked back downstairs with Teddy in her arms, heading for the kitchen and his bottle of milk.

Archie followed her in a few minutes later, his curiosity getting the better of him. "You have a child," he said as she concentrated on holding the bottle at Teddy's preferred angle.

"Yes."

"I see."

She heard a long sigh escape Archie's lips.

"Does the father live here with you?" he asked eventually.

"No, he died."

"He was your husband?"

"No."

"Then . . ."

She left enough time for Archie's imagination to take over, although she had not uttered one word of a lie. And only then did she speak.

"He is a foundling. He has lived with me for just under a month. I am hoping to adopt him."

She looked up then, only just managing to stifle a chuckle at the relief on Archie's face. "His name is Teddy," she added for good measure.

"Of course . . . for Edward," he said, understanding the link to her real father's name immediately. "I admit, I am dumbfounded."

"So was I at my initial decision to take him in. But now . . ." She glanced down at a sated Teddy, his eyes rolling with the pleasure of a full stomach, and kissed him fondly on the head. "I wouldn't be without him."

"So, Teddy is how old?"

"Almost six weeks. He was born in the last week of May."

"Then only a few days before Louise arrived, at the beginning of June. They could be twins."

"But they come from rather different worlds. This little one's father was a shepherd who died in the Great War."

"I can tell you, Flora, that whether you are a lord or a beggar, death does not observe social barriers. Whatever class Teddy's father was, if he fought and died for his country, he was a hero. You must tell his son that one day," Archie said vehemently.

"I haven't yet decided what to tell him."

"So now you are well versed in child care and . . ."

Archie's words hung in the air and Flora was aware where they were heading.

"Where is Louise currently?" she asked.

"Sarah is taking care of her at High Weald. And if you feel unable because of your . . . altered circumstances to consider moving to take care of Louise, then I will do my best, with Sarah's help, to be mother and father to my daughter."

"But even if I agree to the proposition, what about Teddy? Would you accept him into the High Weald nursery? For if you feel you could not welcome my child, then I must tell you that I could not under any circumstances agree to come."

"Flora, don't you see? It could not be more perfect! Louise would have a playmate—a brother, no less—for company. They would grow up together . . ."

It was then she saw the desperation in Archie's eyes. Whether it was for his daughter, his dead wife, or himself, she couldn't say.

"Can I hold him?" he asked suddenly.

"Of course." Flora lifted Teddy and placed him in Archie's open arms.

"What a handsome chap he is, with those big blue eyes and blond hair. Ironically, Louise takes after my side of the family and is dark. Teddy looks more like Aurelia. Hello, old chap," he murmured as he put a finger toward him and Teddy grasped it firmly in his tiny fist. "I think we would rub along well together, you and I."

Flora stood up, feeling as though she was being railroaded into a decision she had not yet had time to make. "I'm afraid I wish you to leave now," she said, taking Teddy back into her arms. "I am unable to give you an answer immediately. However empty an existence you presume I have here, there is much I would have to sacrifice. I run a farm; many animals are dependent upon me. And despite moments of solitude, I love my home and much of my life, especially as I now have such a wonderful companion. You are asking me to give it all up without a second glance."

"Forgive me, Flora, for my selfishness. You know that I always did wear my heart on my sleeve, and just because there seems to be an ideal solution I accept that it may not be so for you."

"Thank you for coming to see me. I shall write to you with my decision."

"And although I will await it eagerly, you must take as much time as you need."

They walked to the front door and Flora opened it. "Good-bye, Archie."

"I just want to reiterate before I leave that I would accept your presence at High Weald on any terms you wished to stipulate. And I would not presume to think there would be any . . . relationship between us. Although I wish to tell you that my love for you burns on. However guilty that makes me feel, I cannot help it. It is simply a part of me. But the most important person in this whole sorry mess is my motherless child. Now, I will do as you ask and leave you alone. Good-bye."

As Archie walked down the path, for the first time, Flora noticed he had a pronounced limp.

Over the following two days, she read and reread her sister's letter. She took Teddy walking up on the fells, asking the blades of grass that tickled her nose as they lay in the shade of a tree, the larks that soared overhead, and the heavens themselves for advice and guidance.

They remained as silent on the question as her own soul. Eventually, her tired mind desperate for a resolution, she strapped Teddy into his sling and walked down the lane to visit her best friend and adviser.

"Well, well," Beatrix said, as they sat together in her garden, drinking tea. She had listened without interruption as Flora had poured out the newest chapter of her life. "I must say, you do seem to have an innate capacity for attracting drama. But then, your background was extraordinary from the start. Firstly, I must give you my condolences on the loss of your poor sister. So young, and, given the letter you read me, so generous. And clever, might I add."

"What do you mean?"

"Surely you can see that her parting gift to the husband and the sister she loved was to find a way of reuniting the two of you? From what you have told me in the past, she has always been fully aware of the mutual feeling between you. And at the same time, it would enable her to give her beloved daughter a proper mother, rather than growing up with an elderly nurse. Can't you see that she wanted to grant all three of you the happiness she felt you deserved?"

"Yes. But even if I did decide to go, what would people think?"

"As if you or I have ever cared about that!" Beatrix laughed. "And what could be more natural than the dead mother's spinster sister arriving to take care of her niece? I guarantee you that not an eyebrow will be raised."

"And what if . . . ?"

"Archie and you were to resume your relationship?" Beatrix finished for her. "Again, I think that after a sufficient passage of time, everyone would be glad for the motherless child and the poor widower, so soon back from the war as a hero and enduring another tragic loss."

"And Archie himself? I wonder how he can even bear to look at me without guilt clouding his vision."

"Flora, one thing I have learned in my many years on this earth is that one must move forward and not look back. And I will guarantee you that your Lord Vaughan saw enough death and destruction in the war to convince him of this. As your sister said in her letter, we can't choose who we love. He does not just have his wife's blessing on such a future; she has positively encouraged it. There are no secrets left, nothing to feel guilty for. And being the pragmatist that you know I am, sadly, the dead are gone, and it's pointless taking what may well be a wrong decision out of guilt."

"So, you think that we should go to High Weald?"

"Flora, dear, it is perfectly obvious that you should. A human being without love is akin to a rosebud without water. It will survive for a time, but never open into full bloom. And you cannot deny that you love him."

"No, I cannot. I do." Flora voiced the words to another human being for the first time.

"And you say he still loves you too. I think this is in so many ways serendipitous. Louise needs a mother and Teddy a father. The only sadness is that I would lose you as a neighbor."

"I would miss you dreadfully, Beatrix. And my animals and beloved Lakes."

"Well, there are always sacrifices to be made somewhere along the line. I would be happy to buy Wynbrigg Farm from you if you wished to sell it. My portfolio of land increases apace. I have just recently made my will, and once I am gone, the land will go to the National Trust to be given back to the people of the Lakes and preserved forever in perpetuity. But back to your conundrum. I can say no more to help you, other than do not dwell too long on your decision. It is so very easy to talk oneself out of changing one's circumstances for the better. Especially when it frightens you. Remember that every day that passes is another day lost to your future. Now, I'm afraid I must get on. I have a new delivery of letters from my young readers in America on the subject of dear little Johnny Town-Mouse. I do so like to reply in person to each and every one of the children."

"Of course." Flora stood up and went to collect Teddy, who was lying under a tree, cooing at the birds singing above him. "Thank you for everything, Beatrix. I don't know where I'd be without you." She felt a lump in her throat as she contemplated life without her friend close by.

And in that moment, she knew she had made her decision.

36

Flora had not traveled to the south of England since the death of the King, her father. Stepping into the entrance hall of High Weald, she was assailed by a wave of memories, and also shock as she took in the state of the house and grounds, elevated for so long in her memory. As Archie showed her around the once magical gardens, careful to keep a respectful distance between them as he limped beside her, she noted the wilderness that had erupted since she'd last been here.

"As you know, the Vaughan family has always had difficulty with their finances," Archie said grimly. "It was hard for Aurelia to keep the estate going while I was away and the young men of the village were fighting in France. Especially as my mother died only a few months after war broke out."

Upstairs in the nursery, Sarah welcomed her with joy and copious tears.

"So tragic," she sniffed as she led Flora over to the cradle to introduce her to her niece. "After all this time, Aurelia has the baby she's always craved, but she's not here to see her. Beautiful she is too, with a gentle nature just like her mother."

Flora lifted Louise into her arms and felt an immediate wave of protective love wash over her.

"Hello, little one," she cooed, as the baby lay placidly in her arms. At that moment, Teddy, perhaps sensing that Flora's attention was elsewhere, began to scream from his travel basket. Sarah swept him up into her arms.

"He's a strong bairn," she said. "Lord Vaughan told me all about his family dying. It's a generous thing you've both done by taking him in, Miss Flora, truly. And I know your sister would have approved too."

In the first two weeks, much of Flora's time was spent with the babies, Teddy demanding the lion's share of her attention. With Sarah there to support her, Flora had placed Teddy with Louise in the nursery at night, unwilling to continue to take him into bed with her. He'd screamed himself blue with indignation as Flora had paced outside, until one evening Sarah had said she would take over the night shift. Flora had gone to bed gratefully, and had woken the following morning from her first undisturbed night in weeks. Running to the nursery in panic, wondering if Teddy had died in the night, she saw Sarah knitting in a chair by the window.

"Morning, Miss Flora," she said, as she watched her dash to Teddy's bassinet and find it empty.

"Where is he?" demanded Flora.

"Look over there." Sarah pointed to Louise's cradle.

And there was Teddy, his tiny head nestled against Louise's, both of them sound asleep.

"He just likes company, I'd reckon," said Sarah. "He started to cry and I put him in the cradle with Louise. I haven't heard a peep out of either of them since."

"Sarah, you're a wonder," Flora sighed with relief.

"Only what I used to do with Aurelia when she fretted at night. I popped her in with you. They look like twins, them two, being the same age an' all."

"Yes, they do," Flora agreed.

Archie arrived later in the nursery to say good morning to his daughter and observed the two babies in the cradle.

"So peaceful," he said. "Maybe it was all meant to be."

Touching Flora lightly on the shoulder, he left the room.

As Sarah began to take over more duties in the nursery, Flora found herself with time to spare. Used to being outside from dawn to dusk in the Lakes, she began to take morning walks around the farmland and gardens to enjoy the summer air, only wishing she could get her hands dirty in the flower beds, whose beauty was choked and hidden by weeds.

But the gardens were Archie's territory, not hers. So far, the two of them had formed a silent tacit agreement to keep to their own spaces out of respect for Aurelia—a task that was not difficult, given the size of the house. They ate together at night, their food badly cooked by a local elderly woman, the only one to accept the paltry amount Archie could offer.

Sitting in the dining room, they would discuss the children's welfare in detail—a neutral topic of conversation that filled the silences, even though so much remained unsaid between them. Flora would excuse herself immediately after pudding had been served and take herself up to bed.

Of course, she was *not* tired. Even a few seconds spent with Archie set her nerve endings tingling. And during the hot August nights, her window open to let in the merest breath of breeze, she even longed for Teddy to wake up and scream—at least it would break the monotony of the impure thoughts that stayed with her until dawn.

However, as September approached, the time when nature—especially of the controlled variety—needed attention if it was to survive the winter, Flora decided to confront Archie. She found him in the orchard, filling a wheelbarrow with windfall from the plum trees.

"Hello," he said, almost shyly.

"Hello."

"Is everything all right with the children?"

"Perfect. They're having their afternoon nap."

"Good. It's wonderful they have each other for company."

"Yes, it is. Archie, can we talk?"

"Of course. Is something wrong?"

"No, not at all. I just . . . well, if I am to stay here at High Weald and it is to become my home too . . . I would like to make a contribution."

"Flora, you already do."

"I mean, a financial contribution. The estate needs an investment of funds, and due to my . . . father's legacy and the sale of Wynbrigg Farm, I have them available."

"I appreciate the offer, but you must remember that your family has already contributed to the bottomless pit of High Weald with the sale of Esthwaite Hall. Perhaps you are not aware of the amount it costs just to run the estate, let alone improve it."

"Well, I could at least offer my own services free of charge in the gardens? And maybe employ a couple of young men to assist us?"

"If you can find any still alive," Archie murmured darkly. "I realize that I am . . . not what I was." He indicated his leg.

"I would like to try, for if we don't do something before the winter, your work here will go to waste. And it will keep me occupied. Sarah becomes more irritated by the day at my constant visits to the nursery."

"Then I would be grateful for any assistance you can give me." He smiled at her. "Thank you."

For the rest of September, the two of them worked every daylight hour in the walled garden. Flora had also managed to find a couple of ex-soldiers in the village who were glad to lend a hand with the clearing.

Back in her element, with a more ladylike set of gardening clothes that Sarah had sewn for her, Flora felt calmer. Nowadays, instead of the strained small talk over dinner, the two of them discussed pruning and weeding and pored over seed catalogs. And the sound of laughter began to trickle back through the walls of High Weald.

Sometimes in the afternoons, Flora would set the perambulator under the enormous yew tree while they worked, Teddy and Louise sleeping soundly together side by side.

"They really are like twins," Archie said as he looked down at the babies one balmy September afternoon. "Who could have believed it?"

Who could? Flora thought as she fell into bed that night, exhausted from a hard day's work in the garden. At least it aided her sleep, although she wondered how long she could go on suppressing her feelings. Spending more time with Archie had made her painfully aware of how the war had changed him. The exuberant young man whom she had loved had matured into a thoughtful and contemplative adult. Often, she would notice him drifting away, his eyes filling with sadness as he perhaps relived a memory of what he had suffered. And watched others suffer too.

Archie had a new vulnerability that had washed away any of his old conceit. And which only endeared him to her more. He had behaved impeccably toward her during the last few weeks, and Flora had wondered recently whether she'd dreamed the fact that he'd said he still loved her.

Besides, they still walked in the shadow cast over High Weald by Aurelia's death. Whatever her letter had said, Flora mused often on whether it would ever disperse.

The nights began to draw in, and desperate to finish the work before the winter frost arrived, Archie and Flora began to toil in the gardens by the light of lanterns.

"I'm all in for tonight," Archie announced one chilly October evening, pulling himself to standing, which Flora could see was an effort. She watched as he lit a cigarette—a habit he'd picked up from the war—and wandered over to the yew tree.

"You go in. I'll finish up here," she suggested.

"You know, the light of the lanterns and the nip in the air reminds me of that night I kissed you here," Archie remarked.

"Don't remind me," Flora muttered.

"Of the kiss, or the circumstances?"

"You know very well which, Archie." Flora turned back to the flower bed.

"Yes."

There was a pause.

"I wish I could kiss you again, Flora."

"I . . ."

A sudden touch on her shoulder made her realize he had moved behind her. He took her hand and pulled her to standing, then turned her around to face him. "Can I? Love is never wrong, darling Flora, it's only the timing that can be. And this time, it's perfect," he murmured.

She looked at him, trying to formulate an answer, but before she could, his lips were on hers. And as his arms pulled her closer, every reason not to kiss him back disappeared from her mind.

After that, the two of them settled into an odd domesticity, keeping their relationship a secret from the rest of the house, although Archie was eager to marry her as soon as possible.

"We've wasted so much time already," he entreated her, but Flora stood firm.

"We must wait for at least a year until we announce any engagement," she told him. "I want no dissenters or gossip when we do."

"Goodness, Flora"—Archie took her into his arms; they were currently reduced to arranging trysts in the greenhouse, which Flora thought rather added to the excitement—"why do you care so much? I am lord of the manor and if I have my way, you will be my lady within a year. And I warn you that, whatever we do, there will be gossip."

"Then we will wait for the sake of Aurelia's memory," she countered.

Eventually, Flora persuaded Archie to let her use some of her legacy to fill the house and grounds with the help it needed. As staff were employed and builders tramped through the house to mend the roof, fix the damp, and wallpaper the interiors to brighten the rooms, she finally understood what Beatrix had seen was missing in her life. Despite the chaos they currently lived in, Flora felt happier than she'd ever been, even though the true nature of their relationship was unknown to anyone else.

"Darling, I have something I must confess to you. A surprise, if you like," Archie said over supper one evening. "I remembered recently that I had not yet registered Louise's birth. The registrar was most helpful, and given the traumatic circumstances of Aurelia's death, even let me off the fine that comes with leaving the registration past forty-two days. *And* . . . ," Archie continued, taking a deep breath, "while I was there, to keep things straightforward, I decided to register Teddy's birth on the date Louise was born. Teddy is safe now, darling, and can never be taken away from us. To all intents and purposes, he is my son, and the twin of Louise."

"But . . ." A stunned Flora looked into Archie's dark eyes. "I now can no longer ever be his legal mother! And you have lied on an official document!"

"Goodness, darling, there is nothing dishonest about love. I thought you would be thrilled! It saves all the dreadful paperwork one must complete, especially given Teddy's provenance—not to mention the court appearances that one must go through to adopt a child. And now our babies can grow up believing they really are twins."

"What about Sarah? And the doctor?" Flora wondered if Archie had taken leave of his senses. "They both know the truth."

"I have already told Sarah, and asked her opinion on what I'd decided to do. She agreed it was the easiest way to make Teddy safe. As for the doctor who attended the birth, he has since moved on to another practice . . . in Wales."

"Good God, Archie, I do wish you had asked *my* opinion on such a huge decision."

"I thought that it was best to present it as a fait accompli, simply because I know your honest heart and mind. And that you would have talked me out of it. Please remember, it is *me* who has handed my title and the estate to Teddy on a plate. One day, the son of a Lakeland shepherd will be the next Lord Vaughan." Archie smiled grimly. "And I cannot think of a better way to honor a man who fell in the trenches than by making his son a lord."

Flora remained silent, finally understanding Archie's reasoning. More and more, she had become aware of his guilt over surviving when so many had fallen. This was his gift to atone for all those lives lost. And he had given it to Teddy.

She knew there was nothing she could say. The deed was done. For better or for worse. And Flora realized that now, she too was culpable in the deception.

Archie and Flora finally announced their engagement the following autumn, in 1920, planning to be married three months later at Christmas.

After much agonizing and gentle persuasion from Archie, Flora had decided to invite Rose to the wedding. Rose had recently returned from India, having gone out to stay with a cousin after her husband's death. On her arrival home, she had sold the house in the Highlands and rented an elegant flat on Albemarle Street in London. She had written to her daughter on receipt of the wedding invitation, entreating Flora to pay her a visit. And there, Rose had wept, apologizing to her for the deception and the difficult childhood Flora had endured. *And* for her subsequent lack of support after the King had died.

"You do understand that, just like Mrs. Keppel, I had to stay away? Any contact with you, given the suspicion you were already placed under, not to mention Alistair's continual bitterness toward the situation . . . I felt that it was for the best. Also, I was frightened of seeing you again, the terrible things you might say. Can you forgive me?"

And eventually Flora *had* forgiven her—in her blissful state, she could have forgiven anyone anything. At least the two of them had been able to share their grief over Aurelia's loss.

"I did not even know she had died until two months later. The post in Poona is so very unreliable," Rose said. "I could not even attend my own daughter's funeral."

Even though her mother had initially questioned the fact that Archie had only mentioned Louise in the letter informing her of Aurelia's death, she had put it down to an oversight due to his grief at the time. And once Rose arrived for the wedding celebrations and saw the "twins" at High Weald, crawling and playing together, any lingering doubt had been washed away.

"Dear Teddy looks so very like his mother," Rose had commented, dabbing away her tears as Teddy sat on her knee, his innocent blue eyes reminding Flora too of her sister's.

"Who would have thought it?" Rose murmured as she helped Flora into her cream wedding dress on the day of her marriage. "We all thought you loathed Archie Vaughan. I am sure Aurelia would be happy if she could see what has happened since. Her babies thriving under your care."

The wedding took place in the old church where Flora had last watched her new husband marry her sister. It was a small and intimate service, out of respect for Aurelia. And the look in Archie's eyes as he finally placed the ring on her finger was one she would hold with her forever.

"I'll love you always," he breathed as he kissed her.

"I love you too."

It was only on their wedding night that Flora saw the damage the Great War had wreaked on his body. Both of his legs were a mass of scars caused by burns from the Bristol 22 that he'd crash landed. He had struggled to release himself from the burning wreck, but his copilot had perished a few minutes later when the plane had been consumed in a blaze of fire.

Flora could only love him more for his courage and bravery, as he gently made love to her for the very first time.

During the first year of their marriage, Flora often wondered that her body could contain the joy she felt with Archie by her side, and Teddy and Louise growing up at a High Weald that was filled with positivity and love.

Louise was gentle and sweet, just like her mother, yet she had also inherited her father's sharp intelligence and natural air of authority. And despite Teddy's more volatile nature, Louise not only tolerated but adored and defended the boy she—and everyone else—believed to be her twin.

Over dinner one evening, Archie told Flora of how he'd taken two-year-old Teddy to the stables, and sat him up with him on his horse.

"Do you know, he did not cry once, even when we began to trot. He kept shouting, 'More, Papa! More!'" Archie said proudly.

Flora was happy to see the bond between the two of them grow and deepen. And thought that perhaps Archie's decision to lie about Teddy's true birth had been the right one.

The Vaughan family settled down to enjoy the golden years between the wars in the paradise of their beautiful home. The "twins" grew and flourished, their closeness remarked upon by everyone in the household and all who came to visit.

However, when they reached the age of ten, Flora's discomfort over lying about the fact she was their blood mother became too much for her.

"I feel like a fraud," she said desolately to Archie. "Louise at least must know that Aurelia was her real mother. Besides, someone from the village is bound to mention her as they grow up. But that means we must lie to Teddy about *his* own mother."

"As we have discussed many times before, surely it's a small price to pay for his safety and comfort here with us?" Archie countered. "Although I agree: we must tell them about Aurelia."

Subsequently, Teddy and Louise appeared hand in hand in the drawing room a few days later, looking for all the world like little cherubs, freshly scrubbed after their bath. Flora and Archie sat them down and told them of their real mother, a pang in Flora's heart as she looked at Teddy's trusting expression. Both of her children looked shocked and uncertain.

"May we still call you 'Mother'?" Louise asked timidly, her dark brown eyes fixed on Flora.

"Of course you may, my darling."

"Because you've always been our mother," added Teddy, his own eyes filling with tears.

"Yes, I have." Flora drew them both to her. "And I will always love you and care for you both, I promise."

As Teddy grew to manhood, Archie taught him all he knew about country pursuits. Teddy, being a child of the Lakes, took to them like a duck to water. But when he reached thirteen, Archie insisted he follow in his footsteps and—against Flora and Louise's fervent wishes—sent him to Charterhouse, a boarding school nearby. It was there that Teddy began to rebel against academia and the routine such an establishment insisted on. Flora tried to tell Archie that Teddy was happiest out in the open air, that it was in his blood to wander across the land, but he would have none of it.

"He must do as any young man of his class does and learn how to be a gentleman," he'd insisted.

Teddy's misery and continued rebellion was the only thorn in Flora's side. She knew that, just like everyone else at High Weald, Archie had forgotten who Teddy really was.

37

December 1943

BEATRIX IS DEAD!

Lady Flora Vaughan, no longer able to see the page in her journal, put down her ink pen and wept. The telegram had arrived only a few hours ago and she could hardly believe that, amid all the renewed death and destruction of war, and the telegrams that arrived regularly to the villagers of High Weald, she herself had received one.

"My dearest, dearest friend . . ." It seemed almost inconceivable that such a force of nature—the woman and the writer, and the kindest, cleverest person she knew—would never walk again across her beloved fells.

"Darling, what is it?"

Archie leaned over her to read the telegram. "I'm so very sorry. I know what she meant to you."

"What she meant to *us*. Beatrix was the one who encouraged me to come here to you and Louise. Not to mention bringing Teddy to my door."

"Yes, it's a terrible loss. Would you like me to stay with you today? I am due at the Air Ministry for a meeting, but I can always cancel it."

"No." Flora kissed the hand clasping her shoulder. "As Beatrix always said, when someone dies, life must go on. But thank you for offering. Will you be back for supper tonight?"

"I hope so. The trains are terrible at the moment." Archie gave his wife a tender kiss on the cheek. "You know where I am if you need me."

"Is Teddy taking you to the station?"

"I'll drive myself," Archie said abruptly. "I will see you later, darling."

He left the study and Flora stared out at the walled garden the two of them had rebuilt. Currently, a thick layer of frost shielded its glory, reminding her of that December day thirty-four years ago when Archie had kissed her under the yew tree. Now both Louise and Teddy were older than she and Archie had been then. And another Christmas was approaching.

Knowing she scarcely had time to grieve today, Flora sent up a small prayer for her dear departed friend, then consulted her to-do list. At five o'clock, the pre-Christmas celebrations would begin with a party for the Land Girls, and she would help Mrs. Tanit set out the homemade cider to go with the freshly made mince pies. Flora wanted an evening of fun for the girls, who had arrived a year ago to replace the men away fighting, and who had worked so hard on the High Weald estate. They would be departing early tomorrow morning on a specially chartered bus, which would take them back to their families for Christmas.

And then, on Christmas Eve, her mother would arrive to spend the festive season at High Weald. Flora marveled at how her relationship with her mother had changed. Rose was a welcome guest at High Weald, and a more regular one now that rationing in London was hitting hard. Flora thanked God for the chickens that laid their eggs, although the fattest chicken would be missing from the coop by this evening. Over time, she'd had to give in to her family's demand for meat and Dottie was this year's sacrifice.

To cheer her spirits, she counted her blessings, including that her family had not suffered during the war as other families had; neither of her beloved men had left to fight: Archie because he'd been invalided out in the Great War and was too old to enlist, and Teddy due to the ridiculous miracle of his flat feet. Flora still did not know how this could possibly have hindered him as a soldier, especially as he was so energetic on them, but neither did she care. The condition had saved her son from possible death.

The news had caused Archie some concern—after all, the young squire of the village was meant to be an example—but it was hardly Teddy's fault and he had sworn that he would play as active a role from home as he possibly could.

Sadly, his attempts at doing so were continually curtailed. Her husband cited lack of discipline, but Flora put it down to the high spirits of a young man who had come of age during a war. With his friends from Oxford leaving to join up, her son's enthusiasm for his studies had waned, and after a term of what the head of his college had called "unsuitable behavior for an Oxford undergraduate," Teddy had been sent down.

Since then, he'd tried the Home Guard, but had found it difficult to take orders, calling the local guard "crusty old fuddy-duddies." Flora then acquiesced to Teddy's request to manage the farm when Albert, the farm manager, had joined up. But Teddy's inability to get up at dawn had irritated the handful of long-serving farm staff under his command.

Archie had then secured Teddy an administration job at the Air Ministry on Kingsway, where he himself worked, but that hadn't lasted long either. Flora wasn't sure of the details—a grim-faced Archie had merely said it had been decided Teddy should leave to find other employment. Reading between the lines, Flora had surmised it was something to do with a girl.

It was hardly surprising that women swooned over him. With his height, strong build, and blond, blue-eyed looks, not to mention his charm, he could hardly fail to attract attention from the female sex. Teddy would be twenty-five soon, and was yet to settle down. Flora was certain that, when he did, all the wrongs would be righted and her darling son would become worthy of the title and the estate he would one day inherit.

Flora walked down the icy passageway into the warm, steamy kitchen, where Mrs. Tanit was conjuring up something that smelled like mince pies but was cleverly made from all manner of alternative ingredients.

"How are you doing?" Flora asked her.

"Very well, thank you, ma'am. What would you like for dinner later? I was thinking I could use the leftover pastry to make a savory pie for the others. I have some spinach, mash, and eggs I can fry for you," she said in her softly accented voice.

"Goodness, a pie! Now, that would be a treat. As long as we can find something to put in it."

"Mr. Tanit has found some beef shin going spare in the village. I thought I could use that."

Flora knew better than to ask its provenance. The local black market for meat was rife. And just this once, she wouldn't resist. "You can indeed," she agreed, grateful once again for the Tanits' presence. The young couple were not afraid of hard work. Mr. Tanit not only drove, he also assisted Flora with the never-ending jobs in the gardens and the orchard, such as collecting the windfall apples, as well as helping to tend the menagerie that Flora had gathered under her protection over the years.

"Can you also make up my mother's usual room?" Flora asked Mrs. Tanit. "Oh, and of course, we will need mulled wine for the villagers' drinks tomorrow at lunchtime. Take some red wine from the cellar, but we'll have to make do without the oranges." Even the *thought* of an orange made Flora's senses tingle with longing.

"Yes, ma'am."

"And tonight, Louise is bringing the Land Girls up at five sharp," she added in afterthought. She left the kitchen and then went back to her study to write a letter of condolence to William, Beatrix's husband. Flora had just put her pen down when there was a knock on the door.

"Come."

"Hello, Mother, am I disturbing you?" Louise popped her head around the door, her shoulder-length auburn hair neatly held back with two combs, her dark eyes so like Archie's.

"Of course not. Although I have just had some very sad news. My friend Beatrix died yesterday."

"Oh, Mother, I'm so terribly sorry. I know how fond of her you were. And such a talent lost to us too. I remember you used to read Teddy and me her animal stories."

"The world will certainly be a lesser place without her."

"It's so sad that she didn't live to see peace. I am sure it will be coming soon. Or at least, I hope it will," Louise corrected herself.

"What is it you wish to see me about, darling?"

"Oh . . . it's nothing. It can wait for another day. The girls are all very excited about tonight's party," she continued brightly.

"And we will do our best to make it as cheerful as we can."

"I have sewn them lavender bags to take home as a gift," she said. "And we are all dressing up!"

"Wonderful, and please do not think that I will be sad this evening. Beatrix would not have wanted any of us to mourn."

"Nevertheless, any loss is a difficult one, and I know that you are simply being brave." Louise walked over and kissed Flora on the cheek. "I will see you at five o'clock."

"Is Teddy coming this evening, do you know? I have asked him to attend."

"He said he'd try, but he's very busy today."

Doing what? Flora asked herself as Louise left the room. And then put away the thought. He was her son and she had to trust him.

The Land Girls gathered later that evening in the drawing room, drinking cider and eating Mrs. Tanit's excellent tribute to mince pies, made from dried plums and apples gathered from the orchard earlier in autumn. Louise was encouraged onto the piano, and they sang Christmas carols with gusto, before ending with Vera Lynn's "We'll Meet Again."

As Louise ushered the girls out to the lobby so they could collect their coats and return to the two cottages they occupied near the stables, Flora saw a look of concern on her daughter's face.

"Is everything all right, Louise?"

"One of my girls—Tessie—seems to be missing. Never mind, I'm sure she'll turn up sooner or later." Louise pecked Flora on the cheek. "If you don't mind, I won't join you and Papa for dinner. I'd like to spend the rest of the evening with the girls."

"Of course. No sign of Teddy then?"

"No. Good night, Mother." Louise herded the girls outside and Flora watched from a window as she marched them down the drive by the light of a lantern. She thought fondly of what a huge help her daughter had been, running the Land Girls single-handedly in a calm and friendly manner, with not a hint of snobbery about her. Flora knew they all adored her.

She headed to the kitchen, and checking inside the range, she saw the meat pie keeping warm along with the mashed potatoes and cabbage Mrs. Tanit had left before returning to her own cottage.

Thinking once more how her solitary, servantless existence in the Lakes had prepared her so perfectly for the war years here, she carried a tray of empty cider glasses through from the drawing room and began to wash them up while she waited for Archie—and Teddy—to return. These days, they ate at the table in the kitchen. It was the warmest place in the house, and even though there were trees suitable to be chopped for firewood, both Flora and Archie had agreed that they must not live above those who were suffering deprivation across the world.

Archie arrived through the back door twenty minutes later, his face worn with exhaustion, but his eyes alight. "Darling, how are you?" He kissed her warmly. "And how was the party? Forgive me for missing it, but I was in a meeting. And I have some good news."

"It was very cheery." Flora donned an apron and began to serve up supper, thinking that they would not wait for Teddy or the pie would be spoiled. "What is your news?"

"Suffice to say, I will no longer have the long commute to London. I am to be posted at Ashford airbase, only a few miles away. You know already from the local newspapers that we have squadrons from the RAF and the RCAF. Plus the Yanks, of course."

"Yes." Flora smiled, remembering the excitement earlier in the year when the Land Girls had heard that Canadian, American, and British squadrons were to be stationed there. There had been a number of dances and the girls had arrived back with chocolates and nylon stockings.

"That's very good news, darling. What will your role be?"

"All I can say is, there's something big coming. I'm to be the liaison officer between the various squadrons, organizing flying rotas and the like, and helping with strategy. You know, darling, for the first time today, I really felt as though the end might be in sight."

"We'll be awfully glad if you're right." Flora put a plate in front of her husband and gazed down at him fondly.

"This looks excellent, thank you," he said as he picked up his knife and fork. "Are neither of the children joining us tonight?"

"No, Louise is down at the cottages with the Land Girls and Teddy is . . . out."

"As usual," murmured Archie.

It was two o'clock in the morning before a sleepless Flora heard the creak of the floorboards and a door closing along the corridor. And knew that her son had finally returned home.

"Where were you last night?" Flora asked Teddy as he wandered into the busy kitchen, where both Flora and Mrs. Tanit were baking and chopping in preparation for the festive season, carols playing on the radio.

"Out. Do you have a problem with that, Mother? I am well over the age of consent." Teddy swiped two jam tarts cooling on a rack on the table. "And how are you this fine day, Mrs. Tanit?"

"I am well, thank you, sir," she replied.

Flora had noticed that their housekeeper was one of the only women she knew who refused to succumb to her son's considerable charms.

"Excellent." He gave Mrs. Tanit a bright smile. "So, what's the plan for today, Mother?"

"We have the villagers' drinks at lunchtime and then your grandmother arrives at five at Ashford. Perhaps you'd be good enough to collect her from the station?"

"That depends," Teddy replied, ambling across the kitchen to lean against the range, close to where Mrs. Tanit was stirring the mulled wine. "The boys in the village have asked me to join them at the pub before supper. After all, it is Christmas Eve."

"It would help us all if you could collect her."

"Can't that husband of yours do it?" he asked Mrs. Tanit, who flinched as he pressed a hand lightly to her back.

"Mr. and Mrs. Tanit have the night off to celebrate Christmas together, as Mrs. Tanit will be here tomorrow helping me cook and serve the lunch. I'm sure that your grandmother would appreciate your effort."

"Is there any bread?" Teddy glanced around the kitchen. "I'm so hungry, I could eat a horse."

Flora pointed to the pantry. "There are three loaves just baked, but please take no more than a slice. We need them for sandwiches for the villagers."

As her son went in search of the loaves, Flora sighed. On occasion, even *her* patience ran out.

"I think this will be a wonderful Christmas," Teddy said as he emerged from the pantry, munching on a fat piece of bread.

"I hope so."

"And of course I will go and pick up Grandmama." Teddy smiled suddenly, walked over to his mother, and gave her a hug. "Only teasing."

And as it turned out, it *was* a happy Christmas. Archie seemed more positive than Flora remembered him being in a long time, engendered, she was sure, by his new posting to Ashford. Louise was, as ever, a dutiful daughter, facilitating everyone's comfort and happiness. And even Teddy managed to control his urge to join his friends at the local pub, and remained at home until Boxing Day.

That night, Flora and Archie fell into bed, both exhausted from the yuletide revelry.

"I feel as though we have entertained the entire neighborhood—rich and poor—at our expense."

"We have," Flora chuckled, thinking of all those who had passed through High Weald in the last few days. "But that's the way it should be, isn't it? After all, Christmas is about giving."

"Yes, and it is you who has given the most. Thank you, my darling." Archie kissed her gently. "And let us hope that the New Year brings the peace that we all deserve."

38

The winter of 1944 seemed longer to Flora than any other. Perhaps because she, along with the rest of the world, was weary of war, weary of bad news, and weary of the falsely cheerful voice on the radio telling everyone to keep their spirits up.

Besides that, an unusual sense of foreboding hung over her, like the tightly packed snow covering the gardens. The one bright spot during the harsh February had been a letter from William Heelis.

Castle Cottage
Near Sawrey
15th February 1944

My dear Lady Vaughan—or may I call you "Flora"?

I do hope this letter finds you well. Up here, the snow is deep around me as I write and it is so very quiet now that my dearest Beatrix is not here to scold me. I write to tell you that Beatrix's will was read out by myself, with only the cat in attendance (who, I note, has received a small bequest in the form of a tin of sardines). This was a formal procedure, legally required by the solicitor (me) and the executor (me). There will be a formal meeting of the trustees and all the beneficiaries in due course, but given the current inclement conditions, I have decided I will refrain from organizing it until the snows have melted, and will conduct it in London, where a number of the beneficiaries—including the National Trust—reside. You can imagine that the list is long, and there is every chance I shall have to hire a banqueting hall to accommodate them all. I jest, but it is a complex will and will take quite some sorting, and made so much more painful for this humble solicitor by the fact it is Beatrix's.

Now then, I wanted to inform you that Beatrix has also left you a bequest. And I enclose the short letter she wrote to you explaining it. I hope you will approve!

Meantime, my dear Flora, let us pray that this endless winter will eventually pass and spring will arrive to give us all hope of a future. I admit that at present I am struggling to accept there will be one without my beloved wife.

Do keep in touch, dear friend.

William Heelis

Removing the other envelope, Flora opened it and steeled herself to read its contents.

Castle Cottage
Near Sawrey
20th June 1942

My dear Flora,

I shall make this brief, knowing that letters from beyond the grave can be maudlin.

So to the point: I have bequeathed you a bookshop in London, which I bought some years ago now, when the family who owned it was struggling financially. Arthur Morston (that is, the great-grandson of the original namesake) died a few years back, and it having been my local bookshop when I was a child living in Kensington, and being fond of its proprietor, I took it off their hands. Sadly, I had to close it at the beginning of the war, due to staff shortages. And it is still closed to this day.

Flora dear, you must do with it whatever you wish. The building is worth something at least. As you are so much closer to London than I, if you decide to keep it, you will make a far better employer and proprietor than I ever did. If you do sell it, I am sure that with your love for books, you will find good use for the stock. The miracle is that it has managed to survive the war—so far at least—when so many other buildings nearby have been destroyed. It is a wonderful little place, and I urge you to at least visit it before you make your decision.

So, dear Flora, it is time to say good-bye. I will always remember the times we shared together with affection. Do keep in touch with dear William. When the time comes, I fear he will be rather lost without me.

Beatrix

"How very generous and thoughtful of her," Archie said over supper that evening. "When you receive the title deeds and the keys, we must go to London to see it."

"I can only hope it *is* still standing. I could hardly bear to find it a pile of rubble."

"Perhaps Teddy may be interested in running it? He seems to have little else to focus on these days. He cannot even rouse himself out of bed before lunchtime. And I hear from the village he is a regular every night at the local hostelry."

"He has had a terrible cold, as you know."

"We have all suffered colds this winter, Flora, but that does not preclude us from doing something useful with our days."

"I think he is depressed. His young years have been clouded by war."

"At least he has years left in front of him, unlike so many of his peers," Archie snapped, trying to keep his anger under control. "I was thinking recently that we must discuss the contents of my will. I haven't revisited it since just after we married. High Weald is currently left to Teddy, as he is our eldest and only son, and therefore, through primogeniture, my heir, but I must admit that I'm starting to wonder about his suitability. I was thinking today that even though there is nothing I can do about the title passing directly to him, perhaps I should leave the estate in perpetuity to you, darling. Then, dependent on Teddy's future behavior, and also if Louise was to produce a male child, you could decide what was best to do. The way he's conducting himself at present makes me wonder if—"

"Can we talk of this some other time? Perhaps when the war is over and all has settled? With Beatrix only just cold in her grave, I really can't stand to think about such things."

"Of course, my darling." Archie reached his hand across the table to hers and squeezed it. "And when it is, we shall celebrate that we have all managed to make it through."

Flora's spirits lifted as England inched out of winter and the first signs of spring appeared. She was also excited to see the seedlings she and Mr. Tanit had planted last autumn beginning to grow. War or no war, a garden—just like a child—needed constant attention. And simply the feel of the solid earth beneath her fingers grounded her.

Despite her cynical view of the skewed positive propaganda churned out by the War Office, even Flora felt a sea change in the Allies' fortunes. She knew from what Archie said—and what he didn't say—that the Allies were gearing up for some form of organized attack in Europe. Even though Archie's hours at the airbase often extended long into the night, she could read the anticipation in his eyes.

There was also some happy news for Louise, who had attended a dance on New Year's Eve with Teddy, after much persuasion from Flora.

"It will do you good to go up to town and take a break from your work here at High Weald," Flora had insisted. She'd lent Louise an evening gown, and Louise had altered it herself, her nimble fingers flying across the fabric, just as Aurelia's had once done. Teddy had accompanied her up on the train and when Louise had arrived home a day later, Flora had noticed a new light in her eyes.

The young man concerned was one Rupert Forbes, a bookish type whose chronic myopia had prevented him from fighting for his country. Teddy had known him vaguely at Oxford, and Louise had reported that he was now doing something in intelligence.

"He can't say what it is, of course, but I'm sure it's terribly important. He's very clever, Mother—he won a scholarship to Oxford to study classics."

"Bit of a dry fellow," Teddy had interjected. "Awfully straight—even refused a second glass of champagne on New Year's Eve!"

"Not all of us have to continually drink the bar dry to find happiness," Louise had snapped at him.

It was unusual for Louise to snap at anyone, let alone her beloved brother, and Flora had wondered if the comment was engendered by an urge to defend Rupert or a growing irritation with Teddy.

The romance between Rupert and Louise had quickly blossomed into something deeper. Both Flora and Archie had liked Rupert immediately upon meeting him and it had warmed their hearts to see the growing love the couple shared. Subsequently, just two weeks ago, the pair had announced their engagement and Rupert had come down to stay at High Weald for the weekend to celebrate. He had been fascinated by Flora's inheritance from Beatrix and begged to be allowed to come with her when she visited the bookshop in a few weeks' time. Inquiries had confirmed that the building had not been bombed during the Blitz, and Flora was expecting the title deeds imminently.

Rupert, although from a good family, had no private income of his own. So Archie and Flora had agreed that the young couple should move to Home Farm across the lane, which had stood empty since the farm manager had left. She knew that, with a lick of paint, and some new curtains and furnishings, which Louise's clever fingers would so deftly create, the house would suit the newlyweds well. And Flora already had the perfect wedding present in mind for the young couple.

"Mother, can I speak to you?"

Louise found Flora in the garden on a sunny May morning.

"Of course." Flora stood up and studied Louise's concerned face. "What is it?"

"Can we sit down?"

Louise indicated a bench in the shade, under a rose arbor that Mr. Tanit had recently built.

"What is it?"

Flora could see Louise's long fingers clasping and unclasping in agitation.

"It's . . . delicate. It concerns one of my Land Girls. And Teddy."

"Then you'd better tell me."

"I've known since Christmas that something was going on between the two of them. Remember the night of the Land Girls' party when Tessie didn't arrive?"

"I do."

"Well, that night I was on my way back home from the cottages when I saw Teddy and Tessie appear from the drive of Home Farm. It was well past midnight and it confirmed what a couple of the girls had already mentioned to me."

"You mean they knew where she was?"

"Yes, and with whom."

"I see."

"I hoped that the relationship would peter out—I am sure that you are aware of Teddy's short attention span, especially when it comes to women—and it seemed to."

"Then why do you tell me now?"

Louise sighed deeply and looked away across the garden. "Because Tessie came to me yesterday in floods of tears. And announced that she was 'in the family way,' as she put it. She's pregnant, Mother, and she swears it's Teddy's child."

"Oh God . . ." It was Flora's turn to clench her fingers together in distress. "And is it?"

"She is four months or so gone and her fiancé has been away fighting in France for the past six months, without leave. All the other girls knew she was out with Teddy until the early hours that night and covered for her. The dates fit, I'm afraid. So I'd say that it is, yes."

"And Teddy? What does he say?"

"She hasn't told him yet. He broke off the relationship after, as Tessie said, he'd finished having his way with her."

"Then I suppose he must marry her."

"He won't. He doesn't love her or, indeed, even like her any longer! Besides, Tessie's a bright and very pretty young woman, but she comes from the East End of London. The two of them have nothing in common. And the child, if it's a boy, would be the heir to High Weald. What on earth would Papa say?"

Flora took in the ramifications of her son's despicable actions, and then thought of Archie's reaction if he heard the news. It would be the icing on the cake of the strained father-son relationship.

"You say the woman has a fiancé?"

"She does, yes. They were childhood sweethearts and have been walking out together for years."

"Do you think he might love her enough to forgive her, and take the child on as his own? She won't be the first girl in wartime to have suffered the same fate, after all."

"I couldn't say, Mother, but I doubt it, don't you?" Louise answered carefully, her tone suggesting that Flora's desperation was making her naive. "I mean, if it was Rupert, he'd leave me without a second glance. And this isn't just about how her fiancé feels about Tessie. It's about how Tessie feels about Teddy. She believes she is in love with him."

"From what you've said, Teddy quite obviously doesn't feel the same."

"Perhaps you could speak to him? You're the only one he seems to listen to. I swear, Mother, he's gone quite wild in the past few months. And is gathering a reputation for his carousing locally that Papa would be shocked to hear of. Forgive me for burdening you with this, but something has to be done. And fast."

"Thank you for telling me, Louise. Leave it with me now and I will try to think what is best to do."

"I will tell Tessie that I have talked to you and that you will discuss it with Teddy."

Flora spent the rest of the day in the garden, wishing that Teddy could be more like the calm, composed Mr. Tanit, who spoke little, yet handled both plants and animals so tenderly.

He has compassion, she thought, wondering if her son would ever learn what the word meant.

During a long night of watching Archie sleep peacefully next to her, Flora tried to decide what she should do. If he heard of his son's dreadful misdemeanor, Flora knew how he would react. Honor was everything to him and she wouldn't be surprised if he threw Teddy out of High Weald on the spot with nothing.

That afternoon, Flora asked for Louise to send young Tessie to see her. The girl arrived in her study, her sweet face pale, her large blue eyes fearful. Flora saw the slight curve of her belly and experienced a sudden ache in her own. Even though she and Archie had tried for a child, she had never succeeded in conceiving one. But then, she had been thirty when they had finally walked down the aisle, and a few years later Flora had known she had missed her chance.

As she studied the girl, a moment of madness made her picture holding this child in her arms and bringing it up as her own. Teddy's child . . . destined to be another fatherless infant. Flora dismissed the fantasy and composed herself for the confrontation.

"Hello, Tessie. Do come and sit down."

"Thank you, ma'am. I'm sorry to bring you into all this, especially seeing how kind you have all been to me and the girls. Have you spoken to Teddy? What did he say?"

Flora readied herself to lie. "Yes, I have, and sadly, he denies all knowledge of such a relationship. Or such an event."

"How can he? Everyone knows we was seeing each other for months in the autumn and all over Christmas. You ask the other girls, they'll tell you. I . . ." Tessie burst into noisy tears.

Flora stood up and went to her, pulling a lace handkerchief out of her sleeve and handing it to her. Her heart went out to this poor girl, but she had to put her family first.

"There, there," she said gently. "Nothing is ever as bad as it seems."

"Yes, it is! How could it be worse, if you'll pardon me for saying, ma'am? A baby on the way, put there by a man who denies the deed, and a fiancé who sure as eggs are eggs will walk back the other way when he sees the bun I've got in me oven. And me mum and dad already have seven mouths to feed . . . they'll have me turned out of the house the minute they know. I'll be destitute, on the streets. I might as well go and throw meself into the river now and be done with it!"

"Tessie, please, I understand you're upset, but there's always a way, I promise you."

"And what way is that, ma'am, excuse me for asking?"

"Well now, the most important thing is that you and the baby have a roof over your heads, isn't it? I mean, your own roof."

"Course. But on my wages, there's no way I could afford me own place."

"No. And that is why I am prepared to give you a sum of money with which you could buy a little house of your own. The money will also provide you with a small yearly income until the child is at school and you can find work for yourself."

"Excuse me, ma'am, but why?" Tessie looked at her suspiciously. "I mean, if that son of yours has told you it ain't his baby, and he never even had . . . knowledge of me, why aren't you casting me out without a second glance?"

"My son has told me that the baby cannot be his, but that does not preclude me helping a young lady in distress, does it? I was once young too, Tessie, and desperate. And I received kindness and assistance in my hour of need. I am only repaying one kind turn with another," Flora replied calmly.

"But houses cost a lot of money." Tessie blew her nose loudly into the handkerchief.

"You could buy something suitable near your parents, if you wish. Where do they live?"

"Hackney."

"I'm sure they will come around once the baby is born. Perhaps even your fiancé too. If he loves you, that is."

"Oh, yes, he loves me. He calls me the sunshine in his day. And look what I've done to him. No." Tessie shook her head. "He won't never forgive me for this, never. So, what would you expect in return?"

"Nothing. Other than perhaps the occasional photograph of the baby. And your promise that you will not drag my son's reputation through the mud by spreading lies about him."

"I swear blind, ma'am, Teddy is the father of the baby. And I reckon you know it too, which is why you're doing this for us. I've got your grandchild in here." She placed a hand on her stomach. "If it's a boy, he could be the heir to all this."

"As you know very well, there is no way of proving it either way. So, there is my offer. Do you wish to take it?"

"You're covering for him, protecting him, ain't you? Your darling son . . . Everyone knows he's the apple of your eye and you won't have a word said against him. Where is he?" Tessie stood up, shaking with anger now. "I'd reckon there's a chance you haven't spoken to him at all. I want to speak to him meself. Now!"

"Feel free." Flora shrugged as nonchalantly as she could, before turning her back and walking to her desk. "But the moment you leave this room, I shall withdraw my offer. And I can guarantee that you will hear nothing different from Teddy's lips. Ask Louise. He's denied it to her too," she added for good measure. She sat down at her desk and drew out her book of checks. "What is it to be? You can leave with a check made out in your name to the sum of a thousand pounds, then go back to the cottage and pack your things. I will send Mr. Tanit to drive you to Ashford station in an hour's time. Or alternatively, you can leave empty-handed and throw yourself on my son's mercy. Which, as you and I both know to our cost, is not a quality he possesses."

Silence reigned and Flora hoped she had done enough to convince her. But she was proud, and bright, and Flora admired her spirit.

"It's blackmail, this . . ."

Flora said nothing, but picked up her fountain pen and slowly unscrewed the lid. A long, defeated sigh emanated through the room.

"As you well know, I have no choice. I'll take your money and go."

"So be it," said Flora as she wrote out the check, relief flooding through her. "You have made the right decision, Tessie."

"There was no decision to make, was there, ma'am? I loved him, you know," she said sadly. "I was always a good girl before, but he told me all sorts, like that he would marry me."

"Here is the check, and the name of my solicitor, who will handle any future correspondence. He will also help with any purchase of a house if necessary."

"Thank you, ma'am," Tessie managed. "You're a kind woman, and that's for sure. Teddy don't know how lucky he is to have a mum like you who does his dirty work for him. He's a bad 'un, he is, I'm telling you."

"Good-bye, Tessie. Take care of both of you."

"I'll do me best, ma'am, swear."

Tessie left the room. Flora sank into her chair, relief and disgust flooding through her in equal measure.

There is nothing dishonest about love . . .

She remembered Archie's words to her all those years ago. Yet her love for Teddy and her need to protect him had turned her into a person she did not recognize. And Flora hated herself for it.

"What is it, Mother? I'm due out at five for a meeting," Teddy said sulkily as he appeared in Flora's study.

"And you are ten minutes late already, so we'd better get straight down to business."

"What is it that I've done now? What gossip have you heard?"

"I think you know very well what it is."

"Oh." Teddy chuckled. "I presume you have heard about my so-called liaison with the Smith girl."

"Yes, I have, from the other Land Girls and from your sister, who claims to have seen you both walking from Home Farm the night before Christmas Eve. And from Tessie herself earlier today."

"She has been to see you?"

"I asked her to come."

"Good God, Mother. You seem to forget I am twenty-four years of age and capable of clearing up my own messes."

"Then you admit that this is your 'mess'?"

"No, I . . ." Teddy faltered. "I don't need my mother to interfere in my life. You do realize that the whole thing is a pack of lies?"

"Having spoken to Tessie today, I sincerely doubt it is. I will get straight to the point. You know that Tessie is pregnant, and the chances are that it is your child she bears. You have refused to take any form of responsibility for your actions, as you take no responsibility for anything. You lie blatantly and routinely to save your own skin."

"Mother . . . I—"

"Please, do *not* interrupt me. You are a lazy, insolent drunk and, frankly, an embarrassment to this family. Only last week, your father spoke about remaking his will."

"And disinheriting me?"

"Yes." Flora knew she had struck gold by the look on Teddy's face. "And I can certainly see why. To be frank, if your father heard even a whisper of the rumor that is circulating about Tessie, it would be the final straw."

"I see." Teddy sank down into the armchair.

"I suggest that, from now on, there are no further lies between us if we are to salvage the situation."

Teddy looked beyond his mother out of the window. "All right."

"I have sent Tessie away, with enough money to make sure she and the baby will be safe."

"Mother, you didn't need to do that, really, I—"

"I think I did. This is almost certainly your child, and mine and your father's grandchild. Admit it, for God's sake, Teddy."

"Yes," he finally agreed. "There is a chance but—"

"I'm not interested in the 'but's. You simply cannot continue in the same vein. I understand that you're bored and struggling with your life, but your reputation as a womanizer and a drunk is growing apace."

"I am indeed bored. And it's hardly surprising I feel the way I do. If it wasn't for my stupid flat feet, I'd have been off years ago doing my duty and serving my country."

"Whatever your excuses, you must now make a choice. You can either stay and become a son that your father and I can be proud of. Or I shall suggest to your father that we send you to Ceylon to stay with your Aunt Elizabeth and Uncle Sidney, where you can help them on their tea plantation. Either way, you have to prove to your father that you are worthy of being his heir."

As with Tessie earlier, there was silence from the armchair.

"You would send me away? There is a war on, Mother." Teddy's voice cracked slightly. "Ships are bombed and sunk constantly."

Flora took a deep breath before she continued. "I would, simply because I am no longer prepared to cover for you or excuse your actions. It is down to my constant interventions on your behalf that things have not reached crisis point with your father before now. However, as much as I love you, the look on that young woman's face today, sitting where you are now when I told her that you had denied having any form of relationship with her, made me realize that I can no longer condone your recent behavior. Do you understand me, Teddy?"

He hung his head miserably. "Yes, Mother, I do."

"I still believe there is a good man inside you. You are young and there is a chance for you to make amends and prove to your father that you can one day inherit this estate."

"Yes. I will stay, Mother," he said eventually. "And I promise I will not disappoint you and Papa any longer." And without another word or glance at her, Teddy left the room.

39

Over the next couple of weeks, Teddy did indeed seem to have turned over a new leaf. He was as helpful as he could be around both the house and the garden. And there was a great deal to do as, the day after Flora's talk with Teddy, Mr. Tanit announced that he and his wife were leaving High Weald immediately. He wouldn't be drawn on the reasons, and when Flora asked if there was anything she could do to persuade them to stay, Tanit remained tight-lipped.

"It's best, ma'am. Mrs. Tanit no longer feels comfortable at High Weald."

They left that night, and Flora was awake until the early hours, wondering what she'd done to offend the sweet-natured housekeeper.

Louise shrugged despondently at the news in the kitchen the next morning.

"Surely you must have seen why?" she whispered. "Teddy has been all over her in the last few months. I mean, I can't be sure, but if I'd been that poor girl, I doubt I could have stood it either."

Flora closed her eyes, remembering her son putting a hand on Mrs. Tanit's back while they had been standing at the range in the kitchen.

The following evening, Flora ate alone, as Archie had telephoned to say he was delayed at the airbase, a common occurrence these days. In bed that night, she heard the drone of German bombers close by, but hardly gave it a second thought. Such sounds had become as familiar as that of the chirruping of the birds at dawn. However, tonight it sounded near, and Flora sighed with irritation that they might have to move down and sleep in the cellar for the night if the bombers came any closer.

Sure enough, just before midnight, the air raid sirens went off, and Flora, Teddy, and Louise trooped down the stairs. Two hours later, the all-clear sounded and they returned to bed, Flora knowing that Archie would almost certainly stay in a bunk at the airbase for the rest of the night.

"Mother! Mother, wake up!" Louise's cry roused her the next morning. "There's a telephone call for you. Someone called Squadron Leader King. He wants to speak to you urgently."

Heart in her mouth, Flora flew downstairs, almost tripping in her hurry to reach the telephone. Yet she already knew the reason for the call.

The squadron leader imparted the news that Archie and fourteen others at RAF Ashford had been killed outright when a bomb had directly hit the tented area that accommodated the reserve fighter pilots and other members of staff.

Despite Flora's previous strength in adversity, she fell apart. The sheer irony of it all overwhelmed her . . . Archie surviving this far, and their happiness at his posting to Ashford rather than working in London—the main target of the German bombers—only for him to lose his life a few miles from home . . . it was a situation her addled mind could not comprehend.

Louise called in the doctor, who prescribed sedatives, and for several days Flora lay in bed, with no will or energy to rise from it. Without her beloved Archie, she'd rather have been dead too. Even the sight of his daughter's haunted face was not enough for her to leave her bedroom. She lay there, reliving every single moment that she and Archie had spent together, and railing at the God she could no longer believe in for taking him away from her forever.

And worst of all, they had not even had a chance to say good-bye.

On the sixth morning after the fateful telephone call, Flora was awoken from a drugged sleep by a tap-tapping on the window. She raised her head and saw a baby thrush that must have fallen out of its nest in the old chestnut tree by the window. The ledge had saved its fall, but in its hysteria, it was in danger of toppling off as it hopped about and squawked for its mother.

"Coming, little one," she whispered, as she carefully opened the window and managed to take the tiny thing into her hands. "There, there," Flora crooned to it. "You're safe now. We'll get a ladder and have you back with your mother in no time." With the bird cupped in her hands, she walked downstairs to the kitchen, where Teddy and Louise were sitting together at the table.

"Mother, you're up! I was just about to bring you some tea," Louise said.

"Never mind that. This poor little thing has fallen from the nest in the chestnut tree. Teddy, can you get a ladder so I can climb up and put it back before it dies of shock?"

"Of course, Mother."

Louise looked at Teddy, who winked at his sister as he stood up. "She'll be all right now," he mouthed as he left the kitchen to follow his mother outside.

The funeral took place in the church on the estate and was well attended by villagers, friends, and family. Archie had been a popular and well-respected figure locally, and Flora sat between her two children, smiling through her tears at the eulogies delivered by his RAF colleagues from both wars. During the service, Flora dug deep for every ounce of strength and courage she possessed. Her week of solitary mourning had at least allowed the torrent of grief to pour out of her, and in turn, she was now able to support her children in their own pain. Her life—or at least, her main source of happiness—may have been curtailed forever. But her children still had theirs to live. And she would not let them down.

The day after the funeral, Mr. Saunders, the family solicitor, paid her a call. After the normal round of condolences, they got down to business.

"You may be aware that Lord Vaughan has not rewritten his will since 1921," began Mr. Saunders, taking a neat pile of papers out of his ancient leather briefcase. "I am presuming that he still wished the estate to go to his son, Teddy?"

"I . . . can only presume so," said Flora, feeling a guilt-induced band close tightly across her chest.

"Then I will set the wheels in motion to transfer such as discussed into

Teddy's name. Sadly, as there is no legal document to grant you a home on the High Weald estate, I must also advise you that it is within your son's legal rights to, er, turn you out. Not that he would do that, I'm sure, but I have known such situations to occur before."

"I will speak to Teddy about his wishes," said Flora tightly. "I am sure that we can resolve it between us. I have only one question for you, Mr. Saunders: if my sister, Aurelia, had only given birth to Louise—in other words, a female—or if Teddy had died in the war," she added quietly, "what would have happened then?"

"Well now, things would get complicated. We would firstly search for a male heir to the estate. And, on finding none, Louise would almost certainly be granted a tenure of High Weald until such time as she produced a son. When he came of age, he would inherit both the lands and the hereditary peerage. If she gave birth to a daughter, that daughter would be granted the same tenure until a male heir was produced. Unless, of course, one of Lord Vaughan's sister's daughters produced a male before her. Et cetera, et cetera."

"I see."

"As you might have gathered, we can only thank the heavens that there *is* a direct male heir." He gave a dry chuckle. "I know numerous families who are bereft of one, due to the two wars devastating generations of fathers and sons. You are lucky, Lady Vaughan. The true bloodline can still continue at High Weald, when many families in a similar situation have not been granted the same easy transition."

"I wonder, Mr. Saunders, whether it would be possible to at least give Louise a portion of the estate? She is soon to be married, and her husband is not a rich man. As a woman myself," Flora said carefully, "I do not feel that the fact she is female should preclude some form of claim on her family estate. Especially as she is Teddy's twin."

"I agree, Lady Vaughan. The rules on such a thing are archaic and I only hope that, in the fullness of time, women will have an equal right to both land and titles. However, I am afraid that this will now be a matter for your son to decide. I'm sad to say that neither of you have any jurisdiction over what happens to the High Weald estate. It is irritating indeed that your husband did not live to rewrite his will. You must now fall on the mercy of your son. And so must his sister."

"Thank you for your advice, Mr. Saunders. No doubt you will be in touch with me and Teddy."

"From now on, all communication from me will bypass your good self and go directly to Teddy," replied Mr. Saunders as he stowed away his papers in his briefcase. "Once again, my condolences for your loss. Your late husband was a very good man. Let us hope his son can be a worthy successor to his legacy. Good day to you, Lady Vaughan." With a deep sigh that indicated the gossip about Teddy must have spread across the neighborhood, Mr. Saunders took his leave.

Flora sat where she was, staring through the window into a garden that would no longer be under her watch. And realized that Archie, through noble intentions at the time, had as good as signed away Louise's genuine claim through her bloodline. And despite his recent murmurings of Teddy's unsuitability to the role of taking over High Weald as his heir, there was absolutely nothing to be done without exposing Archie's original deception.

She was at least grateful that she had had the sense to keep the majority of her inheritance from her real father in secure investments, originally with the advice and help of Sir Ernest Cassel. In the years since, she had taken a knowledgeable interest in stocks and shares and her funds had weathered the ups and downs of the volatile financial markets well. In short, she was a wealthy woman.

And Home Farm itself was already in the process of being transferred into Rupert and Louise's names. Archie had signed the authorization for the transfer of deeds, and the farm was ready for the young couple to move into after their wedding in August. Surely Teddy could not object to that?

Flora knew that the fact that she could even *consider* he might only underlined the gravity of the situation.

She sat down that night with Teddy and Louise and related the conversation she'd had with Mr. Saunders. She watched Teddy's expression carefully, and was comforted to see vestiges of both grief and relief.

"Well, Rupert and I will be extremely happy over at Home Farm," Louise said brightly. "It's a sweet place and I'm sure that we can make it homely."

"Yes, I'm sure you can," said Flora, loving Louise for her obliging and grateful nature. And, Flora supposed, her niece had expected nothing more, unaware of the true circumstances as she was. "So, Teddy, all this is to be yours." Flora swept a hand around the kitchen gaily. "How do you feel?"

"Mother, I am only getting what is rightfully mine, am I not?" he said with an air of entitlement.

"Yes, but you know all too well that the High Weald estate takes a lot of work. As Mr. Saunders will explain to you, there are scarce funds to maintain it. Especially the farm. You will need to employ a new farm manager," Flora added. "And some help in the house itself, what with Louise moving to her own home in the summer."

"You'll be here with me to sort all that, Mother. That is, until I marry." Teddy smiled slyly. "And I may just have someone in mind."

"Really?" Louise's face lit up. "It would be wonderful if we both had children of a similar age who could grow up together. Wouldn't it, Teddy darling?"

"I'm not sure she's the motherly type, but I'm certainly very keen on her."

"What a dark horse you are, Teddy. What is her name?" asked Louise.

"All will be revealed in time. She's not from round here."

"Well, of course I shall move out as soon as you have a wife," Flora said. "I can always go to the London house temporarily until we can perhaps refurbish the dower house? It hasn't been lived in for many years."

"The London house will be for my use only from now on. Perhaps when you go up to town, you could stay with your own mother in Albemarle Street? Now," Teddy said, checking his watch, "I must be off. The London train leaves in half an hour. I shall drive myself to Ashford station in Papa's Rolls-Royce."

"But he hadn't used it for years, Teddy. It eats up too much gas and we need the coupons for the farm machinery," said Louise, casting a nervous glance in her mother's direction.

"I am sure that my estate can afford it just this once. I'll be home in a couple of days." He stood up, pecked both his mother and sister on the tops of their heads, and left the kitchen.

There was a stunned silence.

"Don't worry, Mother." Louise turned to her. "There will be always be a place for you with us at Home Farm."

In the following month, Flora steeled herself to say good-bye to High Weald, while Teddy was conspicuous by his absence, up in the London house for most of the time. Flora and Louise struggled to move on from their grief and run the estate between them. Mr. Saunders had written a letter to Flora—out of diplomacy rather than need—to advise her that the transfer of the High Weald estate, the London house, and the peerage into Teddy's name was proceeding smoothly and should be finalized by November at the latest.

If Flora and Louise had thoughts on the subject of Teddy's inheritance, neither wished to admit her doubts. And at least June brought with it a burst of fresh spirit, due to the success of the D-Day landings in France. Flora did her best to focus on Louise's forthcoming wedding, deciding that she would present her gift to them when Rupert arrived for the weekend to discuss prewedding plans. She was gratified to see the delight on their faces as she told them about Arthur Morston Books.

"Good grief!" Rupert took out a handkerchief and wiped his eyes. "And there was me worrying about how I can keep your daughter in the style to which she is accustomed. Well now, you have just given me the answer. I can never thank you enough. I am . . . quite overwhelmed."

Tears came to Flora's own eyes as she watched the young couple—so happy and in love—embrace each other. And she knew for certain that she had done the right thing.

"There is also a small flat above it, which can be modernized to use when you need to stay in town," she said. "Although I'm sure your brother will offer you the use of his London house."

"I doubt it, Mother," said Louise. "And even if he does, I think the rooms above the bookshop—whatever state they may be in—would suit us far better."

A few days later, Flora received a telegram from Teddy:

married dixie at chelsea registry today stop very happy stop off to italy for honeymoon stop see you soon for celebrations stop tell louise i beat her down the aisle stop teddy stop

Louise read the telegram in silence, her face betraying everything she felt. "Oh dear," she said.

"Do you know this girl?"

"Not well, no. But I certainly know *of* her. The whole of London does. I was introduced to her briefly by Teddy at New Year."

"Who is she?"

"Lady Cecilia O'Reilly. She's Irish by birth, and from a good but rather . . . bohemian family. She is without a doubt a head-turner. Every man in the room became silly the second she walked into the Savoy on New Year's Eve. She has waist-length red hair, and a temperament that is apparently just as fiery. Teddy was mad for her that night, and I reckon that's why he's been spending so much time in London lately," Louise added. "They'll certainly make an . . . interesting couple."

"I see." Flora read between the lines of Louise's comments and her spirits sank even further.

"Forgive me, Mother. As you have always said to me, one must never judge a book by its cover. Or its reputation. Dixie may be regarded as 'fast,' but she might also be a good person. And she'll certainly liven up High Weald and keep Teddy on his toes." She smiled wanly.

That night, Flora lay in bed, her heart aching for the warmth and comfort of the body that used to lie next to her. As she lay back on her pillows, she began to make plans for her *own* future—and wondered how she could salve her guilty conscience about Louise.

A month later, the new heir to High Weald brought home his equally new bride. Contrary to her expectations, "Dixie" was a young woman Flora liked immediately. With her throaty laugh—engendered, Flora was sure, by the endless strong French cigarettes she smoked—and her gorgeous milky-white complexion and willowy frame, she was certainly a force to be reckoned with. She was also ferociously bright, judging by how she proceeded to tear a strip off Teddy for any disingenuous comments he made.

After a viciously alcoholic evening of celebration, where poor Louise turned to wallpaper as Dixie aired her opinions loudly on everything from the Irish situation to the war, and shared her "insider" knowledge of Churchill's depressive personality, Flora said her good nights and walked up the stairs to bed. She was at least comforted by the fact that Archie would have appreciated his new daughter-in-law's vivacious company.

The following day, Flora called Teddy into her study. She kissed him warmly and bade him sit down.

Before he could begin to speak, she took the lead.

"Congratulations, Teddy. I think Dixie is perfectly adorable. You have made a good choice and I am sure that the two of us will become firm friends. I simply wished to tell you that I am happy to pay for the necessary refurbishments to the dower house myself. And I would like to know if you are prepared to sell the two hundred acres of farmland that surround it to me. Being on the other side of the lane, the land also abuts Home Farm. I am prepared to take it on and farm it in your stead. I have consulted a local land agent and can offer you a fair price, which would then provide you with some funds for the upkeep of High Weald and the London house."

"I see." Teddy's expression showed his surprise. "I'd have to discuss it with Dixie and my solicitor first."

"You do that. I shall move out of High Weald after Louise's wedding."

"Of course."

"That is all I have to say."

"Right." Teddy stood up. "Please feel free to take anything you wish from the house."

"My needs are few, and I am very good at starting again. All I will say is that you have been handed a beautiful legacy. High Weald is a very special place and I hope that you and Dixie treasure it as your father and I have done."

And before Flora burst into tears, she swept from the room.

On a sweltering August day, Flora watched Louise marry Rupert Forbes in the church where she had so recently buried her husband. As she prayed for the couple, she could only beg the higher powers to bring the peace that had been promised so often. Both in her own life and the world.

In late autumn, Flora wandered around High Weald, feeling ridiculous for saying good-bye to a house that she knew she would visit many times in the future, but would no longer be hers. But then, she thought sadly, it never had been, as it had never been anybody's. It simply belonged to itself, as old houses did. And it would stand into the future, long after the present incumbents were dead.

She looked through the kitchen window at the walled garden, remembering the many happy times she and Archie had shared there.

"*Moments of happiness . . .*," Flora whispered to herself. Nothing lasted forever, she mused, even though human beings expected it to. All they could do was to enjoy the moments while they could.

The pony and trap stood outside, piled high with her most precious possessions. She let herself out through the front door and climbed up onto it.

"Good-bye . . ." She blew High Weald—and Archie and all the memories—a kiss. Then she turned her head away and, taking a moment to forgive herself for all the mistakes she had made, gave the pony a light tap on its flanks and rode off down the drive into another new future.

Star

November 2007

Rosa × centifolia
(cabbage rose—Rosaceae family)

40

The chimes of the grandfather clock brought me out of the past with a jolt. I looked at my watch and saw it was four in the morning. Opposite me, Orlando's eyes were closed, and he looked gray with exhaustion. I tried to focus on all he had told me, but I knew I needed sleep before I could make sense of it.

"Orlando?" I whispered, not wishing to startle him. "It's time for bed."

His eyes shot open, looking glazed. "Yes," he agreed. "We shall discuss what I have told you on the morrow." He stood up and staggered to the doorway like a man drugged, then turned and looked back at me. "You do see why I thought it best to keep these away from my brother, don't you? He was so very bitter. And knowing for certain that our side of the family had been cheated out of High Weald could only have made him feel worse."

"I think so." I indicated the journals. "Shall I put them away somewhere?"

"Take them with you. My paltry attempt at recounting such a complex story has only given you the bare bones. Those can fill in the detail. Good night, Miss Star."

"But I still don't understand why this story is relevant to me."

"Good grief," he said, eyeing me speculatively. "I am surprised. I would have thought that your able mind would have deduced exactly how. Tomorrow." He waved his hand at me and left the room.

It was past eleven the next morning before Orlando appeared in the kitchen.

"Today, I feel every one of my thirty-six years, plus another two score and ten," he said as he sat down heavily in a chair.

I too was weary, having spent what was left of the night tossing and turning. Managing to fall asleep only half an hour before my alarm went off, I was up at seven to make Rory breakfast and drive him to school.

"How about brunch? Eggs Benedict and smoked salmon?" I suggested to Orlando.

"I can think of nothing more perfect. We can pretend we are at the Algonquin Hotel in New York, having tipped up there from a speakeasy where we have danced until dawn. And how are you today, Miss Star?"

"Thoughtful," I replied truthfully, as I prepared the eggs.

"I am sure that feeding the digestion will ease the ingestion of facts."

"What I don't understand is why Mouse gave me the impression that Flora MacNichol was a devious person. I think she was rather wonderful."

"I agree entirely. If it hadn't been for her injection of funds to restore the house and gardens after Great-grandmother Aurelia died, not to mention the work she herself put in by restoring and then steering the estate through the Second World War, no Vaughans *or* Forbeses would be resident today. She also left the farmland she had purchased from Teddy to Louise and Rupert on her death. That land generates the main income for Home Farm today."

"She did her best to make amends to Louise," I mused.

"Yes, and how. During the difficult postwar years, my father said Flora held the family together. She did the accounts for Arthur Morston Books, and was there to help Dixie bring up her son, Michael, and assist in the running of High Weald. As you can imagine, Teddy wasn't much use in either role. She lived a long and fulfilled life."

"How old was she when she died?"

"She was in her late seventies. My father told me that she was found sitting under the rose arbor in the afternoon sun."

"I'm glad her later years were happy. She'd earned it. How could Mouse feel it was she who was to blame for all of it? After all, it was Archie's decision to register Teddy as Louise's twin on the birth certificates."

"And out of understandable altruistic reasons," Orlando added. "In his own way, he was honoring all those who had died around him in the war. Please remember that Mouse only heard the bare bones of the story from our father when he flew to see him in Greece before he died. He came home distraught—if you remember, I told you our father died only two years after Annie. And that was when I removed the relevant journals to the bookshop. The worst thing, I felt, was for Mouse to wallow even further in the past."

"He felt he'd been cheated out of everything," I murmured. "His wife, his father, and his rightful inheritance."

"Yes. Depression is a terrible thing, Miss Star," Orlando sighed. "And at least *one* affliction I don't seem to have been blighted with."

"Perhaps he *should* read them, Orlando, and discover what really happened. I feel it was Flora herself who lost the most."

"Agreed, although it is a crying shame the estate wasn't passed to Grandmother Louise in trust, waiting on any children she may have had in the future—namely, our father, Laurence. And Rupert, my grandfather, was a smashing fellow."

"Maybe love for a child blinds us all."

"In many cases, yes," Orlando agreed. "Flora was a sensible and pragmatic woman. She knew that Archie, and subsequently she herself, had been culpable in the lie concerning Teddy's birthright. He had been brought up to believe he was the natural heir. Hardly his fault, after all. If she had tried to deny him the inheritance, chances were she would have lost him forever to the fleshpots of London, where he would have spent the rest of his life indulging in wine, women, and song. Which, from what her journals recount, he did anyway at High Weald. It was his wife, Dixie, who saved the day. She gave birth to Marguerite's father, Michael, and kept the estate going while Teddy drank himself to death. It strikes me that High Weald has always been saved by generations of strong females."

"And now, Rory will inherit the title and the estate through Marguerite," I added as I placed the breakfast on the table and sat down.

Orlando picked up his knife and fork, and began to eat. "Ah, the perfect restorative. Personally, I am overjoyed that Lady Flora bequeathed the bookshop to Rupert and Louise. He managed it carefully through the bleak postwar years and I was eventually handed down a wonderful legacy. Mouse tells me the property is almost certainly more valuable than what is left of High Weald."

"Flora had no blood children, did she?" I voiced one of the thoughts that had been nagging at me in the early hours of this morning.

"No." Orlando eyed me. "So you have made the connection?"

"I think so."

"Yes, well, it is indeed a shame, Miss Star, for I feel you would have made an extremely elegant British aristocrat. But it seems from the facts at hand that there is not an ounce of royal blood in you."

"Then why did my father give me the Fabergé cat as my clue?"

"Aha! From the moment you told me of your quest, that is the thing that has puzzled me most. From what you have told me of your father—and mark my words, I have listened to everything you have said and, might I add, *haven't* said—I believe it must have been for a reason."

"What do you think it was?" I thought I knew, but I wanted to hear it from Orlando first.

"He needed something that would definitively link you to the Vaughan line, rather than the Forbes. And Teddy was Lady Flora's adoptive son. So one must look to *his* bloodline . . ."

"You mean the Land Girl's illegitimate baby?" I finally voiced my suspicion.

"There! I knew you wouldn't let me down." Orlando put his two fists under his chin and studied me. "You told me that fateful day at the bookshop when you returned to retrieve your precious plastic folder that the coordinates from the armillary sphere had placed you as being born in London."

"Yes."

"And where did our Land Girl live?"

"In the East End of London."

"Yes. And what address did your coordinates pinpoint when you researched them on the Internet?"

"Mare Street, E8."

"Which is . . . ?"

"In Hackney."

"Yes. The East End of London!" Orlando tipped his head back and thumped the table, overjoyed by his own insight and cleverness. It irritated me, for my heritage wasn't a laughing matter. "Do forgive me, Miss Star, one can't help finding the irony amusing. You came to me with a Fabergé cat, which linked you to a king of England. And we discover that you are almost certainly no blood relation of either royalty or the Vaughans. But just possibly, the illegitimate great-granddaughter of our much-maligned cuckoo in the nest."

I felt sudden tears welling up behind my eyes. Even though I understood Orlando's nonemotional and analytical brain, the fact he found it all so hilarious cut me to the core.

"I don't care *where* I came from," I countered angrily. "I . . ." And as a thousand suitable ripostes entered my exhausted brain, I stood up instead. "Excuse me, I'm going for a walk."

Grabbing an ancient Barbour and a pair of wellies from the lobby, I threw on both and marched out into the freezing morning. And as I passed out of the gates, I berated Pa Salt sitting somewhere up there in the heavens, and questioned his reasoning. At best, I was apparently the illegitimate great-granddaughter of a man who had unwittingly stolen High Weald from under the nose of the legitimate heir. At worst, I was nothing. Nothing to do with any of it.

As I turned right along the lane, my feet took me automatically onto the blackberry path, as Rory and I had named it. Tears blurred my vision as Orlando's laughter rang in my ears. Had he meant to humiliate me? Had he enjoyed the fact that he could prove unequivocally that I had come from nothing? That his so-called *aristocratic* blood made him superior? Why were the British so obsessed with social position?

"Just because they stampeded through the world and formed an empire and had a royal family doesn't mean anything. People are equal, wherever they come from," I hissed angrily at a magpie, who cocked its head at me, blinked, and then flew away. "It doesn't matter in Switzerland," I told myself. "It wouldn't have mattered to Pa Salt, I know it wouldn't. So why . . . ?"

Stomping down the path, I hated myself for my desperate need to belong to somewhere or someone that wasn't CeCe or the surreal fantasy world Pa Salt had created at Atlantis for his disparate flock of doves. To forge a world of my *own*, that just belonged to me.

Having reached an open field, I sank onto a tree stump, put my head in my hands, and cried my eyes out. Eventually, I pulled myself together and wiped my eyes harshly. *Come on, Star, control your emotions. This is getting you nowhere.*

"Hi, Star. You okay?"

I turned and saw Mouse standing a few feet away from me. "Yeah, I'm okay."

"You don't look it. Want a cup of tea?"

I gave him the kind of shrug I'd normally credit to a recalcitrant teenager.

"Well, I've just boiled the kettle." He indicated behind him, and I realized I'd wandered blindly into the field that backed onto Home Farm.

"Sorry," I mumbled.

"Why are you sorry?"

"I wasn't looking where I was going."

"No problem. Do you want that cup of tea or not?"

"I have to go home and do the washing up."

"Don't be ridiculous." He approached me, then took me by the elbow and marched me unceremoniously toward the house. When we reached the kitchen, he pressed me down into a chair. "Sit. I'll pour the tea. Milk and three sugars, isn't it?"

"Yes. Thanks."

"There."

A boiling-hot mug of tea was placed in front of me. I couldn't bring myself to look up, and instead stared hard at the wood grain on the old pine table. I heard Mouse sit down opposite me.

"You're shivering."

"It's cold outside."

"Yes, it is."

Then there was silence for quite a long time. I sipped the tea.

"Do you want me to ask you what's happened?"

Again I shrugged, channeling that recalcitrant teenager.

"Well, up to you."

Cupping the mug in my hands, I could feel the warmth of the room starting to penetrate my freezing veins. The oil tank must have been filled since I was last there.

"I think I know why my father sent me to Arthur Morston Books," I said eventually.

"Right. Is that good?"

"I don't know," I said as I wiped the back of my hand across a nose that was about to drip inelegantly into my mug.

"When you first appeared at the shop and told Orlando your story, he called me."

"Oh, that's just great," I said tersely, hating that the two brothers had been discussing me behind my back.

"Star, stop it. We didn't know who you were. It's natural that he would tell me about you. Wouldn't you tell your sister?"

"Yes, but . . ."

"But *what*? Despite what you might have heard or seen recently, Orlando and I have always been close. We're brothers; whatever goes down between us, we're there for each other."

"Well, blood is always thicker than water, isn't it?" I replied desolately, thinking that the only person I currently knew for certain had my "blood" was *me*.

"I understand you must feel that way at present. By the way, I knew Orlando had taken those journals."

"So did I."

He caught my eye across the table and we shared the thinnest of smiles.

"I suppose we have all been playing each other. I hoped that you might be able to find out from him where they were. I knew why he'd taken them, too."

"I didn't, up until last night. I thought it was because you'd upset him over the sale of the shop," I admitted. "He was apparently trying to protect you."

"So, who does he think you are?"

"He can tell you. He's your brother."

"You might have noticed he's not talking to me at the moment."

"He will. He's forgiven you already." I stood up, tired of these conversations. "I must go."

"Star, please."

I made for the door, but he took my arm as I reached for the handle. "Let go!"

"Look, I'm sorry."

I shook my head. I couldn't speak.

"I understand how you feel."

"No you don't," I said through gritted teeth.

"I do, really. You must feel completely used by us all. Like Flora—a pawn in a game you don't know the rules of."

I could not have described it better myself. Blinking away more tears, I cleared my throat. "I have to go back to London. Can you tell Orlando I've left and to pick up Rory at three thirty, please?"

"I can, but, Star . . ."

He reached for me, but I wriggled violently out of his grasp.

"Okay," he said with a sigh. "Do you want a lift to the station?"

"No thanks. I'll phone for a taxi."

"Whatever you wish. I'm so sorry. You didn't deserve . . . us."

I walked through the door and shut it smartly behind me, doing my best to control my desperate urge to slam things, then walked back to High Weald. Orlando, thank God, was not in the kitchen, and I saw that everything had been tidied away from brunch. I called the taxi company to collect me as soon as they could, and then raced upstairs to throw my stuff into my luggage.

Fifteen minutes later, I was driving away from High Weald and telling myself that the future was all that mattered, and not my past. I hated that Pa Salt—whom I loved and trusted more than anyone—had only caused me more pain. All I had learned was that I could trust nobody.

When I arrived at Charing Cross, I walked automatically toward the bus stop that would take me to Battersea. As I stood there, I couldn't bear the thought of returning home once more to CeCe, after another failed attempt to find my own life. *And her inevitable glee that I haven't*, I thought meanly.

I berated myself for the thought, for even though there was undoubtedly part of her that would be happy to have me back all to herself, I also knew that she was the person who loved me most in the world, and would want to comfort me in my pain. But that would mean telling her what I had discovered, and I really wasn't able to disclose that to anyone—not even her—just yet.

Instead, I got on a bus toward Kensington, and stopped in front of Arthur Morston Books, where this whole sorry story had begun. Finding the keys in my rucksack, I opened the door and walked into a room that was colder than outside. Night was falling fast and I fumbled to switch on the lights, then pulled the old shutters closed across the windows. Then I lit the fire, my hands shaking with cold. As I sat down in my regular chair, the heat warming my fingers, I tried to rationalize the misery that I felt. Because deep inside me, I knew it *was* irrational. Orlando hadn't meant to hurt me—he'd wanted to help me by telling me the story. But I was so deeply tired, confused, and sensitive that I'd overreacted.

Eventually, pulling out my sweaters from my luggage to cover me, I curled up on the rug in front of the fire and slept.

I woke in the same position, and was astonished to see it was almost nine o'clock. I must have slept the sleep of the dead. I stood up and went to make some coffee to revive me; drank it hot, sweet, and black; and finally felt calmer. *Perhaps I could squat here for the next few days*, I thought wryly. Peace and space were what I needed just now.

I pulled my laptop out of my luggage and switched it on. The signal was weak down here on the shop floor, but at least it worked. I went to Google Earth to tap in my coordinates again and make sure I hadn't made a mistake.

And there it was: "Mare Street, E8."

So . . . after everything I'd discovered, was it likely to be a coincidence that Tessie Smith had lived in Hackney?

No.

I took out the notebook in which I'd begun to write my novel, and turned to the back page, thinking how my own history was fast becoming more interesting than any fiction I could write.

I scribbled down the names in two columns—one for Louise's bloodline and one for Teddy's. And realized that of course the current male Forbes line was also distantly related to Flora through her sister, Aurelia: Flora was Orlando and Mouse's great-great-aunt.

But . . . if I was Tessie's great-granddaughter, then I was directly related to Marguerite through Teddy. And, therefore, to Rory. At least that thought made me smile. The next dilemma I faced was whether I wanted to take this whole thing farther. As the chances were, my parents were still alive.

I stood up and paced the room, trying to decide whether I wanted to trace them. Given I knew Tessie's name and the area where she had lived, it would probably be quite straightforward to find out about the child she had given birth to in 1944. And any children after that.

But . . . why had my parents given me away?

I halted abruptly in my mental meanderings, as I heard voices at the front door and a key being inserted into the lock.

"Shit!" I ran toward the fireplace in a desperate attempt to hide the evidence of my overnight stay. The front door opened to reveal Mouse, followed by a diminutive Chinese man, whom I recognized from the antiques shop next door.

"Hello, Star," Mouse said, surprise on his face.

"Hello," I said, clutching a cushion to my chest.

"Mr. Ho, this is Star, our bookshop assistant. I didn't realize you'd be in today."

"No. Well, I thought I should come and check on the premises," I said as I walked to the window and hurriedly drew back the shutters.

"Thank you," he said, casting his eyes over to the fireplace, where the sweaters I'd used to keep me warm in the night were strewn in a heap by the open luggage.

"Shall I light the fire?" I asked him. "It's chilly in here."

"Not on our behalf, no. Mr. Ho wants to take a look at the flat above the shop."

"Right. Okay, now you're here, I'll go," I said, bending down to stuff my things into my luggage.

"As a matter of fact, I was going to drop in on you at your apartment anyway. Orlando gave me something for you. Hang on for a bit, we won't be long," he said, as he turned and ushered Mr. Ho to the back of the shop, and I heard them mount the stairs.

I lit the fire anyway, my cheeks burning with the agony of embarrassment. When they returned, I busied myself at the back of the shop as they talked by the front door, and tried not to listen to the details.

The door opened and closed to let Mr. Ho out, then Mouse strode toward me.

"You stayed here last night, didn't you?"

I couldn't tell if it was anger or concern in his green eyes. "Yes, sorry."

"No problem. I'm just interested to know why you didn't go home."

"I just . . . wanted some peace."

"I understand."

"How's Rory?"

"Missing you. I collected him from school yesterday, and after he'd gone to bed, Orlando and I sat down and had a long chat. I told him about Mr. Ho's offer. As a matter of fact, he took it much better than I thought he would. He seemed far more concerned about upsetting you."

"Good. I'm glad for you both." I could hear the petulance in my voice.

"Star, stop it. You're verging on the self-indulgent. And I know all about being self-indulgent," he said gently. "Orlando was very concerned about your state of mind, as was I. We've both left messages on your mobile, but you didn't pick up."

"There are no mobiles allowed in the shop. So I didn't."

A smile tugged at his lips. "Anyway . . ." Mouse dug into the pocket of his Barbour. "This is for you." He handed me a large brown envelope. "Orlando told me he's been doing some investigating on your behalf."

"Right. Well," I said, tucking the envelope into the front of my rucksack and picking up my luggage. "Tell him thanks."

"Star, please . . . take care of yourself. At least you have your sister."

I didn't reply.

"Have the two of you fallen out?" he asked eventually. "Is that why you didn't go home last night?"

"I don't think we should be so reliant on each other," I said abruptly.

"When I met her, she certainly struck me as very possessive of you."

"She is. But she loves me."

"As Orlando and I love each other—even if we do fall out. If he hadn't been there for me in the past few years, I can't imagine what I'd have done. He has the kindest heart, you know. Wouldn't hurt a fly."

"I do know."

"Star, why don't you open the envelope he sent you?"

"I will."

"I mean, here and now. I think it would be good to have someone with you."

"Why are you suddenly being so nice to me?" I asked him quietly.

"Because I can see that you're hurting. And I want to help you. As you've helped me in the past few weeks."

"I don't think I have."

"That's up to me to decide. You've shown all of us kindness, patience, and tolerance, when I in particular haven't deserved it. You're a good person, Star."

"Thanks." I was still hovering uncertainly with my luggage.

"Look, why don't you come and sit by the fire while I go upstairs and collect the bits and pieces Orlando has asked me to take back for him to High Weald?"

"Okay." I surrendered, simply because my legs felt like jelly. As Mouse disappeared through the door at the back, I pulled the envelope out of my rucksack and opened it.

High Weald
Ashford, Kent
1st November 2007

My dearest Star,

I am writing to beg your forgiveness for the clumsy way I spoke to you. Believe me, I was not mocking you—far from it. I was merely amused by the irony of genetics and fate.

I must now admit that ever since you first walked into the shop and showed me the Fabergé cat and your coordinates, I have been on the trail to trace your heritage. For, of course, it may be inextricably bound up with our own. Enclosed is another envelope with all the facts you need to know about your real family.

I shall say no more (unusual for me), but rest assured, I am here to assist you if you need further explanation.

Again, I beg your pardon. And Rory sends you his best love too.

Your friend and admirer,
Orlando

My fingers passed over the expensive vellum envelope, which was closed with a wax seal. So, here it lay in front of me: the truth of my birth. My fingers began to tremble and I felt horribly sick and dizzy.

"You okay?" Mouse asked as he found me with my head resting against my knuckles.

"Yes . . . no," I confessed.

He walked over to me as my head spun, and put a hand on my shoulder. "Poor Star. Dr. Mouse deduces that the patient is suffering from shock, emotion, and almost certainly hunger. Therefore, as it's lunchtime, I'm going to nip across the road and feed *you* for a change. Won't be a moment."

I watched him leave and, despite myself, managed a smile as I banished the image of the Sewer Rat and—for today at least—turned it into a soft white creature with cute ears and a pink nose.

"Sit there and don't move," Mouse said when he returned through the door with our foil tins. "Today, I'm caring for you."

Although I was slightly suspicious, given his past track record, it was nice to be looked after by someone. As we ate, and I drank a glass of Sancerre that went straight to my head, I searched for an ulterior motive, but couldn't find one. Then a thought struck me.

"Who's picking up Rory this afternoon?"

"Marguerite. She arrived home from France late last night. Never seen her look so happy either. Isn't it incredible, how one can tread water for years with everything the same, and then suddenly there's a tidal wave of events that pushes you either farther out to sea, or brings you in gently to shore? There's been a definite seismic shift happening for all of us Vaughans and Forbeses recently. And you seem to have been the catalyst."

"I think that's just coincidence."

"Or fate. Do you believe in fate, Star?"

"Probably not. Life is what you make it."

"Right. Well, for the past seven years, I've believed that my fate was to suffer. And I indulged that one hundred percent. In truth, I've wallowed in it. And I can't ever make up for the harm it's caused my family. It's all too late."

I watched his eyes darken and the tense expression return.

"You could try."

"Yes, I could, couldn't I? Anyway, enough of me. Are you going to open that envelope so we can discuss it, or not?"

"I don't know. It will only tell me my parents gave me away, won't it?"

"I have no idea."

"Either that or they died. But if they did give me away, how can I ever forgive them? How can any parent give away their child? Especially a tiny baby, which I know I was when I arrived at Atlantis."

"Well," Mouse said, sighing deeply, "perhaps you should hear the reasons before you judge. Some people aren't in their right minds when they do such things."

"You mean like postnatal depression?"

"I suppose so, yes."

"It's not quite the same thing as not having enough food to go around or no roof over your head."

"No, it's not. Anyway, I'd better get back. Things to do. You know."

"Yes."

"Anything I can help you with," he said, standing up, "just call."

"Thanks." I stood up too, sensing the sudden shift in his emotions. "And thanks for lunch."

"Don't thank me for anything, Star. I'm not worth thanking. Bye."

And then he left.

I sat there, shaking my head and swearing at my gullibility. What was it with him? He blew hot and cold in the blink of an eye. All I knew was that there was something . . . *something* that haunted him.

41

That night, as CeCe and I ate together, there was a thick tension between us. Normally, she'd blurt out everything that was on her mind, but tonight her eyes were like an impenetrable fortress.

"I'm off to bed. Long day tomorrow," she said as she rose to go upstairs. "Thanks for dinner."

I cleared away the dishes and stepped out into the cold night to watch the river flowing beneath me. And thought of Mouse and his wave analogy. I too was undergoing a seismic shift; even my relationship with CeCe was finally changing. Then I thought about the unopened envelope slowly burning a hole in my rucksack, and knew I needed to speak to someone I trusted urgently. Someone who wouldn't be judgmental, who would give me calm, sensible advice.

Ma.

I took my mobile out of my back pocket and dialed home—my *real* home—and waited for her to pick up, as she always did when we girls called her, even if it was late. Tonight, the line went to voice mail and an automated message told me no one was at home. My heart plummeted. Who else could I call?

Maia? Ally? Tiggy? Certainly not Electra . . . Even though I loved and admired her for what she'd achieved in her life, empathy was not in her nature. Pa had always called her "highly strung." CeCe and I privately called her a brat.

In the end, I tried Ally, knowing that, unlike Maia, at least she was in the Northern Hemisphere.

She picked up on the third ring.

"Star?"

"Hello. I haven't woken you, have I?"

"No. Are you okay?"

"Yes. You?"

"I'm good."

"That's nice to hear."

"When I see you, I'll tell you all about it. So, how can I help you?" she continued.

I smiled at my big sister's automatic response. She knew that when we younger sisters called, we weren't contacting to ask after her health. And she accepted it, because that was her role as "leader" in our family.

"I have an envelope," I told her. "And I'm scared to open it."

"Oh. Why?"

I explained as succinctly as I could.

"I see."

"What do you think I should do?"

"Open the envelope, of course!"

"Really?"

"I promise you, Star, however painful it is, Pa wanted to help us all move on. Besides, if you don't do it now, you're only putting it off for the future. You'll open it at some point, of course you will."

"Thanks, Ally. How's Norway?"

"It's . . . wonderful. Wonderful. I . . . have some very good news."

"What is it?"

"I'm pregnant. By Theo," she added quickly. "Ma knows, but I haven't told any of our other sisters yet."

"Ally," I said with a catch in my throat. "That really *is* wonderful! Oh my God! It's amazing!"

"Isn't it? Oh, and I've also found my birth family here in Bergen. So even though the two most important people are missing, I have support, and there's a new life on the way."

"I'm thrilled for you, Ally. You deserve it, you're so brave."

"Thanks. And, Star, I'm playing the flute in a concert in the Grieg Hall here in Bergen on the seventh of December. I'm inviting all of our sisters, of course, but I'd so love you to come. And CeCe if she's around."

"I will, I promise."

"Ma said she'll come too, so maybe you could speak to her about the travel arrangements? I'm happy, Star, even though I never thought I would be again after . . . what happened. But listen, back to you. All I can say is that you need to be brave now, if you want your life to change."

"I do."

"I'm warning you that it might not be exactly what you want to hear; the fairy tale was Atlantis . . . but that was our life *then* and it isn't like that anymore. Just remember, you're the only one in charge of your destiny. But you have to help it to happen. Do you understand?"

"Yes. Thank you, Ally. I'll see you at the beginning of December."

"I love you, Star. You know I'm always here for you."

"Yes. God bless," I added.

"God bless."

I ended the call and wandered inside as I realized my fingers had turned blue with cold. And, checking my messages, listened to a number of them from Orlando and Mouse. After taking a quick shower, I crept into the bedroom where CeCe was sleeping silently.

"A seismic shift," I muttered as my head touched the soft pillow gratefully.

I would take a leaf out of my big sister's book.

And be brave.

CeCe had a nightmare around four o'clock, and, after I had slipped into bed with her to comfort her, I felt wide awake. I got up and went downstairs to make myself a cup of tea. I looked over the velvety dark of London, the Seven Sisters of the Pleiades—at their most brilliant in the Northern Hemisphere in winter—shining brightly above me. Tracing the river to the east, I wondered if my *real* relatives were asleep somewhere, perhaps wondering how I was. Or where.

Gritting my teeth, I took the envelope out of my rucksack, and not daring to stop to analyze my actions, I opened it, with the still-sleeping city as my only witness.

There were two sheets of paper inside. I unfolded them and placed them on the glass coffee table. One was a family tree covered in Orlando's flamboyant hand, with arrows pointing to his various comments. The second was a copy of a birth certificate:

Date and place of birth: 21st April 1980
The Mothers' Hospital of the Salvation Army, Hackney

Name and Surname: Lucy Charlotte Brown
Father: ________________
Mother: Petula Brown

"Lucy Charlotte," I breathed. "Born on my birthday."

Was this me?

I referred to the family tree, carefully drawn by Orlando, and studied it. Tessie Eleanor Smith had given birth in October 1944 to a girl named Patricia, whose surname was also Smith. No father was mentioned on the tree, although Orlando had written *Teddy's daughter?* in the margin. Which indicated that Tessie had not managed to make it up with her fiancé. And had brought up her daughter, Patricia, alone . . .

Then, in August 1962, Patricia had given birth to a daughter by the name of Petula. The father was named as one Alfred Brown. And on April 21, 1980, Petula, at the age of eighteen, had given birth to Lucy Charlotte.

I double-checked the family tree and saw Orlando had recorded that Tessie had died in 1975, and Patricia only recently in September of this year. Which probably meant that my mother—even *thinking* those words sent a shudder of fearful anticipation up my spine—was still living.

Hearing the bathroom door slam above me, I stood up and began to prepare breakfast, wondering whether I should ask CeCe's advice.

"Morning," she said as she came downstairs freshly showered. "Sleep well?"

"Not bad," I lied. CeCe never remembered her nightmares, and I didn't embarrass her by reminding her of them. She looked unusually pale and subdued as she sat down to eat. "You okay?"

"Yep." She nodded, but I knew she was lying. "Are you back home for good now?"

"I don't know. I mean, I might have to go back again if I'm needed."

"It's lonely here without you, Sia. I don't like it."

"Maybe you could invite some of your friends from college round when I'm away?"

"I don't have any friends, and you know it," she replied morosely.

"Cee, I'm sure you do."

"I'd better go." She stood up.

"Oh, by the way, I spoke to Ally last night and she's invited us both over to Bergen to hear her play in a concert at the beginning of December. Do you think you'll be able to come?"

"Are you going?"

"Yes, of course! I thought we could fly out together."

"Okay, why not? See you later then." She shrugged on her leather jacket, collected her portfolio case, and barked a "bye" at me as she left the apartment.

The oak tree and the cypress grow not in each other's shadow . . .

Even if I was making a complete hash of walking out from behind *hers*, at least I was trying. And I was still convinced it was right for both of us, even if CeCe couldn't see it yet.

I showered, then checked my messages. Orlando had left one, saying he was heading back from Kent up to the shop today and wanted to know if I was going to be there.

"*Dear girl, please come. I so wish to speak to you. Thank you. Oh, it's Orlando Forbes here, by the way*," he'd added unnecessarily, which made me smile.

As I was still officially in his employ, I decided I should go. But as I got on the bus to Kensington, I admitted this was just an excuse; I needed to talk to Orlando about the family he had found for me.

"Good morning, Miss Star. How wonderful to see you back here. And how are you this fine foggy day?" Orlando greeted me on the threshold, looking positively perky.

"I'm okay."

"'Okay' will just not do. I aim to improve on that ghastly word forthwith. Now, sit yourself down, for we have many things to discuss."

As I did so, I noticed the fire was already lit and I could smell fresh coffee brewing. Orlando meant business. He brought us both a cup of coffee, then laid a thick plastic file on the table in front of us.

"First things first: will you accept my apologies for my insensitive approach to your current familial crisis?"

"Yes."

"I really should stick to talking to myself or shouting at characters in books. I don't seem to have the human touch."

"You're very good with Rory."

"Well now, he is another story, but thankfully not my own. So, did you open your envelope?"

"I did. This morning."

"My goodness!" Orlando clapped his hands together like an excited child. "I am glad. And may I say, Miss Star, you are far braver than I. Having been 'Orlando' all my life, it would be hard to discover I was a 'Dave,' or a 'Nigel,' or, God forbid, a 'Gary'!"

"I rather like 'Lucy.' I once had a lovely friend called that," I countered, not in the mood to tolerate Orlando's snobbery.

"Yes, but you, Asterope, are destined to fly up to the stars. As your mother did before you," he added mysteriously.

"What do you mean?"

"Well now, apart from her birth certificate, I could find no record of a 'Petula Brown' during my long and arduous search into your background. No Internet paper trail whatsoever, which is strange, given her unusual Christian name. In the end, I wrote to the National Archives, and anyone else I could think of, to try and find out what had happened to her. And yesterday, I finally received a reply. Can you guess what it told me?"

"I've really no idea, Orlando."

"That 'Petula' changed her name by deed poll. Hardly surprising, being burdened with a name like that. She is no longer 'Petula Brown' but 'Sylvia Gray.' Miss Star, the person who I believe is almost undoubtedly your mother is currently a professor of Russian literature at Yale University! Now, what do you make of that?"

"I . . ."

"According to her biography on the Yale University website"—Orlando rifled through the file on the table and pulled out a sheet of paper—"Professor Sylvia Gray was born in London, then won a scholarship to Cambridge. Highly unusual, Miss Star, for a girl from the East End to achieve such a thing. She went on to complete an MA and a PhD and was there for the next five years before she was offered a position at Yale, 'where she met and married her husband, Robert Stein, a professor of astrophysics at Yale. She now lives in New Haven, Connecticut, with her three children and four horses, and is at work on her new book,'" Orlando quoted from the sheet of paper.

"She's an author?"

"She's published some critical texts through Yale University Press. There! Isn't it amazing how genes will out?"

"I hate horses. Always have," I mumbled.

"Don't be so pedantic. I thought you'd be overjoyed!"

"Not particularly. After all, she gave me away."

"But I am sure you've worked out from the family tree I drew so carefully for you that 'Petula'—now 'Sylvia'—was only eighteen when she gave birth to you. She was born in 1962."

"Yes, I had worked it out."

"She must have been in her first year at Cambridge, which meant she became pregnant at some point the previous summer—"

"Orlando, please, slow down. I'm doing my best to take all this in, but it's hard."

"Forgive me. As I said earlier, I should stick to fiction, not reality." He lapsed into silence then like a chastised child, as I tried to process what he'd told me.

"May I speak?" he said timidly.

"Yes," I sighed.

"There is something you should see, Miss Star."

"What is it?"

He handed me a printout. "She's here in England next week. Lecturing at Cambridge, her old alma mater."

"Oh." I read it blindly, then put it down.

"Isn't it incredible? To come to where she is now, without the backing of privilege. It just shows you how the world has moved on."

"And you hate it."

"Admittedly," he said, "I've been against the march of progress. But as I was only discussing with my brother the other night, you have helped to change me. For the better, might I add. Investigating your origins . . . well, it has taught me a lot. Thank you, Miss Star. I am in so many ways indebted to you. Will you go?"

"Where?"

"To meet her in Cambridge, of course."

"I don't know. I haven't thought, I . . ."

"Of course you haven't." Orlando laced his long fingers together, finally taking the hint. "So now, how about I tell you what I have decided regarding my *own* future?"

"All right."

"Well, I mentioned that Mouse and I had a long conversation the other night. And you will be glad to hear we made amends."

"I heard from Mouse, yes."

"Then you will also know that dear Mr. Ho has offered us what is an astonishingly healthy amount of money for the shop. Which will enable both Mouse and me to clear the debts accrued against our various assets. And for me to find alternative premises for myself and my books. The good news is, I think I may have found such a thing already," he announced.

"Really?"

"Yes indeed."

And then he told me about Mr. Meadows's bookshop in Tenterden and how he had already offered to take over the lease. And that Mr. Meadows had agreed immediately.

"There is also a set of rooms upstairs where I can live," he added. "And I do believe after all this time in the trade, I've earned the right to name it 'O. Forbes Esquire—Rare Books.' What do you think?"

"About the idea, or the name?"

"Both."

"I think that they are perfect."

"Do you really?" Orlando said, his face opening like a burst of sunshine. "Well, so do I. And perhaps it's time for a fresh start for all of us in the family. Which includes you. After all, you are related to dear Marguerite."

"And Rory," I added.

"Mouse and I discussed whether we should tell her everything about the past. I mean, it hardly makes any difference now, given it was so many years ago, but the irony is, she never wanted High Weald anyway. After Teddy's tenure of extravagance, the estate was left flat broke. My father's cousin Michael—Teddy and Dixie's son—had to sell off portions of what was left of the farmland, plus the dower house and the cottages, just to keep afloat. But, of course, there was nothing spare for renovations. Mouse and I have talked about giving Marguerite a share of the proceeds of the shop to help with the basics like plumbing and heating. Who'd have thought it . . . ?"

"Thought what?" I watched Orlando as he drifted off into his own world.

"That sixty-odd years on, it would be us, the poor relations across the lane, mere shopkeepers and farmers, that would be offering charity to the incumbent lady of the manor. But that is what can happen in time. Just like your mother and her rise in fortunes, a lot can change in two generations."

"Yes, it can."

"Will you go to Cambridge and listen to her lecture?"

"Orlando." I rolled my eyes at the way he'd managed to steer the conversation back. "I can't just turn up and tell her I'm her long-lost daughter."

"I insist that you see one more bit of evidence. One could say it is the denouement of my thorough detective work. Now, where did I put it?" He rifled through the pile of papers once more. "Aha! Here!" He handed it to me with a flourish.

I looked down at the page and saw a face gazing back at me. The face was as familiar as my own, only older and more well groomed, with blue eyes enhanced with subtle makeup, and the alabaster skin framed by a shiny white-blond bob. I could feel Orlando's eyes boring into me, his excitement palpable.

"Where did you get this?"

"The Internet, of course. On one of those networking sites. Now, tell me that Professor Sylvia Gray isn't your mother, Miss Star."

I stared again at what I would undoubtedly look like in my midforties. Despite all the written proof Orlando had collated for me, it was this photograph that made it real.

"She's very beautiful, isn't she?" he prompted. "Just like you. And fate has conspired to have her right under our very noses in a few days' time. Surely you must take the opportunity presented to you? Personally, I'd love to chat to her. She's one of the foremost authorities on Russian literature—which, as you know, I have a particular penchant for. Her biography tells me she lived in St. Petersburg for a year while doing her PhD."

"No, Orlando, stop it, please! It's too soon. I need time to think . . ."

"Of course you do, and again, I beg your pardon for my excitement."

"I can't just walk into a lecture at Cambridge University! I'm not a student there."

"True," Orlando agreed. "But luckily, we are blessed with knowing someone who is. Or at least, was."

"Who?"

"Mouse. He studied architecture there and knows the form for these things. He's agreed to smuggle you in."

"He knows about this too?"

"My dear girl, of course he does."

I stood up abruptly. "Enough, please, Orlando."

"The subject is closed forthwith until you wish to reopen it. Hopefully before next Tuesday," he added with a sly grin. "And now, back to work. Mr. Meadows is happy for us to move into our new home as soon as we wish. I have suggested two weeks' time to cash in on the pre-Christmas trade. The lease is being prepared as we speak. These," Orlando said, pointing to the bookshelves, "must be carefully packed into numbered crates, which I've already ordered and will arrive here tomorrow. I've told both Marguerite and Mouse that they must not make any claim on your time until we are done. We shall have to work night and day, Miss Star, night and day."

"Of course."

"It's all happened rather quickly, what with the sale of this shop going through—Mr. Ho has been most keen and is eager to complete it before Christmas. You must come and see the interior of Meadows's Bookshop. I fancy it's even more quaint than this. And, most importantly, has a fireplace. As we pack, we shall have to sift out the stock—sadly, there is less shelf space, but Marguerite has kindly agreed to store the remainder at High Weald. And then there's Mr. Meadows's stock too, which I've agreed to buy. We shall be inundated with the written word!"

I tried to concentrate on Orlando and be happy for his excitement and relief at the turn events had taken. But my eyes constantly shifted to the sheet of paper lying in front of me. The photograph of Professor Sylvia Gray, my mother . . .

I turned the sheet facedown and pasted a smile on my face. "Right, where shall we start?"

At least packing up the shop kept me busy, both physically and mentally. And as the days ticked by toward Tuesday, I blanked out any thoughts on the subject. And so it was that we arrived at Monday evening, exhausted and covered in dust from days of solid packing.

"Time for a break, Miss Star," he said as he appeared from the cellar, where he had been fastidiously wrapping the most valuable books from the ancient safe. "Good grief, I am not in the least used to all this physical work. And neither does it suit me. Methinks we deserve a glass of good red wine for our troubles."

As Orlando went upstairs, I flopped into my chair, the fireplace area providing an oasis in the morass of crates stacked high around us.

"I uncorked it two hours ago to let it breathe," Orlando announced as he proceeded along the thin corridor between the crates with a bottle and two glasses and sat down opposite me.

"*Tchin-tchin*," he said as we clinked them together. "I cannot thank you enough for your help. I simply could not have done it without you. And I am, of course, hoping that you are prepared to move with me to my new premises."

"Oh."

" 'Oh'?! Surely, the thought must have crossed your mind before now? I'm also going to tempt you by offering you the superior title of manager, with the pay rise such a promotion deserves."

"Thank you. Can I think about it?"

"Not for too long. You know how highly I value your skills. I think we are an unbeatable team. And you must have realized what it means?"

"What *what* means?"

"That the two disparate strands of the Vaughan/Forbes family are reunited, sixty years on, in a joint venture."

"I suppose it does, yes."

"And given that this was, after all, Flora MacNichol's shop, and she is technically your great-great-grandmother—if not by blood—you have as much right to be here as I do. See? Everything works out in the end."

"Does it?"

"Come now, Miss Star, it's unlike you to be negative. Now, I must ask you—"

"No!" I knew what he was about to say. "I'm not going tomorrow. I . . . can't."

"May I ask why not?"

"Because . . ." I bit my lip. "I'm frightened."

"Of course you are."

"Maybe I'll contact her in the future. But it's just too soon for me right now."

"I understand." Orlando gave a sigh of defeat as I drained my glass and stood up.

"I'd best be getting off, it's past eight o'clock."

"See you bright and early tomorrow then? And do think about my offer. I've already asked Marguerite if you could stay at High Weald until you find your own home in the area. She's thrilled at the idea. And so is Rory."

"You haven't told her yet about . . . my connection to her?"

"No, but maybe Mouse has. Besides, she lives for the present, not for the past. Especially at the moment. Well then, good night, Miss Star."

"Good night."

I would be lying to myself if I said I hadn't gone through the following day—and night—thinking about Professor Sylvia Gray and hating myself for my cowardice. At half past seven precisely, I imagined her stepping onto the podium to a surge of applause.

To my shame, I knew there was another reason I hadn't made the journey to Cambridge that night: the opportunity I had missed ten years ago when I hadn't taken up the place they'd offered me. I sat up long after my sister had gone to bed, and confessed to myself that I was *jealous* of this mother I'd never known. The mother who had let nothing stop her attending Cambridge, which had facilitated her path to greatness in the academic literary world. Not even me, her baby . . .

Her determination to make something of herself from her humble beginnings made me feel I'd achieved so little in my life in comparison to this paragon: mother to three probably exceptionally bright and driven children, wife, keeper of horses, with a career that had taken her to the very top of her profession.

She'd be just as ashamed of me as I am of myself . . .

I wandered to the window and looked out at the frosty clear sky, peppered with stars.

"Help me, Pa," I whispered. "Help me."

42

Now then, I will need you down in Kent to help me begin unpacking the books at the new shop this weekend," Orlando said as we ate our three o'clock cake the following day. "I'm leaving in the morning to oversee things there, and I'm hoping that by the time you arrive, the shop front will have been repainted and the sign writer will have begun his work. Then I can welcome you to O. Forbes Esquire—Rare Books."

Orlando shone brightly with excitement as I felt my own star fading further into a dull pinprick in the sky.

"It will be all hands to the pump," he continued. "Mouse has said he'll help, as will Marguerite, who, by the way, is off again to France on Sunday. So it really would be awfully convenient all round if you are willing to stay on at High Weald for a while to assist me and Rory. Perhaps you might see it as a trial run, further to taking up a more permanent situation with me?"

"Yes, I'll come," I agreed. After all, what on earth would I do here once the shop was closed for good?

"Wonderful! That's settled then."

We discussed how I would oversee the packing of the crates onto the van here in London, while Orlando cleared unwanted stock from the new premises to High Weald, and prepared for the van's arrival.

That night, I told CeCe I was off to Kent in a couple of days' time.

"And then you'll come back, won't you?" If her words didn't beg me, her expression certainly did.

"Of course."

"I mean, you're not thinking of moving there, are you? For Christ's sake, Star, you're only a shop assistant, I'm sure you could find a far better-paid job in London. I walked past Foyles bookshop the other day, and they were advertising for staff. It won't take you long to find something."

"No, I'm sure it won't."

"You know how I hate being alone here without you. Promise you'll be back?"

"I'll do my best," I said. It was time to think of *me*, and I didn't want to give CeCe false hope. After all, she wasn't a helpless baby, like I had been when my mother had put her own life first . . .

As CeCe was sulking, I spent the next day at the shop from dawn to well after dusk. And by Friday morning, when the van pulled up outside the front door, I was ready. Orlando insisted on calling every few minutes to issue instructions, and in the end, I broke the golden rule and answered my mobile in the shop.

Some of the "regulars" appeared, looking on in sadness at the books being carted onto the van. I was prepared for that too, as Orlando and I had chosen a book for each of them as a parting gift. Once the van had left, with Orlando's few possessions from his flat crammed onto the back, I wandered around the deserted shop, feeling it really was the end of an era, one that stretched right back through the family threads to Beatrix Potter herself.

My last job was to remove the framed letter Beatrix had written to Flora when she'd been a young girl, and wrap it in brown paper to carry it personally to Kent with me. As I did so, I promised myself that I would one day travel to the Lake District to see where Flora had lived. Even though I knew there was no blood connection, I felt a kinship with her. She too had been unusual—an outcast, belonging nowhere. But she had survived through sheer grit and determination. And had eventually found where she belonged, with the man she loved.

"Good-bye," I whispered into the gloom, looking for the last time at the room where my life had changed forever.

I arrived by taxi in Tenterden later that evening, and stood outside the new shop, its lights blazing out into the foggy night. I looked up at the freshly painted front—Orlando had chosen a bottle green, the same color as the Kensington shop. Above the window was the vague outline of the sign writer's initial lettering. And I was glad that at least one member of the Forbes/Vaughan clan was happy tonight.

Orlando weaved his way through the crates toward me.

"Welcome, Miss Star, to my new home. Mouse and Marguerite are due down here at any moment. I have sent next door for champagne. The Meadowses will be joining us too. Do you know, I think I might even prefer this to the old place? Just look at the view."

I did so, and saw the trees on the green beyond the narrow path, the old-fashioned street lamps twinkling gently between them.

"It's lovely."

"And there's even a connecting door to the café, so no more foil tins for lunch. It will arrive steaming on plates instead, straight from the oven. Ah." Orlando looked behind me and waved. "They've arrived."

I saw that Mouse's old Land Rover had pulled up outside. Both Marguerite and Rory followed him into the shop.

"Just in time," Orlando announced as I recognized Mrs. Meadows appearing out of a door at the back of the shop, carrying a tray of glasses and champagne, accompanied by a squat older man wearing a spotted bow tie.

"Mr. and Mrs. Meadows, I believe you know my brother and my dear cousin Marguerite. And Rory, of course. You have met my assistant briefly, Mrs. Meadows," Orlando added as he led me forward. "This is the perfectly named Asterope D'Aplièse, more commonly known as 'Star.' And that she is," he finished, looking down at me fondly.

Orlando left me with the Meadowses to greet the rest of his family. I sipped a glass of champagne and chatted with the elderly couple, who were overjoyed that Orlando was taking over.

"Hi, Star."

"Hi," I said, as I saw Mouse standing beside me. And then I felt a pair of thin arms clasp my waist from behind.

"Hello, Rory," I said, a genuine smile rising to my lips.

"Where have you been?"

"In London, helping Orlando move all the books here."

"I've missed you."

"I've missed you too."

"Can we bake brownies tomorrow?"

"Of course we can."

"Mouse tried to make some with me, but they were rubbish. All sticky. Yuck!" Rory made exaggerated sick noises.

"They were, I agree." Mouse shrugged. "At least I tried."

"Star!" I received a hug from Marguerite, who kissed me not once, not twice, but three times on my cheeks. "That is how they welcome you in Provence!" she laughed.

I looked at Marguerite, with her wide violet eyes and long-limbed body, wondering at our genetic link. Outwardly, we were so different, although I noticed she did have a similar complexion to my own. But then, so did many people unrelated to me.

"Mouse tells me you've had an interesting few days." She bent down to whisper in my ear. "Welcome to our crazy family," she chuckled. "No wonder we all took you to our hearts so quickly. You belong with us. It's as simple as that."

And that night, as I stood in Orlando's new bookshop, surrounded by "family," I tentatively felt as if I did.

I woke later than usual the next morning, probably due to the mental and physical strain of the past few days. I walked downstairs to the deserted kitchen, which had swiftly returned to its habitual chaotic state in my absence, and found a note on the table:

> *We're all out helping Orlando at the bookshop. Mouse over at eleven to collect you, so be ready. M and R. X*

Seeing it was gone half past nine, I went up to take a hasty bath in the freezing water, wondering if I *could* build a life here in Kent. I dried myself as fast as I could, shaking my hair and scrunching it with my fingers, then pulled on jeans and my blue sweater.

The one that Mouse had said suited me . . .

Not that it mattered, of course.

Then why are you trying to please him?

I hushed my psyche back into submission, and by the time I heard a car pull up and familiar heavy footsteps at the kitchen door, I was standing by the range with a fresh tray of brownies.

"Hi, Star," said Mouse as he walked through the door.

"Hi. Are we leaving straightaway? I've made some brownies, and there's coffee on the boil."

"That sounds wonderful," said a voice that was both familiar and new all at the same time. It sounded like *me* speaking in an American accent.

"I've brought somebody to meet you," Mouse said, guilt written across his face.

And then, from behind him, a facsimile of the photograph Orlando had shown me stepped from the lobby and into the kitchen.

"Hello, Star," the facsimile said.

I stared at her—at her face, at her body—and then I couldn't see anymore because my eyes were blinded by tears. Of anger, fear, or love; I didn't know which.

"Star," said Mouse gently. "This is Sylvia Gray. Your mother."

I don't remember much of the next few minutes, only that Mouse's arms shielded me as I cried onto his shoulder.

"I'm so sorry," he whispered into my ear. "I went to Cambridge to listen to her lecture, then introduced myself to her afterward. She was desperate to come and meet you. Tell me what to do."

"I don't know," I said, my voice muffled by his Barbour.

Then I felt another pair of arms folding around me. "I'm so sorry too," she said. "Forgive me, Star, forgive me. I've never forgotten you for a moment. I swear. I thought of you every day."

"NO!" I shouted, and shrugged her off.

I ran through the lobby and outside into the bracing November air, down into the garden, where I paced through the maze of weeds and plants. I didn't need a past, I didn't need a mother . . . I just wanted a future—one that was safe, real, and clean. And that woman waiting to pounce on me inside High Weald was none of those things.

I made my way blindly to the greenhouse, where Archie had once nurtured his seedlings, which Flora had carefully planted so they'd grown strong and firm out of love. And sank to the floor, shivering with cold.

How dare she come chasing after me! And how dare Mouse bring her here? Does this family really think they can control my life like this?

"Star? Are you in here?"

I don't know how much time had passed when I heard Mouse enter the greenhouse.

"I'm so very sorry, Star. It was badly thought out. I should have warned you, asked your permission . . . When I went to Cambridge that night, and then saw Sylvia afterward and told her who I was and who Orlando and

I thought you were, she begged me to bring her here to High Weald to meet you."

"She probably wants to see the house her grandfather owned, not me," I spat.

"Well, maybe she wants to see that as well, but she wanted to see you more, I swear."

"She hasn't wanted to for twenty-seven years, so why now?"

"Because her mother lied to her and said you had died when you were a baby. She even has a faked death certificate for you that her mother gave her."

"What?" I looked up at him then.

"It's true. But . . ." He gave a deep sigh. "I think it's her job to explain all this to you, not mine. Star, forgive me. This was wrong, the whole thing . . . we should have respected your wishes. But when I saw her, her desperation to meet you overwhelmed me."

I didn't reply. I had to think.

"Well, I'll leave you be. And again, I apologize."

"It's okay." I wiped my nose on my sleeve and stood up. "I'll come with you."

Garnering every sinew in my body to help me to stand up, I did so. I wobbled toward him and he clasped a strong arm around me, taking me back through the walled garden and into the house.

Arriving back in the kitchen, I could see that Sylvia had been crying. Her perfect, subtle makeup had slid underneath her eyes, and she suddenly looked far more fragile than when she had first walked in.

"How about I put the kettle on?" Mouse suggested.

"Good idea," said the woman who was apparently my mother.

Mouse duly filled the kettle as I stood shivering with my back to the range, trying to pull myself together.

"Will you come and sit down?"

"Why did you give me away?" I blurted out.

Her face crumpled, and there was a pause as she delved deep for the words. "I didn't, Star. After you were born during the Easter vacation, my mother insisted I should return to Cambridge to take my first-year exams. She was ambitious for me. I was bright, clever . . . In me she saw a future that she'd been denied. She'd had a hard life—my father had died young, leaving her to bring me up alone . . . She was bitter, Star. Very bitter."

"So you blame your mother now, do you?" I shot back, horrified to hear the bitterness in my *own* voice.

"You have every right to be angry. But I swear to you, when I left you that May in the care of my mother, you were a healthy, bouncing, and very beautiful baby. The plan was that she would look after you until I'd finished university and completed my degree. I hadn't even *thought* about giving you away. Not once, I swear. But yes, if you want the truth, I needed to make *both* of our lives better. Then just a few days after my exams were over, I got a letter saying you had died—from cot death apparently." She reached into her slim leather handbag and pulled out an envelope. "This is the death certificate she gave me. Take a look at it."

"How can something like that be forged?" I demanded, not taking it from her.

"Easily, if you happen to be as good as married to the local doctor. After my father died, she was his daily for years. He was probably as eager to assist my mom as she was to deceive me. He was a horrible man—a staunch member of the local Catholic community; he probably felt I should be punished too."

"By telling you your baby was dead?" I shook my head. "This is difficult to believe. How did you even know I was alive now, if you thought I . . . wasn't?"

"Because my mom passed away a few weeks ago. I didn't attend the funeral—I hadn't spoken to her in almost twenty-seven years. But I did receive a letter from her solicitor, to be opened after her death. In it, she confessed what she had done all those years ago. Of course she did," my mother said, more to herself than to me. "She probably thought she was off to hell, after the terrible lie she had told me."

"Did the letter say who had adopted me?"

"She said the doctor had given you to the priest at the church, who had taken you to an orphanage somewhere in the East End. But when I went there only two days ago, just before I met Mouse, they said they had no record of any baby by the name of Lucy Charlotte Brown."

"My adoptive father would never have taken me if he'd known the true circumstances," I said defensively.

"I'm sure he wouldn't have. But my mom always was a pretty efficient liar. Thank God I took after my grandmother Tessie. What a wonderful lady she was. Worked hard all her life, and never once complained."

My legs felt weak. I slid down the range to the floor, my arms crossed over my chest. "I don't understand how Pa Salt found me."

"Pa Salt is your adoptive father?"

I ignored her. "Why couldn't you find my name at the orphanage?"

"The priest may well have registered you under a different name, but interestingly, there wasn't a single baby who came in during the two weeks after she'd told me you were dead. I checked the original records with the secretary while I was there. I truly don't know, Star. I'm sorry."

"And now my father's dead too, and I can never ask him." My head was swimming. I folded my arms across my knees and rested my head on them.

"Well," came Mouse's voice. "Your coordinates point to Mare Street, which is where Patricia Brown—your grandmother—lived until her death. That's where your coordinates sent you, not to an orphanage. Perhaps some form of private adoption was arranged. It's ironic, isn't it?" he added after a pause. "That you both began to search for each other at a similar moment in time?"

"If she's telling the truth," I muttered.

"She is, Star. Trust me, no one could have made up a story like this on the hoof, when I confronted her after the lecture," he murmured as he put a steaming cup of tea on the floor next to me.

"And Mouse wouldn't have let me near you if he hadn't believed me," said Sylvia. "He even checked the National Archives to see if your death had been officially registered. It hadn't. Oh, Star, I was so, so happy! I'd tried and failed to trace you, coming over early on this trip to England to try again. I'd all but given up hope when your young man appeared."

"He's not my young man."

"Your friend then," she corrected herself.

"Why did you change your name?"

"After my mom told me about your death, I lost it for a while. Really, I wouldn't have put it past her to have murdered you with her own bare hands. She even told me she'd arranged your funeral herself so as to spare me the pain. I went home immediately, of course, to make sure she wasn't lying, which was when she gave me the death certificate. Then I accused her of not caring for you . . ." My mother bit her lip and I saw genuine pain in her eyes. "And she threw me out of the house. I swore I'd never return home again. And I didn't. I stayed in Cambridge, working during the holidays to support myself. I wanted to disassociate myself from her completely. And I figured if I changed my name, she'd never be able to find me."

"Who was my father?"

"He was my boss at the clothing factory I worked at during the summer before I went to Cambridge to gather some money to support myself through university. Married of course . . . Christ! I'm so ashamed to tell you this . . ."

I watched as my mother put her head in her hands and wept. I did not comfort her. I couldn't. Eventually, she recovered herself and continued.

"It's not me who should be crying. I have no excuses, but he seemed so glamorous to me at the time, took me out to dinner at fancy restaurants, told me I was beautiful . . . Jesus! I was so naive. You have no idea what my mother was like: so overprotective, and all that church stuff she insisted I attend all the way through my childhood. I hadn't any real idea of how to stop myself from getting pregnant. Take it from me, the Catholic version doesn't work. You were the inevitable result."

"Would you have aborted me if you could have done?"

"I . . . don't know. I'm trying to be as truthful as I can here, Star. The point was, after that summer, I got to Cambridge, and in November, I finally twigged something wasn't right. I asked a friend and she bought me a pregnancy test. A doctor confirmed I was already over four months gone."

As she picked up her cup to take a sip of the tea, I saw her hands were shaking violently. And felt the first stirrings of sympathy for her. *She doesn't have to put herself through this*, I thought. She could have denied any knowledge of me to Mouse.

"I'm sorry if I'm being rude," I offered.

"She isn't normally," Mouse chipped in for good measure. "Your daughter has changed us all since she arrived in our lives."

I looked up at him and saw he was gazing down at me with something akin to affection.

"Well then, I'll leave you to it." He walked from the kitchen and I had a sudden urge to call him back.

"Here, I brought you something I had made for you when I arrived back in Cambridge just after you were born. I was going to put it round your wrist when I next went home to see you." Sylvia stood up and walked over to kneel down next to me. "It was a little keepsake for while I couldn't be with you myself."

She handed me a small leather jewelry box. I opened it and saw the name of a Cambridge jeweler printed in gold on the inside. Lying on the blue velvet was a tiny bracelet. I took it out and studied the one heart-shaped charm dangling from it.

Lucy Charlotte
21/04/1980

"I was going to add a charm to it every year on your birthday, but I never had the chance to give it to you. Until now. Here." She took the box back from me, then pulled out the central velvet display and produced a yellowing piece of paper. She handed it to me, and I read it. It was a receipt for the bracelet, dated May 20, 1980. The amount was for £30. "That was a lot in those days." She smiled at me weakly, and I noticed the enormous diamond engagement ring twinkling on her finger, and smelled her sweet, expensive perfume. I sat silently as I played with the tiny bracelet. And admitted that if this was all a hoax, it was a pretty good one.

"Lucy . . . *Star*, would you please look at me?" Reaching out, she tipped my chin up toward her. "I loved you then, and I love you now. Please, please believe me."

She smiled at me, her blue eyes still blurred with tears.

And suddenly, I did.

"Could I . . . can I have a hug? I've waited so long," she entreated me.

I didn't say no, and she moved toward me, her arms pulling me into an embrace. After a long hesitation, my arms moved around her of their own accord, and I felt myself hugging her back.

"It's a miracle," she murmured into my hair, as she stroked it with her gentle hands. "My baby . . . my beautiful baby girl . . ."

"You okay?" Mouse asked me as he wandered into the kitchen a good hour later to find us both still sitting on the floor with our backs pressed to the warm range.

"Yes." I smiled up at him. "We're fine."

"Well," he said as he surveyed us, "call me if you need me." He walked to the door, then turned back. "It's like looking at two peas in a pod." Then he left the room.

"That Mouse is a good guy," my mother said as she continued to stroke my fingers, as if imprinting them on her memory. She hadn't stopped touching me in the past hour, apologizing by saying she just had to convince herself that I was real and she wasn't dreaming. "Is he related to us?"

"No."

I'd tried to give her a brief history of myself and my childhood growing up with my five sisters at Atlantis. Then we had moved on to High Weald and the complexities of the Forbes/Vaughan family.

"I hear Mouse has a rather unusual brother. Orlando is his name, I believe?" she said.

"Yes, and he's wonderful."

"I think that Mouse has a real soft spot for you, Star. And by the way, I'm so happy that your adoptive father gave you such a beautiful name. It suits you. You know 'Lucy' means 'light'?"

"Yes."

"So, you are a 'star' that shines brightly." She smiled.

We continued talking, often veering off track when a question came to mind. I learned about my three half siblings—all a lot younger than me, and named James, after Joyce, Scott, after Fitzgerald, and Anna, after Tolstoy's tragic heroine. She told me she was very happily married to Robert, their father. Their life sounded truly idyllic.

"Robert knows about you, of course. He was very supportive when I got the letter from my mom's solicitor a few weeks ago. He's going to be thrilled when I call him to say I've actually found you. He's a good man," she added. "You'd like him."

"I was offered a place at Cambridge," I confessed suddenly.

"You were? Wow! That's some achievement these days. It was easier to get a place in my time, especially as I came from what was classed as an underprivileged background. The government was very hot on egalitarianism back then. You did far better than me. Why didn't you take it up?"

"It would have meant leaving my sister. And we needed each other."

"Is that CeCe? The one you live with in London?"

"Yes."

"Well, you could go back now if you wanted to. It's never too late to change your destiny, you know."

"You sound like Pa Salt." I smiled. "That's the kind of thing he'd always say."

"I'm liking the sound of your Pa Salt. What a shame I can never meet him."

"Yes, he was a wonderful parent to all of us girls."

I felt her shudder slightly next to me, but recover quickly.

"So, have you any idea what you want to do with your life now that you've settled in England?"

"Not really, no. I mean, I thought I wanted to write, but it's harder than it looks and I'm not sure I'm any good."

"Maybe it's not the moment right now, and it'll happen later, as it does for many writers. It certainly did for me."

"I actually like the simple stuff a lot: keeping house, cooking, gardening . . ." I turned to her suddenly. "I'm not very ambitious. Is that wrong?"

"Of course it's not! I mean, we're all glad that female emancipation has moved on, and let me tell you, in the 1980s we girls really were the pioneers, the first generation of educated women to put a foot—or should I say a stiletto—firmly in the male-dominated workplace. But I think that what we did simply offered choice to the women who followed us. In other words, enabled them to be who they wanted to be."

"Then is it okay to say that, just now, I don't really want a career?"

"It's fine, honey," she said as she squeezed my hand tightly and kissed the top of my head. "That's the freedom my generation has given you, and there's nothing wrong with being a stay-at-home mom, although I know all too well it makes it easier if you can find someone who is prepared to support you while you bring up the kids."

"Well, I haven't got that," I chuckled.

"You will, baby, you will."

"Er, hi," Mouse said from the kitchen door. "Just to say that Orlando called: he, Marguerite, and Rory are on their way back from Tenterden."

"Then I'd better go."

As my mother made to stand up, I pulled her back. "Is it okay if she stays, Mouse?"

"Yes, Star," he said, smiling at me. "It's absolutely fine."

43

That evening, I decided as I slipped into bed much later, was one of the best I'd ever had. The Vaughans and Forbeses had arrived en masse, and—obviously well primed by Orlando and Mouse—had welcomed Sylvia with open arms.

"After all, she is family," Marguerite had laughed as she lit one of her endless Gitanes and drank countless glasses of red wine, while I cooked a joint of beef that Orlando had brought home with him from the farm shop. At the dinner table, we'd all explained further to Sylvia just how she—and I—fitted into the family jigsaw puzzle. And as the wine flowed, I'd felt some form of ease seep through the ancient, damp walls of High Weald. As though the secrets of the past had finally shaken down like a flurry of snowflakes and were starting to settle calmly on the ground.

And later, as I wriggled my feet to find a warm spot between the freezing sheets, I realized that tonight, with my mother there beside me, I'd finally felt that I belonged.

"Jesus Christ!" my mother said as she entered the kitchen the following morning, where I was already stationed at the range, making breakfast. "I have a hell of a hangover. I'd forgotten how the English drink," she said as she walked toward me and gave me a spontaneous hug. "Something smells good," she commented, looking down at the sausages I was frying for Rory, who had snuck off to watch Harry Potter—his new favorite DVD—while nobody said he couldn't.

"You're an amazing cook, Star, really. Just like your great-granny Tessie was. I still dream about her homemade chips."

"I make those too," I said.

"Well, I'd love to try them one day," she said, her eyes wandering to the *cafetière*. "Can I take some coffee?"

"Help yourself."

"Thanks. You know, Marguerite and I stayed up after all of you had gone to bed. We spent most of the time trying to work out what we were to each other. We got as far as half second cousins, but who knows? And who cares?! Boy, that girl can drink the shoes off a sailor." She sat down at the table and, despite her professed hangover, looked elegant in a pair of jeans and a cashmere sweater. "She was telling me how she's fallen for the owner of the chateau where she's painting her murals in France. And that she's sick of High Weald and trying to keep it going. I got the feeling she'd like to move."

"Where to?"

"Why, France, of course!"

"What about Rory? He'd have to learn French sign language, and it's so very different from the British version . . ."

"I really don't know, Star, but maybe she'll talk to you about it. You know, by coming here, I've realized how normal I am. And what a simple life I lead, compared to my newly discovered English cousins."

"When do you leave for the States?"

"I take the night flight later today. So if it's okay with you, can we spend the time I have left together?"

"I'd like that," I said.

After I'd served up breakfast and washed the dishes, we entrusted Rory with showing us around the gardens. He cycled along the hard, frosted pathways ahead of us, signing "slow coach" to me if we lagged too far behind.

"He's a cute little boy, that one. And bright," my mother commented. "Not to mention very fond of you."

"I love him too. He's so positive."

"He is. God bless him, I only hope life treats him kindly in the future."

"He has his family around him to protect him."

"Yes, he does. For now, at least," my mother added with a sad smile.

Later that afternoon, I asked Marguerite for the loan of her Fiat and drove my mother into Tenterden, where Orlando—who looked hungover too—was stacking books onto shelves.

"Ah! The ladies of leisure deign to visit me in my humble abode. Welcome, Professor Gray. Perhaps I can now say a Yale professor of literature is my first customer? Now, I must show you my wonderful first edition of *Anna Karenina*."

"Orlando, I told you last night, please call me 'Sylvia.'"

As Orlando and my mother indulged their shared passion, I took over the shelf stacking, feeling rather like Rory as I struggled to understand what they were talking about.

"Of course, the expert on early twentieth-century English literature is Star here." Orlando glanced over at me, sensitive enough to realize that I might be feeling left out. "Ask her anything about the Bloomsbury Set—in particular, High Weald's ex-neighbor, our dear Vita Sackville-West, and her associated lovers. Which is ironic, given Lady Flora Vaughan's own past."

"Star told me vaguely about the connection last night," my mother commented.

"The next time you return to these shores, Miss Sylvia, you must read the journals in full. They are a fascinating glimpse into Edwardian England."

"Well, perhaps Star should edit them into a book. I'm sure the whole world would be fascinated by Flora's story."

"I say! Miss Sylvia, that is an excellent idea. What with her in-depth knowledge of the literature of that period, plus her personal connection to Lady Flora, I can think of no one better qualified," Orlando agreed, and I felt two pairs of eyes upon me.

"Maybe in time," I said with a shrug.

"If you do, I'm sure that Yale University Press would be mighty interested in publishing it."

"As would a number of commercial publishers here too," countered Orlando. "The story has all the elements of what one might call a 'bodice ripper,' never mind that it's true!"

My mother glanced at her watch. "I'm afraid I'm going to have to get back to the house—my train to London leaves soon."

Back at High Weald, my mother came down the stairs with her suitcase.

"Mouse is giving you a lift to the station," I said.

"Oh, Star." She took me in her arms and held me tightly. "Please keep in touch with me as often as you can manage. Otherwise I might begin to think I dreamed all this. You have all my numbers? And my e-mail?"

"I do, yes."

A horn beeped from outside.

"Right, I'm going to have to say good-bye. But the moment I get home, we're planning another trip. Either you come to me in Connecticut and meet your half brothers and sister, or I return here to you, yes?"

"I'd like that."

My mother gave me a big hug, then blew me a kiss as she walked out of the door, and I watched her get into the Land Rover beside Mouse. As the car drove off, I felt suddenly bereft without her. This woman seemed to know me so intimately—in a way that nobody else did—whereas I was only just getting to know her.

Later, after Rory had gone to bed, I served up the bubble and squeak I'd knocked together from the leftovers and we ate in comfortable silence, all of us exhausted from the past two days. Orlando excused himself and ambled off to bed, while Mouse went upstairs to take a look at a leak that Marguerite had discovered on her bedroom ceiling.

"And currently collecting in a saucepan," she sighed as she helped clear the table. "I'm back off bright and early to France tomorrow morning, by the way. Mouse will give you some cash for any groceries you need while I'm gone."

"When will you be back?"

"Never, if I have my way, but there we are. God, how I hate this house. It's like caring for an ancient, ailing relative who you know is beyond any help." Having dried off a plate, Marguerite reached for her Gitanes, lit one, and flopped into a chair. "I was saying to Mouse that I really ought to consider selling it. I know it's meant to go to Rory, but I'm sure there's some city boy and his aspirational wife who'd love to chuck their millions at a country pad like this. At least Mouse has said he and Orlando will throw some money my way from the proceeds of the bookshop. No less than I deserve under the circumstances," she added darkly.

"Rory's happy here."

"Yes, he is, because it's become his home. Ironic, really . . ."

Her eyes fled to the window and she sighed heavily, releasing a stream of smoke. "Anyway, I'm out of here tomorrow for a while and a lot of that is thanks to you, Star. Seriously, you've stabilized the house and its inhabitants. Especially Mouse."

"I don't think so," I mumbled.

"You didn't know him before your arrival. He's different, Star, and at least that's given me hope that things can change in the future. He's actually making an effort with Rory, which in my eyes is a miracle. And even Orlando has become less detached from the real world since you arrived in his life. I've often wondered whether he's gay, but I've never seen him with anyone, male or female. My guess is that he's asexual. What do you think?"

"I think he's in love with his books. And they are all he needs," I said, not comfortable with discussing my employer's sexuality.

"You know what? I think you're absolutely spot-on." Marguerite smiled.

"Rory will miss you when you're gone," I offered, wanting to return the conversation to safer territory.

"And I'll miss him, but the good news is, he's always been used to new people taking care of him. He had a flood of nannies before I decided it was time to take over. Now, if you don't mind, I'll leave you to it." She stood up and stubbed out her cigarette in the hapless cactus pot. "Here's a tip: It's wonderful being in love. It lights us all up. Night, Star." With that, she blew me a kiss and left me with my hands in the soapsuds, my head spinning.

Once I'd finished clearing up, I wandered along the corridor toward the sitting room with a cup of hot chocolate, feeling I needed some time to catch my breath.

"Hi." Mouse walked in just as I'd sat down.

"Hi."

"I'll have to call a plumber in tomorrow to look at that leak. Not that he'll be able to do much. My guess is that it's the roof."

"Oh," I said, as I focused my eyes on the flames leaping from the logs on the fire.

"Mind if I sit down?"

"No. Can I get you a hot chocolate?"

"No thanks. I . . . want to talk to you, Star."

"What about?"

"Oh, all sorts of things, really," he said as he sat down in the chair opposite me, looking as uncomfortable as I felt. "Well," he breathed, "it's been quite a ride since you first appeared in the bookshop, hasn't it?"

"Yes, it has."

"How are you feeling now about finding your mother?"

"Fine. Thank you for taking the trouble to go to Cambridge on my behalf."

"It was no trouble, really. As a matter of fact, it did me good to go back to a place where I'd been so happy. It was where I met Annie."

"Really?"

"Yes. I drove up to Cambridge a couple of hours before the lecture, and had a beer at the pub where I'd first spoken to her."

"That must have been comforting," I ventured.

"No. It wasn't actually. It was horrific. I sat there, and all I could hear were her thoughts on my behavior since her death. And what a selfish and ultimately cruel human being I've been since she left me. I've been wicked, Star, I really have."

"You were grieving. That's not wicked."

"It is when it affects everyone else around you. I've almost destroyed this family, and I'm not exaggerating," Mouse added vehemently. "Then later that evening, I met your mother, and saw the love she'd held for you through all these years, even though she'd believed up until a few weeks ago that you were dead. And I imagined Annie, somewhere up there, looking down at me and what I'd done. Or hadn't done," he checked himself. "I stood on the bridge by King's College and almost threw myself into the Cam. I've known for a long time the chaos my behavior has caused, but just like an alcoholic who knows he's a dirty drunk, then has another drink to make himself feel better, I haven't known how to put it right."

"I understand," I said quietly, and I did.

"That night in Cambridge was seminal," he continued. "I understood that I had to put my past to rest and say a final good-bye to Annie. And stop wallowing in self-pity. What good was holding on to her memory when it had so negatively affected those still living? And then I drove home with a new determination to try and put things right."

"That's good," I encouraged him.

"And the first port of call is *you*. On the bridge that night, I admitted to myself that I have . . . feelings for you. Which have confused me—I honestly thought I'd never love again. I've been racked with guilt; having spent the past seven years putting my dead wife on a pedestal, I felt I was somehow betraying her, that the fact I actually felt happy in your company was wrong. And I was—and am," he continued, "scared shitless. You might have gathered that once I love, it's all-consuming." He gave me a small, wry smile. "And, Star, inconveniently, I'm sure, for you, I've realized that I *do* love you. You are beautiful in every way."

"I'm not, Mouse, I can assure you," I said hurriedly.

"Well, to me you are, although even I realize you must have your faults, just as Annie did. Listen . . ." He leaned forward to reach for my hands, which I reluctantly gave to him, my heart beating so fast I thought it might burst out of my chest. "I have no idea how you feel about me. That calm exterior of yours is impenetrable. I asked Orlando last night, as he seems to be the one who knows you best. He said he thought that my behavior toward you has been so erratic as I've slid between love, then guilt for feeling love, that you were probably as scared as hell of feeling anything, even if you did."

Mouse, usually so eloquent and sparing with his words, was rushing on. "So, I decided that the first thing I should do on the journey to rehabilitation and to hopefully creating a new and better 'me' was to man up and tell you. So? Do you think you might? Feel something for me?"

What I felt was that Mouse had an unfair advantage with his bridge epiphany. He'd had time to put his feelings—real or imagined—into some kind of order. Whereas I'd had none.

"I . . . don't know."

"Well, that was hardly a line from *Romeo and Juliet*, but at least it's not an outright no. And"—he pulled his hands away from mine, then stood up and began to pace—"before you decide whether you do or you don't, I have something else to tell you. And it's so dreadful that even if you *do* discover you have some feelings for me, it's bound to finish them off immediately. But I can't deceive you from the start, Star, and if we've got any chance together in the future, you have to know."

"What is it?"

"Right . . ." Mouse stopped pacing and turned to me. "The thing is, Annie was deaf."

I looked up at him as he willed me to make the connection. I knew it was there, but I couldn't grasp it.

"In other words, Rory is our . . . *my* son."

"Oh my God . . . ," I whispered, as everything I hadn't understood about this family finally fell into place in one stark moment of revelation.

I stared into the fireplace as I heard Mouse breathe out and sit down heavily.

"When she was pregnant, we were both so excited. Then she went for her first scan, and they found she had ovarian cancer. Obviously she couldn't have any form of treatment, as it could harm the baby, so we were left with a horrific choice: continue with the pregnancy and take the consequences of a delayed course of chemotherapy, or abort, and have treatment immediately. Being the optimist she was, Annie decided on the former, knowing that whether she lived or died, it would be her one chance to have a child. The doctors had told her that everything would need to be removed as soon as she gave birth. Are you following me, Star?"

"Yes."

"Rory was born, and they performed Annie's operation almost immediately. But by then, the cancer had spread to her lymph glands and her liver. She died a couple of months later."

I heard his voice break before he continued.

"The truth is, when her illness was first discovered, I'd begged her to abort the baby and give herself the best possible chance of saving herself. You already know how I adored her. So when she left me, every time I looked at Rory, I didn't see an innocent baby, but his mother's murderer. Star, I hated him. Hated him for killing his mother . . . the love of my life. She was everything to me."

He choked on his words, and it took him time to recover. I sat frozen in my chair, hardly daring to breathe.

"After that, I don't really remember very much, but I had some form of breakdown and was hospitalized for a while. That was when Marguerite, bless her, had no choice but to take Rory and have him at High Weald. I eventually came out on endless drugs, and Rory was brought back to me, with a nanny to care for him. I was encouraged to—as my therapist put it—'bond' with him. But I couldn't. I couldn't even bear to look at him. Then my father died too and that just about did it. Eventually, after a series of unsuccessful nannies, whom I frightened off with my aggressive behavior, Marguerite suggested that Rory should come to live at High Weald with her full-time. They'd all given me up as a lost cause. And I was. I let both my architect's practice and the farm go to rack and ruin. The upshot is, Marguerite has had the burden of taking care of Rory for the past five years, and has been unable to move forward in her own life or career. And Rory himself . . . God, Star, he thinks I'm his uncle! And worst of all, he knows nothing about his own mother! I haven't let anyone mention Annie to him his entire life! He's so much like her; she was a talented artist too . . . How can I ever make it up to him?"

There was silence then, as Mouse sat, breathing heavily, with his head in his hands.

"Well," I said eventually, "at least you made him brownies the other day."

He looked up at me then, the agony in his eyes obvious. Then he raised his hands.

"I did. And thank you," he signed perfectly back to me.

44

I told Mouse that I needed to go to sleep. I was exhausted from my own trauma of the past few days, and now his. I lay down on the bed and wrapped the blanket and eiderdown around me like a cocoon, needing to analyze the facts before my heart made a decision.

Although I felt deeply for Mouse and the complexity of the loss he'd endured, I also felt for Orlando, Marguerite, and especially Rory. Innocent of all charges. Damned only by being born.

And yet . . . he was a happy, untroubled soul, who engendered love simply by his generous giving of it. He had accepted his unusual circumstances as children do—as *I* had—without question. And despite his father's behavior toward him, there had been others there to cradle him if he fell, as there had been for me.

As for Mouse's confession about his feelings, I steeled myself not to take them too seriously. He'd had an epiphany, due to returning to Cambridge. And all the years of loneliness and misery had almost certainly collected into a misplaced love for the only single female within reach: *me*. I'd worked for his brother, put food in his stomach, and cared for his son . . .

It was an easy mistake to make.

Yes, I thought, *that is the reason.* And there was no way I was going to unlock my tender heart and allow it to pour its feelings into the turbulent waters of Mouse's emotional storm.

But I will stay here, I thought, as I closed my eyes. *For Rory.*

I'd just returned to High Weald after taking Rory to school the next morning when Mouse arrived through the door. I noticed he was wearing the same clothes I'd seen him in yesterday, as if he hadn't gone to bed at all.

"Hi."

"Hi," I said, as I collected the eggs and bacon from the pantry for Orlando's breakfast. I glanced at him briefly as I walked toward the range and thought that this morning, he looked completely broken. Part of me felt he deserved it.

"Did you think about what I said to you last night?" he asked.

"Yes."

"And?"

"Mouse, please, there's been so much for me to take in over the past few days, I can't do this now."

"Of course."

"Besides, this isn't about you, or me. It's about Rory. Your son."

"I know. Look, I've been thinking too. And you're right. I can't expect you to trust me, let alone love me, after the way I've behaved toward both of you. But . . . are you going to stay here?"

"Yes. Rory needs stability. Also, I do have a job here at the bookshop these days."

"Well then . . ." I watched him shift from foot to foot. "What I'd like to do, with your help, is to try to mend my relationship—or at least *begin* a relationship—with my son. There's not a lot I can do until the sale of the bookshop goes through and the funds arrive in the account, so I thought I could use the time to be with Rory. I won't be very good, I know, but I can get better, I'm sure of it."

"If you want to, then yes, you can."

"I want to, Star, believe me, I do."

"Well, that solves one of my problems. You could collect Rory from school, then I can help Orlando at the bookshop for longer and drive him home. There's a lot to do there before we open."

"Great," he said immediately. "Though I'm not sure my cooking's up to much."

"I'll cook when I get back, but there is bath time . . ."

"And story time. I know." He gave me a tentative smile.

"Good morning, all," said Orlando, walking into the kitchen. He looked at both of us, sensing the tension in the air. "Have I blundered in here at an inopportune moment?"

"Not at all," I said. "Breakfast is nearly ready. You'll collect Rory at three thirty?" I confirmed with Mouse, damned if I was going to offer him breakfast too.

"I'll be there. Bye now," he muttered, and promptly left.

Orlando cocked his head at me quizzically.

"Mouse told me last night. About Rory being his son."

"Ah. Well now, that's certainly a move forward, given that he wouldn't acknowledge it to himself up until recently. You've worked a miracle, Miss Star, truly you have."

"I've done nothing, Orlando," I said as I put the plate of bacon and eggs in front of him.

"Then should I say that *love* has worked a miracle. Of course I've known since the moment he first set eyes on you that—"

"Enough, Orlando."

"Forgive me, but please, Miss Star, at least give him a chance to mend his ways and endear himself to you."

"I'm more interested in him endearing himself to Rory," I countered as I slammed a frying pan into the sink to wash it.

"Do I finally see some fire rising in that belly of yours? Perhaps Mouse isn't the only one around here who's changed recently, due to affairs of the heart."

"Orlando . . ."

"I shall say no more. Other than the fact that when sinners repent and try to atone for their mistakes, it is our Christian duty to forgive them. I have, at least. My brother is a jolly decent man, and if it hadn't been for Annie's death—"

"*Enough!*" I turned to him with the wet frying pan in my hand, and he held his hands up in mock self-protection.

"No more, I promise. My lips are sealed. It's up to Mouse now."

"Yes," I agreed fervently. "It is."

For the next few days, Mouse did exactly as he'd said he would. He took Rory to school each morning, then collected him afterward. They were home a couple of hours earlier than me, having bought the food on the shopping list I wrote every morning. I would drive Orlando home from

Tenterden, then I'd cook supper for the four of us, watching from the sidelines as Mouse did his best to atone for the missed years of his son's life. After supper, he'd take him up for a bath and read him a story. Rory was still amazed by Mouse's sudden new talent for signing.

"He's even better than you, Star. He's a fast learner, isn't he?"

"He's certainly determined, because he loves you," I said as I kissed him good night.

"And I love him. Night night, Star. Don't let the bedbugs bite."

I walked to the door to switch off the light. All these years, I thought, Mouse had known exactly how to sign, having learned in order to communicate better with Annie. And I hoped that one day Rory would begin to know about his mother, who had loved him so fiercely that she had given her life for him.

On Thursday, Mouse informed me that Marguerite had called while I was at the bookshop. "She'd like to stay in France until the beginning of December, returning for the opening of the bookshop. I told her that I'd look after Rory this weekend. You probably need to go back to London?"

"I do, yes." I nodded in agreement. It was important Mouse and Rory spent as much time as possible together without anyone else around.

"Right, then we'll give you a lift to the station tomorrow night when you've finished at the bookshop."

"Thanks. Perhaps you and Rory can give Orlando a hand over the weekend? He wants to move into the flat above the shop on Sunday."

"We will. Good night then."

"Good night."

The following evening, as I got off the London train and sat on the bus back to Battersea, I saw the streets already adorned with Christmas decorations. And wondered vaguely where I'd be spending *my* Christmas. I couldn't think of anything worse than Christmas Day in the sterile, soulless apartment, after years of the glorious Christmases we had celebrated at Atlantis, or on moonlit beaches in far-flung parts of the world.

Christmas at High Weald would be perfect . . .

I ordered my newly disobedient psyche to shut up. And equally refused to let it acknowledge how I had glanced at Mouse sitting patiently with Rory on his knee, signing and reading a book to him, and felt . . . yes, *felt*, a small wave of emotion for him. But it was far, far too soon to open up my heart and let out what I was so fearful it contained.

When I arrived at the apartment, CeCe was enormously happy to see me, and we arranged to spend the weekend together.

"I must get my hair cut this weekend too," she said. "It's getting far too long."

I looked at CeCe, and remembered how, as a child, she'd once had a mane of gorgeous dark chocolate curls that had hung well past her shoulders. Then, at sixteen, she'd arrived home having had the lot chopped off, saying it was too much bother.

"Don't get it cut, Cee," I said, thinking how pretty she looked tonight, with the soft waves framing her lovely dark brown eyes. "It suits you longer."

"Okay," she agreed, surprising me. "I also need to buy some warmer clothes, but you know how I hate shopping."

"I'll come with you. It'll be fun."

So the next morning, we ventured up to Oxford Street to battle with the other Christmas shoppers. I splashed out and bought a dress to wear for Ally's concert, and even persuaded CeCe into a pretty silk blouse to wear with a pair of tailored gray trousers and high-heeled ankle boots.

"This really isn't me," she grumbled as she surveyed herself in the changing-room mirror.

"You look lovely, Cee," I said truthfully, admiring her trim figure. She must have lost weight in the last few weeks, but I hadn't noticed before now because she usually dressed in oversized sweatshirts and baggy jeans. And besides, I'd been away so much.

On Sunday, I cooked a traditional roast lunch, took a deep breath, and told her about meeting my mother.

"Jesus Christ, Sia! Why on earth didn't you tell me about any of this before?"

I could see the hurt in her eyes. "I don't know. Perhaps I had to get used to the idea myself first before I told anyone."

"I'm hardly 'anyone,'" she countered. "We used to tell each other everything, especially 'private' stuff."

"It was so strange at first, Cee," I tried to explain, "but she seems lovely. I might go and visit her in the States. As a matter of fact, I had an e-mail from her this morning inviting me over for Christmas and New Year."

"You won't go, will you?" she said, looking horrified. "It's bad enough with you away all week, let alone Christmas. We've never spent it apart. What would I do?"

"Of course we'll spend it together," I comforted her.

"Good. Actually, I have something to tell you too. I'm thinking of leaving college."

"Cee! Why?"

"Because I hate it. I don't think I'm very good at being institutionalized, especially after all our years of being free spirits."

"What will you do?"

"Try my hand as an artist, I s'pose." She shrugged. "Anyway, forget that. I'm so happy you've found your mum. And now I can tell you about—"

I checked my watch and saw it was past three o'clock. "I'm so sorry, Cee, I have a train to catch. But we'll talk when I'm next back, yes?"

"Sure."

CeCe watched me desolately as I went upstairs. I packed in a rush and came back downstairs to find her painting in her studio.

"Bye now," I said breezily to her as I headed for the front door. "I'll let you know if I'm coming back next weekend. Have a good week."

"And you," came the muffled response.

Back in Kent, I was kept busy, preparing for what Orlando called his "grand opening" in two weeks' time. He stood outside the shop, dressed in his best velvet suit, as the local paper took photographs of him to go with the interview they were running, and I felt desperately proud of him.

Life at High Weald continued in a similar vein, and I saw that both Rory and Mouse were beginning to relax into their new routine. I did my best not to interfere if, on occasion, Mouse was short-tempered with his son, because that too was only natural. Even if Mouse had to learn what "natural" was.

As the "grand opening" was taking place on a Saturday, I took the coward's way out and texted CeCe from Tenterden, explaining I wouldn't be home that weekend. I got a brusque reply in response.

Fine. Call me! Woud like to talk.

I refused to let her put me on a guilt trip. I realized that in some ways, it was like the ending of a love affair—a gentle easing, a letting go—painful, but ultimately right for both of us. And even if I left High Weald tomorrow, never to return, it was essential this happened. For I couldn't go back to where I'd been. And nor must CeCe. I just hoped we could eventually find our way forward to a different and more natural relationship.

Mouse had honored my request for time to think about what he'd said to me. Every evening after he'd said good night to Rory, he would leave by the kitchen door, with a wave and a "see you tomorrow." With Orlando now ensconced in his tiny flat above the bookshop in Tenterden, the evenings began to yawn like an open chasm before me, and I realized that I was just as much a novice at being alone as CeCe was.

Well, I simply had to learn, and even though it was often on the tip of my tongue to ask Mouse to stay on for a beer before he left, I didn't. Instead, I lit the fire in the drawing room and sat in front of it, reading Flora's journals and wondering whether I *could* edit all these detailed years of her life into a book that people would want to read. Yet I was distracted constantly, as my thoughts flew across the lane to Home Farm. And I wondered what Mouse was thinking and doing right now . . .

This tortured, damaged man who had professed to love me.

The question was, did I love him?

Possibly.

But . . . there was also something about *me* that he didn't know. And the thought of telling him—of telling *anyone*—was something I couldn't contemplate.

"All ready?" Orlando asked me, looking wonderful in a newly purchased vintage Edwardian frock coat, complete with a starched collar and a maroon cravat.

"Yes."

"Right then," he said as we both gave last glances around the immaculate shop and I proceeded behind him toward the door. I only hoped there would be people outside to watch him cut the red ribbon I'd placed at his insistence across the threshold earlier this morning.

He opened the door and I saw Mouse, Rory, and Marguerite, who was standing beside a petite blond woman I didn't recognize. Behind them were a group of fascinated passersby, who halted with their shopping bags, astonished by the sight of Orlando in fancy dress.

"Ladies and gentlemen, I'd like to announce the opening of O. Forbes Esquire—Rare Books. And now I shall pass the scissors to the manager of my shop, without whose help I would not be here. Take the scissors," he hissed at me, as he all but prodded me in the stomach with them.

"No, Orlando! It should be you."

"Please, Miss Star, you've been my lynchpin, whatever a 'lynchpin' actually is, and I want you to cut the ribbon."

"Okay," I sighed.

So, I cut the ribbon and our assembled "family" applauded and cheered loudly, as did the passersby. People crowded into the shop and a photographer arrived to take more pictures as we all drank champagne.

"Star, hello." Marguerite kissed me on both cheeks. "This is Hélène, by the way. She's the owner of the chateau, and what you might call my significant other." She smiled fondly at Hélène, squeezing her hand.

"I am very 'appy to be 'ere," said Hélène in hesitant English.

"Star speaks perfect French, among her other accomplishments," Marguerite informed her.

Hélène and I chatted for a while about her chateau near Gigondas, a village in the center of the glorious Rhône Valley; about Marguerite's marvelous murals; and in general about how marvelous Marguerite was.

"She tells me that it is you who has made it possible for us to spend some time together," Hélène added. "Thank you, Star."

"Hi," said a voice behind me.

"Hi." I turned around and Mouse kissed me formally on both cheeks. Rory stood beside him.

"What do you think of Orlando's new shop?" I asked Rory.

"I painted a picture of it for him."

"And I had it framed. Isn't it wonderful?" Mouse said as Rory handed it up to me to admire.

It was a watercolor of the front of the bookshop. "Wow, Rory, it's fantastic," I signed to him. "He's so talented," I said to Mouse.

"Isn't he?"

I heard the genuine pride in his voice. And immediately wanted to cry.

"Listen . . ." He bent down to whisper in my ear. "Can I take you out tonight? I'm sure the rest of High Weald can fend for themselves for once."

"Yes," I said without hesitation.

Perhaps it was the midday champagne that made me answer in the affirmative earlier, I thought grimly as I rifled through my paltry selection of clothing that evening. I had the choice between my two sweaters and a couple of pairs of jeans. Going for the blue sweater, I walked into the kitchen, where the occupants of High Weald were still celebrating the opening of the bookshop.

"Mouse just called to say he'd pick you up from the front door in a few minutes," said Orlando.

"Thanks," I said, clocking the smell of burning sausages in the frying pan and instinctively reaching to remove them from the range. There was the sound of a horn beeping from the front of the house.

"Have a good time," Marguerite said, smirking. Hélène's arm was draped around her shoulder and Rory sat on her knee, contentedly eating a tube of Smarties. "And don't you dare come home before dawn," she added. To which the entire kitchen laughed uproariously.

Red-faced, I walked to the front hall and opened the door, feeling like the proverbial lamb to the slaughter.

"Hi," Mouse said, kissing me on both cheeks as I got into the car. He had shaved, and for a brief moment, I felt his smooth skin against mine. "Ready to go?" he said.

"Sure. Where?"

"To the local pub. Is that okay? They do great bar food."

The White Lion was crowded and charming, with a roaring fire in the grate and a heavily beamed ceiling. Mouse ordered a beer for himself and a glass of white wine for me, picked up a couple of menus, then led me to a table in a quiet nook to the side of the main bar.

"Thanks for coming, I appreciate it," he said. "I thought we should have a chat about stuff."

"Such as?"

"The fact that Marguerite wants to go and live in France with Hélène. Permanently."

So, this is a "business" chat, not a date, I thought.

"What did you say?"

"I said yes, of course. Rory is my son, after all. And I've got to face my responsibilities. Rory will inherit the title—it passed to me when my uncle died, as they'd only had Marguerite. And ironically, I'll inherit High Weald if Marguerite dies before me, since she's forty-three now and unlikely to have any kids. But ultimately, it will eventually be left to Rory."

"So you are actually 'Lord Vaughan'?" I said with a grin.

"Technically yes, but of course, I don't use it. This lot in here would never let me forget it." He gave a half smile as he indicated the crowd at the bar. "Anyway, to cut a long story short, Marguerite's suggested that we swap houses. Given that she intends to be here as little as possible, and the fact that High Weald is Rory's home and will be his in the future, she thinks it's for the best. She'll take Home Farm, and what with the sale of the Kensington bookshop, if we sell what's left of the farmland, it'll give us each quite a bit to pay for the restoration of both properties. And I've had enough of 'tractoring,' as Rory calls it, I can tell you. Orlando and I have also agreed that all his stock becomes his alone if that's what we decide to do. What do you think?"

"Well, Rory loves High Weald, so it's probably the best thing for him if he could stay there."

"And one hell of an undertaking for me to set about restoring it. Or, I could sell it and find somewhere more affordable."

"Don't," I said. "I mean, you can, but I don't think you should. You—your family—belong there."

"The question is, Star . . . do you?"

"You know how much I love the house . . ."

"That's not what I meant. Look, call me impatient, but these past three weeks have been torture. Having you at High Weald—so near, but yet so far—has driven me nuts. So I've brought you here tonight to ask you what your thoughts are on the subject. I mean, the subject of *us*. I have to accept it if you don't want to be with me. But *if* you don't, I think it would be best if you found yourself somewhere in Tenterden to live. This isn't a threat," he said hastily, "although I suppose it is an ultimatum." He ran a hand through his hair. "Star, please understand that every day you're there at the house with us, I'm getting in deeper. And for Rory's sake, I really can't afford to lose it again."

"I understand."

"So?" He looked at me across the table.

Come on, Star, be brave, say YES . . .

"I don't know," I heard myself say yet again.

"Right. Well then." He stared into space. "That just about says it all."

It says absolutely nothing, apart from that I'm terrified to let my feelings out and trust you . . . and myself.

"Sorry," I added pathetically.

"It's okay." I watched him drain his pint. "Well, as there's nothing more to say, I'll take you home."

I followed him back out of the pub, the food we were going to order now forgotten. It had only been twenty minutes since we'd entered, and I got into the Land Rover feeling utterly miserable. Driving back along the road in silence, he turned into the drive, slamming the car to a halt in front of the house.

"Thanks for the drink." I opened the door and was about to get out when I felt his hand grasp mine.

"Star, what is it you're scared of? Please don't go . . . For God's sake, speak to me! Tell me what you're feeling!"

Half in and half out, metaphorically and physically, I opened my mouth, but no words came out of it. They remained locked inside me, just as they always had done.

Eventually, he gave a long, deep sigh. "Here," he said. "Take this. I thought you might like it." He pressed an envelope into my hand. "If you change your mind . . . If not . . . thanks for everything. Good-bye."

"Good-bye."

I slammed the door and walked toward the front entrance, determined not to look behind me as he reversed and pulled out of the drive. I opened the front door quietly, hearing laughter emanate from the kitchen. I walked straight up the stairs, too embarrassed to alert anyone to my presence, then down the corridor to double-check that someone had thought to put Rory to bed. I kissed him gently on the cheek and he stirred, opening his eyes.

"You're back. Have a nice time with Mouse?"

"Yes, thank you."

"Star?"

"Yes?"

"Will you get married?" Rory mimed smooching and grinned at me. "Please."

"Rory, we both love you—"

"Star?"

"Yes?"

"Mag got cross when the telephone broke and said Mouse was my dad and he should pay. Is he?"

"I . . . You'll have to ask him, Rory. Now, sleep tight," I said as I kissed him again.

"Wish he was my dad," he whispered sleepily. "And you could be my mum."

I left him, marveling at how truly forgiving young children were. And also, at how simple everything seemed to them. I walked to my own bedroom and huddled under the blankets, not bothering to take off my clothes because it was simply too cold. Then I tore open the envelope Mouse had given me.

Dear Star,

I'd like to take you away for a couple of days next weekend. I have somewhere in mind. I think we need to spend some time alone together without everything going on here. No strings attached. Let me know. O X

PS Sorry for writing, it's just in case I don't pluck up the courage to ask you in person at the pub.

I woke with a start the next morning, my mind replaying what had happened the night before. Perhaps, I thought, as I pulled on a second sweater to protect me from the cold, I should just march across the road and tell him yes.

Do it, Star, just do it . . .

I dressed, hurried downstairs, and walked into a deserted kitchen full of dirty plates and pans, not to mention wineglasses and numerous empty bottles. I was just heading for the back door, knowing I had to say the words before my courage failed me, when I saw a note propped up in the middle of the table.

Star! Your sister called here last night. Can you ring her? She said it's urgent!!! PS Hope you had a good time. M X

"Shit!"

All thoughts of a possible future with Mouse were wiped away as I went to the telephone, picked up the receiver, and, with a shaking hand, dialed the apartment number. It rang and rang. When I tried CeCe's mobile, it went straight to voice mail. Putting the receiver down, I told myself that she had probably turned off her mobile and hadn't heard the landline, although CeCe could usually hear a pin drop from a mile away. I tried both again and again, but there was no answer.

Running upstairs, I searched for my mobile, willing it to find a signal for me, just this once, so I could hear any message she'd left for me. But, of course, it didn't. Throwing my stuff into my luggage, I raced back downstairs, then called a taxi to come and collect me immediately.

It was only on the train that I was able to access my messages as they dinged through in a huge wave, to the point where other passengers threw me irritated glances.

"Star, it's CeCe. Please can you call me?"

"Star, are you there?"

"They said you've gone out. Need to talk to you . . . Call me."

"In a bad way . . ."

"PLEASE! CALL!"

Shit, shit, shit!

I willed the train to trundle its weary way to London faster. Tears filled my eyes as I thought of my utter selfishness in the past few weeks. I had abandoned my sister. There was no other way to describe it. And when she'd needed me, I hadn't been there for her. *What kind of person am I?* I asked myself.

Arriving at the apartment, I opened the door, my heart beating like a drum in my chest. Seeing the sitting room and kitchen were deserted, and oddly tidy, I ran up into the bedroom. There was no sign of her there either. Unusually, even her bed was made, as if it hadn't been slept in.

After checking the bathroom, the spare bedroom, and even the wardrobe, which—even allowing for CeCe's meager collection of clothes—seemed remarkably empty, I retraced my footsteps downstairs, checking outside on the terrace just in case.

Then I saw the note on the coffee table.

"Please, please, *please*," I begged as I approached it and picked it up, my hands shaking with fear. Sinking onto the sofa, I speed-read it once to make sure it wasn't of the suicide variety and, with relief, found it wasn't. Then I reread it again slowly.

Sia,

I called that place you are staying but they said you were out. I gess you didnt get any of my messages. I wanted to talk to you because I decided to leve collige. And I wanted to no what you thort. Anyway I did leve. Its been a funny time since Pa died hasant it? I no you need to live your own life. And so do I I supposse. Im lonely here and I miss you. And I decided I needed to go away for a bit to think stuff thru. I want the best for you really. So I hope your happy. I hope we both can be happy.

Dont wory about me. Im okay.

I love you.
Cee

Ps can you say sorry to Ally. I wont make it to Norway. And I bought your camelia tree in as it looked coled.

My tears fell on the page as I read it. With her dyslexia, I knew how CeCe struggled to write a sentence, let alone a letter. It was the only one she'd ever written to me—had ever *needed* to write—because I'd always been there before, by her side. I looked then into her studio and saw the camellia standing by one of the windows. There was a flower lying on the floor, its delicate white petals turning to the wilting beige of decay. It too had suffered from neglect and looked as forlorn as I knew its savior must have felt when she'd written the letter, and I hated myself even more.

I immediately typed her another text to add to the panicked ones I'd sent her from the train. But there was no response. And as I sat there in the empty, silent apartment, staring out at the river, I imagined the endless nights she'd been here alone, while I'd been wrapped in the bosom of my dramatic, but loving, new family.

Dusk fell, and still I waited for my sister to contact me. But my mobile remained as silent as it had without a signal at High Weald. Somehow, the fact that it *did* have one now only made things worse. A person, rather than a device, was choosing to remain silent. Eventually, I crawled into bed, or, more accurately, CeCe's bed, and lay there shivering, even though it was blissfully warm in the apartment.

It wasn't CeCe who had the problem. It was me. After all she'd done for me—loved, protected, *spoken* for me—I had left her without a second glance to fend for herself. I thought back to the way I'd casually told her about finding my mother, and then, in my rush to get back to High Weald, hadn't even spared the time to listen to *her* story. And realized how hurt she must have felt.

The morning came, as it inevitably did, and I left a telephone message for Orlando, saying I was unable to attend work due to a family crisis. To my surprise, he texted me back a few minutes later.

I understand.

His unusual brevity upset me further. Perhaps he'd seen Mouse, who had told him he'd asked me to leave High Weald if I couldn't commit to him. I walked numbly down the road to the nearest supermarket, knowing I needed to feed my brain, if not my stomach. Christmas decorations taunted me with their gaudy gaiety, and the radio in the shop played jingly schlock through its speakers. Back home, I cooked scrambled eggs I didn't want to eat, then took a call from Ma, who wanted to make arrangements to meet at the hotel she had booked us both into in Bergen. I told her CeCe couldn't make it now, but held back from telling her I was half-mad with worry, as I didn't want to explain. I was too ashamed.

When my mobile rang again that afternoon, I dashed to it, only for my stomach to plummet in disappointment when I heard Shanthi's honeyed tones at the other end of the line.

"Star, I was just calling to ask how you were. I haven't heard from you in a while. And I just had a . . . feeling something was up."

"I'm . . . okay."

"I can hear in your voice that you're not. Want to talk about it?"

"I . . . my sister's gone," I said. And, prompted gently by Shanthi, I poured out what had happened, feeling the pain of CeCe's loss with each word.

"I just . . . you don't think she would do anything stupid, do you?"

"From the sound of the letter she left you, no, I don't. Star, I'm so sorry you're going through this, but it sounds to me as if CeCe is doing what you yourself have done—she is finding herself. She probably just needs some time alone. Listen, would you like to come over here and have a glass of wine? It might do you good to get out."

"No thank you," I gulped. "CeCe might come back. And I have to be here."

Three excruciatingly long days passed, and she didn't come back. I wrote and rewrote a letter to her to leave at the apartment in case she returned to it while I was away in Norway. And still there was silence from her, despite my rampant phone messaging and texts. I tortured myself, wondering if, like a wounded animal, she needed to be by herself to do something terrible. At one point, I thought about contacting the police to report a missing person, but common sense told me CeCe had left me a letter explaining her absence. And, given she was twenty-seven, I doubted the police would be interested.

I also missed High Weald. I thought constantly of Rory . . . and also Mouse. I realized that, in the last few turbulent weeks, he had somehow managed to be there for me at the precise moment I'd needed him.

Well, he wasn't there now, and despite my initial resolution to go and tell him yes last weekend, the fact I'd heard nothing from him since made me guess that he had given up on me.

By the end of the week, what was left of me collected my luggage—packed days ago, for want of something to do. Just as I was leaving the apartment for Heathrow, my mobile rang. And I ran to pick it up.

"Hello?"

"Star? It's Mouse. Sorry to disturb you, but I went to High Weald this morning—I hadn't been there since the weekend. Marguerite wanted some time with Rory before she leaves for France. I also had the sale of the bookshop going through and all the last-minute comings and goings between the solicitors that entailed. When I telephoned earlier in the week to check on Rory, they said you'd gone to London on Sunday."

"Oh."

"Anyway, this morning when I went over there, I found a note addressed to you still propped up on the kitchen table. Is everything all right? With your sister, I mean?"

"Yes . . . I mean . . . no, she's left and I don't know where she's gone."

"I see. You must be in a state."

"I am a bit, yes."

"Is that why you left on Sunday?"

"Yes."

"Honestly, I wish someone had told me *why* you'd left! You can imagine what I thought. Don't you just love families?"

"Yes," I gulped, relief flooding through me.

"Look, do you want me to come up to London? Marguerite's staying with Rory until next Tuesday, so I'm free until then."

"I'm just off to Norway for a couple of days to hear my sister perform in a concert."

"Which sister?"

"Ally. The one whose fiancé was killed. She's pregnant," I added.

"Oh." There was a pause on the line. "Is that good news?"

"Yes, it is," I said firmly. "Ally's thrilled."

"Star . . ."

"Yes?"

"I miss you. Do you miss me at all?"

I nodded, then realized he couldn't see me, so I took a deep breath and opened my mouth.

"Yes."

There was a long pause. And then, "Wow. So, did you read what was in the envelope?"

"Yes."

"And will you come away with me for a couple of days when you get back?"

"Can . . . I think about it?"

A sigh of frustration came down the line. "Okay, but can you let me know by tomorrow lunchtime? Marguerite's leaving on Tuesday, so I have to be back in Kent for Rory by midafternoon. If you do want to go, I'll come and collect you on Sunday on my way up from Kent."

"I will, yes."

"Well, have a safe trip, and I hope you hear from your missing sister."

"Thanks, bye."

"Bye."

I raced down the stairs to the front door, hoping the taxi I'd ordered was still waiting for me. As we drove off, my mobile pinged to alert me to a text.

Sorry, Sia, only just got all yor mesages. Been traveling. Im fine. Tell you all about it when Im home. Love u, Cee.

I texted back immediately.

Cee! Thank God! Been worried sick. I'm so, so sorry for everything. I love you too. KEEP IN TOUCH. xxx

And I then sat back in the taxi, euphoric with relief.

45

The lights dimmed in the auditorium and I watched my sister rise from her seat on the stage. I could see the contours of the new life inside her clearly defined beneath the black dress. Ally closed her eyes for a moment as if in prayer. When she finally lifted the flute to her lips, a hand reached for mine and squeezed it gently. And I knew Ma was feeling the resonance too.

As the beautiful, familiar melody, which had been part of my and my sisters' childhood at Atlantis, floated out across the hall, I felt some of the tension of the past few weeks flow out of me with the swell of the music. As I listened, I knew that Ally was playing for all those she had loved and lost, but I understood too that just as the sun comes up after a long, dark night, there was new light in her life now. And as the orchestra joined her and the beautiful music reached a crescendo, celebrating the dawning of a new day, I felt the same.

Yet in my *own* rebirth, others had suffered, and that was the part I had yet to rationalize. I'd only understood recently that there were many different kinds of love.

At the interval, Ma and I went to the bar, and Peter and Celia Falys-Kings, who introduced themselves as Theo's parents, joined us for a glass of champagne. As I watched the way Peter's arm rested protectively on Celia's waist, they still looked like a young couple in love.

"*Santé*," said Ma, as she chinked her glass against mine. "Isn't this the most wonderful evening?"

"Yes, it is," I replied.

"Ally played so beautifully. I wish your other sisters could have been here to see her. And your father, of course."

I watched Ma's brow furrow in sudden concern and wondered what secrets she kept. And how heavily they weighed on her. As did mine.

"CeCe couldn't make it then?" she asked me tentatively.

"No."

"Have you seen her recently?"

"I'm not at the apartment very often these days, Ma."

"So, you're the 'mom' who cared for Ally during her childhood?" asked Peter.

"Yes," she replied.

"You did a wonderful job," he said.

"That's down to her, not me," Ma replied modestly. "All of my girls make me very proud."

"And you're one of Ally's famous sisters?" Peter turned his gimlet eyes on me.

"Yes."

"What's your name?"

"Star."

"And which number are you?"

"Three."

"Interesting." He looked at me again. "I was number three as well. Never listened to and never heard. Yes?"

I didn't reply.

"Bet a lot goes on inside that head of yours, right?" he continued. "It sure did in mine."

Even if he was right, I wouldn't tell him. So I shrugged silently instead.

"Ally is a very special human being. We both learned a lot from her," said Celia, giving me a warm smile as she changed the subject. I could tell she thought my silences meant I was struggling with Peter.

"Yes, indeed. And now we're to be grandparents. What a gift your sister has given us, Star," said Peter. "And this time, I'm going to be there for the little one. Life is just too damned short, isn't it?"

The two-minute bell rang, and everyone around me drained their glasses, however full they were. We all filed back into the auditorium to take our seats. Ally had already filled me in fully by e-mail on her discoveries in Norway. I studied Felix Halvorsen closely as he walked onto the stage, and decided that the genetic link to him had had little impact on Ally's physical characteristics. I also noticed his rolling gait as he walked toward the piano and wondered if he was drunk. I sent up a small prayer that he wasn't. I knew from what Ally had said earlier how much this evening meant to her and her newfound brother, Thom. I'd liked him immediately when I'd met him earlier.

As Felix lifted his fingers to the keys and then paused, I felt every member of the audience holding their breath with me. The tension was only broken as his fingers descended onto them and the opening bars of *The Hero Concerto* were played in public for the first time. According to the program, just over sixty-eight years after they had been written. For the following half an hour, each one of us was treated to a performance of rarity and beauty, created by a perfect alchemy between composer and interpreter: father and son.

And as my heart took flight and soared upward with the beautiful music, I saw a glimpse of the future. " 'Music is love in search of a voice.' " I quoted Tolstoy under my breath. Now, I had to find *my* voice. And also the courage to speak out with it.

The applause was deservedly tumultuous, the audience on their feet, stamping and cheering. Felix took bow after bow, beckoning his son and his daughter out of the orchestra to join him, then quieting the audience and dedicating his performance to his late father, and his children.

In this gesture, I saw living proof that it was possible to move on. And to make a change that others would eventually accept, however difficult.

As the audience began to rise from their seats, Ma touched my shoulder, saying something to me.

I nodded at her blankly, not taking in her words, and murmured that I'd see her in the foyer. And then I sat there. Alone. Thinking. As I did so, I was vaguely aware of the rest of the audience walking up the aisle past me. And then, out of the corner of my eye, I saw a familiar figure.

As my heart began to pound, my body stood up of its own volition and I ran through the empty auditorium to the crowd milling around the back exits. I searched desperately for another glimpse, begging the unmistakable profile to reappear to me among the milieu.

Pushing my way through the foyer, my legs carried me out into the freezing December air. I stood in the street, hoping for another sighting just to make sure, but I knew the figure had disappeared.

"There you are!" Ma said, coming up behind me. "We thought we'd lost you. Star? Are you all right?"

"I . . . I think I saw him, Ma. Inside the concert hall."

"Saw who?"

"Pa! I'm sure it was him."

"Oh, *chérie*," Ma said, wrapping her arms around me as I stood there, catatonic with shock. "I'm so sorry. These things happen after someone we love dies. I think I see your father all the time at Atlantis . . . in his garden, on the Laser, and I keep expecting him to walk out of his study at any moment."

"It *was* him, I know it was," I whispered into Ma's shoulder.

"Then perhaps it was his spirit present in the auditorium, listening to Ally. Didn't she play beautifully?" Ma said as she guided me firmly along the path.

"Yes. It was a wonderful evening, until—"

"Try not to think about it. It will only upset you. Poor Ally thought she'd heard his voice on the telephone while she was at Atlantis. Of course, it was the answering machine. Now, there is a car ready to take us to the restaurant. Theo's parents are already waiting inside."

I let Ma do the talking on the drive there, still reeling from shock. Doubtless, Ma was right, and it had simply been an older man of similar build whom—given he had been some distance away—my desperate heart had morphed into Pa Salt.

The restaurant was cozy and candlelit, and when Ally arrived with her twin brother, Thom, we all stood up and applauded them.

"Is there someone missing?" Ma looked at the empty seat at the head of the table.

"That place is for our father," explained Thom in perfect English, as he sat down next to me. "But we doubt he'll turn up, don't we, Ally?"

"Tonight, we can just about forgive him." She smiled. "When we left, he was surrounded by reporters and admirers singing his praises. He's waited a long time for this. It's his night."

"Ally forced me into giving him another chance." Thom turned to me. "And she was right. I'm so proud of him tonight. *Skål!*" He clinked his glass of champagne against mine.

"Everyone deserves another chance, don't they?" I whispered, almost to myself.

For the rest of the evening, I was entertained by Thom's story of how Ally had turned up on his doorstep, and their subsequent discovery that they were twins.

"And it's all due to this," he said, reaching into his pocket, and placing a small frog on the table. "Everyone in the orchestra had one tonight, as a tribute to the great man himself."

It was late by the time we left the restaurant and stood outside saying our good-byes.

"What time are you leaving tomorrow?" Ally asked Ma and me as we all embraced.

"My flight to Geneva leaves at ten o'clock, but Star's isn't until three," Ma told her.

"Then maybe you could come and see me at the house, and we can catch up properly?" Ally suggested. "You can take a taxi straight to the airport."

"Or I can take her," said Thom.

"We'll organize it tomorrow. Good night, darling Star, sleep well." She waved at me as she climbed into a car parked outside, and Thom followed suit.

"See you tomorrow," he said, smiling, and they drove off.

I watched with interest as the taxi drove me up to Ally and Thom's home the following morning. Last night, it had been too dark to see the snow-covered peaks that ringed Bergen, but now I could appreciate their Christmas-card perfection. Up and up we went, until we reached a narrow road and stopped in front of a traditional clapboard house, freshly painted in cream, with pale blue shutters.

"Star, come in," Ally said, greeting me on the doorstep. I did so, and stepped into a toasty-warm entrance hall.

"Ally, this is beautiful!" I said as she led me into a bright sitting room filled with a squashy sofa and pale Scandinavian pine furniture. A grand piano sat in the huge bay window, which overlooked the lake below and the snow-capped hills beyond it.

"What a view," I said. "It reminds me of Atlantis."

"Me too, but gentler somehow, as everything is here in Bergen, including its residents. Coffee or tea?"

I asked for coffee, and sat down in front of a modern glass fireplace, the logs within it burning merrily.

"There you are." Ally put a cup down in front of me and sat next to me on the sofa. "Goodness, Star, where do we begin? There's so much to catch up on. Thom told you most of what's happened at this end. I want to hear about you. How's CeCe, by the way? And more to the point, *where* is CeCe? I'm not used to seeing you two apart."

"I don't know. She's left London and gone away. And . . . ," I confessed, "it's my fault."

"You've fallen out?"

"Yes . . . I just . . . well, I've been trying to find a life of my own."

"And CeCe hasn't yet?"

"No. I feel terrible about it, Ally."

"Well, maybe she needs to find herself too. Something had to give—all of us sisters have worried about your relationship."

"Have you?"

"Yes. And personally, I think this parting of the ways is really important for both of you. And I'm sure it will only be temporary."

"I hope so. I'd just like to know where she is. She was upset because I didn't tell her about meeting my mother."

"You found your mother?! Wow, Star! Will you tell me about her?"

So I did, as always struggling to find the words, but with Ally prompting me, I gave her the most accurate potted version I could.

"Goodness. And there was me thinking my journey had been complicated and traumatic," Ally breathed. "So, what about this Mouse? Are you going to give him another chance?"

"I . . . think so."

"Give it a try, while you can," she said vehemently. "I know only too well that nothing lasts forever."

"Yes." I reached instinctively for her hand. "They need me. Both of them. Father and son."

"And we all want to be needed, don't we?" Ally passed a hand fleetingly across her burgeoning stomach. "I'd better call you a taxi. Thom was very disappointed he had to go into work to have a postmortem on last night's triumph." She smiled as she stood up, and went to the telephone. "You've made a fan there, that's for sure. Do I have to tell him you're taken?"

"Yes," I said. "I think you do."

At Bergen airport, as my flight was boarding, I took out my mobile. And just before we took off, I texted Mouse.

Yes, please.

Back in London, I woke the next morning and saw it was nine thirty. Mouse was coming to collect me at eleven.

My stomach did a somersault and then a double backflip as I stood under the shower contemplating his arrival. And then the day *and* the evening that would follow. I repacked my luggage, leaving in the black dress I'd worn to the concert last night just in case, and donned the thick woolen sweater I'd treated myself to in Bergen. Adding my walking boots, I then placed two sets of clean underwear on the top, and gave a shudder as I did so.

When he knows, I might not even get as far as the car, I thought to myself as my panic began to rise.

The door buzzer rang at eleven o'clock exactly and I pressed the entry button to let him in. My heart was banging like a tom-tom as I heard the lift ascend, then the sound of his footsteps crossing the narrow corridor.

"The door's open," I called, sounding like my vocal cords were being strangled by a python.

"Hi," he said, and gave me a smile. He walked toward me, then stopped a few meters away. "Star, what's wrong? Has something happened? You look completely terrified."

"I am."

"Why? Is it me?"

"No . . . and yes." I tried to breathe, as I gathered every ounce of courage I had. "Can you sit down, please?"

"Okay," he said, and walked to the sofa. "Have you changed your mind? Is that what this is all about?"

"No. I just . . . I need to tell you something."

"I'm all ears."

"The thing is . . ." It was my turn to pace. "The thing is that . . ."

"Star, whatever it is, it can't be worse than what I told you. Please, just say it."

I turned away from him, closed my eyes, and said the words:

"I'm . . . a virgin."

The silence seemed to last forever as I waited for his response.

"Right. Is that it? I mean, what you needed to tell me?"

"Yes!" I jumped as I felt the gentle touch of a hand on my shoulder.

"Have you ever had a relationship?"

"No. Me and CeCe . . . we were always together. There was never the chance."

"I understand."

"Do you?"

"Yes."

Burning with embarrassment, I felt myself being turned around and a pair of arms enveloping me.

"I feel so stupid," I muttered. "I'm twenty-seven and . . ."

We stood in silence for a bit, his hand gently stroking my hair.

"Star? Can I say something?"

"Yes."

"It may sound odd, but the fact that you are, for the want of a better phrase, untouched by anyone else, is a gift, not a negative. And besides, in the particular . . . 'department' we're discussing, it's been years since I . . . Anyway, I can honestly say you're not the only one who's had sleepless nights about this."

Mouse's confessed nervousness definitely made me feel better. He pulled away and reached for my hands.

"Star, look at me."

I raised my eyes to his.

"Before we go any farther, you have to know that I would never, *ever* try to force you or put you under pressure, as long as you'll grant the same favor to me. We have to be kind to each other, don't we?"

"Yes."

"So . . ." He gazed down at me. "Shall we give this a try? Two damaged people trying to put each other back together?"

I looked out of the window at the river, flowing unstoppably forward, its progress unchecked. And felt the protective dam I'd built around my heart begin to crumble. I turned my eyes back to him and felt the love finally start to trickle out through the fissures. And hoped that one day it would become a torrent.

"Yes," I said.

"Where exactly is this?" I asked as Mouse grabbed our luggage from the boot and a porter appeared from the front entrance to take them from us.

"Don't you recognize it from Flora's description?"

I looked up at the vast gray house, warm light pouring from the windows into the darkening night. And suddenly, I *did* know.

"It's Esthwaite Hall, Flora MacNichol's childhood home!"

"Spot-on. When I was looking for somewhere to stay up here in the Lakes, I discovered it had recently been turned into a hotel." Mouse kissed me on the top of my head. "This is where your story—and, in a way, mine—originally began. Shall we go in?"

At reception, he politely offered me a separate room, but instead, we compromised on a suite, and Mouse ordered a fold-up bed for the sitting room and said he'd sleep in there. "I don't want you to panic," he reassured me.

Upstairs, I put on my new black dress for dinner in the formal restaurant. I emerged from the bathroom and Mouse whistled.

"Star, you look stunning. I've never seen your legs uncovered before and they're so long and slim . . . Sorry," he checked himself. "I just want to tell you that you're beautiful. Is that okay?"

"It's okay." I smiled.

Over dinner, Mouse explained how his former career as an architect meant he wouldn't have to pay anyone else to draw up the plans for the renovation works at High Weald. His vivid green eyes lit up as he spoke about taking the house into the future, and I suddenly realized that he loved it too. Seeing the passion he must have once possessed reignited, I felt the trickle in my own heart begin to pour out like a tap turned on to full.

"Before I forget"—he reached into his dinner jacket and pulled out a familiar jewelry box—"I just got this back from Sotheby's. It is indeed a Fabergé, commissioned by King Edward VII himself. It's worth a great deal of money, Star."

He handed it to me, and I took out the little figurine, marveling at how Flora MacNichol herself had once cherished it, and the journey she had been on.

"I'm not sure it really belongs to me."

"Of course it does. To be honest, I presumed Teddy had pawned the figurine years ago. He certainly did that with other family treasures. However you came by it, you are Teddy's great-grandchild. It's *your* legacy, Star . . . You know, I've been thinking more and more about the past," Mouse said, looking at Panther sitting in the palm of my hand. "And I understand what Archie was trying to do when he took Teddy as his own son . . . the trauma that he experienced during the war . . ." He shook his head. "Whatever the consequences were, he wanted to atone for all the random death and destruction he'd seen, by passing on the gift of High Weald to the offspring of an unknown soldier. Just as I hope I can atone by renovating it for Rory."

"Yes. I think it was a beautiful thing to do."

After dinner, he led me back up to our suite.

"Right," he said, as we entered it, "I'll say good night then."

I watched him as he took off his jacket in the sitting room. Then I paused and walked over to him, stood on my tiptoes, and kissed him on the cheek.

"Good night."

"Can I hug you?" he asked, his breath on my skin.

"Yes please."

As he did so, I felt a sudden stirring inside me.

"Mouse?"

"Yes?"

"Could you kiss me?"

He tipped my chin up to him and smiled.

"I think I could manage that, yes."

When we woke the next morning, the glorious Lakeland surroundings had opened up like an unwrapped present through the windows of our suite. We spent the day exploring, visiting Hill Top Farm, Beatrix Potter's old home and now a museum, then driving on to find Wynbrigg Farm, Flora's home, where she'd suffered so many years of loneliness. And I squeezed Mouse's hand extra tightly, glorying in the fact that I had so narrowly avoided her fate.

Back at the hotel, we walked through the trees by Esthwaite Water, and saw a lark gliding through the mist over the lake as the sun set. Our noses pink with cold, we stood hand in hand and looked at the absolute serenity of the view, its beauty rendering us both silent.

That evening, we went to the Tower Bank Arms, the local pub where Archie Vaughan had originally stayed when he'd come to visit Flora.

"Perhaps I should have checked in here, like he did." Mouse gave me a wry smile.

"I'm glad you didn't," I replied, and realized I meant it. Although I had left Mouse to sleep alone after the kiss, I'd lain there feeling a delicious tingle racing through my body. And knew that with time—and trust—I'd get there. In fact, I might even enjoy the journey.

Checking out of Esthwaite Hall the following morning, Mouse drove us to the Langdale Valley, and we took a walk through the majestic mountain pass.

A thought suddenly occurred to me. "Mouse?"

"Yes?"

"What's your real name? I know it begins with 'O.'"

His lips curved into a wry smile. "I thought you'd never ask."

"Well?"

"It's Oenomaus."

"Oh my God!"

"I know. Ridiculous, isn't it?"

"Your name?"

"Yes, that as well, of course—blame my Greek-mythology-obsessed dad—but I meant the coincidence. According to the myth, Oenomaus was married to Asterope—or some stories say he was her son."

"Yes, I've heard the legends surrounding my name. Why didn't you tell me before?"

"I asked you once if you believed in fate. You said you didn't. Whereas I knew that day when I first set eyes on you at High Weald, and heard what your real name was, that we were destined to be together."

"Did you?"

"Yes. It was written in the stars," he teased me. "And it seems you have father *and* son at your feet."

"Well. I hope it's okay if I still call you 'Mouse'?"

And then the sound of our joint laughter rang through the Langdale

Valley as Oenomaus Forbes, Lord Vaughan of High Weald, hugged me to him tightly.

"Well?" he said.

" 'Well' what?"

"Will you come back to High Weald with me tonight, Asterope?"

"Yes," I said without hesitation. "Remember that I've got work tomorrow morning."

"Of course you have, you old romantic. Right then," he said, releasing me and taking my hand. "It's time for us both to go home."

CeCe

December 2007

Camellia
(Theaceae family)

46

I sat at Heathrow airport waiting for my flight to be called, watching the other passengers walk by me, chatting to their kids, or their partners. Everyone looked happy—full of expectation. And even if they were traveling by themselves, I reckoned they probably had someone waiting for them at their destination.

I had nobody any longer—either here or there. I suddenly felt for all those old men I'd seen sitting on benches in London parks as I'd walked to and from college. I'd thought they were enjoying the company of life passing by them in the winter sunshine . . . but now I realized how much worse it felt to be alone in a crowd. And I wished that I had stopped to say hello. As I wished someone would stop and say hello to me now.

Sia, where are you?

I wish I could write down what's in my head and send it to you, so that you could read the things I really feel. But you know the words come out wrong on the page—it took me forever to write that letter I left for you at the apartment and it was still rubbish. And you're not here to talk to, so I'll just have to think it all to myself in the middle of Terminal Three.

I thought you would hear my cry for help. But you didn't. All these weeks I've watched you drift away from me, and I've tried so hard to let you go. To not mind you leaving me all the time to see that family or how irritated you've been with me, like everyone else is.

With you, I could always be myself. And I thought you loved me for it. Accepted me for who I was. And what I tried to do for you.

I know what others think of me. And I'm not sure where I go wrong, because it's all here inside me—the good stuff, like love. And wanting to care for people and make friends. It's like there's a trip switch between who I am on the inside and what comes out on the outside. By the way, I know that would be a bad sentence because it has two "out"s in it, and you used to correct word repetitions in my essays before they went to the teacher.

We were kind to each other. You didn't like speaking, but I could say the words for you, like you wrote them better for me. We were a good team.

I thought you'd be so happy when I bought that apartment for us. We were safe forever. No more traveling—because I knew you'd had enough; time to settle down and be who we were, together. But it just seemed to make things worse.

And it's only in the last few days when I've sat in the apartment alone, waiting for you to call me, that I've understood. I made you feel like a caged tiger who couldn't escape. I was rude to your friends—male or female—because I was so scared of losing the one person who seemed to love me, apart from Pa and Ma . . .

So, I've gone, Sia. Left you alone for a bit, because that's what I know you want. Because I love you more than anyone in the world, but I think you've found someone else to love you and you don't need me anymore . . .

I looked up and saw the flight was boarding. And my tummy turned over, because I had never, *ever* got on a plane without Sia by my side. She sat in the window seat with me next to her in the middle, because she liked being up in the clouds. I'd always preferred the earth under my feet and she'd give me a pill twenty minutes before the flight took off so I'd fall straight to sleep and wouldn't be scared.

I fumbled in the front pocket of my rucksack to find my purse, where I was sure I'd put the pill before I left the apartment, but it wasn't there.

I'd just have to do without it, I decided as I continued to search through the muck inside the pocket to find my passport and boarding card. I'd just have to do without a lot of things from now on. My fingers touched on the envelope with Pa Salt's letter in it. I drew it out to find bits of an old jam doughnut attached to it and saw the envelope was now sugarcoated and stained. Typical me, I thought: I couldn't even keep the most important letter I'd ever been written clean. Dusting the sugar off it, I took out the small black-and-white photograph and stared at it for the hundredth time.

Well, at least there had once been *someone* in the world that I'd belonged to properly. And, I comforted myself, at least I had my art, which was the one thing no one could ever take away from me.

I stowed the envelope back in the front pocket, then stood up and hoicked my rucksack onto my back. I followed the human wave slowly toward the departure gate, wondering what on earth I was doing throwing up everything I'd planned. But if I was honest, it wasn't just Sia who'd found the change so difficult. Even after just a few weeks in London, my feet had become itchy and the wanderlust had started to hit again. I was very bad at staying in one place for more than a few weeks—always had been—and I'd realized I harbored an innate terror of being institutionalized.

You should have thought of that before you enrolled at your art college, you dunce . . .

I liked nothing better than carrying my home on my back and the excitement of not knowing where I'd end up sleeping that night. Being free. And the good news was, I supposed, that this was certainly going to be how I lived from now on.

I thought how weird it was that one of the only two places in the world I had always avoided visiting was where I was headed for now.

Wandering along the concourse and stepping onto the moving walkway, I glanced at a poster advertising a bank and was mentally deriding the art director for his lack of imagination when I caught a flash of a very familiar face walking past me. My heart almost jumped out of my chest as I turned around and craned my neck to search for him. But he was walking away and I was traveling fast in the other direction.

I began running along the moving walkway my rucksack jostling people as I passed them, but in my desperation to get off, I didn't care. Reaching the end of it, I did a U-turn and continued to run back along the concourse, my breath coming in gasps through shock and the weight of my rucksack. I dodged in and out between the people walking toward me, eventually reaching the entrance to the departure lounge.

My eyes searched desperately through the crowds for another glimpse of him, but as I heard the final call for my flight, I knew it was too late.

Acknowledgments

This project would not have been possible without the kind help of so many people, and I am deeply indebted to them for supporting me in this marathon of a seven-book series.

In the Lake District: Many thanks to Anthony Hutton of the Tower Bank Arms, Beatrix Potter's local pub in Near Sawrey, for his in-depth knowledge of local history and his warm hospitality. Also to Alan Brockbank, who at the age of ninety-five took the time to be interviewed about village life when Beatrix was still alive, and who had us in stitches with his deadpan stories of adventure. Also, to Catherine Pritchard, National Trust house manager at Hill Top Farm, for her expertise on all things Miss Potter. I would have liked nothing more than to include all the whimsical details of Beatrix's life in these pages, as she kept busy until the day she died: as wife, farmer, writer, illustrator, researcher, preserver of nature, lover of animals, and friend to many.

Thank you to Marcus Tyers, proprietor of St. Mary's Books, Stamford, for his invaluable knowledge on the intricacies of the rare-book business, and for advising me on how much Orlando would have spent on that *Anna Karenina.* (An exorbitant amount!)

I would also like to thank my fantastic PA, Olivia, who bravely climbed the fells of the Lake District alone in the rain to find a monument to Edward VII, which I insisted was there, but wasn't! And my hardworking editorial and research team of Susan Moss and Ella Micheler, who helped me get to grips with all of Star's recipes as well as British Sign Language and deaf culture.

My thirty international publishers from around the world—whom I'm honored to say I now count among my friends—particularly Catherine Richards and Jeremy Trevathan at Pan Macmillan UK; Claudia Negele and Georg Reuchlein at Random House Germany; the team at Cappelen

Damm Norway: Knut Gørvell, Jorid Mathiassen, Pip Hallen, and Marianne Nielsen; Annalisa Lottini and Donatella Minuto at Giunti Editore in Italy; and Sarah Cantin and Judith Curr at Atria in the USA.

Writing Star's story has been an absolute pleasure, as I have been able to do so from the comfort of my own home for once, with the support of my family. They have learned to ignore me as I wander around the house like a wraith at all times of day and night, talking into my Dictaphone and weaving the threads of *The Shadow Sister* together. Harry, Bella, Leonora, and Kit—you all know what you mean to me—and thank you to Stephen, my husband/agent, who keeps me on the straight and narrow in all sorts of ways! What would I do without you? A special thank-you to Jacquelyn Heslop, who holds the Riley fort so capably and looks after all of us. To my sister, Georgia, and Janet, my mother. And to Flo, to whom this book is dedicated. I miss you.

And lastly, to my readers. Writing a seven-book series seemed like such a mad idea in 2012—I never guessed that the stories of my sisters would touch so many people around the world. I have been honored and deeply humbled to receive all your e-mails, letters, and words of support, and to have been lucky enough to meet some of you on my tours around the world. Thank you.

Author's Note

When I first had the idea of writing a series of books based on the Seven Sisters of the Pleiades, I had no idea where it would lead me. I was very attracted to the fact that each one of the mythological sisters was, according to their legends, a unique and strong female. Some say they were the Seven Mothers who seeded our earth—there is no doubt that, in their stories, they were all highly fertile!—and they had many children with the various gods who were fascinated by their strength, beauty, and ethereal air of mysticism.

And I wanted to celebrate the achievements of women, especially in the past, where so often their contribution to making our world the place it is today has been overshadowed by the more frequently documented achievements of men.

However, the definition of feminism is equality, not domination, and the women I write about, both in the past and the present, accept that they want and need men in their lives. Perhaps the masculine and feminine are the true yin and yang of nature and must strive for balance—in essence, to accept the individual strengths and weaknesses of each other.

And of course, we all need love; not necessarily in the traditional form of marriage and children, but I believe it to be the life source without which we humans wither and die. The *Seven Sisters* series unashamedly celebrates the endless search for love, and explores the devastating consequences when it is lost to us.

As I travel around the world, following in the footsteps of my factual and fictional female characters to research their stories, I am constantly humbled and awed by the tenacity and courage of the generations of women who came before me. Whether fighting the sexual and racial prejudices of times gone by, losing their loved ones to the devastation of war or disease, or making a new life on the other side of the world, these women paved the way for us to have the freedom of thought and deed that we enjoy today. And so often take for granted.

The world is sadly still not a perfect place and I doubt it ever will be, because there will always be a new challenge ahead. Yet I truly believe that humans—especially women—thrive on this challenge. We are, after all, the goddesses of multitasking! And every day—with one hand holding a child and the other a manuscript—I celebrate the fact that my freedom to be who I am was won by thousands of generations of remarkable women, perhaps leading right back to the Seven Sisters themselves . . .

I so hope you have enjoyed Star's journey. Often, everyday quiet courage, kindness, and inner strength go unacknowledged. Star has not changed the world, but has touched the lives of those around her and made them better. And through the process, she has found herself.

Bibliography

The Shadow Sister is a work of fiction set against a historical background. The sources I've used to research the time period and details of my characters' lives are listed below:

Munya Andrews, *The Seven Sisters of the Pleiades* (North Melbourne, Victoria: Spinifex Press, 2004).

Susan Denyer, *Beatrix Potter at Home in the Lake District* (London: Frances Lincoln, 2000).

Roy Hattersley, *The Edwardians* (London: Abacus, 2014).

Philippe Jullian and John Phillips, *Violet Trefusis: Life and Letters* (Bristol: Hamish Hamilton, 1976).

Sonia Keppel, *Edwardian Daughter* (London: Hamish Hamilton, 1958).

Raymond Lamont-Brown, *Edward VII's Last Loves: Alice Keppel and Agnes Keyser* (London: Sutton Publishing, 2005).

Linda Lear, *Beatrix Potter: The Extraordinary Life of a Victorian Genius* (London: Penguin, 2008).

Leslie Linder, *A History of the Writings of Beatrix Potter* (London: Frederick Warne, 1971).

Tim Longville, *Gardens of the Lake District* (London: Frances Lincoln, 2007).

Peter Marren, *Britain's Rare Flowers* (London: Academic Press, 1999).

Marta McDowell, *Beatrix Potter's Gardening Life* (London: Timber Press, 2013).

George Plumptre, *The English Country House Garden* (London: Frances Lincoln, 2014).

J. B. Priestley, *The Edwardians* (London: Penguin, 2000).

Jane Ridley, *Bertie: A Life of Edward VII* (London: Chatto & Windus, 2012).

Vita Sackville-West, *The Edwardians* (London: Virago, 2004).
Diana Souhami, *Mrs. Keppel and Her Daughter* (London: HarperCollins, 1996).
Judy Taylor, *Beatrix Potter: Artist, Storyteller and Countrywoman* (London: Frederick Warne, 1986).
Violet Trefusis, *Don't Look Round* (London: Hamish Hamilton, 1989).

About the Author

Lucinda Riley is the *New York Times* bestselling author of *The Orchid House*, *The Girl on the Cliff*, *The Lavender Garden*, *The Midnight Rose*, *The Seven Sisters*, and *The Storm Sister*. Her books have sold more than eight million copies in thirty languages globally. She was born in Ireland and divides her time between England and West Cork with her husband and four children.

www.lucindariley.com
www.thesevensisters.com
www.facebook.com/lucindarileyauthor
www.twitter.com/lucindariley